A loss of innocence . . .

For Tawny adolescence had not been a gradual change. It was happening this moment. She was sharply aware that she was touching a male. Now, feeling the pulsations beneath her hand, she felt her own body strangely stirring to life.

He took his hand off hers and she in turn pulled her own away from him. She knew she must stand up and walk away but her knees were like rubber.

Lance sat up and put his hands on her slender shoulders and looked into her eyes. "You are a lovely creature, Tawny. I'm sorry if I frightened you. I couldn't help myself."

"I'm sorry Pa brought me here. He shouldn't have done it. He made me come. He would have beaten me if I hadn't."

He leaned forward and kissed her again, very gently, on the lips. Tawny's heart turned over.

"Mr. Oliver, I'd better leave." Before she could pull away his mouth was on hers, and this one was different from the previous kiss. She found herself responding as she never had before. When they broke apart they were both breathless. He took his arms away as she lifted hers and without a word took the pins from her feathered bonnet and lifted it from her head. She put it on the table and then turned to face him.

He picked her up and carried her back to the sofa. He laid her down, and this time it was he who knelt on the floor. . . .

Also by June Wetherell from Pinnacle Books:

A Time for Desire
The Privateer's Woman

PINNACLE BOOKS • LOS ANGELES

This is a work of fiction. All the characters and events portrayed in this book are fictional, and any resemblance to real people or incidents is purely coincidental.

TAWNY McSHANE

An original Pinnacle Books edition, published for the first time anywhere by arrangement with Jay Garon-Brooke Associates.

First printing, March 1979

ISBN: 0-523-40340-2

Cover illustration by Bill Maughan

Printed in the United States of America

PINNACLE BOOKS, INC.
2029 Century Park East
Los Angeles, California 90067

TAWNY MCSHANE

PART I

1870

1

As the girl was ushered into Lance Oliver's study and the door closed behind her, the first thought that crossed his mind was *this is certainly no child.* Somehow he had expected one, since that was the way the old man in the Broadway saloon had spoken of her. He had referred to "my little girl."

Lance had been alone, staring at his reflection in the bar mirror opposite, drink in one hand, beating a tattoo on the mahogany with his other. He was angry with himself for drinking alone, and at the reasons that had sent him there.

"Mornin'."

Next to him was a shabby little old fellow with big ears and a button nose. He must have once been rather a good-looking man in a devil-may-care Irish way. Nevertheless, his smile was friendly. Lance nodded to him and lifted his glass.

"Couldn't help noticin'," the man went on. "Nervous, ain't you?"

Lance smiled. "I suppose that's what you could call it."

"Couldn't help noticin'. Got problems, son, something you'd like to talk about?"

His manner was pleasant but Lance was not drunk nor the sort of fellow who poured out troubles to a stranger.

"Just nerves," he said. "Let's leave it at that."

"Sorry. Didn't mean no offense. Name is McShane. Jake McShane. Just got into town. You're Lance Oliver, aren't you?"

"Yes."

"That's what the fellow down the bar told me. How's the world treatin' you these days, Mr. Oliver?"

"Not too badly."

"Long time since I been in New York. Seems bigger and dirtier than ever. And now they gonta build a bridge across the East River, I hear. Didn't see a paper this mornin'. Anything new?"

"Just talk about the possibility of war in Europe. Napoleon stirring up trouble. Bismarck not liking it. Not exactly news." Lance smiled, glad to get off the subject of himself.

"This Napoleon, now, he any relation to that other Napoleon?"

"Nephew, I believe. But I don't think he's quite the man the first Napoleon was."

"Them Frenchies always cause trouble." Jake shook his head. "I had a run in with a few down New Orleans way once. Don't like 'em much."

"I had a good time in France," commented Lance. Suddenly bored, he finished his drink and turned to leave. McShane touched his arm.

"About them nerves of yours. I won't pry about what causes them. But it just come into my head that maybe my little girl could help you."

Lance laughed. "Your little girl?"

"She's pretty good with this magnetic healing business. She's got the touch, she has. Can heal most anything from rheumatism to chronic bellyache."

Lance laughed again. The man was amusing.

"Let me buy you a drink," Lance suggested, "and you tell me more about this little girl of yours."

Lance was not the least fooled by Jake McShane. He knew a con man when he saw one. This McShane knew who he was, the son of the owner of the Oliver Shipping Lines, and one of the wealthiest young men in New York City. But he found McShane a different and somehow likable specimen of swindler.

He also learned that Jake had traveled over half the United States selling McShane's Marvelous Medicine, which obviously couldn't have been very effective or he wouldn't have moved so often. Apparently somewhere along the road he met a woman who practiced magnetic healing.

"Well, one day I found my little girl Tawny a practicin' with her little hands on her dolls, and I said to her, 'Tawny, why don't you try that on people? There's people who take my medicine and get well because they believe in it. Now if we could get them to believe in your magnetism, maybe they'd lose their aches and pains.' "

"I see."

"Magnetism might just fix your nerves."

Lance looked down into his drink. "For a fee."

"For a fee. Twenty-five dollars. I can bring Tawny around this afternoon, if you like."

Out of sheer curiosity, Lance had agreed.

The butler had said merely, "Miss McShane," before he closed the door.

"Good afternoon, Mr. Oliver." She had a surprisingly low and husky voice.

"Good afternoon, Miss McShane."

She looked perhaps fifteen. Her blue poplin dress was drawn taut across the ample curves of her young breasts.

He stood up, came around his desk, and took a better look at her. A mass of mahogany-colored hair topped by a little bonnet with a jaunty blue feather. Mischievous, very adult eyes.

"So you are Mr. McShane's little girl."

"Is that what he called me?" She smiled.

"How old are you, if I may ask?"

"Fifteen. Almost sixteen."

His eyes swept over her. "Not so little," he told her.

Tawny was beginning to feel uncomfortable. Pa had not told her that Mr. Oliver was young and handsome. And so big. He loomed a giant here in his black walnut wainscoted study.

He was standing closer to her now, smiling, and she smiled back. His hair was black as midnight and his eyes were surprisingly blue, with long curled lashes any girl might envy.

"Please, Miss McShane, have a chair and tell me about your magnetic healing."

He pointed to a big winged chair, and as she settled into it he sat down opposite her. All of a sudden the whole business of magnetic healing seemed rather ridiculous to Tawny. She had not practiced it since she was a very small girl, when it had been merely a game she liked to play.

"Magnetic healing resembles electricity," she began. "The right hand is positive." She fluttered that one. "The left is negative." She repeated the gesture. "I give people a sort of electric massage. People . . . people claim to feel better afterward."

"Indeed." His eyes twinkled.

"It depends, of course, on what your ailment is."

"Your father tells me it's my nerves. I have no real ailment."

Across the room a clock ticked slowly, and beyond the heavily draped and shuttered window she could hear the hum of Manhattan.

She looked at him, wide-eyed. "Then why did you have me come?"

"Curiosity."

Her innocence was childlike and seemed to add to her appeal. She was pretty, but in no ordinary way. The eyes he had first thought of as mischievous were gray with little brown flecks. He never had seen eyes like that. They and her voice and the provocative pointed breasts titillated him. It was pleasant to be alone with such a creature in the sanctuary of his study, where no one, not even his wife, ever disturbed him.

Tawny looked across at his smiling face. The way he was staring at her made her more uncomfortable than ever. "Is your curiosity satisfied?" she asked in a low voice.

"No, it's not." The smile faded from his face. "I agreed to pay your father twenty-five dollars later this afternoon. Meanwhile, I want my magnetic treatment."

Tawny sighed. She remembered now the times when she had performed the abracadabra as a child. Sometimes men would command her to stop, or suddenly break away and grab hold of her with strange looks in their eyes that made her scream for help and brought Pa running from the other room. But he was not in the other room now, and she was no longer a child. She would have to go through with it. Pa had impressed upon her the importance of this "case."

"First . . . first you must take the proper position."

"And what is that?"

She flushed. "You must lie down."

"Of course." He nodded in mock sobriety. "Will the Belter sofa suffice?" He pointed to it.

She glanced over at its ornate brocade and all the curved wood.

"If it's long enough."

He laughed. "I suppose I can hang my legs over the end."

He crossed the room with his long stride and lay down. His legs did hang over one end.

"Ready!" he told her.

Tawny got to her feet. She pulled off her gloves and put them on a mahogany table next to her reticule. She thought: *I can't do it. I simply can't!* She picked up her gloves and purse and turned toward the door.

"Miss McShane!" His voice was imperious. "I said I was ready."

"I don't want to, Mr. Oliver. I just don't want to."

"I promise to hold very still."

I can do it very quickly and then run, she reassured herself, putting down her gloves and purse again and slowly crossing the room. She knelt beside him. She could see the amusement in his eyes.

Her right hand crept like a coy animal, from his right shoulder, down across his chest, his waist, his hip, his leg. Her left hand began the same journey from his left shoulder. One hand and then the other, slowly at first, then faster and faster, until she pulled both hands away in embarrassment.

"I feel better already," he told her. "Please don't stop the treatment."

She was so close it was all he could do not to reach out and take her in his arms.

She put her right hand on his right shoulder again and repeated the descent, more slowly this time.

Lance reached for the hand and placed it over his organ.

Tawny's mother had died in childbirth so Tawny had never known her, but she was given a clear mental picture of her during her childhood. Her pa would say, "Now, mind your manners. Your mother would have been ashamed of you." Or when Tawny lost her temper he would say, "Now, none of them tantrums! Ladies don't have tantrums. Your mother was a lady."

And often, in his cups, he would talk about his wife. Talking more to himself than to the child. "She was a lady. A rich lady. Her parents said I wasn't good enough for her, me a roustabout. Maybe I wasn't. But she loved me, enough to run off with me. Enough to move into this little old wagon and do her own work and never complain. I can still see her standin' at that table peeling potatoes or washing dishes, or sitting in that rocker darning my socks. It was like havin' a princess for a housekeeper. She was beautiful. Yellow hair and big blue eyes. And so slender. Like some sort of flower she was. Why did she have to die? Why? Why?"

When Tawny was old enough and brave enough to ask, "How did my mother die?" the look he gave her was frightening.

"She died havin' you. *You* was why she died."

Suddenly there was hatred in his voice. When she began to cry he took her in his arms. "Oh, Tawny, Tawny, I didn't mean it. Poor little homely kid, you're all I have left in the world."

After that for a long while she did everything she could to earn her father's praise. The most precious thing in the world was his praise, and it was rarely given.

She was a lonely little girl, traveling in that medicine wagon. There was no time for friends except during the few times her pa set up shop in some small town and she was permitted to attend the local school. She would be on the verge of establishing a real friendship with another little girl when all of a sudden, overnight, they would leave.

The villains of their world were the lawmen. Sooner or later word would reach a sheriff that McShane's Marvelous Medicine wagon was operating on the edge of town. The deputy would descend upon them with a warrant, and Jake's choice was jail or getting out of town. So get he would. Tawny would wake to the noise and shaking of the moving wagon and know that they were on the road again.

When she was old enough, she would stand beside her father when he delivered his harangue about his medicine and then hand down the bottles to customers. It was also her task to help him stir his bad-smelling brew.

After she learned to read that became her greatest pleasure. She read any book or periodical she could get her hands on. Each time her pa made what he called a killing, he would be lavish with gifts. When he asked her what she wanted she always said, "A book." And he would oblige. There was a little shelf in the wagon designed to hold dishes, but the dishes had to go elsewhere as her collection grew. "Looks like a goddamn library," Pa would mutter.

Then one day he caught her singing "Rockaby, Baby" to one of her dolls. Business had been slow and he decided for a curtain raiser, to attract a crowd, he'd have his daughter standing on the back of the wagon, singing familiar little songs like "My Bonnie Lies Over The Ocean" or "The Bear Went Over The Mountain" or even "My Country, 'Tis of Thee," before he made his spiel.

At first Tawny said she wouldn't sing. Pa got very cross and told her she would sing or else. ("Else" meant a harsh spanking with a switch.) So to please him she finally agreed. Shy at first, when she saw the happy looks on her father's face as well as others in the crowd she forgot her timidity and even began to enjoy herself.

Pa had called her a homely little kid, but after she started singing for an audience her inferiority complex gradually evaporated. Frequently above the applause she caught scattered remarks: "The little darling," "Isn't she pretty," "What a charmer!" She was about eight years old and it was from then that her self-confidence began to grow.

She was about ten when the woman who claimed to do magnetic healing crossed their path. She was practicing her art near where Jake had placed his wagon, on the outskirts of a carnival outside of Dayton. Jake had sold his batch of bottles. He and Tawny were roaming the carnival and stopped to listen to the woman's spiel.

She was a roly-poly little number with twinkling eyes. "Electricity is the answer, the answer to everything, dear people. There is a power in my two hands"—she waved them dramatically—"a magic power with which I can cure your ailments, whatever they are."

She was looking straight at Jake McShane and he, laughing, agreed to have a treatment. She lifted the flap of her tent and he followed her in. Tawny sneaked around back of the tent and crawled inside. She was fascinated as she watched the woman stroke Pa and mumble incantations. Pa whispered something to the woman that Tawny could not hear, and got up to leave. The girl crawled hurriedly from the tent. The next thing she knew her father had invited the woman to visit his wagon, sending Tawny outside to play. If it had not started to rain that afternoon Tawny might not have learned the facts of life so soon.

Tawny pushed back the flap at the rear of the wagon and jumped in out of the rain. The wagon boasted no beds, only two mats which were now stretched on the floor. Entwined upon them, completely naked, were her father and the magnetic lady.

Tawny had observed what dogs did to each other, and knew what it meant. Pa had said bluntly that the bitch was in heat and the male was having his fun and that was where puppies came from. But she had not bothered to speculate on what human beings did.

Now she watched the whole process and it seemed incredibly ugly. The woman was moaning strange animal noises, and Jake, now on top of her, was plunging himself up and down with grunts of satisfaction.

Tawny lifted the wagon flap and went out on the step and sat there in the rain.

After a bit she could hear them talking inside.

Jake said, "The best piece of ass I've had in a long time."

"Likewise," said the magnetic lady. "You sure cured my ailment."

"What ailment?"

"Hunger. I was nigh to starving and you have fed me a full meal, soup to nuts."

"No nuts. I've still got them."

What could they be laughing at? the little girl wondered.

Tawny heard her father say, "Sounds like it's raining. The kid'll be back any minute. We better get dressed."

That evening Pa was in very good spirits. In fact, he was happy-go-lucky for several days, until the carnival broke up and everyone went their separate ways. After that one afternoon, he had responded to the woman's call from her room in a hotel, leaving Tawny alone in the wagon. It was then that she started imitating the treatment she had watched the woman administer. "Now you lie still," she would tell her favorite doll Suzie. "This won't hurt a bit and when I'm done you won't have any stomachache at all." She had always treated her dolls as if they were babies, undressing them at night, dressing them in the morning, overseeing their imaginary meals. So this treatment became part of the routine.

That was when Pa discovered her.

"If you can do it to dolls, you can do it to people," he had told her. "When you're putting on your act I won't try to sell my medicine. That'll be for the people you can't cure."

She would always remember that season. "Ladies and gentlemen, may I present my daughter Tawny. This little lady is possessed of a power beyond belief. Yet if you want to see evidence of it, you must believe. By the magic of electricity she will, before your very eyes, arouse your spirit so it will rise triumphant, mind over matter. Your headaches will vanish in the breeze, your rheumatism will flow out of your veins, your broken bones will mend like new again. Your indigestion will melt as if you had taken a strong cathartic, but this will be painless and harmless. God has blessed my little girl with the power to make your mind overcome physical disabilities. All this for a small fee. Who would like to be the first to step into my wagon?"

Because many of Tawny's treatments proved unsuccessful, the McShanes were continually on the run. Finally Pa decided it was time to stop them. Results had to be more or less immediately obvious. With his medicine, by the time the customer had consumed enough of it to know whether it was good or not, Jake would be on the road miles away, selling his stuff to another group of suckers.

Tawny was glad to stop. She was saddened by the trusting people who came into the wagon for a treatment and went away the same as they came in. The way they looked at her as they left haunted her.

When they reached New York City in the spring of 1870 McShane was almost broke. They left the wagon across the river in New Jersey and took the ferry to Manhattan.

Tawny was overwhelmed by her first sight of the city. She stared at the rows of chimney pots that framed the sky, at the carriages and wagons with their iron tires rattling over the cobblestones. There was every imaginable kind of carriage, forming a rainbow of color. There were wagons with casks labelled BEER, and others filled with baskets of vegetables, or sometimes sides of pork. Most impressive were the colorfully painted horsecars, tearing up and down the avenue, bells clanging.

Tawny and her father started crosstown, passing stands selling peanuts, lemonade, clams, threading their way through the jostling masses of people. There was so much noise that it was practically impossible to talk over the shouts of peddlers, scissor-and-knife grinders, newsboys and bootblacks. Tawny's mouth gaped in amazement.

Finally they came out of the hustle-bustle into a residential district. They reached Washington Square and sat down on a bench. Jake looked about him, approving of what he saw: respectable-looking people, children with hoops, women with baby carriages and parasols.

"Tawny," he said, "I want you to stay here for a while. Wait for me. Don't talk to nobody. Understand?"

"Where are you going, Pa?" she dared to ask.

"Never you mind. I've had an idea. Now, just wait. And when I come back we'll have lunch. Somewheres."

When he finally came back and told her she was going to give a magnetic treatment she protested. "Pa, I haven't done that in years!"

"I know. But it'll come back to you."

"But I don't want to! That was kid stuff. I'd feel like a fool."

"We need the money. We need it bad."

"I know, but . . ."

"But me no buts. I'm your father and I say you're going to do it. And take that pout off your face or I'll give you what for right here in front of God and everybody."

She knew he was capable of doing just that. The spankings he had frequently administered when she was small had since then became swift cuffs on the ears that made her head spin.

Her face was downcast. He took hold of her chin and lifted her head so she was looking directly at him. "Well, Tawny?" he asked.

"I'm hungry, Pa. Can we have lunch first?"

"Darn tootin'. Come along."

After lunch he had delivered her to Lance Oliver's doorstep.

* * *

Lance Oliver had grown up in Manhattan, the only son of wealthy Sanford Oliver. He was the sort of person of whom people say, "He was born with a silver spoon in his mouth."

He never had to work; he never wanted to. He had gone to Princeton and happily flunked out during his senior year because he preferred gambling and whoring to studying. He had come home and entered Gotham's social whirl and become a popular guest. He had married well; he had a beautiful home. But at the age of twenty-five he was bored and unhappy.

His wife had been Sue Ellen Appleby, the belle of the ball when he met her. A little Dresden doll of a girl with silky blond hair and wide, innocent eyes, a turned-up nose, and a dimple in her chin.

A friend of Lance's, Jim Bentley, was in hot pursuit of Sue Ellen when Lance first met her. Bentley had been Lance's rival since prep school days, for school offices, in sports. Good-natured rivals. It was a game they played.

Lance had not had marriage in mind when he decided to usurp Sue Ellen's affection from Jim. He began arriving early at parties in order to fill most of her dance program. Jim was a working man, and Lance seized the opportunity of taking her for carriage rides in the day-time, buying her ices at the pavilion in Central Park. She was a pleasant enough little thing, Lance thought, although not too bright. It would be fun to dally along with her for a while.

He reckoned without Sue Ellen, who fell hopelessly in love with him.

He had not tried to touch her; he had gone no farther than holding her hand at the theater, or under the table when they dined at Delmonico's. Then, one rainy night when they were running for a carriage, she slipped and stumbled on the curbstone and would have fallen had he not caught her.

"Sue Ellen, are you all right?"

She threw herself against him. "Oh, hold me, Lance, hold me close!" When he did she sighed, "I've wanted that for so long!"

He was surprised, but not displeased. It was such a soft little body pressed against him. She pulled away suddenly, as if embarrassed, and then took his arm as they walked toward the waiting cab. Once inside and once he had given the destination to the driver, it seemed the most natural thing in the world to take her in his arms and kiss her.

"Oh, Lance," she whispered, "why didn't you do that before?"

"I should have. I certainly should have."

"I love you, Lance."

That's a pretty strong word, he thought. But he was not in the mood for a rhetorical discussion. Instead he kissed her again and held her close, as she had asked him to.

Jim Bentley gradually faded from the picture. If Lance did not call on Sue Ellen or invite her to dinner or the theater or for just a carriage ride, she would invite him. Almost every morning there were letters from her in his mail box. "Darling, I've missed you so; it seems ages since last night." Or "The flowers you sent were simply too beautiful; I slept with one of them under my pillow."

He continued to squirm, but he still enjoyed kissing her.

One night, on her doorstep, after one of her most passionate kisses, she stepped back and looked up at him, starry-eyed. She was wearing a low-cut evening gown that tantalizingly revealed a great deal of her breasts.

He put his hand on her throat, his fingers reaching down. "May I?"

"When we are married, darling. Yes, oh, yes!"

Married! The word struck him like a blow. So that's what this little tease wanted. He had not contemplated marriage in this game of cat and mouse. Rather stupidly he echoed her. "When . . ."

She threw her arms around his neck, pressing that bosom tightly against him. "Next month, Lance. Next month is June. We can have a June wedding. My sister will be back from Europe and she can be my maid of honor and you can have Jim Bentley for your best man. And we can have the reception in the garden—the garden will be beautiful by then."

Lance couldn't help laughing. "Do you realize, you little ninny, I haven't even asked you yet!"

She clung even closer, not speaking, almost as if she had not heard what he said and all at once he knew it was going to happen, and just the way she had described it. In a way he did not feel too bad about it. She was a provocative little bitch, she might even be good at lovemaking if she threw herself into it as impetuously as she threw herself into a mere kiss. His mouth reached for hers again, and this time his kiss burned into her. She pulled away. "Lance, you frightened me!"

"You frighten me," he said dryly.

And so they were married, but did not live happily ever after.

He soon discovered how demanding she was. Her whims knew no bounds. She was also terrified by a host of things. Mice, mosquitoes, ants, as well as unidentified nocturnal noises petrified her. She was a fair bed mate, when she was in the mood, but all too often, when he touched her in bed, she would mumble, "Not now, Lance, I'm so tired." A short while later she'd awaken him with, "Hold me, Lance, I'm so afraid. I thought I heard a burglar." If he then tried to make love she would usually refuse, repeating that perennial cry of "Hold me!" of which he rapidly grew sick.

Then he discovered, all too belatedly, that if he tried to be forceful about anything from lovemaking to deciding on a restaurant, she invariably lost her temper.

"You don't care how I feel! You don't care what I want to do! You're a cruel brute and I hate you, I hate you!"

And she would slap him, fling herself from him, and burst into tears. In the beginning he tried to comfort her, but after a while he just stalked out of the room and let her sob it out.

She constantly flirted, smiling in a way that emphasized her best features and standing temptingly close to every male with whom she was talking. Yet if Lance so much as glanced at another woman in her presence, she would fly into a fit of jealousy, storm to his side, and suggest that they leave the party. If the gathering was at their home she might send him on a hastily invented and nonsensical errand. If she could devise no excuse to separate him from the other woman, she would stand there linking her arm in his, maybe dusting his lapels, even smoothing a lock of his hair.

He soon stopped being nice to other women in her presence, but he did not stop seeing them. With the excuse of going to his club, he managed to include visits to Greene Street, where girls were always available. These expeditions usually took place on the nights when she lost her temper over some slight displeasure. He would simply walk out of the room, and out of the house.

In the beginning she asked him, "Where did you go, Lance?" After repeated curt answers of "To my club," she got the picture; then when he did come to bed, she'd mumble, "Back to your old club again, weren't you? I've been waiting for you . . ." She'd snuggle against him but he'd pretend to be asleep.

The morning he met Jake McShane in that Broadway saloon, Sue Ellen had thrown another tantrum. He had just finished his breakfast and was enjoying the *New York Herald* over his last cup of coffee when she stormed into the room, furious that he had started without her.

"I waited a long time." He pulled out his watch and looked at it. "Over an hour. And I got hungry. That's all."

"What you mean is you'd rather eat alone."

She swung around and snatched the newspaper from him. "Stop hiding your face behind that! You got up early deliberately, didn't you?"

"No. Shall I ring for your breakfast?"

"I say you did. I say you're a selfish, uncaring brute who comes and goes as he pleases, with no thought for how I feel about anything."

"Sue Ellen, stop it!" He got to his feet.

She reached up and slapped the newspaper across his face. He grabbed her by the shoulders and shook her, and then slammed her into a chair.

"Ring for your own damned breakfast. I'm going for a long, peaceful walk."

It was an angry walk, winding up in that Broadway saloon with what McShane called a case of nerves.

When Lance took Tawny's hand and put it on his already throbbing organ he could feel the girl trembling as she knelt there, and he could see the panic in those strangely flecked eyes.

"Mr. Oliver, please!"

"Don't be afraid, child."

"I am not a child."

For Tawny adolescence had not been a gradual change. It was happening this moment. It had in fact begun when she commenced the treatment. She was sharply aware that she was touching a male. Now, feeling the pulsations beneath her hand she felt her own body strangely stirring to life. Her breasts had become taut.

He took his hand off hers and she in turn pulled hers away from his body. She knew she must stand up and walk away but her knees were like rubber.

Lance sat up and put his hands on her slender shoulders and looked into her eyes.

"You are a lovely creature, Miss McShane. I'm sorry if I frightened you. I couldn't help myself. It must be the magnetism." He smiled.

She smiled back. "I'm sorry Pa brought me here. He shouldn't have done it. He made me come. He would have beaten me if I hadn't."

"I'm not sorry you came. Not at all." He leaned forward and kissed her very gently on the lips.

Tawny's heart turned over.

Then he helped her to her feet and stood up himself. For a moment he towered there, holding her arms, looking down at her.

"I never before kissed a woman when she was wearing a hat. Not even my wife. Won't you take it off?"

"Mr. Oliver, I'd better leave. I think I have finished the treatment."

"One more kiss."

Before she could pull away his mouth was over

hers, this one different from the previous kiss. She found herself responding, kissing as she never had before. When they broke apart they were both breathless.

He took his arms away as she lifted hers and without a word took the pins from her feathered bonnet and lifted it from her head. Her bustle twitched from side to side as she crossed the room to put her hat down on the table beside her reticule and gloves. She stood by the table, looking down at her hat for a moment before she turned to face him.

"Tawny McShane. I like your name. Would it be out of order for me to call you Tawny?"

She shook her head. Right then he could have called her anything and she would not have minded. But she was thinking: *this is not the way it should happen.* In the books she had read one did not feel like this until the man had gotten down on his knees and declared his love. She brushed tears from her eyes, tears of shame for her feelings, and of confusion.

There was the sound of footsteps outside the study door. Lance hurried to turn the lock, then came over to where the girl stood, and put his arms around her.

"Don't cry. Don't cry, Tawny, my love."

He kissed her wet cheeks, the lobes of her little ears, and her throat; then their lips met once more and the world was wonderful again.

He picked her up, carried her back to the sofa, and laid her down, and this time it was he who knelt on the floor.

He kissed her again. He could feel her breasts rising against him. After the kiss he touched, oh so tentatively, the top button on the front of that blue poplin dress.

She had closed her eyes. She did not move or protest. He unbuttoned the dress to her waist, pulled down her shift from her shoulders. Her breasts were still rising and falling, lovely, firm, pink-nippled, the loveliest he had ever seen, virginal to be sure.

He fondled them first, feeling the nipples grow firm.

Never, Tawny thought, had anything felt so wondrous.

Then he kissed the breasts, one and then the other, over and over again. He could wait no longer. He unbuttoned the dress the rest of the way and pushed it, the bustle, and shift aside on the floor.

Her eyes flew open and she looked up at him in panic.

"Don't be afraid," he whispered. "I won't hurt you."

"But I . . . I never . . ."

"I know, my darling, I know." Those blue eyes of his with the incredible eyelashes had hypnotized her.

But now he was starting to pull down his trousers, and she shut her eyes again. He began kissing and stroking every part of her body, and every part began to come alive. He parted her legs and kissed her between them, and she trembled with pleasure. He lay on top of her, his jacket and his cravat scratching the breasts now tender from his kisses.

She cried out, and he left her for a moment. Then she could feel his naked body against hers. Another kiss, long and ardent, before he again parted her legs. As if they had minds of their own her legs arched. Slowly and carefully he entered her.

There was a moment's pain and she cried out, but when they were completely joined the pain miraculously was gone and she felt nothing but happiness, happier than she ever had been before in all her life. She felt like an empty vessel that is suddenly filled;

she felt complete, as if until up to now she had not been a whole person.

The girl played only a small part in the lovemaking; she was too young, too inexperienced to do more. Lance, however, was getting almost complete physical satisfaction with such a beautiful body. And the girl could learn—he felt sure she could learn. A magnetic treatment at twenty-five dollars—more expensive than having a whore but much sweeter. Perhaps he could set her up in a little flat on the West Side. Perhaps . . . again and again he plunged inside her, letting her swallow him up.

At last he moved away from her. There was not room on the sofa for two to lie side by side. She felt him slip away from her, and a moment later when she opened her eyes she saw that he was getting dressed. The realization of what she had done then struck home to her. She had reenacted the scene she had watched as a little girl; she had behaved like an animal. She felt ashamed and soiled; she wanted to jump into a tub of water and scrub herself clean. She began to dress, but her tears made it difficult to see what she was doing and her fingers fumbled.

"Do you need help?"

She looked up to see Lance Oliver grinning at her.

"No, *thank* you!" she told him, blinking back the tears, keeping her chin high.

"Tawny, it was worth every penny of the twenty-five dollars I promised your father."

Her whole body was shaking with shame and then anger. She picked up her scattered hairpins and jabbed at her hair until it was mostly in place. Then she went over to the table where she'd left her hat and other things.

"Tawny, wasn't it worth it?"

"It was wicked!" she cried, as she put her bonnet on her head and pinned it in place.

"You seemed to enjoy it as much as I did, you must admit."

"No!" She was picking up her gloves as he came across the room.

"You acted as if you enjoyed it." He put out his arms.

She slapped him across the face with her gloves. "Don't you touch me! Don't you dare touch me!"

Lance only laughed. He found her anger amusing and attractive. The girl had spirit. He gave a little bow and backed a step away. He had seen this happen before. And God knows, he was used to tantrums. However much she denied it, she had welcomed his body. Her own body was candid, even if she was not. Her body would remember and want him again.

"When may I have another treatment, Tawny?"

"Never! I never want to see you again!"

"Someday you will. And not for money."

"Will you please unlock that door so I may leave?"

He did not try to touch her. He unlocked the door, opened it, and stood to one side. She swept past him into the hall and he closed the door.

A moment later he was at the street-side window, pushing back the curtain. He saw her standing hesitantly on the curbstone, clenched fist against her cheek. She looked young and pitiful there alone on the sidewalk. Despite the pleasure he had known that afternoon, he was a little ashamed of what had happened.

It had started to rain.

The rain will wash away my sin, Tawny thought as

she started down the street. She was supposed to wait for her father on that same bench at Washington Square. It was not far and Pa had shown her the way. But when she reached the first corner her feet abruptly dragged to a stop.

She was mad at herself, she was mad at Lance Oliver, a married man committing adultery in his own house. But she was also mad at her father. It was his fault, his fault from the very beginning, getting her to practice magnetic healing. There had been no sense to it when she was a child, and even less sense now. Her father must have known what would happen. It was as if she were a prostitute and he were a—what was the word for it? Pimp. He would arrange it again. With someone else.

She wouldn't go to the bench in the park. She wouldn't be waiting there, like a dutiful child. She had no friends in New York City, and she had only a few coins in her purse. But she would not go back to her father.

Chin up, she turned the corner and headed west.

2

Sue Ellen Appleby Oliver had been a spoiled brat who always got everything she wanted since she had stood up in her high chair and demanded pudding instead of porridge. The second and younger daughter of well-to-do parents, she was cherished and doted upon. Her older sister, a placid, unassuming girl, had no resentment. She, too, adored little Sue Ellen.

In the big house on Gramercy Park, Sue Ellen had a nursery full of dolls, a nursemaid at her beck and call. A born flirt, little Miss Appleby got her way with everyone. And if she did not, she stomped her foot, she screamed, and the world tumbled to her feet.

As she grew up she developed no interests beyond living for pleasure. She cared nothing for art or music; most books bored her. She loved fashion: *Godey's Lady's Book* was her bible. With an armoire already bursting with clothes she always demanded a new frock for any occasion. She spent hours in her bath and at her dressing table. And she loved men, men in the plural, dancing attendance, sending her flowers. But she kept them at arm's length until, at the age of eighteen, she set eyes on Lance Oliver.

He was what she wanted.

He was a big man. She preferred big men, probably because her dear papa was one. She had loved for Papa to sweep her up high in the air and then let her cuddle down in his lap and play with his mustache and beard. She imagined Lance picking her up and carrying her off like a prince in a fairy tale. She thought of it the moment she set eyes upon him.

Another attraction was that he did not immediately dance *his* attendance when they first met. He was cool and polite, his eyebrows usually raised in a sardonic fashion. When she tried to flirt with him he only smiled indifferently.

She was bored with Jim Bentley. She knew that he and Lance were more or less friends and she supposed that Lance did not make a fuss over her out of consideration for Jim. It was not in Sue Ellen's nature to play the game of pretended aloofness, however, which was what would have intrigued Lance immediately. Nor did it occur to her that the reason why he finally started courting her was in fact the friendly rivalry between the two men. Lance's continued coolness, his lack of emotion, Sue Ellen finally attributed to shyness. When he did hold her hand her whole body shivered and when he kissed her she knew she wanted him more than anything else in the world. With great effort, during this period, she kept her temper. She must do nothing, nothing to displease him.

She was a little frightened when she thought of what it would be like to go to bed with a husband. But she was confident that Lance would be gentle. Despite his size he was not a rough man; his very touch was tender. Somehow she must persuade him to propose.

The night he put his hand at the top of her bodice was her great opportunity to let him know how she felt, what *her* intentions were. It was a trick, but it worked!

After the engagement had been announced she allowed him to fondle her much more than before. If he wanted to slip his hand inside her dress while kissing her she did not object. She always managed to end such sessions abruptly, pretending it was because she was a "nice girl," but knowing in her heart that it was pure teasing to make him want her more than ever. He never said "I love you" voluntarily, and when she pressed him with "Do you love me, Lance?"—which she did many times—his answer always was "Of course I do."

On the eve of the wedding, when he had escorted her from a party and kissed her good night she whispered, "Tomorrow. Oh, Lance, tomorrow we'll be married!" Lance whispered back, "Tomorrow night we can go to bed together," and gave her a bear hug. She realized then that bed was all he was thinking about. He had bought a house on lower Fifth Avenue but he had been disinterested in the choice of furnishings. He left all that up to her. He had shown little interest in the wedding gifts that had been pouring in, nor had he cared about the details of the wedding at all. It was just the only way he could get to bed with her!

She cried herself to sleep that night.

In the morning, however, she felt better, mostly because of the excitement of it being her wedding day. Her parents appeared happy with her choice of a mate, but all the same Mother cried a little over losing "her baby" and Papa said, "It won't be the same without you, sweetheart. I only hope he can make you happy."

"I know he will!" Sue Ellen cried. But she was beginning to wonder.

The ceremony at Grace Church was dignified, and for Sue Ellen it seemed the climax of her life. The garden reception was all she had dreamed it would be. But when it was time for her to change to her traveling dress, she began to be nervous.

It had been a beautiful day, but the rain started as they left the house in the rice-sprinkled carriage. They took the ferry across the Hudson to New Jersey and the train down to Atlantic City, and she got a cinder in her eye. Lance finally removed it with the corner of his handkerchief, but it took long enough to dampen any amorous hand-holding that might have brightened the journey.

They supped in the hotel dining room and smiled at each other across the candlelit table. Sue Ellen looked lovely in her traveling dress, a soft green silk trimmed in smart loops of black grosgrain ribbon. Lance's blue eyes were shining with pleasure at the sight of her.

As they finished dessert Lance said, "I'm getting awfully sleepy, aren't you?" He winked.

Sue Ellen found herself blushing. "I think the wine has made me sleepy, too," she said shyly.

He reached over and patted her hand. "It's not the wine in my case, my dear. It's the thought of being alone with you."

As they left the dining room and headed for the stairs, Sue Ellen suddenly stopped and looked up at him. "Lance, would you give me the room key? I'd like to go up alone, first."

"Oh?" He frowned.

"You . . . you have a cigar or something in the

lobby. Then come up in a little while. It takes me a bit to get ready . . ." she hesitated ". . . for bed."

"Not *too* long."

"Oh, no. Half an hour?"

He was still frowning as he handed her the key and walked away.

Up in the room she had to open her suitcase and find her lotions and creams and other toiletries and take them into the bathroom. She went through a beautification process every night, and this night was not going to be different. She undressed, put on her new white satin nightgown, and admired herself in the mirror. She looked different without her bustle, smaller and thinner.

She had barely finished before Lance knocked on the door.

"I'm coming," she called out, hurrying to put on her matching white satin robe with its fringe of marabou before she opened the door.

He came in quickly and shut the door behind him, swinging the latch. He took her in his arms and kissed her, pressing her close against him. It was strangely different to be held like that without her usual layers of clothing, particularly her corset. Her breasts felt small and tender.

He released her. "Took you long enough. But you're beautiful." His voice was gruff.

"Thank you, Lance!"

"Why don't you get into bed while I undress?"

"Lance, will you undress in the bathroom? Please?"

"If you like."

He went into the bathroom and closed the door.

Feeling very timid, Sue Ellen slipped out of her robe and laid it across a chair. She decided not to turn off the lamp beside the bed, crawled in on the other side, and pulled the covers up.

The door to the bathroom opened and Lance came back into the room. Sue Ellen gasped. He was naked.

"Lance, where is your nightshirt?"

He laughed. "I didn't bring a nightshirt. I didn't think I'd need it."

She had never seen a naked man before and the sight of the strapping body, as well as his big penis, was frightening. He crossed the room and pulled the covers off, staring down at her. "Surely you're not going to wear that!"

"Of course I am!" She averted her face so as not to see his nakedness.

He sat down on the edge of the bed and ran his fingers over her satin-covered body. "Please, Sue Ellen. I've waited so long to see you, to touch you."

She was frightened of his body now. His touch did not make her feel as his kisses had. She sat up in bed and pushed him away. "I will not sleep naked!" She moved over and got out of her side of the bed. The temper she had held in control for so many weeks now flared. Tears poured down her cheeks and she began screaming, incoherently, hysterically.

Lance stared at her in amazement. Finally he said, "Come back to bed, Sue Ellen."

"I won't! I won't!"

"I'm terribly sorry," he said quietly. "Perhaps I should get another room for tonight."

"Oh, no! No! Just . . ." Her voice was lower now. "Turn out the light?"

Lance did. She slipped back into bed again and into his arms. After a while her crying stopped and she let him put his hand inside her gown and touch her breasts, and under the hem of the gown to caress her there while he kissed her. And after another long while the nightgown was pushed high up to her waist and he entered her.

He did not ask her to take off her nightgown again.

No, marriage was not at all what Sue Ellen had expected. She had anticipated constant devotion and companionship. Instead she found herself leading a split life. She was in morbid fear of becoming pregnant. Some nights the fear was so great that she refused to have intercourse. Each month when her period came she thanked God.

She loved the house—her house—for she had selected the furnishing. She loved having servants to order about, and order she did, and scold if things were not exactly to her liking. Once Lance remonstrated with her for lighting into a maid who had left a dust mop on the stairway and she had whirled on her husband and told him to mind his own business. He reminded her that it was his house as well and another tantrum had resulted.

In spite of it all, she still was in love with him. To be in his arms continued to be the most wonderful thing in the world. It never occurred to her that there would or could be other women in his life. He was her husband. He was hers. She owned every inch of that big beautiful body.

She was busy at her dressmaker's the afternoon that Tawny McShane came to the house. She did not see the girl arrive or depart.

Two days later, sitting in the parlor, Sue Ellen read an item in one of the gossipy newspapers that she adored, an item that made her sit up straight with shock:

"There is much speculation about the recently established Woman's Center. The place is in charge of that well-known Women's Rights lady, Miss Evangeline McClintock, whose flamboyant opinions rival those of Victoria Woodhull. Woman's Center purports to be a sanctuary, a haven for fallen women, but there are those who say it is in truth no sanctuary, that gentlemen are discreetly received and are given the assistance in which the occupants are well practiced. This, of course, is stoutly denied by Miss McClintock. Everyone is aware of the fact that Commodore Vanderbilt is Victoria Woodhull's benefactor—sponsoring her and her sister Tennessee Claflin's brokerage house and the *Woodhull and Claflin Weekly*. What is not so well known is the name of Miss McClintock's fairy godfather, but rumor has it that he is a well-to-do sybarite. By any chance could the first name be Lance?"

Sue Ellen stared at the paper in shocked disbelief; then she read the paragraph again, slowly and carefully, before tossing the newspaper aside. Gossip. Just gossip. But was it? She thought of all the nights Lance went to his club. She thought of all the times, day and night, when he simply walked off, out of the house. Could he have some relationship with that terrible woman? Not Lance, not *her* Lance! She picked up the newspaper. She would come right out and ask him if the gossip were true.

He was in his study, into which she was not allowed to go. He had made that clear the day they moved into the house. She had been furious, but on that point he stood his ground. "Man's domain," he called it; it was where he took gentlemen guests for their cigars and brandy after dinner.

She looked down at the newspaper in her hands. *Lance and Evangeline McClintock.* The thought sickened her. And angered her. She must show it to him, she must watch his face as he read it. Please God she would see anger there, anger at an untruth. She marched out of the parlor and across the front hall and knocked on the study door.

Lance was not alone in the study. On the other side of his desk sat Jake McShane, cigar in hand, his hat still on the back of his head. Two days before, after Tawny left, Lance went to the Broadway saloon where he and Jake had met, had a drink with him, paid the twenty-five dollars, and, when asked if the treatment had been satisfactory, merely nodded. He had begun to see it now, as Tawny had seen it, a pretty dirty business, a father procuring for his own daughter, and now he disliked Jake.

"I'll fix up another, whenever you want it," McShane told him.

Lance shook his head. He would very much like to see Tawny again, but he would not arrange it through her father.

This afternoon when the butler announced a Mr. McShane to see him, Lance had been most displeased. He stood up behind his desk as Jake came in.

"And what can I do for you, Mr. McShane? If you recall, I did not request another treatment."

"That ain't what I came about."

"No?" No doubt the old coot had some other scheme for separating him from a few dollars. He wondered what it might be this time. Suddenly he wondered: could it be that he was going to accuse him of raping his daughter and threaten suit? He wouldn't put it past him.

Jake sat down and lit a cigar, so Lance sat down again. After a puff or two on the cigar, Jake said,

"I've come to see what you've done with my daughter."

Lance gasped. "I haven't seen your daughter since day before yesterday."

"I ain't either. She was s'posed to meet me in Washington Square but she never turned up. I went on back across the river figuring she'd turn up some time, but she didn't. I didn't think of it right away but then it come to me. You'd decided to hang onto her." His eyes were crafty now. As if he would not have objected to Lance hanging onto her.

"I can assure you, Mr. McShane, I did no such thing. She left here less than two hours after she arrived. Do you think that if I had decided to hang onto her, as you put it, I would have walked over to Broadway and paid you that disgusting twenty-five dollars?"

McShane was aware of the chill in Lance's voice, and guessed what Lance thought of him. "I think you would have. Or could have. I guess she skipped out on you, too." McShane actually smiled.

"She left in rather a hurry. I am sorry that she is lost." *But not sorry that you lost her, old boy,* Lance thought. *Just sorry that she is alone somewhere in the big city, so young, so pretty, so innocent.*

That was when Sue Ellen knocked on the study door.

Anticipating some urgent call from the butler, Lance crossed the room and said behind the closed door, "Yes? What is it, Milton?"

"It's not Milton, it's Sue Ellen!" The high-pitched tone indicated anger. "Lance, I've got to talk to you!"

If he refused to let her come in he knew she would start pounding on the door and in a moment would be screaming vilifications. Behind him McShane chuckled. "You got woman trouble, don't you, boy?"

Lance opened the door and she burst into the room, flapping her newspaper. She spotted McShane and lowered her hand. "I'm sorry, I didn't know; I thought you were alone."

"This is Mr. McShane. He's just leaving."

Jake was on his feet. He tipped his hat. "And this must be Mrs. Oliver?"

She looked at McShane with extreme distaste, wondering what sort of business Lance could be doing with such a shabby creature.

Jake, grinning now, said, "Well, I must be meanderin'." He looked at Lance. "Sorry I can't fix it up for you to have another treatment." He bowed to Sue Ellen as she stepped aside to allow him to walk through the door.

"Who is he? What is this all about?" Sue Ellen wanted to know.

"Nothing important."

"What's this about a treatment? What sort of treatment did that dreadful old man give you?"

Lance, somewhat amused by her vehemence, explained casually, "He didn't give the treatment. His daughter is the child wonder."

"His *daughter*!" Sue Ellen choked out the words.

"It's nothing for you to bother about. I met Mr. McShane in a saloon. He noticed my nervousness. It was after your explosion at the breakfast table the other morning. He suggested a treatment. It's all some nonsense about magnetism. I took the treatment. My nerves did improve. However, that's beside the point. What is it today that set you off? That sent you pounding on the door to my private study?"

His offhand manner of explaining his relationship with the old man only made Sue Ellen more curious, and more furious. She held out the newspaper, folded to the page and column.

"This," she said. "Read it!"

He recognized the newspaper. "Sue Ellen, you know I never read those scandalmongering sheets." He deplored the fact that his wife actually enjoyed reading trash, turning up her nose at respectable newspapers like the *Times, Tribune*, or *Herald.*

She stood there holding the newspaper out as if she were a child with a composition book. With her free hand she pointed to the place on the page. "There!" she commanded. "Read that!"

Reluctantly he took the newspaper.

She watched his face as his eyes followed each line. He was frowning and when he finished reading and handed the paper back to her his gesture was an angry one.

Sue Ellen sighed with relief. "Then it's not true?"

"Of course it's not true. The Woman's Center is exactly what it's purported to be, a haven for outcasts. A place where these poor creatures have a chance to be rehabilitated. Evangeline McClintock has done a brave and noble thing to establish such a place. Evangeline is a fine woman. She doesn't deserve such slander."

Sue Ellen's hands holding the newspaper were trembling. Startled by his outburst she finally managed to ask, "You know her, then?"

"Yes," he said shortly, turning toward the window.

"Then the rest of the article is true?"

He whirled around defensively. "What if it is?"

"Oh, Lance, Lance!" she cried. "Not you and that dreadful woman. I couldn't bear it!"

"Evangeline is an old friend of mine, whether you like it or not. I knew her long before I met you."

"You were in love with her?"

Lance, who was growing sick of this inquisition, snapped, "She is my friend. I told you that."

Her pinched face was eager as she asked, "But it's all over now, isn't it?"

Lance looked down at her. How little she understood about life, about anything! How lacking she was in any kind of generous understanding! It was all Sue Ellen and what she wanted or didn't want.

He spoke as gently as he could. "What if I told you that I still do see Evangeline occasionally? That real friendship isn't turned off like a faucet? That I did help finance her Woman's Center?"

She was in tears now, hating the possibility of all of his "what ifs."

"I couldn't bear it, Lance! I simply couldn't bear it!" Her voice had risen.

"What would you do?"

"I'd kill myself!"

Lance laughed. "Oh, no!"

"I would! I would!" She was thoroughly angry now, stamping her foot, her small breasts rising and falling with her deep breathing.

"You haven't got the guts for that, little girl."

"What did you say?"

"I said, you haven't got the guts. You're a stinking little coward, scared of half the world."

She threw herself down on the sofa, sobbing, beating her fists into the upholstery. Her hair tumbled out of her chignon and spread over her shoulders.

Lance went to the cabinet in the corner and poured himself a stiff shot of brandy. He watched her as he stood there sipping it. *Jealous little fool.* He cursed her for having come into the study, for having entered his private world. She belonged upstairs in their bedroom.

"Stop the bawling!" he growled at her. "Go upstairs to your room."

"I won't!"

"Oh, yes you will!"

He put down his brandy glass and strode across the room. He picked her up from the sofa by her shoulders, swung her around and shook her.

She struck at his face. "I hate you! I hate you! You're a brute and you're wicked; you've ruined my life!"

He slapped her face.

The hysteria suddenly stopped.

"I don't really hate you, Lance. I couldn't!" She looked up at him with trembling lips.

"Sometimes *I* hate *you*," he told her, and went back to his glass of brandy.

3

After she left Lance Oliver's house Tawny walked along a street of similar brownstones, all with polished brass door knockers and shining steps. None of them was as big as Oliver's had been, but all were impressive. Tawny wondered what kind of people lived behind those heavily curtained windows.

As she headed west and then south the brownstones were replaced by shingled buildings of various sizes, with many awnings that protected her from the rain. The streets were crowded with people, most with umbrellas which they held so low over their faces as to render them half-blind, and Tawny was constantly jostled.

She was getting hungry, but she could not see any acceptable-looking restaurants, only the swinging doors of countless saloons. At last she spotted a little shed on a corner, like a stand at a carnival, and when she came closer she could smell coffee and grease.

She was standing there trying to decide if this was where she would have supper when someone asked, "Would you like a butter cake, dolly?" She turned to see a roughly dressed man tipping his battered hat.

"No, thank you!" She walked on, hurrying as fast as she could across the crowded street.

Dusk was beginning to fall. She paused to watch a lamplighter. The rain was lessening but the streets were still wet and the lamplights shone in circles on the cobblestones.

On the next corner there was an organ grinder, and Tawny stopped to listen. The man's pet monkey was bouncing up and down on the cobblestones, and when the music was finished he took off his little red cap and held it out.

"You darling!" Tawny cried and, forgetting how few coins she had, put one in the monkey's cap and walked on.

She came to a restaurant, a clean-looking place with many shiny windows and some tables and chairs on the sidewalk under an awning. It was called The Red Horn, and had a picture of a horn on its flapping sign. The people at the little tables were well dressed and respectable-looking.

She went in and sat down. She was tired as well as hungry, and it was pleasant to sit there in the twilight and watch the lighted carriages and people pass. Traffic was still heavy, still noisy. It seemed a fast-moving parade, a show put on for her benefit.

A waiter materialized at her elbow, and she said, smiling, "May I have a menu, sir?"

The waiter looked down at her. He seemed embarrassed. At last he spoke. "I'm sorry, ma'am, but we do not serve unescorted ladies."

"Oh?" She got to her feet.

"I *am* sorry," he again apologized. He did look sorry. He had a kind face.

"Where can I go?" she asked. "Where can I eat?"

He thought a moment before he said, "There's a

place up the street. Ma Kelly's Kitchen, it's called. She don't have the rule."

"Thank you! Which way?"

He pointed. " 'Tisn't far."

"Thank you," she said again.

Ma Kelly's Kitchen was a crowded, dirty hole-in-the-wall, with a small bar at one end. The menu was fly-spotted and the waiter was ugly. The fare was limited, and cheap. While the waiter watched, Tawny took the coins from her reticule and spread them out on the red-checkered tablecloth, looked back and forth from her change to the menu until she finally decided on corned beef and cabbage. She had enough to cover that.

While she was eating, complete darkness fell on the city. The next step would be to find somewhere to sleep.

Where could she go? She lacked enough money for a hotel. She couldn't just knock on people's doors and beg them to take her in. Nor could she approach a policeman; he might put her in jail for vagrancy. Pa had trained her never to speak to policemen. And these in Manhattan were particularly intimidating with their clubs and their hard hats and long beards. She decided she would approach the first woman she saw.

She came out of the restaurant into the almost black night. The streetlamps with their circles of light served as guideposts. She started walking, trying to look into people's faces as they passed, but they were oblivious to her glances. She might have been invisible.

Then she spotted a haven, a church with the doors standing open. She had never been in a church, but from what she had read they were safe shelters.

Inside, the church was lit by soft candlelight.

There was a soothing silence, and an odor of incense. The benches were not exactly comfortable, but it was a place to sit. Two other people up front arose after a few moments; they went forward to the altar, knelt and crossed themselves, and left the church. In the back row Tawny felt very much alone, and very tired. She curled up on the hard bench, using her reticule for a pillow, and went to sleep.

She jerked awake when someone touched her shoulder. She sat up and stared at the old man in the cassock, a lantern in his hand. At first she could not remember where she was; the man with the lantern was like something in a dream.

"Closing time, child."

Slowly she remembered everything. She stumbled to her feet, sighing, and walked out into the night.

She would remember that night for the rest of her life. Walking, sitting on doorsteps when she was weary, ducking into doorways when she saw a man approaching.

When the stars first started to pale in the sky, she found herself almost to the Hudson River. She could smell it and hear it, and she thought of the ferryboat she had ridden on that morning. Should she try to find it? Should she try to go back to Pa? No, she told herself stubbornly. Never!

Ahead of her was a large building. The curving banisters on each side of its row of steps gave evidence that once it had been a mansion. The big sign above the front door said WOMAN'S CENTER. Tawny did not know what that meant, nor did she care; she was too bone-weary, too discouraged. Halfway up the long staircase she collapsed.

Evangeline McClintock was a light sleeper, an early riser. She awakened each morning to the sound of the bell on the milkman's wagon in the alley at the back door. She would stretch and yawn until she heard the wagon clatter away and then tell herself it was time to get up.

She always went first to the window, raised the shade, and looked at the day, mumbling a quotation to herself: "So here has been dawning another blue day. Think, wilt thou let it slip useless away?" Never had Evangeline let a day slip away useless. "Action!" was her motto.

She was only staying in charge of the center until she could find a suitable person to take her place. Then off would she go on one of her lecture tours, on which she would hold forth on women's rights, women's suffrage, freedom of the press, and other subjects, a jumble of matters her audiences loved. It was not so much what Evangeline McClintock had to say as Evangeline herself, a plump little person with expressive eyebrows, sharp, inquisitive black eyes, and a piercing voice.

She pushed back the curtain, raised the shade, and looked out. The sky was a lucid blue this morning, without a cloud. Beyond the smaller houses across the street she could see the early sun glittering on the Hudson. And then, before she turned away, she looked down at the front steps.

Someone was sprawled there. A drunk? She looked closer. No, it was a woman. Another guest for the center.

Evangeline did not stop to dress. She put on a robe over her nightgown and hurried out of her bedroom and downstairs.

She was surprised to see how young the girl on her doorstep was. Most of Tawny's hair had tumbled from under her bonnet and reached her shoulders. But otherwise she did not have the disheveled look of most girls who turned up at the center. Nor was her dress flamboyant, as many of them were. Her simple blue poplin dress was not the sort a prostitute would wear.

Very gently Evangeline bent down and touched the girl's cheek.

"No, Pa, No!" The girl gave a little groan before she opened her eyes and looked up. Strange, beautiful, wild eyes, Evangeline thought.

Evangeline smiled at her. "If you have the strength to stand up, I'll take you inside."

"Where am I? What happened?"

"You're safe. I'm Evangeline McClintock. I have a place for you."

She took the girl by the arms and dragged her to her feet. Tawny was struggling to remember all that had happened yesterday. She was clinging to her reticule as if it were the only reality in her world. She let the plump little woman lead her the rest of the way up that long flight of stairs, through the open front door. They stopped for a moment in the hall and then the woman called Evangeline said, "One more flight, to reach a bed."

It was a small, sparsely furnished room, but there was a bad. Tawny had never slept in a real bed in all her life. Just on that mat on the floor of the wagon.

Passively she allowed Evangeline to unbutton her dress. She remembered, only yesterday, that man doing it. She gave a little shudder.

Evangeline hung the dress over the back of a chair. Then she pulled off the rumpled and faintly bloodstained shift, and the bustle, and ordered Tawny to remove shoes and stockings and to lie down on the bed. She filled the wash basin and oh so carefully washed the girl's body from face to toe. There were small bruises on her breasts, and the inflamed crotch told Evangeline what had happened. But Evangeline was familiar enough with young girls' bodies to know that this girl was no whore. She must have been the victim of rape, which would also account for her state of near exhaustion.

Tawny was given a clean cotton nightgown, a cup of warm milk with a spot of brandy in it, after which she fell into a sound sleep.

When Evangeline came downstairs the other "guests" were at the breakfast table. They were a motley crew, all sizes and shapes, looking bedraggled without the paint on their faces. Evangeline insisted on scrubbed faces. Six of them this morning.

"Another fallen angel?" one of them asked as Evangeline joined them at the big round table.

"Not exactly." Evangeline smiled. "I don't believe she has professional status. Let us be careful what we say to her until I've talked with her. Right now she's sleeping."

Evangeline McClintock was a minister's daughter. She was well raised and educated and, at an unusually young age, was teaching in a female college in New England. All her life Evangeline had had strong opinions, and had voiced them. Her classrooms became her audiences. She could manage to ring in women's rights even in a course on medieval poetry. When the door to the classroom was shut, the room was her own little world. Of course her career as a teacher was doomed. Her originality made her popular with the students, but not with the housemistress. Also discovered was her friendship with Susan B. Anthony and Isabel Beecher Hooker, not to mention Victoria Woodhull, which did not set well with the authorities. Furthermore, not only did she preach free love, in a quite way she practiced it.

She fell head over heels in love with a man in the

college community. They were seen walking together in the woods outside of the town. He was a married man with a hopelessly insane wife, and was not free to marry Evangeline. She knew that and accepted it.

When her lover, desperate because of the situation, committed suicide, her affair became a scandal and she was summarily dismissed. Barred from teaching, she soon found out how difficult it was for a woman to support herself. She could have gone home to her family, become the old-maid sister who lives at home and helps out, but that was not Evangeline's wont. Or would it have been fair to inflict a now-notorious person like herself on her father, who did have his reputation to maintain with his congregation. She had damaged that enough already.

She earned part of her living with her lecture tours. But she also received support from various well-to-do gentlemen. She did not allow herself to fall in love again. She was a practical woman; if men were willing to pay, she was willing to sell—for a limited engagement. She might have been dubbed a high-class whore, but she did not think of it that way.

Now in her thirties, a certain maternal instinct was developing. She felt a great sympathy for women who had stumbled into prostitution by accident, through poverty, or through seduction and abandonment, women who knew no other way to go but down, but who, on the other hand, longed to start new lives without the stigma.

That was why, with Lance Oliver's help, she had been able to rent this big old house and take in women who sincerely wanted to be rehabilitated. It was true, she had not had success with too many; they had left her house and gone back on the streets.

But others she had helped; they had found respectable jobs or even, some of them, husbands.

When Tawny finally woke up she felt almost like herself again. Her eyes first fell on her dress and her shift, washed and ironed and neatly laid out across the chair.

There was a knock at the door and as she said, "Come in!" Tawny sat up in bed and tossed back her mass of dark red hair.

It was Evangeline, accompanied by a wide-eyed maid with a breakfast tray. She put the tray on the table beside the bed and disappeared. When the door closed behind the maid, Evangeline sat down at the foot of the bed and smiled.

"If you're hungry, eat. Then we can talk."

"Thank you. It looks good. Dinner last night seems a long time ago."

"It *was* a long time ago. It's almost noon, now."

Evangeline watched the girl's long graceful fingers as she spread butter on the croissant, noticed the easy grace when she lifted her coffee cup. She was wildly curious, but she said nothing until the girl had finished eating and lain back down on the pillows.

"My name is Evangeline McClintock," she began. "I told you early this morning but you may not remember. You were pretty groggy when I found you on the doorstep."

Tawny nodded. "How do you do, Miss McClintock."

"And what is your name? I think we should get acquainted."

"My name is Tawny McShane."

"McShane. McClintock. A pair of micks."

Tawny laughed. "I guess so."

"Where did you come from, Tawny McShane?"

"From New Jersey, yesterday."

"So you're a Jerseyite."

Tawny shook her head. "We . . . I only came to New Jersey last week."

"You've been traveling."

"Yes. Always, I guess. At least as far back as I can remember."

"You started to say *we*. Who is we?"

"My father and I." Tawny bit her lip and frowned. She was not sure if she wanted to tell this stranger all about Pa and herself.

Evangeline got up and crossed the room, took Tawny's chin in her hand, and lifted her face. "Look, child, you don't have to tell me anything you don't want to. People who come to this center come because they want to forget the past, because they want to start a new life. But sometimes a little confession is good for the soul. So anything you really *want* to tell me, you may. You may trust me."

Tawny believed her. Those sharp black eyes were blatant with honesty. "My father sold medicine. Medicine he made himself. We traveled all over. We lived in a wagon."

Evangeline, listening, could picture the wagon. She had seen such during her travels.

Tawny had paused, and Evangeline said, "You speak of it all in the past. What is your father doing now?"

Tawny shook her head. "I don't know. But he'll probably go back to his medicine. He always did. You know, now and then he'd get some other idea of how to make money. But always he went back to McShane's Marvelous Medicine."

"I see."

"Miss McClintock . . ." Tawny was rubbing her hands together, nervously.

"You may call me Evangeline, Tawny, if we're to be friends."

"Evangeline, when you asked what my father is doing now I was being honest when I said I didn't know. You see, I've left my father. I ran away from him yesterday. And I'm never going back. Never! No matter what becomes of me!"

"I see," Evangeline said again. After a moment she asked, "What happened yesterday, Tawny?"

"He made me go back to magnetic healing." Her voice was bitter.

"What on earth is that?"

"It's hokum. Pure hokum! You touch people in a certain way, one hand and then the other, and you pretend it's a kind of electricity that will cure them of almost anything."

"Fantastic. A kind of faith healing?" Evangeline mumbled.

"I guess you'd call it that. It's like Pa's medicine: you have to believe in it to make it work."

"I never heard of such a thing."

"I never had until once when I was still a little girl. We met a woman who claimed to be doing magnetic healing. It was near a carnival, where our wagon stopped. And being a kid, I pretended to do it with my dolls. And Pa got the idea I could do it to people. It would be part of his show. Like the songs he used to have me sing before he started in talking about the medicine. And so I did it. I always did what Pa said, if only to get out of beatings."

"You poor child."

"I am *not* a child! I'm almost sixteen!" She lifted her head high.

Evangeline, looking at those breasts under the thin nightgown, conceded, "No, you are no longer a child. And yesterday?"

"He arranged for me to give a treatment to a rich man in New York City. In the man's house."

She flung herself face downward on the bed and burst into tears.

Evangeline patted her shoulder. "I can guess the rest," she said quietly.

When Lance said, "Sometimes *I* hate *you*," in such a quiet way, Sue Ellen could only stare at him. No one had ever told her that before. It sent a cold shiver down her spine. Lance, of all people. Lance, her love, her life. It seemed the end of the world.

He had told her to go to her room and she had refused. Now, without a word, without a look, she turned and walked out of the study, into the hall, and up the broad, curved stairway, one hand on the banister because she could not see for the tears that filled her eyes.

She lay on her bed, feeling cold and lonely. Gradually the tears stopped and she stared wide-eyed at the brass chandelier that hung from the ceiling.

Meanwhile Lance finished his brandy, lay down on the sofa, and also stared up at the ceiling.

At first all he could feel was his anger. How dared Sue Ellen come into the study? How dared she intrude on his private world? Most men had mistresses as well as wives. Not that Evangeline was his mistress, she was his friend. True he had slept with her, true they had enjoyed a few romps together. They understood each other. Their relationship was private; it had nothing to do with Sue Ellen.

But after a while, as he lay there, his anger faded. He had said cruel things to his wife. He had called her a stinking little coward; he had told her he hated her. He thought of the look on her face when she walked out of the room.

Slowly he got to his feet and took one more glass of brandy. He was a bit heady when he left the study and climbed the stairs. He opened and closed the door to their bedroom very carefully, in case she might be asleep.

She had taken off her bustle and loosened her dress at the bodice. Her hair hung down in ringlets. Lying there, wide-eyed, she looked even younger and smaller than he remembered her. She did not speak; she did not even look at him.

He crossed to the window and drew the shade, then sat down on the edge of the bed. "Sue Ellen . . ."

She did not answer.

"Like you said, I was a brute and I'm sorry."

At last she turned her head and looked up at him. She reached up to touch his cheek. "Oh, Lance, I love you so!"

It was not love he felt. Nor had it ever been. He felt pity, he felt tenderness, that was all he could give her. He bent and kissed her lips and her arms were around him and she was pulling him down beside her, clinging to him like a hurt child.

As ever, her cry was "Hold me!" But a moment later she took him by surprise. She moved away and began tearing at her clothes, and in no time at all she was spread out on the bed, naked.

Slowly Lance began undressing. He was not prepared for this; he was not in the mood for this.

Sue Ellen, watching him, was thinking: *if this is what he wants, this is what he gets. I'll do anything to keep him. I'll debase myself. I'll grovel. I'll keep him from ever wanting to go to that whore.* Her whole body was not suffused with passion as much as sheer determination to possess him.

Lance sensed this and resented it.

It was the first time he had seen her naked. In the soft afternoon light that filtered through the shutters her pale white body was too thin, too childlike. Only her lips were sensuous, those lips that could pout so easily, now half-open, moist, waiting for his.

He sat down on the side of the bed and put his hands over her small breasts, closing his eyes as he bent to kiss her. She had called him wicked and right now he felt wicked, felt as if he were sinning.

Again she surprised him. She reached out and stroked his organ.

But he did not respond. He could not respond. Lance, who had lain with dozens of women, was this afternoon impotent.

4

Tawny had been at the Woman's Center for two days. Evangeline had insisted that she rest, and eat, and not think about anything but recuperating. She was treated like a patient in a hospital, confined to her room.

But Tawny could not help but think.

The second morning, when Evangeline and breakfast appeared together, Tawny was up and dressed and standing by the window that overlooked the alley that ran behind the house, watching the chambermaid emptying pots into the privy.

"And how are you this morning?" Evangeline asked.

"I'm fine! Fine! You don't have to treat me like an invalid anymore."

"Good."

"And therefore I've got to talk to you. I'm worried."

"About what?"

"About how I'm going to pay you for taking me in, for giving me a bed, for feeding me. For everything!"

"There's no need to pay me."

"But . . ."

"Look, Tawny," Evangeline interrupted. "The girls who come to me here do not pay. They have no means with which to pay."

"They're like me?"

Evangeline smiled. Her eyes sparkled. "No, my dear, they're not at all like you. They're prostitutes."

"But I . . ." Tawny flushed.

"Eat your breakfast, and then we'll talk."

Tawny ate with dispatch. When she had finished, wiped her mouth on her napkin, and tucked the napkin back in its celluloid ring, she said, "Now. Somehow, some way, I've got to find work. And save my money. And pay you back."

"Work," Evangeline mused. "What kind of work can you do—besides magnetic healing?"

Tawny pondered for a moment. "I can cook a little. And wash dishes."

"It wouldn't do for you to work as a housemaid, young lady. You're much too attractive." *She'll be raped again within a week,* Evangeline thought.

"I can sing a little. As I told you, I used to sing before Pa's sales talk. But I wouldn't want to perform someplace. Pa might find me."

"That's right."

Tawny sighed. "There's so many things I don't know how to do. Like sew. Like make a bed, even. We didn't have beds in the wagon. I watched the maid do it here and I felt guilty and stupid."

"You're neither of those, Tawny McShane! You're young and beautiful and, what's most important, intelligent. I'm going to do my best to find a place for you!"

Toward the others who came to the Woman's Center, Evangeline had always been at first sympathetic, then firm. If they wanted to change their lives, if they were sincere, she would help them in any way she could—in finding employment or moving west to a new environment, even to finding a man, a not too particular widower with children who was standing in need of a wife.

With Tawny her attitude was more maternal. To her the young woman was a lost and lonely child who needed help and guidance—and love.

That evening Tawny came down to dinner and was introduced to the others. There was shyness on both sides. It was obvious that Tawny was Evangeline's new protégée. And Tawny, who had had so few friends in her life, was slow to make casual talk.

The next morning Evangeline took Tawny shopping.

First they rode a horsecar across town. The fare was a nickel each. Tawny stared about her in open amazement. The car resembled a little house, having as it did a potbellied stove, a ceiling painted with a flowery design, and a floor covered with dirty straw. The people, much like those who ignored her on the street her first evening, sat like automatons on either side of the car, paying no attention to their neighbors. The trolley jarred and jolted like a boat on a choppy sea.

When they came to a corner the driver would ring a bell and bellow out the name of the street they were about to cross, and passengers wanting that corner would cry out "Off! Off!" as if on signal.

Tawny turned her head to try to look out the little window at the buildings passing by.

When the driver cried "Madison Square Garden!" it was Evangeline's turn to answer "Off!" and then say to Tawny, "This is for us."

They had to push their way off as they had pushed their way on.

Across the street there was an imposing six-story white marble palace, a colonnaded facade facing the square.

"The Fifth Avenue Hotel," was Evangeline's reply to Tawny's wide-eyed stare.

"It's beautiful. Oh, everything's beautiful!"

"Come along, we've got to get moving. We've a lot of walking ahead of us, and plenty more things for you to look at. This is Madison Square Garden, where Fifth Avenue and Broadway cross each other at Twenty-Third Street. The top of the Ladies Mile."

"The Ladies Mile?" Tawny repeated.

"Well, they call it a mile, but it's not quite that long. The shopping paradise of the city. Everything's down there," she pointed, "from here down to Eighth Street. You'll see. Establishments like Lord and Taylor, Arnold Constable, McCreery, winding up near the end with Mr. Stewart's famous emporium. Not to mention a dozen or more small specialty shops. Come along," she said again, and took Tawny's arm as they crossed the street and started south.

There were plenty of ladies along Ladies Mile, stepping down from, or up into, their carriages, walking in and out of stores, or just walking along the street, stopping in front of display windows. The windows extended nearly to the sidewalk and were frequently guarded by waist-high brass bars. The street was alive not only with shoppers but was lined with sidewalk peddlers of toys, artificial flowers, and sundry other small objects.

Most of the shopwindows featured yard goods or ribbons or lace. Now and then a millinery shop caught Tawny's eye, or a shop with nothing but long, soft-colored, soft-looking gloves. Now and then came a masculine touch, a red-and-white barber pole with its gold ball on top, or a cigar store with a big wooden Indian at its door.

Tawny had to look at everything. She even studied what the peddlers were selling, until Evangeline sighed and hurried her on.

On one corner a man with a basket at his feet was holding something in his hands that caught Tawny's eye. A puppy. "Oh, Evangeline, look!"

The sign tacked to the basket said, PUPPIES FOR SALE. And inside the basket, curled up in little balls, were more puppies.

"The lady likes him?" the man asked, handing the puppy he was holding to Tawny. She cuddled the puppy against her.

"I love him! Oh, I love him!"

She was remembering long ago when she was a child and found a stray puppy, soft and furry like this one, along the road. She had carried it back to the wagon in delight, only to be told by Pa that she could not keep it, that he was not going to have a dog cluttering up his wagon, that he didn't want another mouth to feed. He had forced her to leave it there beside the road and they had driven away. She had heard it whimpering, and the echo of that soft cry haunted her for weeks.

"Very cheap," the salesman said. "Twenty-five cents to you, lady."

"Tawny, no!" Evangeline commmanded. "This is no time for you to encumber yourself with a dog. We don't know exactly what you'll be doing, where you'll be going. Later, maybe. The world is full of puppies. Give him back to the man."

Tawny slowly obeyed. Evangeline was right, of course. She, Tawny, without a penny to her name, was in no position to argue.

At first, when they reached McCreery's, Tawny

was still so full of thoughts about the puppy that she was lackadaisical about the array of yard goods. Soon Evangeline's chatter revived her, the older woman asking what her favorite colors were and whether she preferred prints to solids, and so on.

They picked out yard goods for a street dress and for a party dress. As Evangeline was paying for the goods, Tawny said, "You shouldn't get so much. Who knows how long it will take me to pay you back?"

"Stop that nonsense." Evangeline snapped her purse shut. "If I'm going to launch you on life you must be properly dressed. The sooner the better. The dressmaker will be at the house this afternoon to start work."

For the next few days when she was not busy with fittings, Tawny was happy to spend her time in the library. Evangeline had many books and Tawny was lost in Dickens and Thackeray, Ouida and Louisa May Alcott. And there were always newspapers: the *Tribune, Post, Herald,* and others. Tawny's favorite was *Woodhull and Claflin's Weekly*. Its motto was "Upward and Onward," and it was devoted to women's suffrage, interests of labor, birth control, less rigidity in divorce laws, spiritualism, and Victoria C. Woodhull for president. But there were also the latest fashion notes from Paris, and serialized stories.

She mentioned to Evangeline that the weekly was her favorite publication and Evangeline smiled with pleasure.

"Victoria is a remarkable individual. Very capable. Very honest. I must take you to one of her soirees. Many interesting people are always there. We might get wind of a position for you. I'll introduce you as my niece. Otherwise she might think you were one of the other girls who live in my house!"

When the invitation came Tawny was more than excited; she had never been to a party in her life. Parties were something that happened in books. Her new party dress was pink moire; it flattered her complexion and her hair. The neck was high and prim, the bustle modest. Evangeline arranged her hair in a graceful waterfall.

Evangeline herself was resplendent in purple taffeta, with diamond earrings to match the sparkle in her eyes. They stood side by side admiring themselves in the big hall mirror.

"I'm so excited!" Tawny cried. "I've never been to a party before!"

"Don't tell anybody," Evangeline warned. "Now, listen to me, young lady. Don't tell anybody who you really are or how you actually came to be here in Manhattan. You are my niece from . . . oh, say Kalamazoo or somewhere, a respectable if poor young lady. Make something up. Do you understand?"

She had been speaking to Tawny's reflection in the mirror. Now she watched the girl nod for an answer. The mischievous look in her protégée's eyes showed that she understood.

They set off in a hired carriage not long after supper, riding north along the river and then east on Thirty-eighth Street. Tawny felt like a princess as they clop-clopped over the cobblestones.

The Woodhull house was ablaze with lights, and the sounds of the party poured out of the windows as Evangeline and Tawny climbed the front steps. A pert little Irish maid let them in.

The parlor was so full of people that the grandeur

was diminished; still Tawny could catch glimpses of statuary and red velvet and gold trim. Mrs. Woodhull was deep in conversation with two gentlemen. Nevertheless Evangeline, followed by Tawny, pushed her way through the crowd to her hostess's side.

Tawny tried her best not to stare. Victoria Woodhull was a beautiful woman—pale skin, deep-set blue eyes, a mass of dark curls. Her dress was simply cut but extremely short. Her ankles were showing!

When there was a break in the conversation, Victoria turned to greet Evangeline and the introduction was made.

"Evangeline, darling, I had no idea you had a niece."

"Well, she's not exactly a niece. She is my cousin's daughter. But that relationship seemed just too complicated, so I settled on niece. It's her first visit to New York. She just popped in and surprised me."

"How very interesting." But Mrs. Woodhull did not look particularly interested. She turned back to the gentlemen.

All the way on the drive up Tawny had been planning her new life story. She was ready to answer questions about herself, if any were asked. Her chance did not come immediately. The little maid had handed them glasses of punch and they were sipping them before a young man approached.

"May I introduce myself? My name is Kurt Hapwood." His face was heavy with sideburns and his eyes enlarged by thick-lensed glasses.

"I'm Tawny McShane."

"You are new to the city?"

Tawny nodded. "I'm visiting my aunt, Miss McClintock."

The young man nodded to Evangeline.

"How did you know I was new to the city?"

Tawny asked him. The punch had given her courage.

"Your accent. I can't quite place it, although I'm sure it's western. It's my hobby, trying to place strangers geographically."

"I come from Davenport, Iowa," Tawny told him. She had grabbed the name out of the blue. She had stayed there long enough to go to school; she had played in the yard of another little girl's house. She could still remember that house, the gabled roof, the climbing ivy, the picket fence.

"I know it well!" Mr. Hapwood cried.

"You do?" Tawny's heart sank. Then, quickly, she explained. "I haven't been there in years. I left when I was a child."

Evangeline touched her arm. "Come along, Tawny dear. There's someone else I want you to meet."

As they moved away from Mr. Hapwood, Tawny said, "Thank you for rescuing me!"

"It's quite all right. He was a bit of a bore, anyhow."

Evangeline went on introducing her to other people, but no one appeared to be as probing as Mr. Hapwood had been. People were too busy talking about the fighting between the Orangemen and the other Irish groups, Vicky's plan to run for president, and when, if ever, that bridge across the East River would be finished.

It was quite late in the evening when a large, handsome woman strode into the room in a manner that turned everyone's head in her direction.

"Amanda always comes in as if she were going on stage." Evangeline laughed.

"Who is she?" Tawny asked.

"You don't know who Amanda Josephson is? No, I suppose you're too young. She's an actress. A decade ago she was the toast of Broadway."

The woman still was standing near the entrance to the room, as if she were waiting to be welcomed.

"Poor Amanda." Evangeline shook her head. "She's still convinced she's the toast of Broadway. I wonder who the young fellow is with her."

Tawny had also noticed the young man. He was gracefully slender, with a mop of curly blond hair.

Evangeline continued, "I met Amanda years ago. My uncle took me backstage to meet her. I believe he was having an affair with her at the time. At any rate, let's go and speak to her."

Tawny followed Evangeline across the room.

In spite of her overgenerous figure and her hawk nose, the actress was still a handsome woman. It was easy to believe that once she had been truly beautiful. Now the lines, the crow's-feet, had been dabbed over not too successfully with paint and powder; the body was tightly, relentlessly corseted. She was wearing a spangly white dress with tassels hanging on the bustle and from her bosom.

She looked blank when Evangeline spoke to her.

"You probably don't remember me, Miss Josephson. I met you years ago. Maurice McClintock was my uncle."

"Yes, yes, of course," the actress mumbled. "How do you do."

"And this," Evangeline went on, "is my niece, Tawny McShane."

"How do you do," Amanda Josephson said again. And then, as the blond young man stepped forward, she added, "And this is my leading man. Timothy Barrister."

He looked young enough to have been her son.

Timothy Barrister was not much taller than Tawny, and not much older, she felt sure. He had an ethereal air about him and a voice that was like music when he murmured his how-do-you-dos. They smiled at each other, youth to youth.

Victoria Woodhull had at last deigned to become aware of her most recent guest. She wended her way through the other guests to reach Amanda's side.

"I am so sorry to be so late," Amanda apologized.

"I am so glad you and Timothy could come." Victoria gave each of them a butterfly kiss. "I know how busy the theater world can be."

Amanda's smile was sarcastic. She said nothing.

"How have you been?" Victoria went on. "I have been so busy I haven't seen you in ages."

"Right now I am thoroughly, utterly distraught." Amanda sighed. "I am leaving on tour next Monday, you know."

"No, I didn't know," Victoria said with acid sweetness.

On tour, Evangeline thought. *How the mighty have fallen.*

"I'm leaving on tour and just tonight my dressing woman left me. Just walked out. She's been with me for years. I don't know what I'm going to do. I simply cannot go on tour without someone to fetch and carry for me."

Evangeline looked at Tawny.

5

In the summer anybody who was anybody left New York City for the country.

Sue Ellen's family had a summer place at Greenwich, Connecticut, and that was where the Olivers were scheduled to go every June to September.

Lance had gone for two summers, the two summers since they had been married, and had hated it. Stifling as the heat of the city could be, it was never as stifling as the family atmosphere of the Appleby summer place. When they reached Greenwich it seemed as if Sue Ellen became a little girl again in the admiring eyes of her mother and father and the stupid old-maid sister. The Applebys had no interests beyond their garden and their dear little girl. Lance was made to feel like an outsider and within two days was restless.

There was so little to do beyond picking flowers, walking to the beach and gathering shells, walking to the post office to look for mail, sitting around drinking tea and talking—most of the talking being done by Mrs. Appleby who could chatter endlessly about trivialities.

Before his marriage Lance had gone to the races

at Saratoga or to Atlantic City for fun at the beach. But Sue Ellen did not care to go to either of those places. The first summer he had stuck it out. The second he began making short trips on his own, leaving his spouse to pout over his absence. Then this summer he decided not to go to Greenwich at all.

Sue Ellen cried, of course, when he told her of his decision. "I'll miss you so, Lance."

"I don't think you will." His voice was dry. "You'll have Mama and Papa and big sister."

"It won't be the same without you. And it's so beastly hot in town. Besides, what will you do?"

"I'll find something." He smiled.

Sue Ellen dried her eyes, pursed her lips. She was determined not to lose her temper. She would be nice, sweet as she could be, so he would want to be with her, so he would change his mind and go to Greenwich.

The last week in May she saw to it that their cook prepared all of Lance's favorite dishes, even the ones such as sweetbreads, which she despised. At dinner each night she wore her prettiest dresses, particularly those with the low-cut necklines, and doused herself with a new and pungent perfume.

Lance seemed unaware of her efforts. Ever since that afternoon when she had lain naked on the bed for the first time, her physical attraction—which was really all she ever had had for him—had been gradually diminishing. He found himself looking at her across the dinner table, not listening to whatever she was babbling about, but counting the days remaining before she left for Greenwich.

He did not make love to her once that week, not even on the last night when, weeping, she threw herself naked against him. He kissed her, he held her close the way she always wanted him to; then he pushed her aside and turned his back to her. She was still crying when he fell asleep.

She left to take the train to Greenwich the next morning without speaking to him, not even to say good-bye.

Lance closed the house for the summer and moved to his club. His widowed father resided there, and on the first evening, instead of going out on the town, Lance played backgammon with the old man.

Backgammon was about all the two had in common. When Lance showed no interest in the shipping line, with which his father was still active, there had been a schism between them. Lance's sister's husband had gone into the firm. Lance was content to be doled out a generous sum each month; he never went near the office.

Old Sanford Oliver was all business. He lived for it. Only when he played backgammon did he forget it.

Tonight he said, "So you've moved in. Not going to Greenwich this year."

"No."

"Why not?"

Lance shrugged. "Greenwich is boring."

"Greenwich? You're sure it's not that flibbertigibbet wife of yours?"

Lance did not answer. He did not intend to give his father a chance to say I told you so.

They both concentrated on the game for a while. Later, after they had finished and were enjoying brandies, his father looked across at him speculatively and surprised Lance by saying: "I think about you every now and then."

"Really? My son, the great disappointment, that sort of thing?"

"Not exactly. You know, you have your mother's

eyes and hair and a touch of her mannerisms. But there the likeness ends. She was a loyal, faithful wife, God rest her soul. You are a born bachelor. You should have remained one."

"Perhaps," was as much as Lance would say.

His father got to his feet, drained his brandy glass and put it down on the table.

"It's off to bed," he announced. He put his hand on Lance's broad shoulder. "Love her or leave her, lad. It's the only way. Good night."

"Good night, Father."

He had never felt so close to the old man before, not in all his life.

He was alone, but he was not in the mood for whoring. What he craved was companionship. The next morning he sent a message to Evangeline McClintock, inviting her to have dinner with him.

They met at their usual rendezvous, a little country inn north of the city, on the Hudson. A reservation for dinner included the reservation of a private upstairs room. The owners of the inn were the soul of honor and discretion.

Evangeline, when she received the invitation, knew exactly what it implied. But she liked Lance Oliver and he had been good to her, so of course she accepted.

The dinner was excellent. They sat at a candlelit table overlooking the river. There was a breeze off the water. They enjoyed oysters and freshly caught trout, a soufflé, fresh strawberry tarts. All accompanied by a succession of excellent wines and finishing with coffee and brandy. What conversation there was concerned the food.

After dinner, when the waiter had taken away the table and closed the door on them, Lance leaned back in a chair and lit his cigar. At home he was obliged to have his cigar in the privacy of his study because Sue Ellen hated the smell of cigar smoke. It was pleasant to smoke this one while looking across at Evangeline's friendly face. By candlelight her blue taffeta gown was paled to almost white.

She said, "I thought you would be up in Greenwich by this time."

"I didn't go this year. Greenwich can be incredibly dull."

"Is it just Greenwich, Lance? I've noticed lately that something seems to be bothering you. You have that troubled, absentminded look that is always a giveaway."

"I'll be frank with you, Evangeline. It isn't just Greenwich. Although the place *is* dull. I'm afraid—and this is the ugly truth—that I am falling out of love with my wife."

"I see. And there is someone else."

"No. It's not that." He puffed on his cigar for a moment or two, trying to find the words. "I've been trying to analyze exactly what happened. Perhaps I never did love her really. Perhaps I only *wanted* her. Enough to be trapped into marriage just to get her. After we were married she irritated me in a thousand ways. I've put up with her whims, her fancies, even her tantrums. I relegated her to the one role of sharing my bed. But now, now, I am ashamed to say, I don't even want to go to bed with her." He looked down at the stub end of his cigar and shoved it into the bowl on the table beside him.

"Then don't!" Evangeline snapped.

"What?"

"One of the first principles of free love is that marriages are not marriages because some justice of the peace or some minister spoke a few words. A real marriage is consummated when there is mutual love, and when there is mutual love no longer, there is no marriage. Marriage takes place between two people and God, with no intermediary. You've heard me preach all this. Apply it to yourself!"

"Are you suggesting divorce?"

Evangeline shrugged. "That again is a mere formality. It doesn't matter. The point is, leave her!"

The room was full of silence. Lance got up and walked over to the window that looked out on the moonlit river. Somewhere, far away, a church bell chimed the hour.

Behind him Evangeline said softly, "Ready for your postprandial prowl? It's getting late."

Lance turned. "I would gather the center still stands in need of money."

Evangeline chuckled. "It does. And you stand in need of a little hugging and kissing."

She had begun taking down her hair. In a moment she had slipped out of her clothes, blithely unashamed there in the moonlight and wavering candlelight. She was a little too plump, her breasts and belly sagged a bit, but her face was aglow with friendship as she began helping him unbutton his trousers.

It was over very quickly, as it always was, a brief, satisfying physical act, and afterward they lay side by side on the big bed, not touching, just talking.

"How *is* the center, Evangeline? Is it turning out to be what you wanted it to be?"

"Yes and no. I've had some successes. Some failures. They are all interesting in different ways. A few weeks ago my heart really went out to one of the girls who landed on my doorstep." Evangeline got out of bed and began putting on her clothes while she talked. "She was a beautiful young thing. Obviously she had been raped. And raped under the most damnable circumstances. Her father had arranged it."

Lance caught his breath. "Her father?"

"Yes. One of those men who goes around the country peddling patent medicine. She'd grown up traveling with her father, forced to help him in his various endeavors. One was something called magnetic healing. Her father arranged for her to give a man a so-called treatment, which quite naturally led to rape."

Lance wanted to cry out, *it wasn't rape, she was quite willing*! But he was sure Evangeline would never believe him. And he did not want to admit that he had seduced the poor child.

"So she ran away from her father," Evangeline went on, now tying her bonnet over her put-up hair. "She had no one in the world, no place to go. I was so glad to be able to help her."

"And what did you do with her?" Lance was hurrying to dress now, looking away from Evangeline.

"She's on tour someplace out west with Amanda Josephson. Little Tawny—isn't that an odd name?—is now Amanda's dressing woman."

"I see."

"Lance, it's late. It's time I went home. I'm still playing mother to all those females. One of these days I'll have to find a replacement. I'm going on a lecture tour in the far west this fall."

"Everyone seems to be going west." He laughed to himself.

They were both standing now, ready to leave. Evangeline gave him a swift hug, a kiss on the cheek. Then she said, "Maybe that's what you should do, Lance. Go west. Get out of New York. Really out of

New York City. You're restless, you're bored, you're unhappy. Isn't that true?"

"Yes. But what would I do out west?"

Evangeline laughed. "What do you *do* here, man-about-town?"

"True enough. But I hate train travel. I hate stage-coach travel."

"Then go around the Horn. Lance, that's a capital idea. Go around the Horn on one of your father's ships. They say San Francisco is a lively town. That's one of my last stops. I'll be there sometime in the spring. We could meet and talk about our travels."

"I'll think about it, old girl. I'll think about it!"

6

The heat of New York City was not as intense as the mid-country weather in which Tawny McShane now found herself.

Amanda's troupe had traveled by train as far as Chicago. Then, for economical reasons, they had transferred to three covered wagons. There were about a dozen in the crew, including stagehands whose duties, in this case, included pitching the tent in which the play was performed, as well as the tents in which the troupe slept each night.

They were presenting a foolish little melodrama billed as *The Ballad of Melanie: A Story of Love in a Paris Garret*, in which Amanda played a very young, very rich girl, giving her a chance to wear dazzling costumes.

The producer-director of the show was traveling with them. Abe Sheldon was a has-been, old, bald, and enamored of Amanda. So in truth it was Amanda's troupe. She made all the decisions.

Tawny was on the road again, but it was quite different from traveling with Pa. The little villages welcomed the players, there was no fleeing from sheriffs. True, Amanda was as demanding as Pa had been, but Tawny's duties were comparatively easy. She helped Amanda pry herself in and out of her corset. She hung up and brought down costumes as needed; she mended when that was necessary.

And there was no cooking. They arranged to eat in restaurants, to have the restaurants pack basket lunches for them if they were to be traveling all the day.

For the most part it was a cheerful, friendly crew but Tawny did not have much chance to become a close friend of any of them because Amanda kept the girl by her side most of the time, except when she was on stage—at which time the whole crew was involved in the production. And, except at night, when Tawny shared a tent with a cross, older woman who played the part of Amanda's mother and a silly, homely young girl who played the role of Amanda's maid. The older woman was known only as "Grannie" and the young girl was named Sally. It was quite obvious that they resented Tawny's very presence. This puzzled the newcomer, who did not guess it was simply because of her good looks.

At night Timothy Barrister shared Amanda's tent. Tawny liked the young man. He was quiet, polite, much more a gentleman than anyone else in the outfit. But she scarcely had a chance to do more than pass the time of day with him.

When she set out on the road, Tawny decided never to tell anyone her real-life story. And, as Evangeline had suggested, she concocted a yarn: Her parents had been theater people, like these itinerant performers. They had been killed in a railroad crash from which she had been thrown free. Evangeline's cousin had raised her in an imaginary village near Davenport, Iowa. The cousin also had died, so Tawny was alone in the world. This story had supplied the answers to Amanda's questions during her first interview. Amanda expressed sympathy at the moment, but her sympathy did not extend to the kind of motherliness Evangeline had shown. Amanda was primarily interested in Amanda. And in Timothy Barrister. That Timothy did not completely share her feelings was quite apparent.

One night they were camped near a little town not far from Rochester, Minnesota. Summer in Minnesota can be as hot by night as it can by day. Tawny found herself tossing and turning, trying with little success to sleep. Particularly because both Grannie and Sally were snoring.

The campsite was near a bit of a river. The sound of the water was appealing. In the dark, Tawny put on her clothes, all but her shoes and stockings, lifted the tent flap, and stepped out into the star-filled night. Following the sound of the river she found her way to it through the dark, sat down on the bank, and watched the fireflies darting through the bushes. After a bit she moved closer and let her bare feet dangle in the water.

She missed Evangeline's library. She missed reading. Their tour was taking them only to tiny towns and she rarely saw even a newspaper. Her salary was small but she was saving all she could. When, eventually, they got back to New York, she could go to Evangeline and pay her.

There was a rustling in the bushes. Someone was joining her. She scrambled to her feet. It was Timothy Barrister, his yellow hair pale in the starlight.

"And who is this?" he asked as he came closer.

"It's me. Tawny McShane."

"Good evening, Tawny."

"G—good evening."

"What are you doing out here, all by yourself?"

"Cooling off. Isn't it hot tonight?"

"I hadn't noticed." He gave a soft laugh. "I come from Louisiana. I'm used to hot weather. But I guess you could say I'm cooling off, too, in a way."

"Oh?"

"Amanda and I had one of our nightly fights."

"I'm sorry."

"It's all just part of life. Sit down, Tawny. Let's talk a bit."

She slipped down to where she had been sitting before, again hanging her feet in the water.

"That's a good idea," Timothy said as he sat down beside her and took off his shoes and stockings.

For a moment neither spoke. Finally Tawny said, "Aren't the fireflies pretty?"

"They are. So are you."

"Thank you." And you are very handsome, she thought to herself.

"You're about the youngest dressing woman I ever met. However, Amanda seems to think you are doing a good job of it."

"I'm glad of that!"

"Have you ever considered becoming an actress yourself? Amanda tells me your parents were in the theater."

She shook her head. "No, I hadn't thought of it."

"You have the looks. And you have a good voice."

"You've never heard me sing!"

"I meant your speaking voice. It has a nice husky quality. If I were you, do you know what I'd do? Get hold of the script and study it. Particularly the part Sally plays. Then, if Sally should fall ill, you could step in."

Tawny's eyes widened. "Do you suppose I could?"

"It's a possibility. That's how I started. I was a

stagehand. Until Amanda spotted me." He sighed, picked up a stick, and started scratching in the dirt beside him. Tawny studied his handsome profile.

"It's hard to imagine you as a stagehand."

"I wasn't a very good one. I'm not a very good actor, either. But I'm working at it.

"I think you're good," Tawny said shyly.

Timothy laughed. "*You're* acting when you say something like that. And doing very well. You just might get a chance to go onstage. Amanda was foolish not to bring understudies. She wanted to economize. But one of these nights someone will get sick and the show won't go on."

After a bit he took his feet out of the water, wiped them with his handkerchief, and put on his stockings and shoes. As he stood up he said, "I'd better get back. Kiss and make up and all that." His voice was bitter. "It was nice talking to you, Tawny."

"It was nice talking to you."

"I'll get that script for you in the morning."

"Thank you!"

"I hate to leave you out here all by yourself. Can't I walk you back to your tent?"

"I guess I should go back, too. And try to sleep."

He reached down and took her hand and helped her to her feet. He did not let go of her hand immediately, just held it and looked down at her, unsmiling.

Finally he let go and took her elbow as they walked through the bushes and back to the camp.

Timothy Barrister was the son of a Louisiana planter who had been impoverished by the Civil War. As a child Timothy had been mad about the world of the theater. A precocious reader, he memorized whole passages from Shakespeare, acting out all the parts with an audience of his parents and his younger sisters. They had encouraged him, hoping to send him to New Orleans to be trained. The war stopped that. Still determined to become an actor, he had gone off to New Orleans and taken the only job for which he was eligible. As a stagehand he did as he had told Tawny to do—studied scripts, memorized roles for which he might be suitable, and watched the people on stage, watched and studied.

For over a year nothing happened and he was getting discouraged. Then Amanda Josephson made an appearence in New Orleans. He was excited about seeing the famous actress. She was older than he had expected, but she was beautiful, and he admired her techniques.

Ever since he had come to New Orleans he had been collecting autographs of actors and actresses. Of course he wanted Amanda's name in his little book. She was one of the most famous performers he had yet encountered. He already had Joseph Jefferson, Edwin Forrest, and Fanny Davenport.

He went to her dressing room after a performance, feeling more timid than usual because she was a beautiful woman, as well as a famous one. The hatchet-faced old lady who was then her dresser answered his knock. As he was telling her what he wanted of her mistress, Amanda, who was at her dressing table, called out, "Who is it?"

"A young man wants your autograph, ma'am."

"A young man with a beautiful voice," Amanda said, as she turned around. "Who are you? Where did you come from?" she demanded.

"My name is Timothy Barrister. I work here in the theater."

"Why haven't I met you? Why haven't I seen you? What do you do in the theater?"

"I'm a stagehand, ma'am. You probably haven't noticed me."

"What on earth are you doing working as a stagehand?" She stood up and came over closer, studying him from head to toe as if he were a prize horse.

Embarrassed, Timothy mumbled, "Trying to become an actor, ma'am."

She shook her head, making a tsk-tsk sound. "Give me that book!"

In it she hastily scribbled, "Go home and change your clothes. You're having supper with me tonight." Beneath it she flourished her name.

Amanda Josephson was a sex-hungry woman, and although she had retained her beauty behind the footlights, offstage the aging showed. In her prime she claimed many lovers; now they were seeking features fresher than her forty-year-old ones. And Timothy Barrister was indeed handsome. When he walked into her dressing room, she thought to herself, "An Adonis, a true Adonis." Such a slender, graceful body, such a profile, the boyish blond hair. And a voice that seemed to caress with every syllable.

She wanted him. She wanted to eat him up as if he were a bonbon.

But she did not throw herself at him that first night. She questioned him about himself and his family. She was all kindness. Timothy was so overawed by having been invited to sup with the famous Amanda Josephson—and mellowed by the wine—that he was in a haze of excitement.

When he left her he thanked her profusely. "This has been the most wonderful evening of my life." She took his face in her hands and kissed him on the lips. And then she said, "Dear boy, dear boy, there will be many more!"

He was still in something of a shock the next day when he was working on the backdrops on stage. The outside door opened and Amanda, with Abe Sheldon, the producer-director, in tow, swept into the theater, down to the footlights.

"Timothy Barrister, come out here! Abe, this is the boy I told you about. Timothy—may I call you Timothy?—this is Mr. Sheldon. He would like you to read a few lines for us." She handed him a script.

He would never forget. It was the balcony scene from *Romeo and Juliet*. He was accepted. He was to go back to New York with them and train as an understudy, at first.

They went by ship to New York. The first night aboard there was a knock at Timothy's door and when he answered, expecting the steward, it was Amanda, her hair about her shoulders, wearing nothing but a dressing gown.

To his surprised face she asked, "Didn't you expect me, darling?"

He truly hadn't. In that moment he realized that he should have, all along. But, Good Lord, she was almost old enough to be his mother.

She closed the door and shot the bolt. Then she crossed the cabin and threw her arms around his neck, pressing her huge breasts against him, kissing him full on the lips before he could utter a protest.

When she finished he looked at her blankly. He had not responded, he had not been ready for that kiss. Amanda's eyes narrowed as she looked at his face and realized his surprise.

"Come now, Timothy, we are going to make an actor of you. A great actor. We are going to find you fame and fortune and everything your young heart desires. For that, can't you love me a little?" She stroked his cheek with one hand while with the other she loosened her dressing gown, reaching for one of his hands and putting it on one of her breasts.

"I promise you, Timothy, I shall be a good lover. I shall be the best lover you have ever known. I shall show you ways to make love that you in your innocence have never dreamed of."

In spite of himself he found he was responding. He clutched her breast firmly in his hand. He kissed her full on the lips, and she pulled him down on the bunk and lay on top of him. She was going to eat him up, like a bonbon, as she had dreamed.

Timothy despised himself for becoming her lover. But the opportunity to further his career was there, and he grimly decided to take it. He thought: *the moment I have one good role, the moment I know that I can stand on my own, I shall leave her*. The part of the leading man in *The Ballad of Melanie* was a good one; with it he had hoped to make good, to be able to break away. It was a huge disappointment when Amanda told him the show was going on the road, away from critics, away from possible producers or talent scouts lurking in the audiences. He would play out the tour because he had been hired and was being paid, but when they got back to New York it would be good-bye to Amanda Josephson.

The morning after Timothy and Tawny talked by the riverside Amanda saw him take his script out of his suitcase.

"Darling, certainly you don't have to study that anymore. By now you must know your lines pluperfect!"

"I think I do. I was going to lend this to somebody."

"Who?" Her eyes sharpened.

"Little Tawny McShane. She might like to become an understudy for Sally's part."

Amanda grabbed the script from his hands. "No!" she told him sharply. "Absolutely not."

It was his turn. "Why?"

"I hired her as my dressing woman and she's going to remain that!"

"You wouldn't want to give the girl a chance to become something more, if she did have talent?"

"Talent or no, I will not have her on stage with me! She's too . . . too pretty." That wasn't the right word, Amanda thought to herself. Tawny wasn't just another pretty youngster. She had a different, distinct personality, the kind that drew the eye.

"And too young," Timothy was saying.

Amanda slapped him across the face. "Mind your manners, young man, or you'll be a stagehand again."

"I'm sorry I said that," Timothy apologized.

Amanda hurried to kiss the cheek she had struck. "I'm sorry I slapped you, dear. Please, don't let us quarrel."

But we will, Timothy thought. He put the script back in his suitcase. Later that same day, when Amanda was not around, he took it out again.

Amanda only required his presence on stage, and in bed. There were many other times when she was conferring with Abe over financial details or taking naps in the daytime when Timothy knew freedom.

After he had smuggled the script to Tawny they met frequently, usually in the big tent where the play would be presented in the evening. He was pretty sure that Amanda would never allow Tawny to replace Sally, but he did not mention it to Tawny. She seemed to get such pleasure out of reading and then reciting the maid's lines. And he got gratification from just sitting there listening and watching. She threw such youthful vigor into the part Timothy felt sure that if she appeared on stage in even a minor role she would steal the show.

They were on the Great Plains, in the Dakotas, when Amanda's toothache developed, and she sent Tawny into town to look for some oil of cloves. *Dressing woman*, Tawny thought, *is really only a more polite way of saying maid.* It was a blistering hot day; the sun beat down relentlessly on the flat ground. It was not far to the town but it turned out to be a long walk because of the heat.

She came to an abandoned cabin, half fallen in, but with the front porch still intact, and its roof whole and she sat down in the shade and mopped her brow.

A little later Timothy appeared on the horizon, on his way back from town, and she called out to him.

He came over toward her, shading his eyes from the sun. "I do find you in the strangest of places."

"As usual, when you find me, I am trying to cool off. Amanda sent me to town for oil of cloves for her toothache."

"I see. I've been to town just to go to town, hot as it is. I found a saloon with cold beer."

"That sounds good."

"Only ladies don't go into saloons."

"I know. Sit down, Timothy."

He looked as hot and tired as she felt. He sat down, sighing.

"Tawny, I'm sick of this tour. I'm sick of this wide, flat nothingness of a countryside. And . . ." He broke off. He did not want to say out loud: *and I'm sick of Amanda.* He said instead, "I'd like to take you by the hand and run back, all the way back to Louisiana." As he spoke he took hold of her hand.

"I have no place to run to," Tawny said sadly. He watched her long lashes blink back the tears. "I have no home. I have no friends, except Evangeline, and she is way back in New York."

"You have me, Tawny." He squeezed her hand.

"But you . . . you and Amanda . . ."

"Amanda doesn't own me." He was stern.

"But . . ."

There was only one way to stop her. He leaned forward and kissed her on the lips. "I've been falling in love with you," he said after the kiss, "ever since that night we met by the river. I didn't give a damn whether you ever became an understudy. I just wanted to be with you."

Suddenly, listening to him, Tawny felt that the world was all right again. The hot Dakota sun did not matter. Her loneliness had blown away. Reluctantly she pulled her hand from his and got to her feet. "I'd better get to town."

"Tawny, wait! Will you meet me here tonight, after the show?"

She nodded and then turned her back and hurried away. Somehow she felt no one could feel afraid of a man like Timothy.

That night Tawny slipped out of the tent while Grannie and Sally were getting ready for bed. They paid no attention. There was moonlight that night and she found her way easily along the road to the old, abandoned cabin and sat down on the front steps to wait. She was thinking how strange it was to be here in the middle of the country, traveling with a motley crowd of strangers, working for such a domineering, selfish woman, her only real friend being that woman's lover.

She should not be attracted to Timothy; she should despise him for what he was doing. Instead, she felt sorry for him. She sensed his unhappiness with himself.

It seemed like a long wait. The big moon rose higher and higher until it floodlit fields and the road. As Timothy came down the road he could see Tawny there on the step. She was wearing a pale pink dress that was white in the moonlight. She was turned to one side so that she was silhouetted. He caught his breath at the sight of her, at the curve of her firm young breasts. She was so sweet, so young, so trusting! She stood up when she saw him coming.

"Tawny!" he called.

"I thought you'd never get here!"

"I'm sorry I'm so late. But you know how Amanda can be."

"Her toothache is still bothering her?"

He nodded. "The oil of cloves helped, but I guess it wore off during the show. Tonight she was moaning about it, wanting to be comforted. But I finally got away." He took hold of Tawny's hands. "Let's not talk about Amanda. Let's not even think about Amanda. Just you and me."

"What about you and me?" Tawny asked.

"What are we going to do about ourselves? We are both dependent upon her."

"Yes. But not forever, Timothy. When we get back to New York . . ."

"If we ever get back to New York," he interrupted bitterly. Then he leaned forward and kissed the tip of her nose. "I love you, do you know that? I love you!"

"Timothy, you . . ."

"And I am unfit to touch the hem of your skirt!"

She pulled her hands away from his, threw her

arms around his neck, and pressed close against him.

"Don't talk like that!" she whispered into his ear. Both of their hearts were beating wildly as they embraced. The moonlight had played magic; there was no longer need for any words. They were just two people, alone and full of love. *This is what love is,* Tawny thought. *This is what it feels like to be in love.*

They sat down on the step, still in each other's arms, and kissed, and went on kissing as if they would never stop.

Her whole body was afire, as it had been that long ago time in New York. But Timothy did not try to touch any part of her. As he had said, he felt unfit, unclean.

When finally the wordless decision arrived that it was time to go back to the camp, they got to their feet slowly, both of them shaking. Timothy escorted Tawny to her tent, gave her a quick good-night kiss, and walked away.

He did not go back to Amanda that night. He walked. He took the longest walk of his life and did not come back to the camp until it was almost dawn. He felt as if he could never touch the older woman again.

As the covered wagons rolled westward that day Timothy dozed. Dozed and woke and dozed and dreamed of Tawny.

When they reached the little town of Loneville, the tents were set up, and the crew ate supper in the town's one shabby restaurant. As they were coming out of the cafe Timothy passed close enough to Tawny to whisper, "There's one big tree on the prairie near camp. Did you see it?" When Tawny nodded, not looking directly at him, he added, "There," and hurried on.

When the whole cast was putting on makeup backstage, Tawny darting in and out with fans and parasol and other properties for Amanda, Timothy avoided looking at her.

Amanda said, "You're awfully quiet tonight, Timothy. Don't you feel well?"

"I'm fine. How is the tooth?"

"Much better, thank you. Much much better, thanks to Tawny."

He winced.

Usually Timothy enjoyed being onstage; it was his natural element. He was no longer Timothy Barrister; he was the man he was playing. But tonight he could not feel the part of Paul. He was only pretending to be a strange young artist in love with a rich girl. The whole business was repulsive this evening: he had to steel himself to say his lines, and when it came to kissing Melanie's hand, at the end, taking her into his arms and kissing her on the mouth, he was in agony. How bitterly the words "The show must go on" rang in his ears.

Just as the play finished, the audience's applause was blotted out by crashing thunder, the dimming gas lanterns outshone by flashes of lightning.

From the wings Tawny had been aware of the change in Timothy's acting and she was worried for fear the others would guess that something was wrong. She had thought of nothing but Timothy since the night before. It was risky, it was madness to meet him again. Soon everyone would know of their meetings; they would not be able to keep them secret. Still, she would be there tonight, under that tree, waiting.

The thunder and lightning, which normally terrified her, did not stop her. When it was bedtime she threw a shawl over her head and dashed out through the rain.

This time Timothy did not keep her waiting. In a few moments the lightning revealed him running toward her. He took her in his arms and kissed her; then, still with his arms around her, he said, "I've made up my mind. And we'll do it. Right now."

She had never heard Timothy speak so positively.

He went on. "Look, Tawny, darling, I'm through with Amanda. I don't care what it means. I didn't go back to the tent last night. I couldn't. And I'm not going back tonight. Or any other night. Tawny, will you marry me? Tonight?"

"Tonight?" She gasped.

"Tonight. We'll walk back into town and rout out a justice of the peace. I'm sure there's one there. And when we were in town for dinner I noticed the Hotel Loneville. Not much of a place, but it will have to do for a honeymoon. Oh, Tawny, Tawny, will you?"

The "Yes" came easily, and she lifted her face for his kiss.

Gradually, as they walked toward town, the rain faded away.

The hotel room was sparse, but clean. There was water in the pitcher beside the basin. The place was lighted with two big candles. The bedspread was turned down.

First Timothy sat down on the room's one chair and pulled Tawny into his lap. He stroked her and kissed her, but a strange shyness had crept between them.

Finally, with a little laugh, Tawny murmured, "I didn't bring anything with me. Not even a nightgown."

"It doesn't matter."

"You're my husband. I'm married. I can't believe it!"

"It's true, my love, it's true. Oh, Tawny, take the pins out of your hair; let me see you, all free and lovely."

She began taking out the hairpins, tossing them aside. Soon his hands were in her hair, caressing, and then he pushed the neckline of her dress away to kiss her shoulder.

She slipped from his lap and stood beside him. She began unbuttoning her dress, turning her face away shyly until the dress fell to the floor.

Timothy stared at her. He mumbled, "God, oh, God!" Then he jumped up, lifted her, and carried her to the bed, kneeling beside her.

"You mustn't be afraid, my love," he told her. "You mustn't be afraid."

"I'm not afraid."

He turned his back to her and began getting undressed. Then he blew out both candles before he came to the bed.

She could smell the snuffed-out candles, and he could smell the perfume of her body as he helped her out of the shift and ran his hands across her breasts, down her slim waist. The world was shut out as their bodies touched.

It was like a slow-moving dream; he was gentle and sweet and patient . . . more patient than he needed to be. Her whole body was quivering with desire.

When he whispered, "Are you ready, my darling?" she cried "Yes! Yes!" as she arched her body.

When they reached the camp the next morning the tents had already been folded and the troupe was getting ready to leave. Timothy and Tawny were so happy, so in love, that they approached the camp with no trepidation whatsoever. They were man and wife and they were ready to shout the news to the whole world.

Everyone stared at them; some of the stagehands snickered. Timothy put his arm around Tawny's shoulders and called out, "Listen, all of you!" in his rich stage voice. "We were married last night in Loneville."

There was a general gasp.

Then Amanda climbed down from a wagon and strode toward them. "What did you say?" Her face was white.

Timothy repeated, steadily, "Tawny and I were married last night in Loneville."

Amanda swayed as if she might fall. Then she straightened and turned back toward the wagon. "Abe, come out here."

Abe was immediately beside her.

"I want you to pay whatever is owed to these two. And fire them. As of this moment."

Within the hour, Timothy and Tawny, surrounded by their few belongings, were standing alone on the prairie, watching the covered wagons fade in the distance.

7

After that evening with Evangeline, Lance was doing more thinking than he ever had in all his carefree life, about himself, and about Sue Ellen. He would sit alone in his room at the club sipping brandy and remembering his father's words: *love her or leave her.*

More and more as the slow summer days passed he realized that he did not love Sue Ellen. He did not miss her at all. But if he left her it would not be possible to return to his old bachelor life, not in Manhattan, where they had the same circle of friends. He would have to take Evangeline's advice and leave town.

Of one thing he was certain: there had been no point in marrying a woman just to get her into bed with him. There were plenty of women who did not insist on marriage, and with them one was not obliged to spend long, boring waking hours.

He reasoned to himself that it was not decent, nor honest, to go on as he had been. It was unfair to both of them. Sue Ellen had her loving family; she was still young, still pretty, she would find another man.

He must go to Greenwich and tell her.

* * *

He arrived at the house unannounced and Sue Ellen met him at the door. She stared at him for a moment in utter surprise.

"Lance! You came, after all!" There was a note of triumph in her voice. She was thinking: *he does care!* And then she saw that he had no luggage.

He guessed what she was thinking. He said, quietly, "I didn't come to stay overnight. I just wanted to talk to you."

"About what?"

"About us." He could hear the voices of her family inside the house. "Where can we be alone?"

Sue Ellen, wide-eyed, suggested, "The garden?"

"The garden would be fine."

She closed the door behind her, and they walked down the steps and around the house to the walled-in garden at the rear. His manner frightened her. She did not know what to say, or how she should behave. She sat down on a bench under the arbor where the wisteria vine trailed its lavender blossoms. She looked up at him, her lips trembling.

He sat down beside her. "Are you having a pleasant summer?"

"Yes. But I've missed you."

She waited for him to say he'd missed her, but he didn't. He said instead, "I haven't missed our quarrels."

She turned her head. His tone had been light, sarcastic. It was true there had been quarrels, too many quarrels.

Lance said, "Sue Ellen, you must admit that things have not been right between us for some time."

"I know, I know."

"Sue Ellen, look at me. We've got to face this together."

She lifted her face and looked into his, blinking the tears from her eyes. "Oh, Lance, we can change everything. I know we can. I'll stop losing my temper. I'll be good as gold. If you'll just try."

"Try?"

"To love me!" she cried. "To really love me!" Her voice was beginning to get high-pitched, the signal that in spite of her promise she might throw a tantrum.

He looked at her with distaste. He felt nothing for her now, nothing at all. He said, "You can't force love, Sue Ellen. You can't will it back, when it's gone."

"Gone!" she gasped. "Lance, what do you mean?"

"I think you know what I mean."

She felt cold inside, cold and empty, as if he had struck her.

"I'm trying to be honest with you," he went on. "And with myself. It's time we both faced up to the truth. We don't belong together."

At first she could not speak. She knew by his tone that he was not pretending; she knew it would do no good to throw her arms around him. Finally, looking down at her tightly folded hands, she asked, "What are you doing to do?"

"I'm leaving New York. I'm going away. Probably out west. At any rate, for good."

Under her breath she whispered, "Oh, no!"

"The house and everything in it is yours."

What did she want with a house, if he weren't in it?

"You are free to divorce me, Sue Ellen. You'll have clear grounds of desertion."

She burst into tears with a cry that was almost a

scream, jumped to her feet, and ran out of the garden.

Tawny and Timothy felt like babes in the wood. Homeless, jobless. Between them they did not have enough money to get back to New York, even if they could find their way through the wilderness to the railroad.

They sat under the big tree where they had met the night before. Beyond them was the debris of the broken campsite. Timothy put his arm around her and leaned his head against hers.

"What are we going to do?" Tawny wondered aloud.

"God only knows. I suppose we could walk back to Loneville and look for work. But it's such a little place."

"Maybe a wagon train will come along and give us a lift."

"Maybe." But there was no hope in his voice. "I've made a mess of my life, and now of yours."

"No, Timothy. We'll make out. Let's go back into town and talk to the man at the hotel. He might know of someone who would give us a lift."

"A lift where?"

"Anywhere!" Tawny cried impatiently. "Any civilized place! We can't stay out here in the middle of nowhere!" She moved away from his arm and stood up.

"Tawny, I'm so sorry."

"Sorry you married me?"

"No! Yet . . ." He looked up at her. "Perhaps I should be. If we hadn't run off last night, we wouldn't be here today—in the middle of nowhere, as you so aptly put it."

Something came over Tawny as she looked down

at her husband: the realization that from now on she would have to be the strong one. Impulsive, moody, temperamental—Timothy was all of those. What she had admired as a gentlemanly manner was also a weakness.

"Timothy," she told him, "we can't sit here and mope. We've got to go to town." She picked up her suitcase and started for the road.

"Tawny, wait!" He ran after her, carrying his suitcase, and took hers from her.

The walk into town was a hot one.

It was a strange honeymoon in the Loneville Hotel. There was nothing to do, no place to go in Loneville. So they spent most of their time in their room, making love. Each morning they consulted the hotel proprietor about the possibility of getting a lift anywhere, and each morning they also counted their dwindling money.

In bed they could almost forget their predicament. But soon it became quite evident that Tawny was an insatiable lover and Timothy was not. The strength of his passion depended on his mood and his moods were mercurial.

Then, one day, the Wilson family came to Loneville and spent a night in the hotel. The proprietor introduced the Wilsons to the Barristers.

There were three Wilsons, Mr. and Mrs., and their daughter Wilma. They hailed from Texas and were headed for California. Mr. Wilson ("call me Joe") explained why they were traveling all the way by covered wagon. "Figgered to save money that way. Carry our belongings with us, camp out, Ma here doing her own cookin' same as home. Once in a while, like now, we stop at a hotel. Take real baths, eat somebody else's cookin'."

"It gets mighty weary sometimes." His wife sighed. "I'll be powerful glad when we get over them mountains that Joe says we'll be comin' to pretty quick."

"So will I," daughter Wilma agreed. She was a big, bony, awkward girl, a little younger than Tawny.

The Wilsons were most impressed with Timothy and Tawny. Never before had they met "a real live actor and actress." They shared the same table for dinner. At the time the five of them were the only guests at the hotel, which made for a homey, friendly atmosphere.

Now that they had the opportunity to ask about a lift both Tawny and Timothy felt shy about coming right out and asking.

Mrs. Wilson said, "Understand you folks are here on your honeymoon. Land alive, how did you ever pick this spot?"

"By accident," Timothy grinned.

"You got privacy, anyhow." Joe Wilson winked at Timothy. "Till we come along. How long you goin' to be here?"

The Barristers looked at each other. Then they both started to speak at once. "We were hoping . . ." Then they broke off.

"Hopin' what?" Wilson boomed out.

Tawny gave him her best smile. "Hoping we might get a lift."

"West," Timothy added.

Now the Wilsons regarded each other.

"Ma, do you suppose we've got room in our wagon for these two nice people?"

Mrs. Wilson smiled at the two of them. "Reckon we could make some. The lady here might help Wilma and me with food fixin'. Hafta get their own tents," she added.

"I'd be glad to help," Tawny said eagerly.

"Young man," Joe Wilson said to Timothy, "you ever spent time drivin' mules?"

"No, but I've driven a horse and buggy."

"Mules ain't much different. You could change off with me on the drivin'. My womenfolk here ain't no good at all about helpin' me out."

They shook hands all around.

Alone in their room that evening Tawny threw her arms around her husband's neck. "California!" She sighed. "San Francisco. There's theaters there. We'll find jobs. Everything is going to be wonderful!"

"Everything *will* be wonderful, darling," Timothy echoed. His spirits were high again, infused now with Tawny's optimism. He held her close and kissed her. Then he blew out the candles and led her to bed.

They met few other travelers as the Wilson's wagon wound its way across the rest of the prairie toward the white-capped mountains in the distance.

The two men rode up front, taking turns with the mules. They didn't talk very much, but back in the wagon the women chattered. Wilma said very little. She was a strange, shy girl. When Tawny spoke to her, Wilma would blush and then beam a smile. Obviously she thought Tawny the most beautiful creature she'd ever seen and watched her every movement with envy.

Mrs. Wilson did most of the talking. It was incredible how the woman could run on and on without saying anything significant.

They carried with them a supply of dried foods and bacon, which they augmented by stopping either at a stream for Joe to fish, or to shoot an occasional jackrabbit. Tawny learned how to clean a fish and skin a rabbit. When she had traveled with Pa they never had gotten this far into the wilderness; there had always been towns and stores. This was wild and rough and sometimes fun.

Sometimes fun and sometimes difficult. The weather was against them. First there was rain and driving was hard. One night as they came closer to the mountains there was a thunderstorm that tore tents open, blew Tawny and Timothy's tent completely off them. Drenched to the skin, they climbed into the wagon to wait until morning.

The exhilaration they had shared the night before they left on the journey was fading that stormy night. "Do you suppose we'll ever get there?" Timothy sighed. "Do you suppose we'll get over the mountains?"

"We'll get there, somehow," Tawny tried to reassure him.

Her bones ached from the bumping wagon day after day. She longed for a real bath, not just a dip in a river or creek. As they began to climb into the mountains the nights grew sharply colder. They often slept in their clothes, wrapped in each other's arms. No longer was there any thought of making love, though that might have helped warm them.

Mrs. Wilson remained unfailingly cheerful throughout it all. She liked to daydream aloud about the house they would build when they got to California. "They say they got mighty good weather out there, not like the awful heat and sudden cold we get back in Texas. I think it'll be nice to have a regular weather, year round."

"Ought to be good land for growin' stuff," Joe said. "We gonna have a nice farm. Now, what are you young folks planning to do?"

"We hope to find work in San Francisco," Timothy said. "In the theater. This country life is not for us."

They came to a river and decided to stop and do their laundry. They would have been tempted to take a swim but the water was icy cold. Tawny's hands were numb and raw when she finished wringing out the last piece and spreading it out on a bush to dry.

When they left they were obliged to ford the river. A wheel fell off the wagon, and Joe and Timothy had to wade in waist-high water to retrieve it.

That night, as they were sitting around their campfire, Joe said, rather ominously, "Might get into a little trouble in these parts. Heard tell there be a few Indians about."

"Joe, you promised me when we left Texas that there wouldn't be no Indian trouble!" Mrs. Wilson sounded indignant.

"Well, that's what I thought then. But back there in Loneville I was talkin' to a feller who said there were a few strays out this way. So it's good I brought along my old shotgun and that I been keepin' in shape. Jest in case I have to aim at something besides a rabbit."

Tawny, with a little shiver, moved closer to Timothy, who put his arm around her.

Joe said, "Ever do any shootin', Tim?"

"Only squirrels, when I was a boy," Timothy answered.

"Got a pistol too. Think you could use a pistol?"

"I believe so." He tightened his arm around Tawny but he was shaking a little himself.

They all stared into the fire. Nights were so big, so black, so silent out here, sometimes only broken by the cry of a nightbird, or the howl of a wolf high up in the hills that lay ahead of them.

Mrs. Wilson broke the silence. "The worst of it is, if a whole pack of them redskins come at us, your two little guns won't be worth nothin'."

"I ain't expectin' a whole pack of them!" Joe snapped back. "Just one or two wild young bucks wantin' to steal my mules and my wagon. Tim and me, we can fend 'em off, scare hell out of 'em. Can't we, Tim?"

"Yes." That was all he could manage to say.

That night, in their tent, drifting toward sleep, Tawny confessed, "I'm scared!"

"So am I," Timothy agreed. "So are we all. But, after all, it's only a chance. A long chance. So let's try not to worry."

For a few days life went on in the usual way. On the third night they camped in a narrow canyon around which the hills rose as vertically as walls. Late that night Tawny and Timothy were awakened by Joe's voice outside their tent.

"Tim! Tim! Wake up!"

They were sleeping fully dressed, and it took only a moment for Timothy to fling back the flap of the tent and look out.

Joe, shotgun in hand, was standing there. "I think I heard horses, Tim. We'd best get the women in the wagon and stand guard. Git your pistol."

The three of them felt their way through the dark to the wagon. They did not want to show a light. Just as they reached the wagon, Joe stood still with his head cocked. "Listen," he said.

Far away there was the *tlot-tlot* sound of horses' feet.

"It don't sound like it's comin' from the road behind us," Joe said thoughtfully. "Or ahead of us."

"No," Timothy agreed.

"It's up in them hills, I'm thinkin'. They gonna ride down from one side or t'other. When I figger out which way they be comin' we'll know which side of the wagon to be on. Git inside, girl."

"Oh, Timothy!" Tawney cried.

He gave her a kiss. He actually smiled before he boosted her into the wagon. Inside it was pitch dark. From a corner Mrs. Wilson and Wilma whispered hello. And then the three fell quiet, listening.

The hoofbeats were gradually growing louder. Then they heard Joe say, "C'mon," accompanied by some movement outside the wagon, and the bray of one of the mules.

Suddenly the hoofbeats roared to a crescendo and then ceased. There came the sound of one shot, and then another, the hoofbeats starting again and fading. And then a scream that pierced the night.

"That's Joe!" Mrs. Wilson cried. "I'm going to him!"

As the woman climbed out of the wagon Tawny heard, from the other direction, a bloodcurdling war whoop. Joe had made a mistake in thinking the Indians would come from only one direction. They were surrounded!

Tawny made her way to the corner where Wilma was whimpering and put her arms around the girl.

"What's happening, Tawny? What are they doing out there?"

"Sh! I don't know. We'll just have to wait."

The silence was now more frightening than the gunfire and screams and war whoops. Not knowing what was happening or what had taken place, was anguish, and on top of that there was the sheer fear. Would the Indians find them, there in the wagon? And if they did, what would they do to them?

Now a faint light was coming into the sky. Through the gaps between the wagon's cover and its sides Tawny could tell that dawn was breaking. She said to Wilma, "You stay here. I'll go outside and look around. I think the Indians must have gone by now."

When she stepped outside into the gray dawn light, the first thing she saw were the bodies of Joe and Mrs. Wilson. Joe was lying face down with an arrow in his back; blood had seeped onto the dirt and was beginning to dry.

Mrs. Wilson had been decapitated.

Tawny turned her head, feeling as if she were going to be ill, and closed her eyes. When she opened them she saw a dead Indian lying back a ways.

Where was Timothy?

She leaned against the side of the wagon. She knew she must walk around the wagon in search of Timothy, but it took a while to build up her courage.

It had been, as Joe had predicted, no big horde of Indians. Only a few. Perhaps only two. But they had been tricky, coming down from the hills on both sides.

The sun was coming up now. It was a beautiful morning in this paradise of a valley; evergreens and weeping willows, shining with dew, birds caroling away with the joy of discovering a new day. Tawny took a deep breath and started around the wagon.

Timothy lay sprawled on the ground, his yellow curls tangled in the dust, his pistol still in his hand.

There was an arrow through his heart.

PART II

1871

1

In the spring of 1871 Bill Ferguson was in his senior year at Princeton University. He had expected to graduate, go up to the big city, and find work in the financial district. But things did not go the way he had planned because his father died suddenly, and he had to go home to San Francisco.

Bill had been devastated when the telegram reached him. He had loved and respected his father; he had not even thought of the possibility of his death. Old Warren Ferguson had been a big, hearty man, self-made and proud of it. He had wandered west during the gold rush of 1849 and struck it rich. And he had stayed rich through his investments and speculation. Or so Bill had thought until he came home to San Francisco for his father's funeral and discovered the sad state of his father's estate.

Warren Ferguson had been a gambler. For years he had taken all sorts of chances and always come out a winner. But during the past year he'd had bad judgement on several deals—he'd gambled, he'd lost, he'd died in debt. About all that was left for Bill and his mother was the old home on Nob Hill and some scattered landholdings, the value of which was yet to be determined. Bill's college days were over.

The youth felt ill at ease, disjointed. He did not know where he belonged, or what he should do next. His mother was anxious to maintain her place in San Francisco society, to keep her head up, and pretended she was much better off than she was, which Bill found to be a terrific bore.

Mother also had high hopes of his marrying a rich girl. That, to her, would solve all their problems. But so far Bill had not met a girl he liked.

Bill Ferguson was a stocky young man, with round brown eyes in a round face. He was a quiet person who took life seriously, and almost totally lacked a sense of humor.

Before he could decide what to do with the rest of his life he was obliged to wait until his father's estate was settled. His mother hovered over him, fussing about his clothes, his food, trying to keep him entertained. She would say, "It's so good to have my boy home again!" to her friends.

Bill was tired of being her boy. As often as possible he left the house to walk the San Francisco hills. By night he wound up on the waterfront. Unlike his father he was not a gambler. Nor was he a heavy drinker. He wandered into saloons and watched card games, or stood at the bar sipping beer and watching people dancing.

He looked with distaste on the Barbary Coast girls. In his opinion whores should not appear in public. He had lost his virginity during his first year at college. He was not inexperienced with women. But such a rendezvous had to be an arranged affair. Never would he approach one of these painted creatures and invite her to share a bed with him. For such, one went properly to a house in the red-light district and spoke to the woman in charge. It was a necessary procedure, akin to having regular checkups with the family doctor.

Bill never stayed very long at any one saloon. Some of them he decided against the moment he stepped through the swinging doors. He could recognize at a glance a waterfront dive, full of sailors and bums. Other places he liked. And finally one night he found his favorite. It had started to rain and he hurried toward the gaslight that illuminated The Golden Parrot. It was mainly to get out of the rain that he went inside.

There were golden globes on the saloon's gas lamps; there was a golden ceiling and red velvet cushions on the chairs. And just inside the door a live parrot in a cage croaked, "Good evening, good evening, what'll it be tonight?"

On the floor were a few tables, but most customers were standing at the bar. Bill saw no bums and only a handful of sailors. He made his way to the bar. When he reached it he almost wished he had chosen a table, even if he were by himself, for he spotted a red-haired waitress with a quick-moving marvelous figure.

The bartender announced, in a perfect imitation of the parrot at the door, "Good evening, good evening, what'll it be tonight?"

Bill ordered beer and watched the bartender fill the mug expertly from the tap in the keg, and then slide it across the top of the immaculate bar without spilling a drop. Bill sipped his beer and looked around him again. It was indeed a pleasant haven from the rain.

In one corner an old man with flowing white hair was pounding a piano in the style of a concert pianist, but playing old favorites like "The Velocipede

Gallop," "The Telegram Waltz," and "Little Maggie May." Most of the time he played softly; now and then he would slip into a crescendo as if his own playing were exciting him, and the bartender would call out to him, "Tone it down, Ned!" and Ned would try to oblige.

Bill was watching for the waitress but she was nowhere in sight now. The place seemed strictly a drinking spot; there was no sign of dinner being served, but a free lunch decorated the bar.

When the waitress finally emerged from the back room she stood hesitant in the doorway. And then, to Bill's surprise, Ned at the piano bonged out a grandiose chord, and the girl crossed the room and stood beside him.

She was still wearing her waitress uniform, black with demure white collar, and a white ruffled apron. But the dress fit her well; it emphasized her curves. She had a very pale complexion and a head of rich, dark, red-brown hair, worn in a waterfall.

As Ned's introductory music faded to silence there was clapping and cheering from most of the patrons.

And then Ned began playing again, softly this time, and the girl began to sing.

> Drink to me only with thine eyes
> And I will pledge with mine
> But leave a kiss within the cup
> And I'll not ask for wine.

She had a rich, deep, yet soft voice, rather strange for one who looked so young. Bill had heard cabaret singers before, but in contrast to this girl they seemed in retrospect to be raucous, teasing, flirting. This one sang from the heart; it was as if she were singing directly to someone. He felt as if she were singing to *him*, and from the looks on the faces of those around him, he guessed she was having the same effect on all of them.

When she finished there was another burst of applause and cries of "More! More!" She spoke to the pianist and he nodded and then she sang "Beautiful Dreamer."

Beer in hand, Bill moved a little closer to where she was standing. Somehow she seemed to be smiling, even as she sang. He was completely enchanted.

There was applause again at the end of the song, and again the crowd wanted more. The girl nodded and smiled, blew them a kiss. "Sorry," she apologized. "I've got to get back to work."

There were more people sitting down now, Bill noticed. But he spotted an unoccupied table and took his empty beer mug over to it.

He watched her move about from table to table, again aware of her quick, graceful movements. At last she reached him, and when she asked, "What will you have?" he could not speak. He just held up his empty mug, and she laughed as she took it away.

When she came back with the beer and put it down on the table in front of him he said, "You sing beautifully."

"Why, thank you! Five cents for the beer, please, and another five for the one you had at the bar. Al says you walked off without paying." Her words were matter-of-fact enough, but her tone was not unfriendly.

Bill reached in his pocket and handed her the dime. "I just might want another, you know."

"I know."

She dropped the dime in her apron pocket and walked away.

That night he felt a strong reaction: *she doesn't*

belong here. She shouldn't be here, singing for her supper.

Before he was ready for another beer, the girl had disappeared and was replaced by another waitress in an identical costume, but not with as interesting a face and figure. Evidently the attractive one had the earlier shift.

He was back the next night, and the next after that. They reached the point of saying good evening to each other, and how are you, and agreeing on the state of the weather, good or bad.

That third evening he drummed up the courage to say, "You get off early, don't you?"

Her eyebrows went up. "Why do you ask?"

"Because, when you are off-duty I should be very pleased if you would sit down and talk with me. If that's not against the rules."

"I guess not."

He watched her go and speak to the man behind the bar, and she nodded in Bill's direction; he saw him in turn nod his permission. She disappeared to the back and when she reappeared she was in street clothes: a neat walking suit of brown silk and a perky little bonnet with a matching brown feather.

A wave of shyness swept over Bill as he stood up and pulled back her chair.

The other waitress, eyes twinkling, approached their table. "What will you have, madam?"

"A glass of wine, Jessie, please."

The wine arrived. She clinked the wineglass against his beer mug, rather solemnly.

"Perhaps. I should introduce myself. My name is Bill Ferguson." He gave her his best smile.

She smiled back. "My name is Tawny," she told him. "Tawny . . ." she hesitated for a fraction of a second. "Tawny McShane," she concluded.

* * *

In the year since the lonely waif had arrived on Evangeline McClintock's doorstep, life had held a lot of changes for Tawny. She had matured, she had hardened; in short, she had grown up. She was trying her best to forget the nightmare last summer on the wagon trail west. She was deliberately putting that episode out of her mind, trying to pretend it never happened. Which was why, after coming to San Francisco, she had stopped calling herself Mrs. Barrister and gone back to being Tawny McShane.

Of course, she never really could forget the sight of the bodies that morning after the Indian attack. She tried to remember Timothy as a handsome, sweet young man who had made love to her in his quiet, ineffectual way, but her clearest memory was of his dead body.

She had no idea what she and the tearful Wilma Wilson would have done that morning had they not been overtaken by three prospectors. She had heard hoofbeats and lifted her face. Would it be the Indians coming back?

The sound of the approaching horses grew louder, coming down the road to the east, and then three men suddenly reined in beside the wagon. Two of them were grizzled old fellows; the third was a young man. "Where are your men?" the oldest man asked.

Tawny did her best to steady her voice. She pointed to Joe Wilson's body as she said, "They were killed by the Indians last night."

"My God!" the prospector cried, looking down at the Wilsons' bodies.

"There's another behind the wagon," Tawny told him, thinking, *I won't show it to him. I couldn't*! "I suppose they should be buried quickly. The vultures . . ." She couldn't go on.

The old man tipped his hat. "We'll get to it right off, miss." He turned to his companions. "Come on, Jack, Ben, get out your picks and shovels."

"Thank you, sir!" Tawny cried out.

"'Tain't work for young girls like you. Mebbe you could brew us up a bit of coffee while we're working?"

"Of course!" She was glad to have something to do. It was while she was building the fire that Tawny realized that the mules were gone. The Indians must have taken them. She tried to make conversation with the three men while they were drinking coffee. Wilma had refused to join them; she was back in the wagon, sobbing quietly.

The youngest of the three kept staring at Tawny, so she hurried to tell them her story, to let them know that the body of the man behind the wagon was that of her husband. "We were headed for San Francisco. The Wilsons had been kind enough to give us a ride. I'm not sure what to do now with only the wagon. Without the mules."

The oldest of the three, apparently their leader, said, "Excuse us, miss, while we have a little powwow?" and he motioned the other two to one side.

Within a moment he was back.

"We have a proposition, miss. How would it be if we hitched two of our horses to your wagon and we all moved west together? If, in return, you two girls do our cooking for us."

Tawny looked into the three faces, one at a time. Could she trust them? It did not take her very long to conclude that she would have to. There was no other way.

She put out her hand as if she were a man. She said to the leader, "It's a bargain." He gave her a firm handshake. "If you'll see to the hitching, I'll see what I can do for her." She nodded toward the wagon.

The next few nights, while they were still in the mountains and Indians were still a threat, one of the men stood guard until dawn. Each day one rode horseback, the others keeping to the wagon, taking turns at the reins.

At first Wilma, a frightened child whose parents had been killed, kept weeping constantly. Tawny wept inwardly. She never had been madly in love with Timothy, but he had been a good and gentle companion and now she was practically alone again, assuming the responsibility for the younger girl. They had some money that Joe and Timothy had stashed away in the wagon, and what was left of the money that she saved when she had drawn a salary. Near the ferry landing before they crossed to San Francisco, where they bade farewell to the three prospectors, they were able to sell the wagon and some of the personal things the Wilsons had been bringing from Texas.

Their two birthdays both took place in September. Tawny turned sixteen and Wilma fifteen. They celebrated them on the day they finally arrived in San Francisco and found a boardinghouse, run by a little old lady named Mrs. Schultz. She was the motherly type who clucked like a hen over the girls' story of their trip west. Since their money was running out, she assured them they could live there on credit until they found employment.

Each morning they bought a newspaper and studied the advertisements. It was Wilma who found a job first, probably because there were more advertisements for domestics. She was content to become a daytime nursemaid for two small children up on Nob

Hill. There certainly were no opportunities for dressers, and that was the only real experience Tawny had. She found herself making the rounds of the theaters, late mornings when the box offices were open and people were working backstage.

Every time she said "dressing woman" she was laughed at. One stage manager winked at her in a nasty way and suggested she try out for the chorus line. She was getting discouraged and didn't try out for the chorus line for that stage manager, but she considered auditioning if she came across somone really decent.

With no experience and no "gentleman backer," she didn't seem to have a chance. Then in one backstage office, the man who was interviewing her asked, "You say you can't dance. But can you sing?"

She was far away from Pa now and she was less apprehensive about his finding her. She took a deep breath, and then told him, "I have sung for audiences."

"Sing something for me."

"Now, just like this?" She looked around. The door to his office was open and she could see people beyond.

"Just like this."

"What shall I sing?"

"Anything, for God's sake. 'Annie Laurie,' if you like."

So she sang the ditty and heard clapping from outside the office.

The man behind the desk said, "You've got a voice, young lady. Too strong a voice for the chorus line. Take a few lessons and you'll be a professional."

The applause was coming closer, and now a man had come into the office. He turned out to be Al

Benedict, owner of The Golden Parrot. He was fat, balding, middle-aged, a family man who meant no monkey business. She liked him on sight.

He said, "She's professional right now, for my money. How about it, young woman, do you want a job?"

She wanted one very much. She worked from noon until ten o'clock each evening. Work was light during the day, and she only sang in the evenings. She got along fine with Al Benedict, who let her choose her own songs, and also with old Ned, the pianist, who taught her to read sheet music so that all her songs would not have to be done from memory.

And she learned how to fend off men.

For men did stare at her; men did want to buy her drinks, or take her home. It was old Ned who walked her home each night, not leaving until she was safely inside Mrs. Schultz's house.

Wilma and Tawny saw little of each other except Sundays, when neither of them worked. Then they would go for a walk, out toward the Presidio, talking about what had happened during the week. Wilma's tales amounted to a dull list of children's pranks and mistress's whims. Tawny's were not much more exciting. They got to talking about their lives before they had met. Wilma's had been confined to the farm in Texas. And when she asked, "What did you do before you were married, Tawny?" Tawny, to her surprise, found herself telling the truth. Wilma listened open-mouthed to the tales of McShane's Marvelous Medicine.

Wilma was not the brightest girl in the world, but she was a wonderful audience. "But what happened, Tawny? How did you ever get to be an actress?"

So Tawny began at the beginning, explaining about magnetic healing and how her father had forced her to go to the man's house and give a treatment. "But, Pa forgot how much I'd grown up. Or pretended to forget. Perhaps a child can touch a man with such a treatment and nothing happens. But not when you're grown. The man . . . took me, Wilma. Do you understand what I mean?"

Wilma nodded soberly. "Oh, Tawny, it must have been dreadful!"

Tawny did not reply. She looked back on that afternoon in Lance Oliver's study with mixed feelings. What would always puzzle her was how she had come to do what she did—let him do what he did—and not fight back. Why had she felt as if she wanted it all to happen? Why had she known such passionate pleasure, such bodily satisfaction—something she'd never known in Timothy's arms? Would she ever feel something like it again? She prayed to find it someplace, somehow, with some man she had yet to meet.

But in the meantime she was being very careful. She did not want to become promiscuous; she did not want to succumb to a man out of sheer desire; nor did she want to make the mistake of marrying the wrong man. Her brief marriage to Timothy had been such a mistake. She realized that if he had lived they could not have been happy together.

So she was biding her time. It proved alien to her nature, and consequently she found herself frequently being short of temper, particularly with Wilma.

The round-faced young man who had been coming in alone for the last few nights was rather appealing. He was not really good-looking; his attraction lay more in his manner. He was a gentleman; he had spoken to her like a gentleman. All he had asked of her was to sit down and talk.

"Pleased to meet you, Miss McShane. Are you a native San Franciscan, as I am?"

She shook her head. "No, I've only been here since last fall."

"I see."

He did not ask where she was from, so at least for the moment, she would not have to go into that Davenport, Iowa, story.

"You're a native San Franciscan? You've lived here all your life?" she asked.

"Except for the last few years. I've been to college back east."

College. He was a gentleman, for sure.

"But that"—Bill looked down into his beer—"is all over now. I won't be going back."

"You sound unhappy."

Bill looked up, looked into her eyes. Lovely, lively, intelligent eyes. Full of sympathy at the moment.

"I'm just a bit at loose ends right now. My father died and I had to come home."

"I'm sorry."

"I'm not brooding over his death, if that's what you're thinking. I'm just at loose ends, as I said, because I'm not sure what I'm going to do until his estate is settled. Now tell me about you. How did you happen to be here in The Golden Parrot, of all places?"

She smiled impishly. "Why, because Al—I mean Mr. Benedict—hired me."

"But you don't belong in a place like this." He was frowning now, looking about.

"What's wrong with The Golden Parrot?" Tawny retorted. "I think it's a nice place. A nice, pretty place."

"But it's a saloon!"

"I know it's a saloon. It's the only saloon I've ever been in. The way people talked about saloons I though they were ugly places full of awful people. Most people who come in here are nice."

"Oh?"

"Well, sometimes, once in awhile, someone will have a bit too much to drink. But Al always makes them leave. And he doesn't let customers bother Jessie or me."

"I'm glad of that!"

"Anyhow, I can take care of myself," Tawny said confidently. "I've had to for a long while."

"You have no family?"

"No."

"An orphan?"

"Yes." Now she told him the story of her parents, the actor and actress, the train wreck, the relative in Davenport, Iowa, who had raised her.

"And how did you get way out here?" Bill asked when she had finished. The story of her life so far was heartbreaking.

I've told him absolutely all I'm going to, Tawny was thinking, so her answer was, "I joined an acting troupe myself."

"But you left them."

She nodded, her face abruptly sad. "I had to."

Some man, Bill thought, *some man went after her.* He hesitated at expressing his thought aloud.

Just as abruptly Tawny's face brightened. She said, "But I like it here in San Francisco. And I like The Golden Parrot, even if you don't! I'm happy here."

She finished her wine, sat back in her chair, and folded her hands in her lap.

Bill asked, "Would you care for another glass?"

"Oh, no thank you. I better be getting home or my roommate will be worrying about me."

"May I escort you? I hate to think of you out alone so late at night."

His solicitude was indeed impressive.

"Ned always sees me home. He's a sweet old thing and he worries about me. Look at him now. He's regarding you with suspicion."

Bill looked across the room. Ned, his hands still cavorting over the keyboard, was keeping his eyes on Tawny.

Bill said, "Should we give him a night off, just once? I should very much like to see you home."

He was in deadly earnest. Those big brown eyes—like a spaniel puppy's, she decided—were most appealing. She suddenly thought it would be nice to have him walking beside her through the dark.

"I'll speak to Ned," she said.

Bill watched her cross the room, her bustle swaying a little as she walked between the small tables. She was lovely, lovely. He never had felt about a girl the way he felt now. Desire welled up in him: *I wish she belonged to me. I wish she were mine.*

Bill couldn't hear what she said to the pianist, but the old man appeared to be smiling as she bent to kiss his cheek, before hurrying back to the table.

"Is it all right?" he asked her.

She grinned. "It is all right for the gentleman—that's what he called you—to escort the lady home."

Bill got to his feet. "Are you ready now?"

Tawny's smile was a bit awry. "You forgot again," she reminded him.

"Forgot?"

"To pay for the drinks."

"Oh." He looked around but did not spot the

other waitress. So he said, "Excuse me!" and hurried over to the bar.

As he handed over the money Al Benedict said, "Take good care of the young lady."

It was a beautiful spring evening. For once it was not raining in San Francisco. He started to hail a cab, but Tawny said, "I usually walk. It's not far, just up the hill a few steps."

Walking would take longer, Bill realized. "Then we'll walk," he told her.

Each time they crossed a street he took her arm, and each time he hated letting go of her. Her arm felt so soft through the silk of her suit jacket. Tawny was enjoying his touch. It was solicitous and somehow comfortable.

They said little as they walked: "Watch out for that curb" or "It's only a little farther," until Tawny stopped walking and said, "Here it is."

Mrs. Schultz's boardinghouse was on the side of one of the steeper hills. One end of the porch had a higher base than the other. A porch light flickered and there was a light in one of the windows on the second floor.

At the bottom of the steps Tawny turned and looked up at him. "Good night, Mr . . . Ferguson, wasn't it?"

He took hold of her elbows. "Bill," he told her. "Please call me Bill."

"Good night, Bill. And thank you. For the wine. For walking me home."

"Thank you, Tawny, for letting me."

His voice was so earnest, his face so serious that she wondered if he were going to kiss her. She could almost feel his wanting to and she wondered if she should let him. He moistened his lips, and said, rather breathlessly, "Tomorrow night . . . tomorrow night . . . will you have a late supper with me when you are through work? It would be all right if your roommate knew you were going to be a little late, wouldn't it? Will you?"

"That would be nice," Tawny said slowly. "I'd like that."

"Tomorrow . . ." He breathed the word, holding her shoulders so firmly that it was almost painful. Then he suddenly let go of her and ran down the hill.

Tawny smiled at his back and then turned and hurried up into the house to tell Wilma about her conquest. For she knew for sure that a conquest it had been.

Bill had no one to tell what had happened to him.

At home there was only Mother, and Mother would not appreciate his falling head over heels in love with a girl who was a waitress-singer in a waterfront saloon.

2

Bill chose a seafood restaurant farther along the waterfront. He did not want a place where he might encounter friends or acquaintances, so that word would get back to his mother. He was not ashamed of being seen with Tawny. How could he be? But he knew that if his mother learned he had been seen dining with a beautiful young girl she would insist on his bringing Tawny home to meet her. And he was not ready to face that scene yet.

Tonight Tawny was wearing a white silk dress with ruffles of lace around the low-cut neckline. Her hair was piled high to support a ridiculous little hat. What a lark it would be to remove that hat, pull the hairpins from that hair, and run his fingers through it!

Tawny was admiring his striped cravat and neatly trimmed mustache. She was proud to be seated there with someone as respectable-looking as Bill Ferguson.

They enjoyed huge bowls of freshly made chowder.

"Where do you usually eat dinner?" Bill asked.

She shrugged. "I don't eat a real sit-down dinner. Just snack off the bar."

"How dreadful!"

"It's good-enough food."

"I suppose. If you're hungry."

"I'm always hungry," Tawny told him. "This chowder is awfully good."

"I'm glad you're enjoying it."

"Aren't you?"

"Oh, yes, yes. I just meant I'm glad that *you* are. I like to see you looking happy."

They were sitting in a curtained booth, one small bracket lamp casting shadows of the two of them, even of the salt and pepper and bowl of oyster crackers, on the table between them. They were in a restaurant, true, but their booth had an aura of utter privacy. Only now and then could they hear voices from other cubicles, or the sound of waiters passing by.

Shaking her head, Tawny said, "I never knew anyone like you, Bill Ferguson."

"I never knew anyone like you. But what about me? How am I different from your other admirers?"

"I don't have any other admirers."

"No? Dozens of secret ones, I'm sure."

"You flatter me."

"You deserve to be flattered. You deserve to . . ." He broke off. Then he added, "I liked that song you sang tonight."

"Which one?"

" 'Come Hither My Baby, My Darling.' Something like that. I'll bet every man in the room wanted to heed the words. I did."

Tawny said shyly, "It's kind of a silly song."

"It wasn't when you sang it." Suddenly, just before she could pick up her spoon, he reached across the table and took her hand. "Tawny, it made me downright jealous!"

"Jealous?"

"Yes. I didn't like it. I didn't like your singing to all those people. I wanted you to be singing just to me, just for me." He held her hand in an almost painful grip, his brown eyes rounder than ever.

"Bill, you're hurting me." Her voice was quiet, but he took his hand away immediately.

"I'm sorry, darling. I'm sorry." He retrieved her hand and kissed it. Then he added, as if it followed reasonably, "We'll take a cab tonight to get you home. But first we'll take a ride. Out onto the peninsula. If you like."

Tawny was smiling.

"If you behave yourself," she said, and went on spooning the chowder.

At first, in the cab, he sat as far away from her as possible. As the horse *tlot-tlotted* along, he looked out the window on his side and said nothing. So Tawny looked out her window as the thinning streetlights bounced by. When the carriage was at last enveloped by blackness, Bill moved closer, very slowly put his arm around her, and held her near him.

"Is this behaving yourself?" she asked.

"I didn't promise. I couldn't. Not with you, Tawny, not with the way I feel about you, the way I've felt ever since I first laid eyes on you. I've wanted to hold you like this. I've wanted to kiss you."

She turned her face toward him.

"Why haven't you?"

"Because I . . . because . . ." And then his hesitation vanished. Her lips were there, waiting, and his own found them.

When they broke apart he whispered, "Oh, Tawny, I love you! I love you so much!"

Tawny did not respond. She had enjoyed the kiss; she enjoyed *being* kissed. But love? She felt nothing like love; she had no longing for him to hold her closer and closer. She felt a curious separateness, as if she were some other girl, or as if she were someone else watching the two of them.

She realized the cab had stopped, that they were at the end of a road. After a moment the cab driver leaned down from his perch and asked, "You folks ready to go back yet?"

Tawny called out, "Yes!"

They did not speak again, but Bill kept his arm around her all the way to Mrs. Schultz's.

There were other men in Tawny's life but not in Bill Ferguson's category. They were the kind of men who tried to pat her buttocks when she passed by their tables, the kind who made lewd remarks when she brought them their drinks, the kind who, to a man, acted as if she were legitimate prey. She despised them all; it was all she could do to hide her resentment, to accept their badinage as part of her job.

Timothy had thought she had the makings of an actress. She had not had the chance to try out for such a career, but she was acting now. She was acting at work, pretending to be a heart-of-gold waitress; she was acting when she sang, pretending to be pouring out her feelings to the faces of the crowd.

What she longed for was a man, one man she could love and trust and depend upon.

She was not sure if Bill Ferguson was the one.

Each night she saw Bill she went home and talked to Wilma. They sat up late in their room at Mrs.

Schultz's. Wilma would already be in her nightgown, her hair in pigtails, sitting up in bed and waiting for Tawny to undress, put on her nightgown, and let down her hair to brush it the required one hundred strokes.

The first night when Tawny reported the kisses Wilma gasped. "You let him? You let him kiss you?"

"Why not?"

"But Ma always told me never to kiss a fellow unless he had proposed. Did he propose to you?"

"No."

"Do you think he will?"

"I don't know. He's awfully serious. He did say he loves me. More than once."

"Oh, how exciting!"

"I ought to be excited," Tawny said. "But somehow I'm not."

"You're remembering Timothy."

"I guess I am." She went on brushing her hair, more than the one hundred strokes, enjoying the rhythmic strokes, remembering how Timothy had loved her hair, remembering his tenderness. What would Bill be like? The way he had held her hand across the table suggested violence. Yet his kiss had been tentative, careful. It was not the way that man back in New York had kissed her. Why did she keep remembering Lance Oliver, comparing other men to him?

"I'm sorry I mentioned Timothy," Wilma said. "It makes you feel bad."

"That's all right. I wasn't thinking of Timothy. I was thinking of that other man, back in New York."

"The one who . . ." Wilma broke off in mid-sentence.

"That one." Tawny smiled. "The one I should forget. I should think about Bill and whether I want him to be in love with me or not."

The pattern of Bill and Tawny's evenings together seemed to become static, except that the kisses grew more frequent and more passionate. But he did not try to touch her in any other way. And then one night she understood his attitude. As they were leaving The Golden Parrot, they passed close to the bar and a man standing there said to his companion in a voice loud enough for Tawny and Bill to hear, "Did you ever hear that old story, 'Did you ever sleep with a redhead?' Answer: 'Not a wink!' "

Bill grabbed her arm and practically dragged her out of the saloon.

"Bill, what is it?"

"You heard what that man said? He thinks you and I are having an affair!"

Tawny wanted to laugh but Bill looked so deadly serious that she repressed it.

"If I could only take you out of that place! I've told you you don't belong in there! Not someone as sweet, as innocent as you!"

"But I . . ." She started to say *but I'm not a sweet innocent; I've been married, Bill.* Then she thought, *Why tell him? Why not let him think that way if he wants to*? She could pretend she was to the manor born, as they put it in the books she'd read.

"But what?" he asked her. "What were you going to say?"

She thought a moment, choosing her words carefully. "But I have to earn my living, Bill. I'm not trained for much else."

They were standing on the sidewalk just outside The Golden Parrot when Bill said in a quiet voice,

"You wouldn't have to earn your living if you were married to me."

She gaped at him, unable to speak. Then he took her arm abruptly and started down the street.

Tonight he walked her as far as Chinatown, not talking all the while, saying nothing until they were in the booth behind the beaded curtain, with pots of tea on little candle warmers, and a menu on the table.

Bill picked up the menu and held it but did not look at it. He said, "I want to marry you more than anything else in the world. But I can't ask you until I know what my prospects are for the future. Until my father's estate is settled and I know what I'll be doing. *Then* I'm going to ask you and pray God you say yes."

Again Tawny did not try to answer. She reached across the table and patted his hand, smiling at him. Then she asked, "Shall I pour you some tea?"

"Please." Still not looking at the menu he went on talking. "Chow mein? Chop suey? Or what?"

"It makes no difference, Bill."

"It makes no difference to me, either."

The waiter appeared and stood for some time before they made up their minds.

That night, on the doorstep, his good-night kiss was longer and more passionate than ever, and when he finished he ran his hands over her shoulders and breasts and down to her narrow waist.

He whispered, "God, honey, how I want you!" and then he turned and ran down the street away from her.

For several nights he did not come to The Golden Parrot. Tawny missed him. She wondered if he was trying to forget about her or if he had found a girl somewhere else, a girl who could satisfy his desires for a price. *He doesn't want to have me that way; he actually wants to marry me. But in the meanwhile,* she thought, *he must be going through agony.*

Tawny knew because that was the way she felt. She had not fallen in love with him, she was not sure she wanted to marry him, but on the other hand his kisses, and the way he had touched her that last night had left her body alive and tingling. She was conscious of her body, constantly conscious, and wondering, if and when Bill came back, she could bear to go on the way they had been.

How long could she go on pretending to be innocent?

Bill did come back, but there was a change in him. His good-night kiss seemed almost perfunctory.

Wilma was dying to meet him, and so it was arranged that he come for Sunday afternoon tea at the boarding house. Mrs. Schultz, giggling, served tea and left the three of them alone in the austere parlor with its scratchy horsehair chairs, its daguerreotypes of dead Schultzes, its drooping fern in a brass pot, and the perennial bouquet of artificial flowers that always inhabited the fireplace in spring and summer.

It was not what would have been called a jolly tea party. Wilma was her usual shy self, Bill seemed awkwardly embarrassed, and Tawny could not summon her usual sparkle.

But after Bill left, Wilma said, "Oh, Tawny, I think he is wonderful! So good-looking. So nice."

"He is that."

"And he is absolutely mad about you. It was written all over him."

"I know."

"But I noticed something else. You're not so crazy about him. Are you?"

"No, I'm not."

"Tawny, what are you going to do?"

"I don't know," Tawny told her. "Now let's take these tea things into the kitchen. It was nice of Mrs. Schultz to serve it, wasn't it?"

That night at supper Mrs. Schultz expressed her admiration of what she termed "your gentleman caller." And then added, "And of course the Fergusons are one of the first families of San Francisco. You knew that, didn't you?"

Tawny shook her head.

"He's a great catch. A *great* catch!" Mrs. Schultz repeated. "You are a very lucky young lady."

Am I? Tawny wondered. She felt as if she were being swept along into something beyond her control, as if her future were being decided for her by others.

And then the next time Bill came to The Golden Parrot and took her out to supper he suggested they go to the seafood restaurant where they had spent their first evening together. It was as if he were trying to make a fresh start.

He scarcely spoke until they had finished eating and then, very seriously, he began with the preface: "I have something I think I ought to tell you."

Tawny couldn't imagine what it could be. Some sort of confession?

Then he said, "My father's estate has been settled, at last. And it wasn't much of an estate. He gambled it away. Neither my mother nor I had any idea what was going on. He actually died in debt. Mother has the house and enough insurance to live on—if she is careful. My inheritance is an odd one."

"In what way?"

"Well, as I said, my father was a gambler. He loved to take chances. And for years he was lucky. He made his first fortune in forty-nine when he came west in the gold rush. *Gold* was a magic word to him. And so, not long ago, he bought, sight unseen, a ranch up in the hills of Washington Territory. He bought it solely on a rumor, mind you, just a rumor, that there was gold on the land.

"In his will he left that ranch to me. The ranch, and nothing else." His voice was bitter.

After a moment all Tawny could think of to say was, "You don't sound very happy about it. I'm sorry, Bill."

"I'm *not* very happy about it."

"And you had to tell someone about it."

"I had to tell you because it shows how bad my prospects are. What am I going to do with a ranch? I'm a city boy; I've always lived in a city, except when I was in college. I know about things like stocks and bonds, not about horses and cows!"

"You could learn," Tawny said quietly.

"You think I could?" His eyes lit up. "You have that much faith in me?"

"I wasn't thinking of that," Tawny said frankly. "I spoke as I did just because I've learned to do a lot of things I never thought *I* could."

Bill leaned across the table. "You mean you could learn to be a rancher's wife? You're saying yes?"

Tawny's eyes twinkled. "You haven't asked me yet."

"Tawny, will you marry me? Will you?"

She swallowed. She said, in a very low voice, "I just don't know . . ."

"Don't know if you could face life in the wilderness?"

"It's not that. I just don't know if I love you."

"You could learn. You just said . . ."

"I know. But give me a little time, won't you? Let me think about it."

"Of course, of course!"

It will have to be a secret wedding, he thought. His mother would never agree. They would have to run away together. But he wouldn't tell her that. Not now. It might influence her decision.

He got up, pushed aside the curtain, sat down on her side of the booth, and threw his arms around her. "Think, darling. Think hard!"

How could she think when he was holding her so tightly, his body pressing against hers?

"I will," she told him. "Bill, you're hurting me again!"

He released her, apologized, and then said, "I think it best if I take you home now. Before I lose all of my self-control."

That night they walked home, Bill holding her hand as they moved silently along the streets. They came to a building site and slowed up to read posters along its makeshift wall, posters advertising everything from patent medicines and perfumes to coming events in the theater. They turned away in embarrassment from one sketch of a voluptuous woman, an example of the wonders of Hiller's Mammarial Balm, which claimed to augment the bust. Next came Dr. Stricklander's cough syrup, which cured "everything from paralysis to scrofula, and is also good for worming the baby." Tawny scanned the theater posters, wondering if Amanda would ever arrive in San Francisco, or if she were forever condemned to play the back roads and small towns.

At the last poster Tawny stopped, let go of Bill's hand, and cried out, "Look!"

It was a drawing of a woman standing at a podium, one arm outstretched dramatically.

"COMING! COMING! COMING!" screamed the

poster. "For the first time in San Francisco, the one and only Evangeline McClintock. At Gardner's Hall, Tuesday next, she will deliver her electrifying, inspiring, indescribable lecture, 'Women of the World Unite.' Listen to Evangeline McClintock tell us how the world should be for women, and what we can do to make it all come true!"

"She's coming; she's going to be here in San Francisco!" Tawny cried excitedly.

Bill frowned. "One of *those* women. Disgusting."

Tawny paid no attention to his mumbling. She went on, "Oh, I shall simply have to ask Al to give me the evening off. I'll have to go and hear her!"

Bill asked, "But why? Why should you want to go and listen to that trash?"

"Evangeline's a friend of mine, that's why."

"A friend of yours! Where on earth did you meet her?"

"In New York City." *Careful now*, Tawny reminded herself, *you can't tell him* how *you met Evangeline.*

"I see," Bill said. But he did not see at all; he couldn't imagine Tawny in the company of one of those wild, free-love women. "But you won't go to the lecture, will you, darling?"

"Of course I'll go! I wouldn't miss it. And I'll go up and talk to her afterward. I told you, she is my friend!"

She had taken him completely by surprise. He thought, *I don't know this girl as well as I thought I did. She has a tiger inside her I shall have to tame, if I am to possess her as I want to possess her*. It was a challenge he was eager to take.

"I'm not going to take you to that lecture," he told her.

"I'll go by myself."

She started walking up the street. He caught up with her and took her arm. *Right now,* he thought, *I can't tell her what she must and must not do. But if this girl decides to accept my proposal, if she becomes my wife, it will be a different story altogether.*

Tawny was more excited by the thought of seeing Evangeline again than she was by his proposal of marriage. To Evangeline she could pour out all that had happened to her in the past year. Evangeline would have sensible advice.

"You never before mentioned being in New York," Bill was saying. "I suppose you were there with your acting troupe?"

"Yes, they were there."

"For a long time?"

"Not very long."

"What kind of parts did you play, Tawny? Heroines? Or little girls?"

"I played the part of a maid," Tawny said quickly.

"That's all?"

"That's all."

"You should have played a fairy princess," he said quietly. "That's what you are to me." He took her arm and squeezed it. His good-night kiss was long and passionate, and afterward his only words were, "Don't forget to think, darling. Think hard. About us." And then he was gone.

Tawny was glad that night that Wilma had not waited up for her when she tiptoed into the room. She was not in the mood for a report of her evening with Bill. And neither was she in the mood to tell Wilma about Evangeline. She felt like being alone this night; she wished that she did not share a bed with the younger girl.

It took a long time to get to sleep, and when she

did, she dreamed. She dreamed of Lance Oliver, of his hands on her body, his lips on hers, his entering her, and the completeness she had felt. She awoke in a cold sweat, her breasts taut beneath her nightgown.

3

Lance Oliver had arrived in San Francisco the week before. By that time he had had enough of life at sea. He had taken Evangeline's advice and set out on one of his father's sailing ships. He had gone around the world, traveling in an easterly direction, port after port from Liverpool to Marseilles, to Zanzibar, to Hong Kong and finally San Francisco. He had lived like a sailor all that year—that is, he had lived like a sailor when they reached a port, drinking and whoring; but on board he had lived as Sanford Oliver's son, dining with the captain in the evening, strolling the decks by day.

His monthly allotment had reached him in each port. That had been his only contact with his past: money from his father. The old man did not write letters and Lance wrote no one until he reached San Francisco and decided to leave the ship. Its next journey was around the Horn and back to New York, but Lance decided not to stay aboard. He was not ready to go home.

He liked the looks of San Francisco. He liked his high-ceilinged hotel room with its veiw of the bay—

even if most of the time the view was blurred by the almost constant rain.

He, too, saw the poster advertising Evangeline's coming speech. He, too, determined to be there that evening.

Al Benedict was as surprised as Bill had been that Tawny wished to attend a lecture by "that notorious woman." "I've always thought of you as too much of a lady to take a fancy for that sort of vulgarity."

"*Evangeline* is a lady!"

"Lady of the evening. Not your sort at all."

"She was very kind to me when I needed help. I want to see her again. And she's only going to be in San Francisco for one evening. I'll make it up to you, Al. I'll work both shifts the next evening."

"You don't have to do that. Go ahead and go to your lecture, but don't come back here and start preaching free love and the rest of the nonsense. Understand?"

"Yes, sir! Thank you, Al!"

Gardner's Hall was easy to spot because of the crowd around it: men and women of all classes, all talking excitedly as they lined up to buy tickets. Tawny had come an hour early hoping to catch sight of Evangeline before the lecture, but a lot of other people seemed to have had the same idea. Still she found herself a good seat, down front.

There was clapping and cheering as Evangeline swept onstage. First she bowed an acceptance and then held up a hand calling for silence. She seemed smaller than Tawny remembered, a little ball of a woman in a schoolteacher's dress with stiff white collar and cuffs. Her hair was pulled back severely and she wore no jewelry. She did not look like the sort of person who could hold an audience spellbound.

But when she spoke her rich strong voice dispelled all doubt.

She started speaking very quietly. "Ladies and gentlemen, I thank you for your welcome! If you came here tonight in the hope of witnessing histrionics I am afraid you are in for a disappointment. This is no performance. This is a woman, speaking for all women who are victims of a man-made society.

"Legend has it that throughout the ages men put women on pedestals. The knight and his lady theme runs through history. But there are few knights today, and few women are given the opportunity of being treated like ladies. The majority of women are slaves to their lords and masters. As Victoria Woodhull has so aptly put it, compared to a Roman matron in the time of the Caesars, a married woman today is no more than a concubine."

Evangeline had said it was not a performance, but gradually, as she went on about the rights denied women, about unfair inheritance laws, the vote, divorce injustices, and so on, her tone became more intense, more outraged, and her listeners, in spite of themselves, in spite of their feelings, were caught up with her intensity. When she finished there was a torrent of cheers and applause as well as catcalls that brought her back on stage for several bows.

At last she just stood there, her head lowered slightly as the people began to leave the auditorium. Not all of them filed out immediately. Several, like Tawny, walked toward the platform, to climb the steps and shake Evangeline's plump little hand.

When Tawny reached her Evangeline recognized her immediately. She grabbed Tawny by the shoulders and kissed her on both cheeks.

"Tawny, dear child!"

"Oh, Evangeline, it's so good to see you!"

"It's been a long time. Too long a time." She was looking Tawny over, nodding to herself. A year ago she had been scarcely more than a child on her doorstep. Here was a grown woman.

"I've so much to tell you, Evangeline."

"Some I know, my child. But, look, I can't talk with you now."

"But you're only here one night!"

"I know, I know. Have breakfast with me in the morning, will you? Eight o'clock too early? I have to catch a train."

"That's not too early," Tawny told her.

"I'll see you then, dear, at the Hotel Elizabeth, where I am staying." Evangeline had passed on to the next person in line.

Tawny turned and walked past the line to the steps. She had come down the steps and was walking past more people up the auditorium aisle when she saw him. . . . She caught her breath and stared at him in utter surprise. What was he doing here in San Francisco?

He was wearing a stylish, high-buttoned waistcoat with narrow lapels, more formally dressed than when she had seen him in New York. But he looked just as she remembered him. She would have known him anywhere—those broad shoulders, that black, black hair, and those blue eyes with their curly lashes.

He glanced at her as they passed, but there was nothing like recognition in his face.

Tawny hurried up the aisle and out into the night.

Lance had not had a good look at Tawny, there in the crowd. He had caught a glimpse of a pretty young girl who looked vaguely familiar. Someone he knew? He doubted it. The girl had merely resembled someone he had known some time, somewhere. Attractive wench. But then, a lot of wenches were attractive. . . . Good old Evangeline. Would she be glad to see him again after all these months?

She was. He could tell the moment they shook hands, despite the formality of their greeting.

"Congratulations, Miss McClintock, on this evening's speech. You were in fine form, as ever!"

"Thank you, Mr. Oliver. What a surprise to see you here in San Francisco!"

"I am living here now. Let me present my card."

The card, of course, was his invitation. She slipped it into her reticule there on the lectern and gave him a small wink as she did so.

He went back to his hotel and ordered a late supper for two, to be served in his room. He had barely had time to pour himself a glass of brandy when she arrived. She'd come straight from the lecture hall and of course was still wearing the prim dress.

As soon as the door was closed behind her she threw her arms around his neck. She had to stand on tiptoe, and he had to lean down to receive her affectionate greeting. But there was no need for words between them. There never had been.

He released her, poured her a glass of brandy, and they sat down opposite each other, raising their glasses in a silent toast.

"Sea life agrees with you, Lance. You look very well."

"And you're looking fine, Evangeline." She wasn't, really. She looked tired, and older. Could less than a year make that much difference?

"When did you leave New York?" she was asking.

"Soon after the last time I saw you, last summer."

"You've been here ever since?"

"Oh, I didn't go around the Horn, as you suggested. I went around the world. Except I got off here. The ship sailed for New York this week, going around the Horn. But I wasn't ready to go back. I never was seasick, but right now I'm sick of the sea."

"So you're going to become a man-about-San Francisco, instead of a man-about-New York."

"Evangeline, I don't know how I put up with you. You have a genius for making me feel like a worthless heel."

"Well, aren't you?"

A knock on the door. Dinner had arrived.

Dinner was up to San Francisco's high standards and Evangeline marveled over each course, from the big west coast shrimp to the fresh-cracked crab to the flaming Baked Alaska for dessert. Afterward, when the waiter had removed the debris and left them with a bottle of champagne and two slender glasses, after Lance had turned the lock on the door, Evangeline snapped off her stiff white collar and laid it aside.

"There," she grinned, "that feels better."

"Why don't you take your hair out of that ugly knot, as well," Lance suggested, as he began loosening his cravat.

Evangeline obeyed him. Her hair, falling about her face, made her look younger—but not young enough, he thought.

"Shall we have some champagne . . . first?" he asked.

"If you like." Evangeline's tone was offhand, but he had surprised her. There was something different about him. Always before he had followed the routine.

After they had sipped champagne for a bit, Evangeline said, "So you left her."

"I left her."

"Divorced?"

"I don't know. I haven't heard from her since I left New York. Or heard about her. Which is, in itself, a pleasure."

"Perhaps you should find out if she did get a divorce. What if you wanted to marry again?"

"I doubt that. My father told me I was a born bachelor, and he was right. I should never have tried marriage."

"You just tried it with the wrong person. But your father has his point. Marriage isn't for everyone."

She put down her glass of champagne and unbuttoned the top of her bodice so that her round breasts were bare. She leaned back in her chair with her arms folded behind her head.

Lance watched, amused and now, with the champagne, somewhat titillated. Those breasts were too big for a small person, but they were beautifully shaped. He got up, crossed the room, and stood beside her, one hand cupped around one of her breasts. It was a gesture less of passion than of comfortable friendship.

"What's going to become of me, Evangeline? What am I going to do with my life? Lately I've been wondering."

"You were bored in New York, and so you ran away to sea. Now you're bored again."

"Not exactly bored. And I wasn't bored on the long voyage. There were strange places to see, exotic foods, drinks, women. A world full of different things that were interesting. But all that, all travel, is just living vicariously with other people's lives and ways. I'm beginning to think an individual should have more to his life than endless fleshly pleasures. One should have a challenge, a cause, like your women's rights."

Evangeline said quietly, "I hoped someday that thought would occur to you. I'm glad it did. I'm glad it's me you're telling it to."

She reached up and pulled his head down to her breast; the two warm mounds caressed his cheeks. He turned his head and kissed one and then the other.

"Now?" she whispered.

"Now."

He turned down the bracketed gas lamps on each of the walls, so that the light in the room was ephemeral as moonlight. There was no moon that night in San Francisco; the rain had started again, a purring *rat-a-tat-tat* mingling with the horsehoofs on the cobblestones of the street below the windows.

In her usual swift way Evangeline undressed, pulled back the coverlet, and lay down on the bed. When Lance came to the bed she sensed he was not ready. She also knew it was up to her to make him ready. She pushed him gently so that he was lying on his back and she bent over him as she kissed him, letting her breasts brush him. She kissed him full on the lips, while one hand found his organ and massaged it in a steady, repetitive motion until she could feel it come to life. Then she changed her position and kissed it, as she had kissed his mouth. And at last he was ready, ready as he always was for a swift consummation.

Afterward, as they lay there, no longer touching, Evangeline thought: *how much better it is when men want me, want me so badly that they make all the overtures, and all I have to do is to accept, to welcome it all. Is this what it means to get old?*

And Lance, exhausted, thought: *intercourse, just for its own sake, is not enough. There must be something to love, something I've always laughed at. Love has always been just a word, something you said to women to get them to give you their bodies, a meaningless word. But is it meaningless? Did Sue Ellen really love me, as she said she did?*

He determined to remain continent, as continent as it was possible for him to be, for a while.

"This is my only night in San Francisco," Evangeline said softly. "It's all yours, Lance."

He wanted no more of it.

When Tawny met Evangeline in the hotel dining room the next morning the latter was wearing her traveling suit, very plain, very sensible, and her hair was tucked under a featherless bonnet. Beside her on the floor was her reticule, bulging with books and papers. She had a morning newspaper on the table. She looked up as Tawny came toward her.

"The editor had the decency to say I was well received, but he deplores my subject matter. Oh, well, that's the way it always goes. Another town, another audience, keep hammering at them; some day the blockheads will wake up. Someday, mark my words, women will vote, women will have equal opportunities. Or my name isn't Evangeline McClintock. Well, what shall we have for breakfast?"

"Whatever you say." Tawny smiled. "I don't care what I eat when I have a chance to see you."

The waiter had come to their table.

"Waffles," Evangeline said crisply. "Waffles and a touch of bacon. And coffee. Plenty of coffee. Make sure that it's freshly made and hot."

Morning sunlight was pouring through the windows of the hotel dining room, glinting on the heavy silverware and dishes.

Evangeline began by saying, "So you and Timothy Barrister are here in San Francisco."

Tawny could only shake her head.

Evangeline went on. "Amanda read the riot act to me when I met her in Chicago—for ever having introduced my so-called niece to her, for having let her hire you. She told me you eloped with her precious leading man."

"I did."

"But you left him?"

"Oh, Evangeline, please! Let me tell you what happened!"

"Here come the waffles. Eat some of your breakfast, at least, before you start talking."

Tawny smiled. "It seems you're always telling me to eat first. I'm not starving any more, Evangeline." She took a few bite of waffle and sipped her coffee before she spoke again.

"Timothy and I were fools, silly young fools who thought we were in love, that nothing else mattered. We should have had the sense to know that Amanda would be furious, that she would throw both of us out of the troupe. And there we were in the middle of nowhere on the Great Plains with practically no money, no way to get anyplace where we could find work."

"How dreadful!" Evangeline murmured. "What on earth did you do?"

"We found some people headed west, homesteaders on their way to California. We lived with them, rode in their covered wagon. A man and his wife and daughter, from Texas. They were very kind." Tawny shook her head and sighed, hating to remember.

"What happened?"

"We were attacked by Indians. Only a handful. But they killed Mr. Wilson. Mrs. Wilson ran out of the wagon where we women were hiding, and they cut off her head. And in the morning when I dared to step out of the wagon I saw them. Mr. Wilson and his wife—and Timothy. All dead."

"Oh, my God! Oh, Tawny. You poor child. What did you do then?"

"Wilma—the Wilsons' daughter—and I made it here to San Francisco and found work."

"You were lucky. What kind of work?"

"Wilma is a nursemaid. I am a waitress-singer at The Golden Parrot."

"A saloon?"

"Yes."

"Do you like it?"

"It's all right, but . . ."

"But?" Evangeline persisted.

"Some of the customers . . ."

"Aren't what you'd call respectful?"

"Oh, Al, that's the owner of The Golden Parrot, doesn't let them get really fresh. And I just pretend I don't mind the way they look at me, or things they say to me. But I don't like it."

"Of course not. It's not the place you should be, Tawny."

"That's what Bill says!"

"Now the plot thickens. Who is Bill?"

"Bill Ferguson. A young man I've been seeing of late."

"One of the not-so-respectful customers?" Evangeline grinned crookedly. There was something so lusty about this lass one couldn't imagine her existing without a man someplace handy.

"Oh, no! No! He's a gentleman, very much a gentleman. He treats me as if I were a lady. He's in love with me, Evangeline. He wants me to marry him!"

"And you?"

"I don't know. I simply don't know. I know he's

what you'd call a real catch. He comes from a good family, he's nice looking, he's, as I said, a real gentleman. And yet . . ."

"You're not in love with him."

"I don't think so."

"You don't have to think about something like that, my dear. You just know."

Tawny nodded. "It was a mistake to marry Timothy," she said. "I know now that it wasn't love, not real love, that made me run away with him. It was kind of an infatuation. And a loneliness. I had no one. But if he had lived, it wouldn't have worked out. He was weak. He was sweet, but he was weak."

"Is Bill like that?"

"Oh, no!"

"What is he like?"

"He's hard to describe. I think he's a strong man. At least physically I'm sure he's strong: the way he grips my hand, the way he hugs me. And I think he may be strong in other ways—I mean positive, I guess. He didn't want me to attend your lecture. I think he is one of those perhaps old-fashioned men who have no time for the question of women's rights."

"Do you mind him hugging you? And kissing you? Touching you?"

"No."

"Then marry him, Tawny."

"What? Just because I enjoy hugs and kisses? With anyone I could . . ." She broke off. Evangeline was laughing now.

"My dear girl, I know! I know what you are like even better than you know yourself. Physically you are all passion and desire. Your whole body, everything about you, tells me that you are a bundle of sensuous emotions. I think you could adapt yourself to any man, in no time at all. You are ready, so terribly ready. And if you don't watch out, if you don't play it safe, you'll wind up the victim of one of those disrespectful men you've mentioned. You'll wind up that way and you'll hate it, but you'll be caught, and before you know it you'll be one of those poor unfortunate creatures I find on the doorstep of the Woman's Center in New York. It's in your blood."

"You make me sound wicked!"

"There's nothing wicked about it! It's just the way you are. It's just you! Nothing to be ashamed of. Just something you must be aware of, and something you must control. I say, marry the man. Marry the man and satisfy his desire and yours. Yes, yours. You have it. I can feel it. I can practically smell it. Some women are better off married and I think you are one of them. People like myself can take a casual roll in the hay now and then—as one takes a bath, or washes one's hair. You are sexually emotional; you probably need a nightly dose of it. Marry the man. Satisfy yourself. If it turns out that a strong man, which is what you want, is really a brutal man, then leave him."

"That's your advice.

"Yes. For what it's worth."

"I don't think Bill would be brutal. I'm just afraid that he would never . . . how shall I put it? Make me come alive."

"As Timothy did?"

"No. Not Timothy."

"Then who?" Evangeline leaned forward, her black eyes bright with curiosity.

Tawny lowered her eyes. "The first man," she said under her breath.

"The first man! You mean the one who raped you in New York?"

Tawny lifted her face, and looked directly into the other woman's eyes. "I never explained, Evangeline. It wasn't really rape. I mean, he didn't force himself upon me, not really."

"Oh?"

"I didn't fight him off. I didn't protest. I was furious afterward, for what he had done and what I had done. But while it was happening. . . I can't describe it, but I was happy. Do you know what I mean? I was so very happy!"

"I think I understand," Evangeline said. "You don't have to be, shall we say, graphic."

Tawny was silent for a few moments. Then she said, "It's strange, but last night, when I was leaving the lecture hall, I thought I saw him. In fact, I know I saw him."

"Here, in San Francisco?"

"Yes. I couldn't believe it at first. But then, I was sure. He is so big; he has that thick black hair and those wonderful blue eyes with long, curled eyelashes. Oh, I know it was him. But he didn't seem to recognize me. If he had, if he had tried to speak to me, I know I would have turned and run, as fast as I could. He is a married man. What we did was bad."

Evangeline, who had been drinking in every word, heard that description of "him" with a catch of her breath. She finally managed to find her voice. "You know, Tawny, you've never told me the man's name. Do you remember it?"

"Of course! He was Mr. Oliver. Mr. Lance Oliver. I'll never forget him."

4

At first it was only the vaguest memory in the back of Lance's mind that he had once known someone who came from San Francisco, who had spoken of it in glowing terms. Then, that sunny spring morning after the night with Evangeline he began to remember who the person was. He recalled the face first, a round, boyish face, and then the name Bill. A young freshman at college who had been assigned to him to introduce around and help with registration. Bill. Bill Ferguson, that was it. Lance had liked the lad.

He spoke to the hotel's desk clerk, who was a fountain of gossip, who assured him that Bill Ferguson indeed was in town, explained about Bill's father's death, and offered to send a messenger to the Ferguson house with news of Lance's inquiry. Within an hour Lance had received an invitation to tea from Mrs. Ferguson.

The Ferguson house was garish, and Mrs. Ferguson matched it. She was angular and draped with black lace, and she was plainly impressed at being introduced to the only son of the shipping magnate. Lance was a disappointment to her, however, because he did not turn out to be full of the latest news of New York society.

Bill looked much the same as Lance remembered him, serious, sober, earnest.

"I am so glad you looked us up," Mrs. Ferguson was pouring tea from a silver pot. "Poor Bill has had a rather dull time of it since he came home from college."

Bill said nothing but he shot a significant glance in Lance's direction.

"Cream and sugar, Mr. Oliver?"

"Just sugar, thank you. And please call me Lance."

"If you wish."

After a bit of awkward silence Lance said, "I've been at sea for so long I scarcely am up with the news. I know that France fell. Contrary to most people in this country my sympathy is with the poor people of Paris. It is too bad such charming people must be the victims, not only of their enemies, but of their own leaders."

"Quite," was Mrs. Ferguson's total comment.

"You have been in the East more recently than I have," Lance said to Bill. "How is little old New York?"

"Still in the grip of Boss Tweed. But Thomas Nast's cartoons in the *New York Times* and *Harper's Weekly* are beginning to show him up for the rascal he is."

"Good!" Lance cried.

"New York is full of rascals," Mrs. Ferguson said contemptuously. "I was reading in this morning's paper about that notorious woman—what is her name?—giving a lecture here."

"Evangeline McClintock," Lance told her.

"As bad as that Victoria Woodhull who plans to run for president."

"I attended Evangeline's lecture." Lance sipped his tea and smiled with amusement at the expression on Mrs. Ferguson's face. For the first time she was regarding her guest in a different way.

"You actually attended? Why?"

"One goes not so much to hear what Evangeline has to say, Mrs. Ferguson. It is the way she says it. She performs, like an actress, and she is a pretty good one."

"You mean she doesn't believe what she preaches?"

"No, I'm sure she's sincere. But she does have a flare for drama that is a delight to watch."

"Indeed."

Bill, too, was shocked by what Lance was saying, although he reminded himself that in college days Lance had been a bit of a devil. He had fascinated young Bill. At that period he had thought Lance Oliver the most sophisticated man in the world.

After a bit Mrs. Ferguson asked, "Do you plan to stay long in our fair city?"

"For a while. I have no definite plans."

"I must introduce you to some of our friends." She frowned and bit her lip. Bill thought: *she's trying to figure how much she can afford, just what sort of soiree would be feasible on her limited income.*

"That's very kind of you, Mrs. Ferguson, but I wouldn't want you to go to any trouble." Her friends! He wondered what they would be like.

"If you aren't attending another lecture tonight," Bill put in, "perhaps we could do the town a bit."

"I'd like that." It would be amusing to have young Ferguson as his cicerone.

Mrs. Ferguson was making no comment, but it was obvious that she did not approve. She offered

Lance more tea, more watercress and cucumber sandwiches; she was polite but withdrawn. When he got up to leave and thanked her for the tea she said, "It was good of you to come," but she did not sound as if she really meant it.

Bill saw him to the door. When they were safely out of the parlor and out of earshot, in the front hall, Lance asked, "Where and when shall we meet tonight?"

Bill didn't hesitate. He said, "There's a place on the waterfront called The Golden Parrot. I'll meet you outside. Nine o'clock?"

"I'll find it."

Just as he turned to leave Bill called him back. "Lance?"

"Yes?"

"Have you ever been married?"

"Yes. Why?"

"I'll tell you later."

All day long, after she had said good-bye to Evangeline and watched her dash away to catch her train, Tawny wondered about the look on the other's face when she told her Lance Oliver's name. It was one of surprise and hurt, as if Mr. Oliver were a close friend. But when Tawny asked if he were a friend, Evangeline had shaken her head and said, "I know who he is, that's all."

Tawny had a distinct feeling that Evangeline was not telling the truth.

She had not promised Evangeline to do anything more than to consider another marriage. And the time for consideration was the next time she saw Bill in the flesh. She was singing the song that Bill had commented upon as being particularly intimate, "Come hither, my baby, my darling." When she sang it she threw out her arms as if she were reaching for something or somebody, and for a moment or so turned her eyes upward, almost as if in prayer.

She lowered her eyes and saw Bill come into The Golden Parrot. Bill, and with him, of all people, Lance Oliver!

It was all she could do to finish the song.

If Lance Oliver were a friend of Bill's, if he told Bill about her and what had happened between them, then consideration of Bill's offer of marriage was pointless. He would not want her. There was also the possibility that Lance would not recognize her. But it was remote. She hadn't changed that much in a year.

She finished the song at last and, after cries of "More! More! More!" she sang another. She was putting off going back to work, going back among the tables, reaching the one where Lance and Bill were sitting. She chose "Gather Ye Rosebuds While Ye May" and she did not look in the direction of their table.

Now Lance recognized her, the minute they walked into the saloon. The eyes, the hair, the curves of her body, all as he remembered, only grown richer, fuller. The child whose body had so pleased him had grown into a beautiful woman.

Bill asked, "Well, what do you think of her?"

"The singer?"

"Yes." Bill leaned forward eagerly.

"She's quite remarkable."

"I'm in love with her. I want to marry her. If she'll have me."

Lance's eyebrows arched in surprise. He looked at Tawny who was now delivering a drink to a table, swishing her provocative hips, smiling. He looked back at Bill. "Does your mother know?"

"No."

"I thought not."

Tawny was now approaching their table. She did not look at Lance, only at Bill.

She said, "Good evening," in that husky voice that Lance remembered. Bill jumped to his feet and Lance followed.

"Tawny, I want you to meet my friend Lance Oliver. Lance, this is Miss Tawny McShane."

They said "How do you do" in unison. Then Tawny said, "Sit down, gentlemen. What will it be?" in her best waitress fashion.

Lance ordered brandy and to Tawny's surprise Bill asked for the same, instead of his usual stein of beer. After the drinks had been brought and Tawny moved on to serve another table, Lance said, "Tawny McShane. What an odd name. Tell me about her."

"Well, she's an orphan. She lives alone in a rooming house with another girl. Her parents were stage people; they both were killed in a train accident. She was an actress herself, for a time. She is very much a lady, much too sweet and innocent a young thing to be working in such a place. I want to take her out of all this."

"Gallant knight, rescuing fair lady?"

"Something like that." But Bill's face was completely serious, unsmiling.

The little devil, Lance was thinking. *Making up a story, not telling him about Jake and the wagon and McShane's Marvelous Medicine, or about the magnetic healing. Clever minx. Out to catch a rich young man.*

But now Bill was saying, "I haven't much to offer her, of course. My father's estate was in bad shape. Mother and I, I must confess, are really almost on our uppers. Don't let my mother know I told you. She keeps on pretending that everything is the same as always. But I won't be finishing college, that's for sure. And I may have to go up north and take over a ranch that my father owned."

"In the meanwhile, you've fallen in love."

"Really in love. Here she comes again."

Tawny asked, "Everything all right?" again keeping her eyes on Bill.

"Won't you join us, Miss McShane?" Lance asked.

She gave him a swift look.

"Not until I'm off duty."

But even at ten o'clock she did not join them. She signaled to Ned, and slipped out the back door.

Bill said, "Usually, when I come here, I take her out to supper when she is off duty." He pulled his watch from his pocket. "But it's after ten now. I wonder where she can be." Then he noticed that the pianist was also missing and he excused himself and went up to the bar and spoke to Al Benedict.

"Where's Tawny?"

"Ned is taking her home."

"But . . ."

"Evidently she was in a hurry. Did she have an engagement with you?"

"No."

Al shrugged.

"I guess she's gone home," Bill told Lance, when he came back to the table. "I don't know why."

"Maybe she didn't want a third party," Lance smiled.

"Maybe."

"At least you and I can visit a few other spots."

"Sure." But the lovesick young man did not seem overly enthusiastic.

Late in the afternoon the next day Lance came alone to The Golden Parrot. The place was empty except for Al Benedict behind the bar, polishing glasses and looking over his stock. And Tawny, sitting at a table in a corner, reading a copy of *Harper's Weekly*.

At the squeak of the swinging doors and the parrot's greeting, Tawny put down the magazine and got to her feet.

But Lance went directly to the bar, ordered a drink, and stood there, so Tawny sat down again. A moment later Al called out to her, "Tawny, will you take charge for a minute? I've got to go down to the cellar."

Reluctantly, she rose and took her place behind the bar.

Lance smiled at her enigmatically. After a moment he drawled out, "Hello, Tawny McShane."

She did not answer.

"You've given up magnetic healing?"

Still she did not speak.

"I know you're pretending it never happened. You're pretending you never came to my house in New York. Because of Bill. I understand."

At last she spoke, her eyes wide with pleading. "Don't tell him! Please don't tell him!"

It was his turn to be silent. He just sipped his drink and smiled at her across it.

She leaned on the bar and looked up at him. He reached across and cupped her chin in his big hand.

"There's no need for me to tell him," he said softly. "It can be our secret."

She jerked away from his touch. It reminded her all too clearly of that long-ago afternoon, and how his sheer physical attraction could cast a spell over her.

"You're something, Tawny McShane. You don't have to practice magnetism. You've just got it. That ridiculous uniform can't hide it. You must drive a lot of the customers here out of their minds."

She was blushing, breathing hard, as he spoke.

"You've grown into a beauty, Tawny." His eyes were on her breasts.

She began polishing glasses that did not need polishing. Her hands were shaking.

"Do you suppose," Lance said, "that on some evening I could take you out to supper—instead of Bill?"

She almost dropped a glass. "No!" She shook her head firmly. "No!"

"I'm sorry about that. I think we could have a very pleasant time together. We did before."

"No! Don't even talk about it! No!"

In her anger she was lovely. Lance sighed in disappointment. He said, "I only asked."

Al Benedict had come back to the bar.

After Lance had his one drink, he left The Golden Parrot.

Soon other customers were pouring in and Tawny was kept busy. But now and then when there was a lull she would think about Lance. He was after her. She knew because of everything he said, because of the way he looked at her. She was sharply aware of his feelings toward her. And he had no right to be like that, to look at her the way he did, to make her lips feel moist and her breasts tingle. He was Satan in the flesh, tempting her and in the same moment repulsing her.

She was glad that Bill came alone that evening. The moment she went over to his table to take his order he asked, "Why did you run off last night?"

"I thought you were with your friend for the evening."

"You could have joined us for supper."

"You hadn't asked me, Bill."

"Do I need to ask? Don't you know that if I come here to The Golden Parrot it is only to see you?"

She nodded, feeling shy.

"Will you have supper with me tonight, Tawny?"

"Of course."

At supper at their seafood restaurant Bill asked, "How did you like my friend Lance?"

"I scarcely talked to him, Bill. He's very good-looking."

"He's good-looking, he's rich. And quite the devil."

"Devil?" she repeated.

"He was wild when I knew him back in college and he's still wild. Last night . . ." Then he broke off. "I shouldn't talk about such things."

"Things young gentlemen do when they're on the town?"

"Yes. I went home early last night. I couldn't stomach all that Lance wanted to do. I haven't wanted to since I met you. All I want is you. I'm still waiting for your answer."

"I know." *And I should give it to him,* she thought to herself.

That night in the carriage he held her in his arms and whispered in her ear. She remembered Evangeline saying, "Some women ought to be married and you're one of them." *I do need a man,* Tawny thought. *I'm not complete without a man.* And Bill was whispering, "I can't wait to teach you about love; I can't wait to show you what love can be."

She turned her face and stopped his whispering with a kiss, pressing herself against him. The kiss was her answer, long and passionate, and when it was finished he held her close, and rocked back and forth.

"I should like to learn about love," Tawny told him quietly.

"You mean . . ."

"I mean I should like to be married."

He held her close; his whole body was alive with ecstasy. He cried, "Soon! Soon!" His voice was hoarse. Then he put his head out the window and called up to the driver, "We're ready to go back now!"

He held her hand as they rode back into town; he couldn't trust himself to do more.

The night before, in the explaining to Wilma why she was home so early, Tawny told about Lance coming to The Golden Parrot with Bill. Wilma had cried out, "Oh, how awful! Did he recognize you?"

"I don't know. It was hard to tell. At least he didn't say he did."

Tonight there was much more to tell Wilma. First about Lance's coming to the saloon in the late afternoon. "He's after me, again. I could tell."

"Oh, dear! Oh, Tawny, what are you going to do?"

"That was only the beginning of the day's adventure." Tawny smiled. "Tonight Bill came alone and took me out to supper and . . ."

"And what?" Wilma sat straight up in bed, flung back her braids excitedly. "What are you smiling about?"

Tawny began taking down her hair, enjoying her eager audience.

"I told him I would marry him."

"Wonderful!" Wilma jumped out of bed, ran across, and threw her arms around Tawny. "So you fell in love with him after all! Oh, Tawny, I'm so happy for you!" Then Wilma stepped back and looked directly at Tawny.

Still pulling hairpins from her hair, Tawny said, very quietly. "I didn't say that."

"But . . ."

"You want it like a story, don't you?" Tawny snapped, now brushing her hair with swift rough strokes. "They fell in love, they got married, they lived happily ever. Well, life's not always like that, Wilma. I told him I would marry him simply because I want to get married. I want to be in bed with a man again. I want to make love again with someone who loves me, who belongs to me. I want a man and I prefer being a wife, to a whore. Does that make it clear to you?"

"Clear. And awful," Wilma said. She got back in bed, pulled up the covers, and turned her back.

Bill tracked down Lance in a saloon not far from the hotel where the latter was staying. Lance, who had been drinking pretty steadily since that afternoon in The Golden Parrot, looked up in surprise when Bill appeared. "What are you doing out so late, my friend? Doesn't Mummy wait up for you?"

"Of course not. Don't be ridiculous. Lance, I've got news. I had to tell someone."

"News? From the look on your face it must concern the little charmer at The Golden Parrot."

"It does. She's agreed to marry me."

"Well, well." Lance could not decide whether he wanted to laugh or to cry. He said, "I suppose congratulations are in order. Let me buy you a drink."

When Bill's drink arrived he sipped it thoughtfully. "There're a lot of arrangements to make," he said.

"Arrangements?"

"I mean, we'll have to elope, of course. You'll have to help me. You will help me? You'll be my best man?"

Lance put his arm on Bill's shoulder. "I'm with you, boy, right or wrong."

"What do you mean?"

"Bill, has this girl told you anything about herself?"

"What do you mean?" Bill said again.

"I mean, just looking at her, I'd lay dollars to doughnuts she's no virgin."

Bill glared at him.

"How dare you say such a thing about Tawny!"

"Sorry."

Love is *blind*, Lance was thinking. *The lad is infatuated. Is it my place to disillusion him, to tell him about the magnetic treatment and the jolly good romp I had with her that afternoon in my study?* He decided against it. Bill was in love. Bill was beyond logic and reason. Maybe it was all for the best.

5

The next morning Tawny was still at breakfast when Mrs. Schultz's maid announced that there was a gentleman caller waiting in the parlor.

Wilma grinned at her across the table.

Tawny finished her coffee leisurely. She felt a little awkward about seeing Bill in broad daylight. She was wearing her old morning dress, loosely cut, full, hardly the garment in which to receive a gentleman. Should she take the time to go up and change? She had no chance, for when she came out of the dining room into the front hall, Bill was standing in the doorway to the parlor.

When she came close to him he took her by the hand, pulled her into the parlor, and closed the door behind her. Then he took her in his arms. Without her corset, without her bustle, she melted against him.

"I've arranged for everything," he whispered into her ear. "Everything. But first . . ." He released her, reached into his pocket, and held out a sparkling ring.

"It's beautiful, Bill!"

"Not as beautiful as I wish it were. But it's the best I can do."

He took her left hand and slipped the ring on the proper finger, and then he kissed her hand. She was thinking: *there was no engagement ring with Timothy. My wedding ring was little more than tin.*

He looked up at her. "We're getting married tonight. I can't wait any longer."

"Tonight!"

"Tonight. When you go off duty. We're going over to the mainland and find a justice of the peace."

"Bill, dear, you can't get married just like that. I need a new dress! I need all sorts of things!"

"Wear an old dress. Any old dress. And have your bags packed before you leave for The Golden Parrot."

"My bags?"

"We're sailing for Astoria at midnight. We're going to that ranch up in Washington Territory. I've already reserved the seats."

Tawny stared at him in amazement. She had never pictured Bill Ferguson as such a man of action. She had expected that he would want a formal wedding, after a respectable period of engagement.

"Bill, you overwhelm me. Deciding everything, arranging everything, so quickly!"

He took her hands in his and held them tightly. "One other thing you've got to do, besides packing your bags. Ask Wilma to be your maid of honor and witness. I've already asked Lance to be best man."

Her heart sank. Her eyes darkened.

"What is it, darling? What's the matter? Don't you like Lance?"

"It's just everything happening so suddenly."

"The sooner the better, love." He brushed a kiss across her lips. "And now I must run. And you must pack. And speak to Wilma." He let go of her hands and walked over to the door.

She watched him leave, still feeling overwhelmed. *That is the man I'm going to marry. That is the man who will lie with me tonight.*

Suddenly she was apprehensive. What had she let herself in for?

Mrs. Schultz wept with delight when she heard the news, but bemoaned the fact that there would be no wedding. "You would have made such a beautiful bride!"

"I'll still be a bride," Tawny reassured her. "I'll even wear my white dress. I think it's appropriate. I wore it the first time I had supper with him."

"Something old, something new . . ." Wilma was reciting the old rhyme. "Your dress is old, but why don't you buy a new bonnet? I'll loan you a petticoat; it's got blue embroidery on it. That will be both borrowed and blue."

Tawny laughed. "All right. It doesn't really matter, all this fuss." It did not matter because she did not feel like a bride.

She was kept busy all morning and was late getting to work. And of course Al Benedict had to be told. "I can offer congratulations," was his response, "but I can't say I'm happy about it."

"Don't you approve of my husband-to-be?"

"He seems like a fine young man. What I don't like is having you leave us. And going so far away. The place won't be the same without you. However, I should have expected this would happen to a girl like you. Good luck!"

It began raining late in the afternoon and a fog rolled in. There were few customers in The Golden Parrot that evening, but when word got around that Tawny was leaving to be married, a bottle of champagne was ordered: She sang the favorite songs they requested; she drank champagne as she sang. She was the star of the evening, and she began to feel, if not exactly happy, at least excited. And she was a little tipsy when Bill came to pick her up. He frowned with displeasure.

"I shall be all right," she assured him. "I'll be quite all right. I promise. I promise to be proper." And to his surprise she threw her arms around his neck, there in the midst of the crowd, and kissed him. "I'm ready, Bill. I'm ready!"

Everyone laughed.

"Let me change my clothes and I'm ready. Just a minute," she continued. She disappeared into the back room while Bill waited, feeling awkward. And when she emerged in the white dress Ned struck up "Here Comes the Bride" on the piano.

Now she must kiss Ned good-bye, even kiss Al on the cheek before she could tie on the frivolous little bonnet Bill had never seen before, and finally throw a kiss to everyone.

He took her arm and hurried her out into the rainy night.

A carriage was waiting, but when they were seated inside Bill did not put his arms around her. He had never seen Tawny like this. He was shocked and disappointed.

She leaned her head on his shoulder. "Please don't be cross, Bill. Kiss me, Bill. I promise to be good. I'm sorry they gave me so much champagne. But I feel so happy now. I'm just bubbly like the champagne was, I just want to . . ."

He moved away from her. He barked, "Be quiet."

Subdued, she stayed quiet. The silence was only interrupted by an occasional hiccup.

Lance and Wilma were waiting for them at the

ferry pier, and Tawny wobbled cheerfully toward them. Wilma had brought a bouquet which she handed to Tawny. Roses and fern and forget-me-nots.

"Oh, Wilma, how sweet of you! Oh, it's beautiful. I missed having a bouquet that other time!"

She was remembering the night she and Timothy ran off together. Again, to a justice of the peace. Who had been their witnesses? She couldn't remember.

Bill was staring at her. "Other time?" he asked. "What other time?"

She held the bouquet under his nose. "Aren't they lovely, Bill? Oh, this makes it a real wedding."

Lance was finding her tipsiness amusing; even her little bonnet had a tilt to it. There was a mischievousness about her in sharp contrast to Bill's sober, frowning visage. The whole performance, including the cast of characters, was strange. This Wilma Wilson girl—big, bony, awkward—where on earth had Tawny picked up such a friend?

Tawny was also thinking somewhat along the same lines. This was a dream from which she would awake and laugh at herself for having conjured up something so impossible. *I said I wanted to get married, but it's my body that wants to, not my mind. Not my heart. It's all my body. It's all because Satan came back into my life and touched me.*

On the ferry the four of them huddled together out of the rain. The bay crossing was a blur in Tawny's mind, a blur as thick as the fog through which the ferry was chugging. She later remembered docking and Bill helping her down the gangplank, then a short carriage ride, and then a little house where a sleepy couple in nightshirts, carrying candles, opened their front door and let the four strangers in out of the rain.

Lance's amusement with the whole procedure was beginning to wane. Tawny looked very much the bride in her white dress there in the candlelight. She was sobering now; her face was as solemn as Bill's, as she listened to what the justice of peace was saying, and when she made her responses in that low, husky, musical voice. *Maybe she's not the conniving wench I've considered her,* Lance thought. *Maybe she is genuinely in love with him* . . . Maybe. His own marriage ceremony was dim in his memory: a kind of charade he went through, only to get Sue Ellen.

Marriage. He had told Evangeline that he would not marry again. Or rather, that he did not *think* he would marry again. Now he wondered. This ceremony seemed meaningful. It made Evangeline's chatter about free love somehow irreverent.

"You may kiss the bride."

Bill took Tawny in his arms and crushed her against him, kissing her full on the lips. When he finally released her he turned to Wilma, to the wife of the justice of the peace. The traditional ceremony went on: everyone kissing the bride, everyone kissing the groom.

Lance bent down and brushed his lips against Tawny's cheek. No more. They looked into each other's eyes. He thought: *I have misjudged her. In my mind I've called her names. She is a genuine, decent person. But she is not happy. She takes this marriage seriously, but she is not in love.* The realization had nothing to do with reason. It had more to do with instinct. He *felt* it.

Back to the ferry, back to San Francisco.

"When does that boat sail?" Lance asked.

"Supposed to be at midnight. But they promised to wait for us if we were late."

Lance consulted his watch. "We're not too late."

"Not now. But first we must pick up our luggage," Bill reminded him. "And I must introduce my wife to Mother."

Lance thought: *what a scene that will be!*

Tawny had not even thought of such a possibility. *He was in such a hurry,* she thought. *He insisted we elope, we marry tonight. I thought we would just run off together. Now I have to meet his mother.*

They said good-bye to Lance at the ferry pier. The two men shook hands.

"Good luck, Bill. Hope all will go well with the ranch."

"It's rumored to have gold. If that's true, things will go very well."

"Gold? Really?"

"It's the reason my father bought it. On a rumor. My father was like that."

Lance turned to Tawny. "Good luck to you, too, my dear. Good luck and happiness."

There was a new expression in those gray brown-flecked eyes. Uncertainty, almost fear. She mumbled, "Thank you," and turned her head.

Bill, Tawny, and Wilma took a carriage to Mrs. Schultz's house, where Wilma was kissed good-bye. She cried and Tawny promised to write. Then, with Tawny's valise, Bill directed the cabbie to his house. Tawny trembled a bit at the sight of the big, gar-goyled house. There was a light in one downstairs window.

"It's almost midnight," Tawny said, as they got out of the carriage. "Will your mother be awake?"

"She'll be awake. I left a note on her bedside ta-ble. She knew I was leaving for the ranch tonight, but she didn't know that you were going with me. She didn't know about you at all. Not until she found the note."

"You never told her about me before that?"

He shook his head. "No, I hadn't."

"But why? Why not?" Even as she asked the question she thought she could guess the answer.

"I was afraid she wouldn't understand."

"You mean wouldn't approve."

"Yes. But when she sees you, I'm sure she will."

Tawny was not at all sure.

Bill unlocked the door and ushered her into a big dark hall. She stood there hesitant. He put his arm around her. "Come, darling!" he said and led her into the parlor.

It was a large, formal room. The furniture was heavy and austere. And the woman who rose from a chair by the window belonged in that room.

"Mother, this is Tawny."

"My boy, my boy!" Tears were cascading from her eyes and she was looking directly at him, ignoring Tawny. Bill took his arm from Tawny's shoulder and hugged his mother, patted her. "Don't cry, Mother. You should be happy for me, happy that I found such a wonderful girl to be my wife."

Mrs. Ferguson wept for a moment more; then she found her handkerchief, wiped her eyes, and took her first real look at the girl who stood in front of her. Her eyes traveled from the top of Tawny's head slowly down over the curves. Tawny, feeling like a piece of livestock, managed to say, "How do you do, Mrs. Ferguson."

Mrs. Ferguson did not respond. Still staring at the girl she said, "I had such high hopes for you, Bill."

The silence was agony. Tawny wished she could turn and run out of the room, out of the house. Then she felt Bill's arm around her again, holding her close. "I love her, Mother. I love her with all my heart. That is all that matters."

There was another awful silence and then Mrs. Ferguson said, "Take her away, William. Take her away and never bring her back." She turned her back on them and looked out the window.

They hurried out of the room. Bill picked up the two pieces of luggage which he had left in the front hall; Tawny opened the front door and closed it behind them.

Once inside the carriage, which had been waiting for them, Tawny burst into tears. Immediately Bill's arms were around her, holding her tighter and tighter, not speaking. He could find no words. His mother had been cruel, and Tawny was badly hurt. Yet for a moment there, before his mother ordered them to leave, Bill had seen Tawny through his mother's eyes. He had seen what he should have from the beginning, that his mother could not, would not, admit Tawny's beauty, nor feel her charm. An old, unattractive, straitlaced woman could never see what he saw in a young, voluptuous girl.

At last Tawny stopped crying. She sat there with her head leaning on his chest.

"All of a sudden I'm tired," she sighed. "So terribly tired."

"We'll be on the ship pretty soon. We'll have a nice stateroom. I asked for the biggest."

"Is it a long trip?"

"Several days. I'm not sure exactly how long."

"Will the sea be rough? I've never been on shipboard. Just the ferries, like tonight." She was also remembering the ferry trip from New Jersey to Manhattan, with Pa, on that fateful day.

"I hope it will be calm all the way."

He stroked her hand as they rode through the rainy night and she thought: he will be gentle, as Timothy was; it will be like being with Timothy again.

Was that what she wanted?

They reached the waterfront and their ship. A cabin boy met them and hurried their luggage aboard. The moment they had finished climbing the gangplank, it was pulled up. The whistle boomed into the night and the ship began to move.

They followed the cabin boy across the deck and down the corridors to their stateroom. Bill motioned her to wait until the boy had put their luggage inside and turned away.

He looked down at her. "Part of the ritual. I must carry you over the doorstep."

He swooped her off her feet and carried her across the cabin to the nearest bunk and laid her down upon it. Then he went back, bolted the door, and leaned against it.

"Would you care for a brandy?"

She shook her head. "Not after all that champagne."

"Of course not. Tawny, what did you do with your bouquet?"

"I don't know. I lost it someplace. On the ferry or in the carriage. Why?"

"I've been thinking about that bouquet. About what you said when Wilma handed it to you."

"What did I say?"

"Something about *the other time*. What did you mean by that?"

"Oh."

He bent over her. "Tell me. You've got to tell me what you meant."

He was breathing hard and his eyes had a strange wild look in them.

There was nothing to do but blurt out the truth. "I was married before, Bill."

"Married!" He gave her a little shake. "You never told me!"

"It's something I've tried to forget. He was killed by the Indians. We were coming west and they attacked us. It was a nightmare, Bill, something I had to forget!"

He stared at her for a moment. Then he jerked off her bonnet and threw it on the cabin floor. He grabbed at her hairpins and tore them free. He spread her hair out over the pillow, also with rough gestures, and then he began pulling at the bodice of her dress.

"Bill, don't, you'll tear it!"

"Be quiet!" he commanded, as he had in the carriage when she was babbling after the champagne.

He tore her bodice open, and when both breasts were bare he stared down at them. "God, God, how wonderful!" he murmured, and then he put his mouth on one and then the other. He ripped her dress down the front until the soft fabric fell away from her; he went on tearing at her clothes until she lay there naked.

His eyes had that strange wild look again. "This is what I've waited for all these days, all these nights!" he went on breathlessly. "You're mine, bitch, you're all mine, every inch of you!" He spread her legs and grabbed at her. Again his mouth sucked upon one breast and then the other.

She watched him step back and pull off his trousers, and then he threw himself on top of her. His weight was suffocating, but almost immediately he was up on his knees. He had separated her legs again and was inside her, before she had time to feel any emotion beyond shock.

6

Lance Oliver slipped easily into San Francisco society, without the help of Mrs. Ferguson. He was popular with hostesses who needed an extra man at dinner parties. He joined a club where he could play backgammon of an afternoon or evening. He enjoyed the theater. His life was scarcely different from what it had been in New York, only on a smaller scale.

His new friends did not know that he knew Bill Ferguson, since his San Francisco relationship with Bill had lasted less than a week. The gossip that summer included the shocking tale of that nice Bill Ferguson breaking his mother's heart by running off with a girl from a waterfront saloon. Descriptions of Tawny were vague and varied. Quite a few of the men had visited The Golden Parrot and remembered her. One said, "Can't blame the boy, the girl was a humdinger. But what will he do for money? He'll never make a go of a ranch."

Lance often thought of Bill and Tawny and wondered how they were managing. He would never forget the look on the girl's face the night of that wedding, a lost look. Was Bill making her happy?

Lance still received money from his father each month; that was the only mail he ever received. Until one morning when he came down to the hotel lobby to hand in his key and the clerk gave him a telegram from his father that had just arrived.

It was brief but its very brevity was a shock.

"Regret report death of Sue Ellen. Stop. Letter follows."

Lance immediately wired condolences to the Appleby family and waited for the promised letter. It was hard to believe that Sue Ellen was dead. It was unreal to him. And then his father's letter came:

> Dear Son:
>
> The enclosed will tell you what happened better than any sentences I could construct. Sue Ellen was found dead on the sidewalk in front of your home in Manhattan. She evidently had jumped from the top floor where a window was found open. The story has madc headlines in all the newspapers and will no doubt appear soon in San Francisco journals. The note she left tells the rest of the story. My sympathy, Son.

Lance's hands shook as he unfolded the enclosed note.

> Dearest Lance, wherever you are:
>
> You once called me a coward, 'a stinking little coward' I believe were your words. The cruelest words anyone ever spoke to me. I've never forgotten them. There were other names you called me that day, and from that time on I did my best not to deserve them. I did my best to please you. But all to no avail. You left me. Would you had stayed around, called me anything you wished to, or even beaten me. You could have done anything you wanted if only

you had stayed. At first I prayed you would come back. I believed in my heart that you would. But as the dreary weeks, then months passed and you did not come, I lost heart. Life without you is unbearable. I can stand it no longer. I love you and only you. You are the only person I ever loved. There can never be another. Perhaps it is cruel, perhaps it is a sin to take my own life. But at least it will prove to you, once and for all, that I am not a coward. All my love to you.

Sue Ellen.

Lance crumpled the two letters and shoved them into a pocket. He walked out of the hotel into the rainy streets of San Francisco and let the rain blend with his tears.

She had really and truly loved him, more than he ever had guessed. He had thought her shallow and selfish, but her feelings had run deeper than he ever had suspected. Now it was easy to remember the good things about his wife—her pretty face, her lovely gestures, the childlike quality that had first attracted him. Her great need for love and tenderness, the way she would cry out, "Hold me!"

He walked into the first saloon he came to and ordered a stiff drink. The drink did not help. But at least he had quit crying. He was still drinking that evening when the woman sidled up to him in a shabby waterfront place.

"Buy me a drink?"

He looked down at her. Even his bleary eyes could see she was shabbily dressed; her eyes were hollow in her painted face.

"You don't want to drink with me," he told her. "I'm the biggest bastard in the world."

"You don't look like a bastard, mister."

"I am. I killed my wife."

She edged a bit away from him. "You what?"

"I might as well have killed her. I treated her badly. And then I left her. And she killed herself."

"How awful! You must be very unhappy."

"I'm unhappy with myself. I never really loved her. But I married her. And she loved me. She loved me enough to take her own life when I left her." It was a relief to say it out loud. He asked the woman, "What do you want to drink?"

"Gin."

"Gin," he told the bartender. "And another whiskey for me."

"You sure you want that whiskey, sir?"

"Sure I want it. It will take a gallon of the stuff to make me stop hating myself."

Shaking his head, the bartender poured.

When the drinks were handed to them the woman said, "Thank you, mister."

"Mister Oliver," he told her. "What's your name?"

"Amy."

"Here's how, Amy!"

"Cheers, Mr. Oliver."

They drank together, rather solemnly. Amy asked, "Did it just happen—what you were telling me—today? Is it in the papers and everything?"

"No, it happened days ago. Back east. In New York City. It was in the papers there. And it will be in the papers here in time. She threw herself out of a window. She left a note addressed to me. My father sent it to me. That's how I know."

"You poor man."

"I don't need pity, Amy. I need a good kick in the pants."

"It's not your fault. You can't help it if you don't

love somebody. No more than you can help it if you do. I quit eating my heart out over one guy who couldn't see me for dust years and years ago. If I couldn't get him I didn't care who I got and that's the way it's been ever since. Love is bad cruel stuff so let's forget about it. Can I have another gin?"

"You are quite a philosopher, Miss Amy. Yes, you may have another gin."

"And after that I'll invite you to visit my little attic room. The sheets are clean and so am I."

Lance signaled the batender and then turned back to the woman. "I don't know, Amy, if I'm quite in the mood tonight."

She grinned. "You will be when I get through with you."

He was drunk for a week, staying in Amy's little room under the eaves. They both drank too much to enjoy intercourse. But he was away from his solicitous acquaintances, away from whatever sensationalism might appear in newspapers, away from any kind of reality. It acted like a purge, and when he finally woke up one morning with the world's biggest hangover, he told Amy good-bye, paid her well, and went back to his hotel.

His few older friends back in New York were sympathetic and wrote him condolences after they got his address from his father.

Life was back to normal.

Until one night when he strayed into The Golden Parrot, for the first time since Bill and Tawny had left. There was no singing waitress now, and Lance sat there remembering her face and her eyes and wondering about her.

7

It was bright blue October weather. The sun shone on the white-capped mountains and the rolling green hills of Washington Territory.

Tawny sat on her front porch stringing beans, the last from her garden. String beans and salt pork and baked potatoes for dinner; the potatoes had been a gift from her nearest neighbor, Nellie Fitzroy. Apple pie from Fitzroy apples. She would be eternally grateful to the Fitzroys for all they had done for her and Bill since they arrived here in the wilderness.

The Fitzroys had homesteaded there for years. They were older and wiser about life on a ranch than the Fergusons ever could be. Dull but kind.

Winter was coming and Tawny dreaded it. Not that the winters here were severe—or so the Fitzroys said—but in the winter Bill would spend much more time inside the house and that she dreaded, as she now dreaded any rainy day.

Bill had taken to ranch life in a way she had not expected. He was in no way a farmer but he loved hunting and fishing, to which Doug Fitzroy had introduced him. They were poor and life was rough, but Bill seemed to be enjoying it.

The trip up from San Francisco had been long and onerous. The Pacific had not been at all pacific, and Bill had insisted on making love no matter how the ship tossed and turned. His lovemaking was never gentle; it was always rough and swift and unsubtle. The first morning she woke to find him touching her breasts, whispering, "Poor darlings, I hurt them!"

She said nothing. She thought: *and you were the man who was going to teach me about love!*

"I couldn't help myself, Tawny. You have no idea how just the sight of you excites me. And I'd waited so long, so terribly long before I ever touched you. I lay awake nights dreaming of it. And when I knew you were my wife, you were mine, you belonged to me, I was beside myself."

He kissed the red marks on her breasts, softly this time, and in spite of herself she found she was responding. He stroked her whole body until she slowly came to life. He spread her legs, and cried out, "Mine! Mine!" and again he possessed her.

His abrupt bedtime behavior was in sharp contrast to his behavior during the daytime, or when other people were present. He went on being the quiet, serious gentleman then. But at night the rough savage in him came to life. She was bone weary by the time they reached Astoria, in Oregon Territory, and boarded the smaller boat to travel up the Columbia River to a town called Wallula.

The mood along the way was never that of a honeymoon. There were no tender, companionable moments. It was as if they were two people traveling together, sleeping together.

When the small boat reached Wallula, they transferred to a stagecoach, which climbed its way up into the hills. Fir trees, between the rocks, reached for the sky. Only rarely did the stage pass any houses. She began questioning him then about the ranch and what he knew about it.

"I don't know very much. The deed is to the land: it only describes the amount of the acreage, and to find it I am to contact a man named Fitzroy. Doug Fitzroy. And I know the land is near a town called Littleton."

"How big a town?"

"I don't know! We'll find out when we get there."

"If we ever do," Tawny sighed.

"Don't be such a pessimist."

He put his hand in her lap, his way of changing the subject. The stagecoach jerked on.

Littleton was what they used to call a one-horse town. There was a small general store, a rooming house deemed a hotel, a church, a post office. The ranch was in walking distance.

Carrying their suitcases they walked in the direction the man in the post office had pointed out to them. The road followed the river and they came first to the Fitzroy place, a big house built of logs with a stone fireplace on each side, a comfortable, homey-looking place. Two big dogs came bounding down to greet them, barking hellos. Their tones were guarded but their tails were wagging.

The Fitzroys already knew by the grapevine that the Fergusons were arriving. Their door stood open as Bill and Tawny opened the gate to their split-rail fence and started up the road to the house. The dogs were now jumping all over Bill and Tawny.

Both Mr. and Mrs. Fitzroy were tall, gaunt people, with roughhewn faces and gravelly voices.

"Don't mind them dogs!" Mrs. Fitzroy called out. "Rover! Rosie! Down, down, both of you!" Then to the Fergusons, "Come in, come in, set down."

Their handshakes were rough and firm. The Fergusons must have coffee before the Fitzroys showed them their property.

"There's a house over there," Doug Fitzroy told them over coffee. "Tain't much of a place."

Nellie Fitzroy added, "It sure ain't. Old Kennedy built it mostly just to keep the rain offen him while he was searching for that gold he never found." She was looking at Tawny, as she spoke, and the girl caught the sympathy in her voice.

Doug Fitzroy said, "That Kennedy was a scoundrel all right, hightailing it away from the territory and palming off the ranch with a story of mebbe there being gold."

They left their luggage at the Fitzroys and walked over to see the house. Like the Fitzroys', it was built of logs, but they had been put together in a haphazard fashion. There were only three rooms—living room, bedroom, and kitchen—with a rickety outhouse, and a porch that was starting to fall off. Inside there was a musty odor of disuse. Rats and mice had been frequent occupants, and the fireplace was a black hole in the wall. There was a minimum of pieces of rickety furniture. The Fitzroys insisted that the Fergusons stay with them until they could get the house in order—their first reason for gratitude to the older couple.

That first summer after her marriage Tawny learned almost a lifetime of practical lessons. And she worked hard, scrubbing and cleaning and painting that awful little house, with Nellie Fitzroy as her teacher and helper.

Meanwhile, after the men had finished with the heavy part of the work, they went off together and, from Doug, Bill learned the joys of hunting and fishing.

When the house was ready for occupancy Bill

again insisted on carrying her over the threshold. He did not put her down until he had crossed the living room to the bedroom. The old brass bed that Tawny had tried her best to clean had a tattered, lumpy mattress, but that made no difference to Bill.

It was late in the afternoon; the sun was slanting through the room's one window.

"Bill, shouldn't I be starting dinner?"

"There's time enough for that, later."

"But I . . ." She started to sit up.

He pushed her back on the bed.

"Will you take off your clothes or must I tear them off you again?"

She knew by the look in his eye that he would do it. She began unbuttoning her dress as she sat up. He was undressed before she was and stood watching her, fascinated yet irritated by the slowness of her movements. Last of all she let down her hair and, as it cascaded over her shoulders, Bill stepped closer and took her in his arms with that tight grip that always startled her but what she had come to accept as part of his lovemaking.

The sunlight in the room was hot; their bodies clung to each other. Still holding her close, he pressed back against the bed and they lay down together, still joined.

If the days it took them to travel from San Franciso to Littleton could be regarded as a honeymoon so had the days they were houseguests at the Fitzroys. Tawny had done no housekeeping, except to help Nellie in the kitchen and learn how to cook various items that were new to Tawny but indigenous to the region: how to prepare a freshly caught fish or recently shot pheasant, rabbit, or even, once, a deer. The lessons she had had from Mrs. Wilson along the wagon trail west came in handy. How to build a fire in the fireplace, how to build a wood fire inside the kitchen stove. How to, how to, how to . . . but always with Nellie's supervision.

All of a sudden she was on her own. In some areas she was not at all prepared for the role of wife.

That first evening it had not mattered. Satiated by sex, Bill had fallen asleep, while she dressed and went into the kitchen. It took her a while even to start the fire, and longer to get the water boiling for potatoes and carrots. And the fish Bill had caught and brought home was a different variety than she had ever seen, or attempted to clean.

She took it outside in the gathering dusk to work at scraping off the scales. She had gone down to the river for fresh water with what she called the fish bucket, and she was lavish with the water as she worked, but the flies still found her, in droves.

When dinner was finally ready she went in to wake Bill. Asleep, he had the look of a young boy who has found just what he wanted for Christmas under the tree. She felt kindly toward him as she leaned over him to kiss his cheek and say, "Wake up, dinner is ready."

He pulled her down on the bed, picked up her skirt, raised it, and within moments had taken her again.

The dinner was ruined.

But that was only their first night in their own house. Once they were settled in Tawny discovered that Bill was a man of routine. He wanted to get up at a certain hour, go to bed at a certain hour, eat meals on time. It was all right for him to go off fishing or hunting or come back either earlier than she had expected, or later, or for him to go to town ostensibly on an errand and linger at the Littleton Hotel Saloon-Bar with traveling men until long after dark. But when he came home he expected dinner to be ready and waiting, as he expected her to get up promptly in the morning and have his breakfast on the table when he was ready for it.

Tawny never had known routine in all her life. Life with Pa had been irregular, ups and downs, late meals, no meals, hurried meals because they were fleeing a sheriff. Life on the road with the acting troupe had also been irregular, and there had been no cooking or housekeeping, nor had there been such responsibilities when she was the waitress-singer.

Routine was absolutely anathema to Tawny's personality. She writhed under it, and frequently rebelled, in small ways.

One night at dinner he asked, "And what is for dessert?"

"I'm sorry, there isn't any dessert," she told him, smiling. "I forgot to make it."

"You forgot to make it?"

"Yes."

"Why?"

"I just forgot, that's all."

"And what was on your mind?"

"Nothing in particular. Maybe people I used to know. Places I used to be. A lot of things. I was just sitting out on the front porch in the rocker, resting after the laundry, and thinking. And I forgot about dessert."

"I always want dessert. You should know that." He sounded most distressed.

Distressed herself, Tawny said, "Excuse me!" and got up from the table and walked out to the front porch.

Bill was immediately beside her. "Aren't you going to clear the table?" were his first words.

"Not yet. Not till I feel like it."

"Tawny, what's the matter with you? I don't like it, at all."

She stood there looking out into the night. So quiet. Only the roar of the river and now and then a frog croaking, or a nightbird serenading. She said, very quietly, not looking at him, "Bill, you didn't marry me to get a housekeeper. You could have hired a housekeeper. So don't complain about the way I do things."

"But as my wife . . ."

She interrupted. "As your wife, you want me to be your slave." She thought of Victoria Woodhull's words about a modern wife being no more than a concubine. She went on, "But just remember this, the only reason you married me was to take me to bed. You only married me to fornicate with me. You called it love, but it's never been love. Never! Only lust."

She walked down the steps and out into the dark.

Bill watched her go with a heavy heart. *But I did fall in love with you,* he thought to himself. *I love you now, despite your irritating irresponsibility, despite your passive lovemaking.*

With practically all that remained of his capital, Bill, with Doug Fitzroy as a partner, had invested in cattle and horse raising. It was not undertaken on a grand scale but it did earn them a living and Bill was content. Doug had convinced him that the vein of gold was a figment of the man Kennedy's imagination.

The Fitzroys were their only close friends. Uneducated, poor whites from out of the hills of Tennessee, they were the prototypes of hardworking, unimaginative farmers. They lived for the day and asked no more of life than food and shelter. Bill looked upon

Doug as a sort of foster-father. But Tawny could not feel anything as strong as that toward Nellie. She liked Nellie, she appreciated all the practical things she had taught her, but she never felt close. As she had, for example, with Evangeline. Or even Wilma.

The first time Tawny decided to invite the Fitzroys to dinner—after all, the Fergusons were more than a little indebted to their neighbors—Bill was worried about doing it properly. The dining table had come with the house, the chairs did not match, what linens they had Tawny had made from material bought at the general store. Their silverware was shabby and cheap, all that that general store had to offer.

"I don't think the Fitzroys will care," Tawny told him. "After all, when we were staying with them they weren't ashamed of their linens and silver. And, if you noticed, theirs weren't any fancier than ours!"

"I know, I know. But this is our house."

"I'm not ashamed of our house. We've done the best we could!" Tawny snapped.

"It would be nice, though, if we could live graciously. Perhaps someday we will. Have a good cook, have a maid to serve us, so you wouldn't have to trot back and forth."

"But in the meanwhile?"

"All right. Go ahead and invite them. And try and think of something your cooking can't ruin. And don't forget to make a dessert. Doug loves desserts too, I've noticed."

With those words he walked out on her, leaving her feeling rebuked.

"I'll show him!" she said to herself as she ran for the book of recipes she had copied down from Nellie's collection. She decided on roast pork and applesauce. She could bake potatoes around the roast.

You couldn't miss there. And for dessert? Once more she would try to bake a cake, and this time she would do what she had watched Nellie do once, douse it with a thick rich chocolate sauce that would disguise any faults in the cake's texture.

The Fitzroys arrived promptly on the night of the dinner. Doug looked a bit stiff in his old-fashioned, tight-fitting jacket and flowing tie. Nellie wore a black alpaca dress that was rusty at the edges. They both sat politely waiting for dinner to be announced.

Nellie was composed of a series of sharp angles. Rawboned, flat-chested, sharp-nosed. She sat with her arms folded across her chest, looking about. "You've fixed up this old place pretty nice, Tawny, if I do say so. Old Kennedy was a sloppy bachelor—you know how men are when it comes to keepin' house. They just plain don't give a darn."

"That's women's work, ain't it, Bill?" Doug laughed.

"I did a bit of painting and hammering," Bill said defensively.

"Of course you did!" Nellie cried. "I just meant that keepin' a place nice depends on the woman of the house. Ain't that so, Tawny?"

"Yes," Tawny answered. "I'll see about dinner." She darted out to the kitchen.

The pork was overcooked and tough, the potatoes soggy, the applesauce more of a soup than a sauce, but Doug nobly said, "This is just the kind of vittles I like," and Nellie added, "Men's kind of food. Myself, I allus prefer men's kind of food."

Bill said nothing.

When the dessert arrived Nellie turned to Tawny and gave her a sly wink. She knew why such a dessert had been chosen, and the wink told Tawny that Nellie had invented the sauce for the same reason.

After dinner Nellie helped Tawny clean up, while the two men went out on the front porch with their cigars.

When they were alone in the kitchen, Nellie put her bony hand on Tawny's shoulder.

"Don't fret, honey. You'll learn. We all hafta learn, sometime."

After the Fitzroys had left Tawny expected Bill to light into her. To her surprise all he had to say was, "Do we have any bicarbonate of soda? I sure need it." The look he gave her was one of sheer disgust; it hurt as much as words might have.

She told him, "The bicarbonate of soda is on the shelf by the sink in the kitchen. Near the tooth powder." And she went off into the bedroom to get undressed.

Her cooking did improve as the summer went on and fall began. But Bill went on being constantly critical.

Tawny wrote lots of letters. Almost every evening, while Bill dozed in front of the fire or trekked over to the Fitzroys for horse talk with Doug, Tawny would sit at the dining table, pen in hand, and write to Wilma, or to Evangeline, describing in detail her life on the ranch. Wilma always answered promptly—stiff little notes that scarcely got beyond the weather. Evangeline never answered.

Writing letters, getting letters, was Tawny's chief pleasure in life, with the exception of one other, newly discovered sport: horseback riding. Bill allowed her to have a little mare named Brownie for her very own. Brownie was gentle and obedient, and whenever Tawny could find the time away from housework she would go riding.

* * *

There had not been time this October day. She finished the last of the string beans and sat there in her rocking chair feeling lonely.

A moment later she saw Nellie Fitzroy trotting down the road, a covered dish in her hand. Good old Nellie, bringing her something.

"Afternoon, Tawny child!" Nellie called out as she opened the gate and snapped it shut behind her. "Brung you some corn bread hot out of the oven. You and your man partial to corn bread?"

Tawny got to her feet. "Of course we are!" she called back. "Nellie, you're too good to us."

"Nonsense. What are neighbors for? Nice day, ain't it? Most like summer but wouldn't surprise me a'tall if there was frost tonight. Never can tell in this country what things are gonna do." She climbed the steps and handed the plate of corn bread to Tawny.

"Sit down, Nellie." Tawny took the corn bread, and picked up her pan of string beans. "I'll put these in the kitchen and be right back." When she came back she perched on the porch railing.

"Better be careful there," Nellie paused long enough in her rocking to say. "Don't want you falling off and hurting yourself."

"I'll be careful. You mother me so, Nellie. I'm a big girl now."

"Got to mother something, don't I now? Never having had any kids of my own. Lord knows we wanted kids. And Lord knows we tried hard enough. But I just didn't have what it takes. Or Doug didn't. When are you and Bill gonna start raising a family?"

Tawny felt suddenly shy. "We haven't talked about it."

"No? That's funny. Most married folk talk about it. We used to lay awake nights after doing what Doug called tryin' to make a baby, talking about names. What we was gonna call 'em when we had 'em. Only we never did." Her face was grim as she finished speaking and Tawny had a rush of pity for the old woman. She jumped down from the railing and touched Nellie's shoulder. "I'm sorry."

Nellie looked surprised.

"No need for you to be sorry. I reckon I got used to the idea, long ago. And maybe it's just as well we didn't bring no more hatchet-faced Fitzroys into the world. But now you and Bill, nice-looking young couple like you ought to be able to make beautiful babies. 'Specially when you love each other like you do."

Tawny took her hand from Nellie's shoulder and turned her head. *So that's what she thinks. That's what the world thinks. But I don't really love him. I don't!*

"What's the matter, honey?" Nellie was asking.

"Nothing."

"Well, I won't pry, but I can tell something's not right. Maybe you got the wrong position."

"Position?" Tawny turned around, puzzled.

"In bed. Doug used to want to try all sorts of different positions and ways because sometimes you just can't start a baby the way you been doing it."

An angry resentment was stirring in Tawny. She took a deep breath to calm herself before she spoke.

"I'm sorry. Nellie. I'd rather not talk about it. After all, it's none of your business."

Nellie lumbered to her feet. "You're right, of course. Shouldna spoke out like that. Excuse me, please?"

"All right."

"Got to be running along now. Like I said, I got to fix dinner."

"Thank you for the corn bread."

"Think nothin' of it. Allus make too much."

Tawny stood on the porch and watched the old woman walk across the yard, open the gate, wave good-bye as she closed it. Tawny waved back. The sun was starting to lower. It was time for her, too, to fix dinner.

While she was working she kept thinking about what Nellie had said, wondering if having a child would be a good idea. If so, would things be different? She'd heard about a child bringing a couple together. Was it true? If she had Bill's child would she fall in love with him? Or was that putting the cart before the horse? At any rate she resolved to speak to him about it when the right moment came.

Bill had been to town and this was one of the times when he was late for dinner. She fretted because she knew keeping baked potatoes warm did not improve them particularly, and overcooked string beans became stringy beans. She was thankful for Nellie's corn bread.

He was in a good mood when he did come in. He had had a chat at the saloon with a man recently arrived from back East.

"Any exciting news, Bill? It's been so long since I've even *seen* a newspaper."

"There was a dreadful fire in Chicago. Almost the whole city was destroyed. Hundreds homeless. The story is that somebody's cow kicked over a bucket, knocked over a lamp, and then it spread."

"How dreadful! Didn't the man have any good news?"

"Well, let's see. A Russian Grand Duke is going to visit New York this fall. Big to-do about it back there."

Tawny thought: *how nice it would be to be back in San Francisco or New York City, a place where there is noise and excitement. That's not your life now,* she reminded herself. *You got yourself into this, you are stuck with it. You must make the best of it.* She looked across the table at her husband. As usual he had said all he had to say for a while. He was concentrating on his food.

"Nellie brought over the corn bread," Tawny told him.

"It's very good. Best part of the meal."

"Thank you kindly, sir," she said. "The reason the rest isn't too good is because you were late."

"Couldn't help it. Got to talking."

"I know. At least the apple pie isn't ruined."

"And I do like apple pie." He reached across and patted her hand. And smiled. All gentleman.

Maybe this was the moment to try it.

"Bill, have you ever thought about children?"

He took his hand from hers. "Children? What about them?"

"About . . . having them."

"Are you pregnant?"

"No."

"Then why are you talking about it?"

"Nellie was saying . . ."

"You were talking with Nellie about that?" he interrupted.

She shook her head. "I wasn't talking. She was. She was talking about how they never had children, and she asked when we were going to start raising a family, and I told her we hadn't talked about it."

"Of course not. That's not something one talks about." He was properly shocked.

"Nellie says most married people do."

"We are not most married people." He put down his knife and fork on his now-empty plate. "Did you say apple pie?"

That night after they were in their nightclothes, before they got into bed, he took her in his arms and held her close. She pressed herself to him in a way that made him catch his breath. Her breasts were firm against him. He could smell the perfume of her hair. He felt as he had the first time he kissed her, the want, the aching want all through his body.

"Bill, I've been wondering about having a child. Would you like it?"

"I haven't thought about it. Not really. Would you want it?" His voice was gruff.

"I think I would."

"I suppose every woman wants a child." He ran his hand around her body. "You would grow fat and ugly, you know. You would never be as you are now, so completely desirable."

"I know." But suddenly it came to her that she did want a child, she wanted their lovemaking to have a purpose, to create something. They must make a baby, as Nellie put it, together.

She put her hand on his organ, which was stiffening. "You say you love me, Bill."

"Of course I love you!"

"Then give me a child."

He stepped back and looked down at her, cupping her breasts in his hands.

"If that's what you want. But no child will ever touch his lips to these. These are mine. They belong to me. Do you understand?"

She nodded.

"You are in for an evening you will never forget. I shall play with your body until it is as hungry as mine is at this moment. I shall take you again and again until you give me what you never have. Yourself."

She knew what he meant. She must feel as she had

felt the first time, the way Lance Oliver had made her feel. And if she did not honestly feel it, she must pretend. She stood tiptoe to kiss him on the mouth. She told herself to pretend that he was Oliver. She closed her eyes to help with the pretense.

He slipped her nightgown off her shoulders and let it fall to the floor. He dropped his nightshirt beside it. He took her by the hand and led her to the bed, gave one last hungry look at her before he blew out the candle on the bedside stand.

He had said he would play with her body, and he did. Always before he had done no more than kiss her breasts, before proceeding swiftly to complete the act. Tonight he was a tease, a terrible tease with his fingers, with his lips, until at last with a cry that was almost a scream she threw herself on top of him and made them one. Now it was he who cried out with pleasure.

There was a frost that night, as Nellie had predicted; the room grew cold, but they did not notice. Over and over again Bill came to her, over and over she responded, until they fell back exhausted.

After a moment, he murmured, "If you're not pregnant now, you little bitch, you never will be."

She did not answer. She had fallen asleep.

PART III

1872

1

January in San Francisco was damp and dismal. Lance, who had taken a room in one of the more fashionable rooming houses, sat before his comfortable fireplace one rainy afternoon.

He was pondering on life in general, as he often did when he was alone. He had yet to find the meaningful career he had spoken about to Evangeline—he was still the man-about-town, the popular bachelor. Sometimes he even thought about going back to New York and approaching his father about some connection with the shipping business. But in his heart he knew that he was not ready to accept that as what he really wanted from life.

Often he thought of Bill and Tawny and wondered how they were getting along up north. He had not heard a word from Bill, but then they had never written.

Once he encountered Bill's mother on the street. Lance tipped his hat and stopped. Mrs. Ferguson stopped, too, but she was not smiling.

"You remember me, Mrs. Ferguson? Lance Oliver."

"Oh, yes, of course. I knew you were still in San

Francisco, because some of my friends have mentioned meeting you."

"How have you been, Mrs. Ferguson?"

"Very well, thank you." But she did not look it.

"And what do you hear from Bill?"

"I do not hear from Bill!" She snapped the words out as if they were a reprimand.

"Oh? He's not much of a correspondent, I gather."

"Mr. Oliver, the night he brought home that creature from the streets I disowned my son. I cast him out. Of course I do not hear from him!"

There were protests Lance would have liked to make. *Tawny is not a creature from the streets. Bill truly loves her. Your son is a decent fellow.* But Mrs. Ferguson did not give him a chance.

She said, "Good afternoon, Mr. Oliver," turned and walked past him, her petticoats swishing.

Lance looked after her. He could picture the scene in that gargoyle of a house, after the wedding. Poor Bill. And poor Tawny. Tawny, who even before she met Mrs. Ferguson, had not looked too happy. He continued to wonder about them but had no idea of how to get in touch with them. Washington Territory was a big place.

On this pondering afternoon he was interrupted by a knock on his door. When he opened it he saw one of his bachelor friends, John Selby, dripping wet, but smiling.

"John, what a nice surprise! Come in, come in."

John shook his hat over the hall doormat and put it on a table just inside and Lance took his overcoat and hung it on the clothes rack in the corner.

John Selby was a thin fellow; his only distinguishing features were his large, thick-lensed glasses and his Adam's apple. He was a practicing lawyer but his private life was in the same category as Lance's: eligible bachelor. They had seen a lot of each other at people's houses. He crossed to the fireplace and stood there a moment, warming his hands.

"Beastly weather, isn't it?" Lance commented. "But I guess it's beastly everywhere this time of year."

"They tell me Los Angeles is much warmer, but I'm not sure I'd like to live there after reading about those race riots there last fall. Surprised we don't have more trouble with the Chinese here. I guess they're a more orderly lot. More of the aristocrats settled in Chinatown."

John turned from the fire and Lance asked, "Would you like a brandy? To take off the chill?"

"As a matter of fact I was on my way to a little afternoon reception at some friends of mine and on the way I thought of you and wondered if you would like to come along."

"In all that rain?"

"It's not far. And maybe you're a sensible enough chap to have an umbrella. I left mine at home."

"Who are these people? Do I know them?"

"I don't know if you do. The name's Hulbert. Charles and Evelyn Hulbert. Very nice young couple with two children. Rather wholesome. But nice. No convenient unmarried spinsters to palm off on us poor bachelors. Good food and drink. How about it?"

Lance laughed. "Fine. I'll put on my newest cravat."

As they climbed one of the steeper hills together, huddled under Lance's umbrella, John said, "It will be great if they ever build that cable car, won't it? The older I get the less I like playing mountain goat. A trolley car on a cable would be a big help."

"All I have against hills," Lance said, "is that I'm

not inspired to walk as much as I used to in New York. What they call Murray Hill, for instance, isn't really much of a hill. I used to do a lot of walking."

I walked to get away from Sue Ellen, he thought. He was running away from no one now, except himself.

The Hulberts turned out to be exactly as John Selby described them. Evelyn Hulbert could have been any of the fashion models in *Godey's Ladies Book*. Her bustle was modest, as was her neckline. She was rounded like most ladies in their thirties, and her husband had the paunch that usually appears on men of his age. They were polite to Lance, asking him how long he had been in San Francisco—less than a year—what news he had had from New York—none—what did he think of the breakup of the Tweed ring this past election—pleased—wasn't he sorry he hadn't been in New York for the visit of the Russian grand duke—such gala times!

Lance was acquainted with some of the other guests and moved about the room, punch glass in hand, making small talk. He spotted and avoided one young matron who, whether or not her husband was in earshot, always tried to flirt with him.

In the late afternoon the Hulberts' children were brought in by their nursemaid to meet the guests.

Somebody cried, "Here come the little darlings!"

A boy and a girl ran into the room to their parents' side. The mother escorted the girl, the father the boy, and they duly circled the room and shook hands and curtsied.

After they had passed Lance moved to one side. He felt awkward with children because he was never sure of what to say to them. These were handsome small creatures, full of giggles and talking in chirpy voices as the adults cooed at them.

The nursemaid was standing in the doorway. She was a plain-looking young girl, modestly waiting, not trying in any way to join the party. And then, as Lance watched her, her face became familiar. He put down his punch cup and walked over to her side. He smiled at her and she smiled back, very shyly.

"I'm trying to remember your name," Lance said. "I know we've met."

"We met at Tawny's wedding, Mr. Oliver. I'm Wilma Wilson."

"Of course!"

"You're still in San Francisco? You didn't go back to New York?"

"I'm still in San Francisco. And so are you."

"Yes."

She seemed a bit more at ease than she had the night of the wedding. But poise and posture could do nothing to help her plain looks. She was not out of her teens, but she was already assuming the guise of a spinster. Some poor women, Lance thought, are born to be spinsters. As I was born to be a bachelor.

"Do you ever hear from them? From Tawny and Bill?"

"I hear from Tawny. All the time." Her eyes brightened. "She writes wonderful letters."

"And how are they?"

"Fine, I guess. She has to work awfully hard. It's all very different for Tawny. I mean, she never lived on a ranch or kept house or anything like that. And I guess it's kind of lonesome or she wouldn't write so many letters. But she says Bill loves it because he likes hunting and fishing."

Lance thought: *so Bill has found a way of life he likes. But Tawny hasn't.* At least he had a hard time picturing that lively, zestful creature being content as a rancher's wife.

"Then they haven't found gold yet."

"Gold?" Wilma puzzled.

"Don't you remember the night of the wedding when Bill told us that the reason his father bought that land was because there was a rumor of gold being on it?"

Wilma frowned a little. "I forgot about that. And Tawny's never written anything about it."

"Strange. If I'd been in their shoes that's the first thing I would have investigated. That makes me curious."

"I'll ask Tawny about it the next time I write."

Lance saw his hostess approaching, holding her children by their hands.

He said quickly, "Wilma, could you give me their address? I'd like to write Bill a letter. About that gold business."

"It's just General Delivery, Littleton, Washington Territory. That's all."

"General Delivery, Littleton, Washington Territory," he repeated. "Thank you, Wilma."

Mrs. Hulbert and the children were beside them. "So Wilma knows you, Mr. Oliver! How nice."

"We met last year at a wedding."

"Why, Wilma, you never even told me you went to a wedding!"

Wilma was blushing. "It was a secret one, Mrs. Hulbert. I promised not to tell."

"Well, it all sounds very romantic. Wilma, take the children out and give them their supper, please."

"Yes, ma'am."

Lance said, "Thank you for the address, Wilma."

"You're welcome."

He was puzzled by the look on her face before she turned and took the children's hands and led them away. She seemed concerned. About Tawny? Or about his asking for the address? He would write that very night.

"Is something wrong, Mr. Oliver?" Mrs. Hulbert was asking.

"No," he reassured her. "You have two lovely children. And this is a lovely party."

By January Tawny was three months pregnant.

When she first told Bill that she suspected her condition he was delighted. There was an awe in his eyes that reminded her of how he had been when first they met. Perhaps things would be good again. Perhaps she had done the right thing to want a child.

Bill was pleased and proud of himself. He immediately hired—and later bought—a buggy to take her to see the nearest doctor in Twuylip. The doctor confirmed her suspicions, and after he had examined her he pronounced her fit and assured her that all would go well with her pregnancy.

As she came out of the doctor's office into the waiting room Bill jumped to his feet and crossed the room to grab her hands.

"Are you?" he asked. "Is it true?"

She nodded.

He took her in his arms and held her close. "We shall take very good care of you, little mother."

Tawny gave a laugh. "I'm not quite a mother yet!" But she shared his happiness and, just then, his pride in what they had done. The doctor's office was in Twuylip's Grand Hotel, and when they came down into the lobby, Bill suddenly decided the occasion was cause for a celebration.

"Do you realize," he said to her, "we haven't been out to eat a meal together since San Francisco? Why don't we have dinner here in the hotel dining room before driving home? It would be like old times."

Tawny nodded. *Old times*, she thought, *when he was the tender, lovesick young man, adoring me.* He had somewhat the same expression on his face now and she was overwhelmingly glad that she was pregnant.

"Come along, then." He took her arm and they walked into the dining room. The Grand Hotel dining room was anything but grand, but it was clean. Light from a big chandelier shone on the heavy silverware and thick dishes, the napkins folded and stuffed into glasses, artificial roses in cut-glass vases on each table.

The room was empty when they came in. The headwaiter bustled up and seated them in a corner, under the impression that they were lovers who wanted to be alone.

As he went away to fetch the menu they laughed at him, and Bill reached over and touched her hand. It was the delicacy of his gesture, almost reverent, that took them back to their first rendezvous, those nights in San Francisco when they sat across a restaurant table and looked into each other's eyes.

The menu was limited, a choice of fried chicken or meatballs. They chose the chicken. When the waiter asked if they wished wine Bill asked her, "Do you suppose you ought to drink it?"

"The doctor said to go ahead and eat and drink anything!"

"A small bottle then," Bill said. "White. And chill it, please."

Tawny felt happier than she had been in months.

"In the spring," Bill was saying, "we shall have to build an addition on the house. After all, my son must have a room of his own."

She laughed. "It might be a girl, Bill."

"I'm sure it will be a boy."

"How can you be sure if even the doctor doesn't know?"

"I know in my heart."

When the food came Bill fell silent, as he usually did at such times. The fried chicken was excellent, and so were the creamed potatoes and peas. Tawny was hungrier than usual: *it's probably because I'm pregnant,* she thought, *and also because I'm in a restaurant and somebody else is doing the cooking.* She emptied her plate with great speed.

The waiter was back, bending over solicitously. "Is everything all right?"

"Everything is very all right," Tawny told him with a smile. "It's so very all right that I am going to have a second helping, if I may!"

"Tawny!" Bill's tone was reproving and he was frowning.

"Certainly, madam," the waiter said. "It's a pleasure to see someone in good appetite. Would you prefer white or dark meat?"

"Either or both," Tawny told him. "I'm just plain hungry. You know what they say: I'm eating for two now."

"May I offer my congratulations to you both." He picked up Tawny's plate and turned to Bill. "Would you care for more chicken, sir?"

"No thank you. Nothing."

He was furious. He had been so happy, so pleased with himself, and with her, too. She was beautiful, lovely, young, all his heart could desire. She had conceived his child, his son. And then she had to belittle herself, embarrass him again.

When the door to the kitchen closed on the waiter, Bill said, "Tawny, how could you!"

He took her completely by surprise. In her boisterous mood she had been ready to shout the news of the day to the whole world.

"How could I what?" she asked. "Bill, what's the matter?"

"How could you be so vulgar as to say such a thing aloud in public, and to a waiter?" He had lowered his voice because other diners were coming into the room.

"That was vulgar?" Tawny asked. "I didn't think it was vulgar. I was happy to tell him, as I'd be happy to tell anyone that I'm going to have a baby!"

"It was vulgar. Just plain vulgar."

"I'm sorry."

"Go ahead and be sorry! Go on, finish stuffing yourself like a pig. And then we're leaving."

His anger took away her hunger. She was only able to dabble with her second helping, and shook her head at the question of dessert.

The joy of being pregnant was almost destroyed. She had hoped that everything would be different, that he really would return to old times. But it was not to be like that. He was back to his old arrogant self. She had displeased him and she would pay for it.

2

Bill began treating her as he would treat one of his mares that was going to foal. He insisted she take good care of herself. His eyes shone with appreciation as her breasts swelled; when he touched them it was almost reverently. And he talked, night and day, about his son. When he kissed her good night he would put his hand on her abdomen and say, "My son is in there."

He was not sympathetic with her morning sickness, only annoyed and repulsed. He felt it was a weakness on her part. He brushed aside her apologies so she quit apologizing. And when the morning sickness stopped, as the doctor had told her it would, all Bill had to say was, "I'm glad you're through with that messy business."

He couldn't have explained his feelings about Tawny to anyone, not even to himself. In the beginning he had fallen in love with her face and her body. It had been a sheer, consuming, physical desire for possession of that body. He could not think of her as merely a possible subject for seduction. He had to have her for his own; she had to belong to him. Marriage meant absolute possession.

It was not until after he married her that he realized that possession of her body did not mean possession of the woman herself. He was aware of her submission, submission without complete surrender. He did not even feel it was surrender that one night when she suggested pregnancy, when she made the advances. In Bill's mind her behavior revealed the heart of a whore, and yet she had aroused him.

At first being pregnant made her more beautiful than ever, particularly her breasts. Then, little by little, as her body thickened, the feelings he had had for her since the first moment he set eyes upon her were diminished. She was no longer the woman he took to bed at night for the joys of fornication. She was a woman having a child. His child.

He had never thought about fatherhood until now when it was suddenly being thrust upon him. And so he began to concentrate on the child, what he would be like, the things they could do together.

For Tawny it was in no way a joyous pregnancy. She felt alone with it. Nellie Fitzroy was kind, but Nellie was childless, and her sympathy could only be abstract.

Tawny felt alone and burdened. Even before the pregnancy began to show she felt heavy, listless. The doctor had told her that for a while it would be all right for her to ride horseback, providing she held the horse to a mild canter and did not do anything like fence jumping or galloping. Bill did not want her to ride at all, so the only times she indulged was when he was in town and could not know about it.

She enjoyed riding Brownie down by the river. It was called the Green River because it was bordered by the most lush evergreens in the area; it was beautiful even in winter. She would get off Brownie and sit by the water's edge. Sometimes she would think of that river back on the plains and that hot night she had sat with her feet in the water when Timothy had found her. Every once in a while, she would remember sweet, gentle Timothy, with his rich musical voice that made anything he talked about, even inconsequentials, seem beautiful.

Sometimes she looked back over her life and wondered what it might have been like if Pa had not made her perform magnetic healing on Lance Oliver. What if Pa had selected another type of man? A fat, ugly old ape who would have repulsed her, instead of a man with the overwhelming attraction of Oliver? She admitted now, to herself, that her first experience, if it had not been with Oliver, would have been with someone. *I was ready for it that day. I have been ready for it ever since.*

But to marry Bill had been the wrong thing. She saw that now. He loved her, she knew, but in such a strange masochistic, possessive way. When he hit her, when he hurt her in any way, it was because of his love. If only he would show tenderness now, tenderness and love.

January. Three months gone by. Six more to come. Bill had gone to town and she went to the barn and fetched out Brownie and rode down by the river. Snow was threatening, had been threatening for weeks. Nellie was sure it would come any minute. Still Tawny went riding.

Six months. How could she bear it? She tried to think about the baby and what it would be like. Would it turn out to be a boy or a girl; would it look like Bill or like herself or, God forbid, like Bill's mother or her father? It was hard to think of the baby as a reality, as someone who was going to be. She did not even know what it would be like to have a baby. And she remembered now that her own mother had died in childbirth. And so she was afraid. If she told Bill she was afraid, would he be kinder? Would he worry about her a little instead of always harping on "my son"?

The sky had darkened. It was time to go home. As she stood up and walked toward Brownie she felt the first snowflakes fall. By the time she had mounted the horse and started along the trail the snow was falling more and more thickly, a white swirling curtain ahead of her, and despite what the doctor had told her she urged Brownie into a gallop. Brownie obliged, but her footing was slippery and she almost fell several times before they reached the gate and Tawny dismounted to open it. To her dismay she saw that Bill's horse was already in the barn.

As she walked up the path to the house, Bill opened the front door and called out to her.

"What the devil are you doing out there in the snow? Do you want to catch your death of cold? You know I don't want you to go riding. 'Specially not on a day like this!"

She climbed the steps, shook the snow off her shawl, and walked into the living room. Bill had the fire started in the fireplace and she went over and stood in front of it.

Over her shoulder she said, "It wasn't snowing when I went out. It was quite nice."

"My dear woman, this is January. You know what the Fitzroys have told us about the weather here. Completely unpredictable. And you, in your condition, risking life!"

She turned then and looked directly at him. "Are you speaking of my life, or the child's?"

"Don't be cruel, Tawny."

She said, "I'll put dinner in the oven."

He made no comment.

When she came back from the kitchen, to her surprise she found him sitting in front of the fire, reading a letter. Usually the only mail Bill ever got was bills; most of the letters were addressed to her.

She said, "There was mail."

"Yes. There's one there on the table for you."

"And you got a letter?"

He looked up, smiling. "Yes, I got a letter."

"Your mother? She's forgiven you, at last?"

"No, not my mother. Guess again."

"I've no idea, Bill."

"Lance. Good old Lance."

She caught her breath at the sound of his name. Slowly she walked over to the dining table and picked up her letter. It was from Wilma.

She read it with less interest than she usually felt. Wilma told how her charges would be starting school the next year, but that Mrs. Hulbert wanted her to stay on, just the same, to supervise them, even to help with their schoolwork. "And she wants me to move into the house, so everything will be quite different next year." The letter went on in its usual way with much attention paid to the weather. Then, at the end of the letter, a P.S.: "By the way, I saw that man Lance Oliver who was best man at your wedding. He was at a party at the Hulbert house. He asked about you and Bill."

That was all. Tawny would have liked to have known more about him, why he was still in San Francisco, if his wife had joined him there. She scolded herself for wondering about Lance Oliver, but when she had finished Wilma's letter she sat there watching Bill's face as he read his.

When he had finished reading, folded the letter, and slipped it back into its envelope, he was smiling, but he was also looking thoughtful.

"Did your friend have any interesting news?" she asked.

"In a way. Do you want to read it?" He was holding out the letter.

She was not sure she wanted to; on the other hand she was not without curiosity. She took the letter and looked at the envelope. "I see he's not at a hotel anymore."

"No? I didn't notice."

"It sounds like a private address."

She was prattling on about the return address when what really caught her eye was his handwriting. It was big and bold and graceful, like the man himself. Big, bold, graceful—and arrogant, she reminded herself.

"Are you going to read it, or aren't you?"

She took the letter out of the envelope. "You can read Wilma's, if you like." She did not like him sitting there watching her read.

"No, thanks. I'll go wash up."

So she was alone in front of the fire.

My dear Bill:

I have wondered so many times how things are going for you and Tawny up there in the wilderness. But I had no idea of an address until by chance I ran into Tawny's friend Wilma, who is nursemaid at a home where I was taken to a reception. Of course I inquired about you two. I received a rather sketchy report of what you were up to, but I did extract your address from the young lady, so that I was able to write. I asked her about the gold vein on your land and discovered that Tawny had not mentioned the subject in any of her letters. It seems, as I understand it, secondhand, you have turned yourself into some sort of gentleman farmer instead of pursuing the possibility of finding gold. If I were in your shoes I would have certainly explored the land with a fine-tooth comb. I would also gather from my vague source of information that you are not exactly flourishing as a farmer, that Tawny is working hard. . . ."

Oh, why did Wilma have to tell him that? Tawny wondered. *Now Bill will scold me for writing such a thing to her. But if he had been truly offended by that sentence he would not have let me read this letter. In fact, he seemed pleased with it.* She went on reading.

I have a proposition, Bill. I am getting restless and bored with San Francisco and I have no desire as yet to go back to New York. I seek adventure, as I sought adventure when I made my round-the-world trip. I should say almost around the world as I did not go all the way. At any rate, I should like to come north this spring and visit you, and help you look for that gold. Please let me know if this would please you.

He had signed it, "Sincerely, Your Friend."

The P.S. was: "Give my best regards to your lovely wife."

The letter still in her hands, Tawny stared into the fire. She felt as if Lance had been there in the room, talking to them. She imagined him saying the words he had written. She could hear that rich voice of his; she could picture the sparkle in those long-lashed blue eyes. Lance Oliver, a man from another world.

She was slipping the letter back into the envelope when Bill came back into the room.

"Interesting, isn't it, Lance wanting to come here," Bill said.

"Very interesting."

"Doug has convinced me that the gold vein was only a rumor."

"I know."

"Lance is such an adventurer. He's such a footloose fool. Just because he is rich."

"What are you going to tell him? What Doug has told you?"

"I suppose I should. It's only fair. And yet . . ." He had that faraway thoughtful look again, his round, now-suntanned face so very earnest. "And yet," he repeated, "I should like to see him again. Doug is a good friend but sometimes I miss someone like Lance."

She knew exactly how he felt but she said nothing. She was not going to encourage him to invite Lance to come north.

Bill, thinking aloud, said, "The thing to do, I guess, is to tell him frankly about Doug's opinion; then tell him if he wants to come anyhow, it's all right. Explaining of course that he would have to stay at the hotel. We don't have the room here yet."

Thank goodness for that, Tawny thought. *I couldn't bear to have him as a houseguest.* "That does seem like a good idea," she said. "Just write him an honest, friendly letter, telling him exactly how things are and what your feelings are."

Outside the wind was roaring with a whistling clatter and swirling the snowflakes against the windowpanes. Bill got up, picked up the poker, and began stirring the coals in the fireplace, and then threw on another log.

"It will be cold in bed tonight," he said. "We must

warm some bricks. And find an extra blanket." He put the poker back in its rack and turned to her.

"Tawny, I'm no good at letter writing. Never have been. I want you to write the letter."

"Me?"

"You seem to be a very proficient letter writer. I've watched you night after night, scribbling away. And as you already have made a very good suggestion as to what to say, I think you should do it."

"But he wrote to you, Bill. Not to me."

"Tell him I'm too busy. Pretend you are my secretary, if you like."

It was the last thing on earth she wanted to do. And she knew it would be difficult. But finally she said, "All right, Bill. I'll write."

He came over and stood beside her. He cupped one of her breasts in his hand, looked down at her.

"Good girl," he said. "Good girl."

An emotion she had not felt for weeks stirred in her.

He quickly took his hand away, asking, "What's for dinner?"

She laughed a bit hysterically, before she told him. "Rabbit pie. And . . . and beet greens."

It took her a whole evening to compose the letter. She crumpled up several sheets of paper after she'd written no more than a sentence or two on them. She chewed on the end of her pen.

She would have preferred to begin it with "Dear Mr. Oliver," but under the circumstances it had best be "Dear Lance." One thing was sure, if he did come he would not look at her the way he had that day in The Golden Parrot, not with her distended belly. And in the spring the baby would be almost due.

* * *

Dear Lance: Bill has asked me to answer your letter, as he finds himself very busy at this time. And, I must confess, I am the letter writer of this family.

Family? Did one call two people a family? Should she tell him she was expecting? She decided not to.

As regards the possibility of gold on our land: It was, in the beginning, only a rumor. Bill's father bought the land because of that rumor, he having been a gambling man who made his first fortune in the Gold Rush of Forty-nine. When we arrived here our neighbors the Fitzroys, who, incidentally, have become very good friends, told us that there is no gold, that the man who owned the land had found that out and decided to get rid of the land by means of using that rumor. That is why Bill has never pursued the matter, never explored his land to make sure. However, Bill wants me to tell you that if you wish to look for this vein of gold, if you wish to take the risk of traveling all the way here for what may turn out to be a fool's errand, you are welcome to come. I am sure he will help you look. One thing more: I must tell you that at the present time we do not have a guest room. I am afraid you would have to put up at the hotel in Littleton. However, we are in walking distance of the village.

What would it be like if Lance Oliver did actually come here to Washington Territory? How would he fit in? She pictured him as completely the city man, part of the world of carriages and gaslight and fine clothes. Perhaps she should warn him.

* * *

This is a very primitive country, you will find. Littleton is a small village. The ranches are large tracts of land. The countryside is beautiful but it is lonely. If you are bored and restless in San Francisco, you may quickly become more so here. I do not mean to sound inhospitable, it is just a warning I felt I should make.

Bill sends his best regards. He very much looks forward to seeing you, if you decide to come.

Sincerely yours, Tawny Ferguson.

She showed the letter to Bill.

"It's a bit formal," he commented. "But it will have to do. I'll mail it the next time I go to town."

Except for the tablecloth and napkins Tawny had done little sewing in her life. She had never really sewn before this year, only mended. She remembered the mending she had done on the road for Amanda, and how Amanda had complained at her big stitches, which never held very well.

Now, with Nellie's help, she began working on baby clothes. The tiny garments were not as pretty as she would have liked them to be, because of her poor sewing. She had made several little nightshirts, cut up a thin old blanket to make small blankets.

Bill, with Doug's help, constructed a cradle from scraps of lumber left over from the building of the Fitzroys' house years ago. Bill painted it white with paint left over from their front gate.

The days passed with no word from Lance Oliver, and Tawny began to think that the letter she had written had discouraged him; she no longer need dread his arrival.

Now and then Bill would voice disappointment at not having heard from Lance, but gradually life began to resume its old pattern, and when Bill talked about anything but the horses and the cows and the weather it was about the baby.

One afternoon he came home from town after having had several drinks at the saloon, crossed the living room to where she was sitting, took her sewing out of her hands and laid it aside, and put his hand across her stomach. "Was talking to a fellow in town. He was telling me sometimes you can feel the baby—feel the baby kick. Have you felt him yet? Has he kicked?" His voice, his eyes, were both excited.

She shook her head. "Not yet," she told him. "I have felt nothing except now and then a slight pain."

"When you feel him, tell me. Tell me right away. I can't wait to feel my son, alive."

"I hope I'll be alive as well."

"What do you mean by that?"

"I mean I'm afraid sometimes. I can't help it, Bill. Sometimes I'm terribly afraid of having a baby."

"Nonsense! Women have babies every day of the year. Besides, hasn't Doctor McGlinn told you that you are in fine condition?"

If only he would put his arms around her, reassure her with affection!

She said, "Perhaps I am. But I can't help remembering that my own mother died giving birth to me."

He took his hand away from her; he stared down at her, wide-eyed.

"Tawny, you told me your parents were killed in a railroad accident. Now, didn't you?"

She nodded, biting her lip. Finally she said, "It's what I've always pretended."

Pretended. Sometimes Bill was shocked by how

little he knew this woman he had married. How many other secrets about her past was she hiding from him? "So you never knew your own mother, then."

Tawny shook her head. "Please, Bill, let's not talk about her. Not now. I don't like to think about it. As I said, it only makes me afraid."

"You mustn't be afraid," he said gruffly. "Or you might muff the whole business."

"And you wouldn't get your precious son. That's what's worrying you, isn't it?"

"I didn't say that."

"But you thought it. That's all you've talked about for weeks. The baby. What if I fooled you and gave birth to a girl?"

She was tired that afternoon, out of sorts. And resentment had been building up inside her for days. Now she was downright angry. She jumped to her feet and picked up her sewing, started to run out of the room.

Bill caught her by her shoulders and held her firmly. "You mustn't get excited, Tawny. It isn't good for you."

"I'll get excited if I want to!" Her eyes were wild, her breasts were rising and falling.

"Tawny, please!"

"Let go of me!"

"Not until you calm down."

"You're hurting me, you know."

"Not as much as I *could* hurt you." His voice was hard and he did not loosen his hold on her. He was furious with himself for having given her cause to say such things in anger.

Tawny took a deep breath. Then she said, "But you're not going to hurt me, are you? Not now, when I'm carrying your child."

Slowly he took his hands from her shoulders. "Damn you!" he cried. "Damn you, you little bitch!"

She walked into the bedroom and slammed the door behind her.

Bill sank down in a chair, his head in his hands. Slowly his fury faded. He had behaved badly. She had a right to be angry. He had not realized she had such strong feelings bottled up inside her. It was true he'd thought much more about the child than about her. He could hear her crying in the bedroom. He must somehow make it up to her.

He went over and knocked on the door, opened it a crack. "Tawny, may I come in?"

She was lying face down on the bed, her hair tumbling over her shoulders. She lifted her face. "Of course you can come in! This is your bedroom. This is your bed. This is your wife!"

He came over, sat down beside her, and smoothed her hair away from her forehead. "Tawny, I'm sorry. I do love you."

She knew he meant it. It was the voice he had used when he was courting her.

"Even the way I look, now?"

"Even the way you look."

She wished she could say, "I love you, too," but she could not. In spite of all that happened between them, in spite of the months of physical intimacy, even in spite of the fact she was carrying his child she could not, with all honesty, say the simple words, "I love you."

He was giving her now what she had wanted: tenderness. It was an awkward tenderness, but it was there.

She said, "Thank you, Bill."

In the days that followed Bill was much more considerate. He restrained himself from talking too much about "my son" and he tried not to criticize Tawny for late meals or burned biscuits or unmade beds or dust on the tabletops.

On the other hand Tawny tried her best not to talk about the aches and pains she sometimes felt, and she tried not to think about the birth itself, certainly never to speak of it. But the enforced silence did not drive her fear from her mind and there were dreams, almost constant dreams of what birth would be like: nightmarish, unformed terror, her body bursting, her being on fire, falling down endless caverns, or being dragged down the icy-cold rush of the Green River.

Then one night there came a different dream. She was by a river, not the Green River, but one like the river on the plains. Only more beautiful than that one had been. It was daytime, the sun was shining and there was a grassy bank full of dandelions and she was lying there, listening to the river and looking up at a bright blue sky, feeling happy. The happiness was a palpable part of the dream, a physical reality. Her body was slender again. She was lying there naked in the sunshine. She closed her eyes for a moment.

A voice said, "Don't be afraid, I won't hurt you."

Her eyes flew open and he was there.

"I won't hurt you because I love you, my darling."

She reached out her arms to Lance Oliver. Then suddenly he was gone; the sunlight and the river's singing had disappeared, the dream dissolved.

She sat straight up in bed, shivering. The dream was still with her, still real. She looked at the man sleeping beside her and he was a stranger.

She realized that she loved Lance Oliver, that she had always loved him.

When the letter came it was addressed to both of

them. She recognized the handwriting the minute Bill had tossed it on the table.

"You haven't opened it yet?" she asked.

Bill was grinning. "I've opened it. He's coming. In a couple of weeks."

It was all she could do to keep calm as she walked over to the table and picked up the letter. She sat down before she started reading. It was no more than a note.

> Dear Bill and Tawny: Ever since Tawny's letter came I have been debating with myself. I have finally decided that in spite of Tawny's warnings, or perhaps because of them, I feel challenged. Getting there was the first problem so I did not post this letter until I knew exactly when I would set sail from Astoria.

Tawny's eyes blurred as she skimmed through the details of his journey. At the end of the letter he said, "I can't wait to see you two nice people again. Love to you both."

"What's the matter?" Bill asked as she slipped the letter back in its envelope. "Don't you feel well?"

"I'm a little tired." Love to you both. She couldn't bear it.

"Lie down, then, for a while."

"I think I will." She knew she had to be alone, to prepare herself to face the fact of Lance's coming.

From then on all that Bill talked about was the things he and Lance would do together. "Oh, we'll look for gold, if that's the game he wants to play, but we can also go fishing together. I wonder if he's ever hunted. I wish it were deer season; it would be nice to let him feast on venison. And, Tawny, you must get the house in order. Perhaps Nellie could help you clean it. After all, this whole ranch is going to seem awfully rustic to someone like Lance Oliver."

When Bill was around Tawny managed to keep her mind pretty much on mundane details of housekeeping, but whenever he left her alone her mind went back to that dream. She paced the floor and fought her nerves.

The snow had long since melted away, and an early spring was on its way. There were new pale green needles on the evergreens and some of the other trees were beginning to show their tender new leaves.

"Not long before planting time," Nellie Fitzroy said one afternoon when she arrived with a tureen of soup. "Always cook too much!" she snorted. "And not too long before you, young lady, will be sprouting."

"Not until summer, Nellie."

"Well, you look like it could be any minute. Feel any kicking yet?"

"No."

"It'll come. Now, take it easy, girl. You look kind of peaked lately. I don't like them circles under your eyes."

"I haven't been sleeping well."

"Drink some hot chocolate when you go to bed. Do you good."

"I'll try that." She thought: *it won't stop those other dreams.*

She had been obeying Bill's request that she no longer ride horseback. But one sunny afternoon her restlessness, with the added pique of spring fever, made her think, *why not? It will do no harm. And maybe I'll feel better if I go down by the river and just sit for a while. No chance of a snowstorm today.*

She rode slowly up the hill and down again to her

favorite spot. There were bits of wild grass springing up around the rock where she usually perched. She looked down at them and her dream came back to her. How was it possible to have dreamed such a feeling? There was no peace by the river today.

She rode away from the ranch on a road she had never tried before. It went higher up into the hills. She reached a point where she could look back, down the hill, and see the little huddle of buildings that was Littleton.

She turned Brownie and went on up the hill. There was a curve in the road and she could no longer look down to the village. She was going deep into the brush; branches hovered over the road; there were ruts filled with water from the last heavy rain.

She was remembering now where this road was supposed to go, to the house of a lone rancher, a hermit who only came into town a few times a year for supplies. She had no desire to call on him, so she turned Brownie back down the hill.

Suddenly there was the sound of growling from the brush. From the side of the road a large dog bounded out, barking wildly. The hair on his back was standing straight up; his teeth were bared. He headed straight for Brownie, his growl rising in crescendo.

With a whinny of fright Brownie reared; the reins slipped out of Tawny's hands and she was thrown onto the road.

At first all she was aware of was the buzzing in her head, the sound of Brownie's hoofbeats as the horse galloped for home, the gradual dimming of the dog's barking as he raced away.

She did not lose consciousness; she felt no specific pain, just an overwhelming weariness as the blood and the embryo poured out of her body.

3

It was late afternoon when Bill got back from town and found an empty house. He was upset to find Brownie standing in the barn, still wearing her saddle. He hurried up to the house, ready to scold Tawny for having gone horseback riding and for not having put Brownie into the barn properly.

He went through the house, calling out to her. No fire in the fireplace, no fire in the kitchen, dirty dishes left from lunch, the bed unmade. To let the house be in such a state and then, in spite of his frequent objections, to go riding!

He had been told, in recent conversations in town, that pregnant women were often full of strange notions, that their behavior was unpredictable, but it seemed to him Tawny exceeded any ordinary woman in her irresponsibility.

Now his anger with her changed to concern. A closer inspection of Brownie confirmed she had been ridden. The horse was home but Tawny was not.

She had fallen from the horse. That was the only answer.

It had started to get dark. He ran over to the

Fitzroy house and told them what had happened. They had not seen Tawny that afternoon.

"She don't usually ride this way," Nellie said. "Not toward town. I ast her once where she went and she said down by the river. That prob'ly means t'other way. Doug better go with you and bring a lantern."

"I'll fetch it," Doug said. "Lemme go to the woodshed."

"Thank you, Doug! I appreciate your coming with me."

"Glad to oblige."

They rode together through the gathering dusk following the river for as far as that road went. There was no sign of her. They turned back and at the crossroads Doug said, "Only other way she coulda gone is up there."

"Up in the hills? To that hermit's house?"

Doug shrugged. "It's the only other idea I got, Bill. We best try it afore we go to town and tell the sheriff she's missing."

"I guess you're right."

As their horses started to climb the first incline Doug said, "She's a damn foolhardy girl to go riding right now anyhow."

"I know."

"Women is women, Bill. Can't never figure them out, all the way. Can't figure out the way they think, or why they do the things they do. Even Nellie's got her quirks."

"I know," Bill said again.

They heard a dog howl, from a distance, and Bill shuddered. And then he spotted Tawny, lying in the road.

The two men dismounted and Doug held the lantern while Bill knelt beside her. For a moment, in his panic, he thought she was dead but now he could see that she was breathing, her chest rising and falling.

He turned. "Doug, please, will you bring my buggy? And a blanket? Take my horse, and hurry."

"Sure thing." Doug put the lantern down on the ground and in a moment Bill could hear him riding away.

How pale she was there in the lantern light! He wondered if he should try to awaken her. She was lying as she had fallen, limp, helpless. One arm was flung up, the palm open—lovely, soft, slender palm. He bent his head and kissed it. Still she did not stir.

"I do love you, Tawny!" he whispered. "I really do. In spite of all the things I have said, in spite of all the things I have done to you. You are my wife; you are carrying my child."

He caught his breath. He moved the lantern away down toward her feet. And then he saw, for the first time, what was lying there in the pool of blood.

"Dear God!"

He moved the lantern away from the spot. He sat down on the ground beside her and he cried—for the ugliness of what he had seen, for the loss.

Tawny was murmuring something. He brushed away his tears and bent over her.

"What is it, darling? What is it?"

"I killed the baby. I'm sorry, Bill, I killed the baby!"

She began crying, hysterically. He reached down and took her in his arms and held her close. "No, darling, no, it was an accident."

She went on sobbing and mumbling while he held her. He was relieved at last to hear the sound of the buggy.

"It's all right, Tawny, I'm taking you home. It's all right."

She was still sobbing when he lifted her into the buggy, and covered her with the blanket.

He told Doug, "Please go home and get Nellie, right off?"

"Sure thing."

Bill drove home with the speed of a madman.

The first thing Tawny remembered clearly was opening her eyes and finding Nellie Fitzroy bathing her. She felt infinite weariness and a slow, throbbing pain. And then, very slowly, she remembered what had happened.

"Bill will kill me," she mumbled to herself.

"What's that, child?" Nellie asked.

"Bill wanted the baby so much."

"Of course he did. Like you did."

"He wanted it more. It's all he's talked about, all these months. The baby. His son. And what he would do with him. And now there is no baby. There is no son."

"There'll be others."

"No! No! I couldn't again. No, not again."

"Don't think about it now." Nellie was busy now with bandages torn from a sheet. "I'll fix you up good so you won't bleed no more all over the earth. The blood you've lost, young lady! I swear to heaven I've never seen nothing like it. But you'll be all right. I'll give you a little shot of what Doug calls Nellie's cure-all. It will put you sound asleep and when you wake up you'll feel all better."

"I'll never feel all better again," Tawny said. "I'll never be happy again. I'll never . . ."

Nellie was holding a cup to her lips.

"Be quiet. Drink this."

It was a bitter-tasting mixture of brandy and

Lord knew what else. Tawny drank it obediently and lay back and looked up at Nellie.

"You're too good to me."

"Nobody can be too good to anyone else." Her bony hand smoothed Tawny's hair back from her face. "You lie still and I'll send that husband of yours in to say good night."

Tawny was starting to doze when Bill tiptoed into the room. Tired as she was, she tried to look penitent when she opened her eyes and faced him.

To Bill her face had never been more beautiful. He knelt beside the bed. "Nellie says you'll be all right. I hope to God she's right."

"Bill, I'm so . . ."

He put his hand over her mouth.

"Don't try to say a thing tonight, my darling. Just thank God that you're alive."

She closed her eyes and drifted off, and Bill could have cried again, just looking at her.

Tawny lost weight as well as blood. Her body became as it had been the previous fall. Perhaps her breasts were a little larger, but her waist was slender again, her abdomen flat. She was feeling better, too, better than she had let Bill know. She enjoyed being lazy and being encouraged to be lazy.

And she enjoyed Bill's abstinence. Even when she was pregnant he had had a way of fondling her that frequently irritated her, especially if she were out of sorts anyhow. Right now his attitude toward her was completely without sexual overtones. She might have been a sick child. She found it pleasant.

The homemade cradle had been packed away in the attic. The baby clothes were put away in a trunk. She tried not to think about the possibility of putting them into use someday. People don't talk about such things, Bill had said once. She certainly did not want to talk about it now.

One morning when Nellie came over to check up on Tawny she stuck her head around the bedroom door before she came in.

"Morning, Tawny. Brung you a present. If you want it."

"You're always bringing presents!"

"This is sorta different. It really comes from old Rover and Rosie," she announced as she came into the bedroom. In her arms was a small, furry puppy. "Not much of a litter this time. Found homes for all but this little feller. The runt of the litter. Would you like him? He'd be somethin' to look after, you know, take your mind off . . ."

Tears came into Tawny's eyes. "I'd love him. Give him to me." She reached out her arms for him. The puppy snuggled against her. He was reddish brown with shaggy, uneven hair, his eyes warm and brown and infinitely innocent.

"We been calling him Fido," Nellie said.

"Then we will call him Fido."

"You know what?" Nellie laughed. "He's got almost the same color hair as you."

Tawny laughed with her. It was the first time she had really laughed since the accident.

"If Fido takes after his ma and pa he'll be a good hunting dog for Bill."

When Bill came back to the house that day he looked skeptically at Fido. "Don't you have enough to do without taking care of a puppy? Look, Tawny, he'll chew up shoes and clothes and make messes all over the house if you don't keep a close eye on him."

"I *will* watch him! Isn't he cute? Isn't he a darling?" She picked up the puppy and held him up close to Bill. "Just look at him!"

Bill reached out and gingerly patted the top of Fido's head, pulled his hand back when the dog tried to lick him. "Do you suppose he'll grow up to be a good hunting dog?" Bill wondered aloud.

"Nellie thought so. After all, look at his parents, Rover and Rosie." But to herself she thought: *I don't want him to grow up to be a hunting dog. I want him to be* my *dog!*

"We'll see," Bill said. "Just don't let him get on the furniture."

Bill did not take to Fido, and Fido did not take to Bill.

One morning Doug arrived on the porch, gun in hand, his dogs at his heels, to ask Bill to go on a foray with him.

"Nothing big about. Nothing more than a squirrel or two, or a rabbit. Maybe a pheasant. But the weather's good and I just felt like a bit of huntin'."

"Sounds great." Bill called out to Tawny, "I'm off with Doug. Bit of shooting."

She came out of the house, still in her morning dress, dustcloth in hand. "Good morning, Doug."

"Good morning, Tawny. Gonna borrow your husband for a little shooting."

"Of course."

Fido was at her heels. He immediately ran up to Doug, remembering his first master, and Doug reached down to scratch the dog's floppy ears.

"Morning, Fido. You big enough to come along?"

"Of course not," Bill said.

Standing there on the porch, Fido beside her, wagging his tail, Tawny watched the two men leave. The next thing she knew Fido had bounded down the steps, run across the lawn, crawled under the fence, and was at their heels. As well as the heels of his parents.

Tawny called out, "Fido! Fido!" but of course the puppy paid no attention.

When next she saw her puppy he was being carried into the house by Doug. "What is it, Doug? What happened?"

One of Fido's paws was encased in a homemade splint.

"Just a litle accident, Tawny."

"Accident?"

"Fido shouldn'a come with us. He's too young. But there he was tearing along after us, no matter how many times we told him to go home. And then this rabbit no bigger than Fido come along, and Fido all of a sudden started chasin' that rabbit. Bill, he had his gun cocked to get the rabbit and fired too fast and not too careful and Fido was in the way . . ."

"Fido! Poor Fido!" She held out her arms.

"Tawny . . ."

"Yes?"

"Don't you take on too much over that pup. I have a feelin' it might make your husband jealous."

Tawny did not try to answer. She held Fido close. She thought: *this crazy little pup is all I have in the world.*

4

Lance enjoyed the voyage from San Francisco to Astoria. In a way it was good to be back at sea again, and this time he was not the only passenger. There were a few assorted individuals from all walks of life. Some were going to Oregon Territory but most of them were headed for Washington. The migrants had one common bond: they were all excited about starting a democratic new life.

Washington Territory, which used to be part of Oregon, appeared to be the coming place. It would supply the world with lumber, with fish, with apples. And the newcomers would be a part of it. They could forget businesses that had failed, farms that had been destroyed by tornadoes or floods, loss of loved ones and homes through the tragedy of civil war. They could erase from their minds crimes they had committed.

The feeling was catching. Lance began to wonder if he, too, could begin all over again. He flirted with a young girl who was on her way to meet her fiancé in Walla Walla, where they were to be married. Her young man had gone ahead and established himself before he sent for her. She was a wide-eyed innocent with a lisp. But she was propriety itself and he knew there was no chance that he could go to bed with her. They walked the deck together and at night after supper when they went out to look at the stars he sometimes held her hand. It was all pleasant, adolescent fun.

There were fewer passengers on the boat up the Columbia River to Wallula. And when he asked people about the town of Littleton very few had heard of it. Walla Walla, yes. Twuylip, yes. He began to feel as if he really were headed for the end of nowhere.

By the time he boarded the stagecoach at Wallula he was travel-tired, and some of the enthusiasm about the future that he had felt on the long voyage was fading. The road now was no better than a dried creek bed; his coach jolted and swung. The only real lift he got was from the scenery. They wound around and sometimes over hills covered with evergreens; they crossed rivers that rushed under flimsy bridges with a roar like that of the sea. Fish were frequently jumping in the rivers and streams. Now and then he would spot a snow-covered mountain, lording it over the rolling green hills.

It was night when he arrived in Littleton, and raining. The Littleton Hotel was a small three-story building with a narrow front porch lined with rocking chairs. The small lobby inside was deserted, and a man was dozing behind the desk. On the other side of the lobby two swinging doors led to the saloon-dining room, which also looked quite deserted.

The desk clerk woke up and Lance registered. He asked to have his bags taken to his room but said that he would visit the saloon before he went up. The clerk nodded and pressed a bell, and the bellhop—an old Indian with a face like a death mask—came out of the woodwork, or so it seemed, picked up the bags, and staggered up the stairs.

There were only two customers in the saloon. They were playing checkers and did not look up as Lance came in. The bartender wore his thin hair in a swirl to cover his bald spot. His bow tie was jaunty, his apron large and very red. He did not smile as Lance approached. He looked respectful enough, but his eyes were full of curiosity.

Of course, Lance thought, *I'm a stranger in town. They will be asking me why I'm here,* as people during his trip had asked him why he was going to Littleton. All along the way his answer had been, "To visit friends."

He smiled at the bartender. "Brandy, if you please?"

"Ain't got no brandy tonight. Got whiskey."

"Whiskey, then."

"Coming up."

He held the glass under the spout of a keg, served up a generous shot, and shoved it across the bar.

Lance lifted his glass and nodded at the man. No response. Lance said, "Lots of rain tonight."

"Hadn't noticed." The man mopped efficiently at the bar, keeping his eyes on Lance. There was nothing like jolly companionship in this saloon! Lance sipped the fiery whiskey. The only sounds were the patter of rain against the windows and the clicking game of checkers in the corner.

Finally, out of the blue, the bartender asked, "What's your line?"

"My line?"

"Yup. Most strangers come in here are selling something."

"Oh, I see. Of course." Lance smiled again. "I'm afraid I don't have any line."

The question, "What the hell are you doing here, in Littleton?" was written all over the man's face so Lance said it again. "I'm going to visit some friends of mine."

"You got friends in Littleton?" He was inspecting Lance's clothes; they had the cut and the style of city clothes. Furthermore they were obviously expensive.

"Mr. and Mrs. Ferguson. Perhaps you know them?"

The bartender smiled for the first time, a broad smile revealing some glittering gold teeth.

"Bill Ferguson? He's the only Ferguson I know of in these parts. Sure I know Bill. I never met his missus. But he comes in here regularly, daytime mostly, sits around and has drinks with the fellows. Nice quiet guy, Bill is. So you're a friend of his."

"Yes. We were in college together."

"College? Bill?" His expression was of incredulity.

"Princeton."

"It's funny, he don't talk like a back easter. Like you do."

"Bill's from San Francisco. I don't think he spent enough time in the East to change his accent. But I was born and raised in New York City."

"You don't say! You're a long way from home."

"A long way." *It was,* thought Lance. *This bar, this hotel, this town could all be on another planet.*

"Your glass is getting kind of low," the man said. "Here, let me add a splash. No extra charge."

"Thank you. I think I need it. It's been a long hard day, getting up here from Wallula. I thought it was too late to try to reach Bill tonight. He says it's walking distance so maybe in the morning I'll just hike out and knock on his door."

As he poured the "splash" into Lance's glass the bartender said, "Ain't seen much of Bill the last week or do. Don't know if he's having some trouble there with the ranch or what. I did hear as how his wife is expecting."

Expecting! Tawny expecting? It gave Lance a jolt. He couldn't imagine her pregnant. He couldn't think of her becoming a mother. In fact, it was hard to think of her being a housewife, doing housework in a place she had described herself, in her letter, as primitive. When he pictured her in his mind he thought of The Golden Parrot and her standing there singing. Or he thought of the long-ago, younger Tawny, walking into his study.

Magnetic healing. Magnetism. She was full of her own. A special, different, unique female.

A pack of nonsense you are thinking, he told himself. *She's the wife of your friend. And she's pregnant.*

Lance finished the drink, declined another. "I think I had better turn in," he said, and paid his bill.

The sleepy desk clerk gave him his room key, attached to a big block of wood with the number on it. "Third floor," the clerk said with a yawn. "Good night, sir."

"Good night."

The two flights of stairs were steep, but Lance's long legs took them easily. There were gaslights at he turns of the staircase and one down the hall by which he was able to make out his room number. The gaslight in his room had been lit for him. It was a sparse room, containing the necessities: bed, washstand with pitcher and bowl, chamber pot, and an armoire. There were two paintings on the wall of "Cupid Awake" and "Cupid Asleep" which might have been amusing but tonight were only nauseating. Up here in the middle of a natural wilderness the man-made world lost all beauty by comparison.

Soon after he got into bed he fell asleep, lulled by the constant drumming of the rain on the roof.

The next morning he was having breakfast in the corner of the saloon that passed for a dining room, when Bill suddenly walked in.

Lance had been enjoying the breakfast, a big one: steak, eggs, hashed brown potatoes, and good strong coffee, as he had been enjoying the sunshine pouring through the rain-splattered windowpane.

Bill dashed across the room, his hand outstretched.

"Lance, you're here! I came as soon as I heard. How long have you been here?"

"Since late last night. How did you know I was here?"

"Messenger from the hotel, this morning. I'd left instructions with them."

Bill was tanned and looking very healthy, but his face was strained, drawn, not the face of a happy man. They shook hands and then Lance invited him to sit down and have a cup of coffee with him while he finished his breakfast. Bill agreed.

First they talked of the obvious: how Lance's trip up the coast had been, and up the Columbia, and so on.

"I'm sorry, we have no guest room, as Tawny wrote you."

"It's quite all right, Bill. I wouldn't want to impose on you that much. I'll make out fine, right here. More coffee?"

"No, thank you. We can have some more when we get out to the house."

Lance chose not to mention the bartender's gossip, so he felt obliged to ask, "How is Tawny these days?"

Bill almost scowled. "Not very well."

"I'm sorry to hear that."

"She's . . . I'd better tell you, Lance, before I take you out there. So you will understand."

Bill had turned his face, his voice unnaturally shy. He was silent for a bit, twiddling the teaspoon in its saucer. When he spoke he was close to stammering. "What I'm trying to prepare you for is that she's not the same Tawny you remember, all sparkle and life. She's . . ." Again he broke off.

"Look, Bill, are you trying to tell me that she is pregnant?"

Bill looked at him, his face anguished. "No, she's not. That's it. She was pregnant, but she had a miscarriage."

"I see. I'm sorry."

Bill's eyes had darkened. He let go of the teaspoon, clenched his fist, and banged it against the table. "The damn fool went horseback riding. I *told* her not to. I told her a *thousand* times. But she paid no attention. And she lost my son."

Lance did not like Bill's anger, which it seemed unjustified. But feeling inadequate he again said, "I'm sorry."

Bill went on. "She's irresponsible. Completely irresponsible. Headstrong. Wild."

Lance made no comment but he thought to himself: *That much is like the girl I remember. Bill has not succeeded in domesticating her. He should never have tried.* After a moment he said, almost as if he were talking to himself, "So the bloom is off the rose."

Bill's head jerked up. "What do you mean by that?"

"I mean, as they say, the honeymoon is over."

"Dammit, I still love her!" Bill cried. "No matter

what I've said, no matter what she's done, I still am in love with her."

"And she?"

"She's my wife," Bill said flatly. "That's all that matters." *She'll be my wife again,* he was thinking, *as soon as she is well, when the bleeding stops. Then I can quit playing the role of gentle nurse and become a man again.*

When the messenger from the hotel had arrived that morning with word that Lance had arrived in Littleton, Tawny's heart gave a great jump.

It was the first time that Bill had seemed happy since the night of the accident. "I hope you feel well enough to straighten up the house, Tawny. And to plan a really nice lunch, while I go to town to bring him out."

She assured him she felt well enough. She only dabbed at dusting, sloshed the dishes through suds and rinse water and stacked them up to dry. Then she concentrated on what, to her, was the important thing: getting dressed.

She had not had a new dress since she left San Francisco, almost a year before. She had no idea how the styles might have changed. She must not dress up too much; it would not be appropriate to be overdressed in this modest little house. Her gray merino would probably be the best, although it was a little warm for this time of year. A brooch at her throat to temper the harsh, high neckline.

She spent some time at her dressing table, arranging her hair. She tried three styles before she was satisfied. She picked up her hand mirror and viewed herself from all angles, approving of what she saw. If only there were a full length mirror! She would just have to hope that she looked all right.

She came out of the bedroom and gave the living room a cursory look-over. It seemed plain and drab to her. Then she had an inspiration. What the room needed was color. She must pay a visit to Nellie's garden.

The sun was shining brightly after the night of rain; it glittered on wet leaves and wet pale green sprouts on the evergreens, and on puddles along the path and the road. She held her skirts high as she hurried to the Fitzroy house, with Fido at her heels.

It was the first time she had walked over there since her accident. Nellie opened her front door and emerged as Tawny opened the gate. "Land alive, what are you doin' runnin' around like this?"

"Nellie, can I pick some of your lilacs?"

"Of course you can pick some of my lilacs. If you'd just told Bill to stop in on his way to town and tell me I'd 'a been glad to bring 'em over. He did stop for just a minute to tell us his friend had got here. Which I already had figgered out when I seen the boy from the hotel go by this morning."

"Thank you, Nellie. I'd better hurry and get them."

"I'll help you."

They were still in the garden when they heard Bill's buggy clatter past.

Lance thought when they approached the Fitzroy house that it was Bill and Tawny's place, and almost said something complimentary about the huge fireplaces flanking its sides. He was glad he had not spoken as they passed the house and rode on around a bend to another place. His first reaction was that it was so small! No more than a shack, with an ugly little outhouse at the rear. "No guest room," Bill had said. There was no room for a guest room!"

Bill stopped the buggy at the foot of the front steps. The front door was open, but Tawny wasn't in sight. "I'll let you off here," Bill said, "while I put this trap away. Go on in the house, Lance."

Lance climbed the steps to the porch and stood there a moment looking around before he went inside. The room into which he stepped was depressingly drab. How could Bill stand to live in such a place, after the grandeur—albeit faded—of his San Francisco home? He stood there hesitant, waiting for Tawny to appear. He cleared his throat to announce his presence, but there was no sound of her.

Bill came running into the house. He called out, "Tawny, Lance is here!" When there was no answer he ran first into the kitchen, where he saw the stack of dishes drying, and no sign of any food preparation having started.

Damn the woman, where was she? He emerged from the kitchen and darted into the bedroom, still calling.

Lance, standing in the living room, saw her first. She stood riveted in the still-open front door, breathless, her arms loaded with lilacs, half-silhouetted in the morning sunlight that shone on the mass of dark red hair. She was fresh and lovely, like the spirit of springtime incarnate.

She murmured, "Lance . . ." It was all she could say. There he was, just as she remembered him. In that small room he seemed bigger than ever.

They stood looking at each other, finding no words, the puppy scurrying around them, as Bill came back from the bedroom.

"Tawny, where the devil have you been?"

"Picking lilacs."

"Picking lilacs! You knew Lance was coming; you

knew I'd be bringing him back from town any moment. And you go pick lilacs!"

"That's why I went!" she cried, hugging the lilacs to her like a shield. "I wanted to make the living room look nicer. Excuse me, I'll go find a pitcher or something to put them in."

She walked across the room and into the kitchen, her head high. While she was pulling down a pitcher for the lilacs she remembered she had done nothing about lunch, not even planned it.

Bill gave a shrug and lifted his hands with a gesture of hoplessness as Tawny left the room. "What can I do?" he asked.

"It was a decent enough impulse, Bill," Lance said gently.

"What was?"

"Picking the lilacs."

"Irresponsible," Bill snapped. "God knows what we'll have for lunch."

"It doesn't matter."

"It does to me!"

Tawny came back into the room, carrying the flower-filled pitcher. She set it on the center of the mantelpiece, stepped back, and looked up at the men.

"The lilacs are lovely, Tawny," Lance said. "Are they from your own garden?"

"No, from my neighbor's. We haven't been here long enough to have a real garden."

"Of course not."

"I meant to start some plants this spring but I didn't get around to it."

"I understand you've been ill."

Tawny flashed a look at Bill. How much had he told Lance? What had he told him?

"I was," she said quietly. "I'm all right now."

That brought a look from Bill.

"What's the dog's name?" Lance asked.

"Fido," Tawny told him.

"Fido? Really? I never knew a dog named Fido, except in books." He smiled.

"He came with the name," Tawny explained. "I didn't want to change it, for fear of confusing him."

"Of course not." Lance bent down and petted the puppy, and the puppy's tail swung back and forth like a pendulum.

"A silly name for a silly dog," Bill said. "Tawny, what are we having for lunch?"

"I haven't decided."

"Well, while you *are* deciding, I'll show Lance around the ranch. All right, Lance?"

"All right."

Lance now knew he was coming face to face, for the first time in his life, with actual poverty. Not poverty you heard about or read about, not the nameless faces of street beggars, nor the sight of smoke rising from the tin chimneys of the little shacks where people camped out in Central Park, but poverty or near poverty that was part of real people, people who were your friends. No servants. No servants at all! He did not like the picture of Tawny down on her knees scrubbing or bending over a washboard. She had lovely, slender, aristocratic hands. He didn't want to glance at them now, he didn't want to see them rough and reddened as they very well might be.

It seemed wrong for the two of them to stalk off on a sightseeing tour while Tawny decided about lunch, planned it, cooked it, all by herself. He was not sure of the protocol in such a situation, but he felt he must make some attempt to rectify it.

He had said "All right," but now, looking at

Tawny sinking wearily into a chair, he added, "Shouldn't we stay and help Tawny?"

"It's two hours until lunchtime," Bill said. "She has plenty of time."

Tawny couldn't get over the way Lance was looking at her today. Not at all as he had before, not ever. He was being polite and considerate. She smiled at him, hoping the smile would express her gratitude. "Lunch will be on time, Bill."

"I certainly hope so."

Bill had started for the door. As Lance passed the chair where Tawny was sitting he paused and touched her shoulder. In a voice scarcely above a whisper he said, "It won't matter if it's late. I ate an enormous breakfast."

She laughed, and said, with only a touch of sarcasm, "It would matter to Bill. It always does."

Bill turned back. "What are you two whispering about?"

Now Lance laughed. "At you, Bill, for being such a fussbudget over lunchtime."

Bill frowned. It wasn't going to be easy having Lance around, encouraging Tawny to be frivolous.

"Come on, Lance, I'll show you the barn first."

"Where, I presume, the cows moo and the horses whinny at your command. All right. Here I come."

Tawny thought: *it's going to be different with Lance around. He can make fun of Bill and get away with it.* She felt as if, in a strange way, Lance had become her ally.

Lunch. What to have for lunch. There were a lot of leftovers: scraps of mutton, vegetables. She would make a soup. A big, thick—put in lots of flour—soup with loads of leftovers floating in it.

She planned it a bit maliciously, knowing that Bill was not fond of soup.

* * *

Lance was polite about the livestock, but Bill was quite sure that he had little interest in them. He asked more questions about the land itself—how big was it, had he explored all of it, just where did the edge of his property lie, and so on. He was surprised and puzzled by Bill's vagueness.

Finally, as they were walking back toward the house, Lance said, "So you've not looked for gold, at all."

"I've been too busy."

"Too busy to want to better yourself?"

"I am bettering myself, as it is. Look, Lance, the gold was only a rumor. My neighbor and good friend Doug Fitzroy has convinced me of that."

"So Tawny said in her letter. That's just one man's opinion."

"He's lived here twenty years or more. He knows this country."

"Look, Bill, I'm going to explore your land, if you won't. With your permission, of course."

Bill smiled. "Of course you have my permission. But, if you'll pardon my asking, what do you know about looking for gold?"

"A little. I talked with old-timers in San Francisco. I have a few tips. I noticed, riding out here, that the road was following a river. Does your land border that river?"

Bill nodded.

"That's the place to start. First I must buy some proper clothing, and hire a horse. That's tomorrow's assignment."

At lunch Lance praised the soup. Sheer politeness, Bill thought. To him the soup was just another of

Tawny's sloppy concoctions. And after lunch Bill dragged Lance off to meet the Fitzroys.

By the time Tawny had finished washing and drying and putting away the lunch dishes she was really weary. She went into the bedroom, closed the door, stripped down to her shift, and threw herself across the bed. She fell sound asleep almost immediately. She did not hear Bill and Lance come back from the Fitzroys, nor did she hear them leave again. She had said she was better, but not all that better, even if the bleeding had stopped.

She awakened at last to Bill's hand, reaching under her shift and touching her between the legs. As she opened her eyes he took his hand away. His eyes were hard. He said, "This morning you told Lance you were all right. But you hadn't told me. You hadn't told me you were clean again."

Tawny did not speak. She was pulling herself out of a deep sleep.

"If you are all right, why are you lying here, in the middle of the afternoon?"

"I was tired. That's all."

"What tired you today? You scarcely touched the house except for those ridiculous lilacs. You made a soup of garbage for lunch. Oh, you were a wonderful hostess!"

Tawny sat up straight. "You needn't be so cross!" she cried. "Lance liked the soup. He liked the lilacs."

"He was only being polite. I was ashamed of you."

Tawny lifted her chin. Her voice was defiant. "I'm not going to give you the satisfaction of apologizing. Now or ever again. Do you understand? No matter how much you browbeat me, how often . . ."

He slapped her. Then, as she fell back on the bed he seized her shift and ripped it from her. With both hands he clutched her breasts in a grip that was painful.

"There is no baby to be protected," he told her in a hoarse voice. "There is no baby now."

He let go of her and began pulling off his trousers. She rolled over toward the far side of the bed but he quickly jerked her back. He looked down at her as he removed the rest of his clothing. There she was again, his Tawny, his wife, his, his, his. Her irresponsibility did not matter, nothing mattered, not when she lay naked in their bed. He would have her again. He would have her as he had that night he impregnated her.

He began stroking her, every part of her, watching her, eager eyes, hopeful.

In spite of her anger with him, Tawny felt herself gradually softening. It had been a long time, a long strange time, and her body was hungry. *I am no better than an animal,* she thought, *letting him do this to me, letting him make my body feel something that my heart cannot.* She closed her eyes against the sight of him, she held back tears of shame, until he entered her and then she cried openly. Tears poured down her cheeks and she began sobbing. But he paid no attention; he just went on plunging and plunging again until, at last, he fell down upon her, panting.

She lost consciousness.

When she came to Bill was kneeling beside her, holding a wet towel to her forehead. "Tawny, are you all right? Tawny, what happened?"

She did not try to answer. She gave him a sardonic smile. She said, "I guess it's time for me to fix dinner."

"No dinner. I'll find something."

She laughed. The idea of Bill going into the

kitchen and fixing himself something to eat was funny. Very funny.

He took the wet towel away and put his face close to hers; his mouth was open, ready to swallow her with a kiss. She turned her head.

"Go away, Bill! Go away! Leave me alone!"

Through half-closed eyes she watched him pull on his clothes and leave the room. After the door had closed behind him she began crying again.

5

When Tawny finally pulled herself together, wrapped a dressing gown around her, and left the bedroom, it was dark.

She lit a lamp in the living room. There was no sign of Bill. She moved on into the kitchen and lit another lamp. There was no sign, either, indicating that Bill had eaten anything. She fixed bowls of bread and milk for Fido and herself and sat down at the kitchen table to eat. She was physically near exhaustion but her head was clear, unemotional. She was through with tears.

Meanwhile, Bill was sitting in front of the Fitzroy fireplace, talking to Doug. He had arrived at the house just as they were sitting down to supper.

"You et yet?" Nellie asked. "If not, come in and pull up a chair. Where's Tawny?"

"In bed."

"She sick?"

"Just tired."

"She's tryin' to do too much, that girl." Nellie shook her head. "Soon's I eat I'll take a run over and look in on her, while you two are yakking away."

"You don't need to, Nellie." He didn't want Nellie Fitzroy to walk into the house and find Tawny crying.

"Will anyhow. You two don't want me around when you get to talkin' horses."

So they ate supper, pork and beans and brown bread, for which Bill had little appetite. But he must eat, he must forget what had happened between him and Tawny, he must talk with Doug about the real reason for Lance being on the ranch. That afternoon Lance had not once spoken the word *gold*. They had exchanged the briefest of amenities with the Fitzroys; the Fitzroys and Lance appeared ill at ease.

Now, in front of the fire, a cup of corn whiskey in his hand, Bill asked Doug, "And what did you think of my friend?"

"Nice gent. Nice, citified gent. Don't see many like him in these parts. Must have had a real hankering to see you, coming all this way up here."

"He didn't come just to see me."

"No? You think mebbe he plans on settlin' up here?"

"I very much doubt that."

"No. He didn't strike me as the kind of fellow what would take to ranching. So what is the bee in his bonnet?"

"That mythical gold."

"*What* kinda gold? What you talking about?"

"The vein of gold that is supposed to be on my land."

"Oh, that! The fellow's crazy, Bill. He don't look like no prospector, either. He don't look like he needed to find gold, if you ask me."

"He doesn't need to, Doug. He's independently wealthy. For him it's just an adventure, just trying to find it. That's the sort of fellow he is."

Doug grunted. "You gonna let him look?"

"I even said I'd help him."

"You're wastin' your time, Bill. I toldya so a thousand times."

"I know you have. And I've told Lance your opinion. It doesn't make any difference, not to Lance. So it looks like you'll have to handle our mutual affairs for awhile. I'll do what I can, but part of the time I'll be at Lance's beck and call."

Doug tossed off his whiskey, got up, reached for the jug on the mantel and poured himself another drink.

"You young guys are crazy in the head," he laughed. "When you get to be my age you won't get such notions. You wait and see."

Tawny was still in the kitchen when she heard the knock on the front door. Fido barked excitedly as Tawny hurried out into the living room. "Who is it?" she asked automatically before she opened the door, although she was quite sure it would be one of the Fitzroys.

"Me. Nellie. Bill said you was in bed. Get back there!"

Tawny half-smiled as she opened the door. "Come in, Nellie!"

The neighbor stepped across the threshhold, gave a little shiver. "Shore is chilly in here. You need a fire on these spring nights or else catch your death of cold."

"I'll make one," Tawny said. "Right away."

"No, you don't. You just set down there. I'll make the fire." She gave Fido a pat, and then pushed Tawny toward a chair and looked down into the girl's face. "You been cryin'."

Tawny nodded. "I'm through now."

"Good." Nellie bustled about with twigs and kindling and in a surprisingly short time had produced a fire.

Tawny said, "I should be offering you tea. Or coffee. But I'm afraid the fire's out in the kitchen."

"Don't bother yourself, child. I jest finished supper. You have any supper?" She gave Tawny a sharp look.

"Yes. I ate something."

Nellie sat down in the rocker opposite Tawny, in her usual arms-folded position, rocking slowly and studying the younger woman's face for a long moment before she spoke. "Why were you crying, honey? Still thinkin' about that baby?"

Tawny shook her head, turned her face away. "No, it wasn't the baby. Not anymore."

"I don't like to pry, Tawny. But I can't help knowing that something's wrong and if I could help I sure would like to."

"I don't think there's much you could do, Nellie."

"No? I could give advice, mebbe. Free advice. Now, without being critical—'cause I don't like to be critical, not of good neighbors like you two young folk—but it don't seem to me that Bill is treatin' you right. Comin' over to our house tonight just to yap with Doug, leavin' you here, all wore out, with no fires goin'. It's enough to make a body cry, like you was a doing."

"Bill is like that, Nellie. I've had to get used to it. A wife has certain duties to perform. No matter how she feels."

It was good to blurt it out to someone.

"But for a while there, after your accident, he was treating you decent, wasn't he?"

"Yes. But you see I made the mistake of saying in front of his friend this morning that I had been ill but now I was all right. I did feel all right this morning when I came over for the lilacs. Remember?"

Nellie nodded. "But I was afeared you were tryin' to do too much, remember?"

"I didn't do too much. That wasn't what made me tired."

"What did?"

"Bill. You see, being all right to him meant only one thing. So when I lay down to rest this afternoon he came to me."

"If you weren't ready, child," Nellie said after a moment, "you coulda told him."

"I had stopped bleeding. That had been all that had held him off!" Tawny's eyes flashed angrily.

"But weren't you ready, Tawny? After all, it musta been a long time since you was together."

"I wasn't ready to be slapped, to be hurt!"

"Bill hurt you? I can't believe that, somehow."

"Of course you can't. Nice Bill. Bill the polite gentleman. You don't know Bill. Nobody knows what Bill is really like, I think, except me.

"On our wedding night he tore off my clothes, the way he tore off my shift this afternoon. He was rough. It's all part of his way of making love. Look! Just look at the bruises from the way he grabbed me this afternoon!" She pulled open her robe and revealed her breasts, and even by fire and candle light the bruises were visible.

"Do you wonder that I was crying, Nellie? Do you blame me?"

"Of course not. Your poor darling. I had no idea."

Tawny covered her breasts again. She looked down into the fire. After a moment she said, "The worst part of it is that I feel depraved by all of it. Depraved. Disgusted with myself for letting him, in spite of his roughness, arouse me."

Nellie could not think of an answer. She got up and pushed at the fire with the poker, threw on another log.

"So now," Tawny said, "what about some advice? The advice you offered."

"Well, I've been thinkin'. Nothing like this ever happened to me, you know. I'm a tough old bird; I've always been that way, even when I was a young bird. But Doug allus treated me like I was a delicate little flower. He never hurt me, not even on our weddin' night; he has always been kind of sweet and shy about lovemaking. I know that sounds odd for a big old guy like him, but that's the way he is. But if he ever had tried to do any of them things you say Bill does, I tell you I would have slapped him down good. I would have let him have it."

Tawny shook her head. "I don't think I could stop Bill. It's not only that he's strong, he's stubborn about having his own way. In anything. I think he'd be happy to rape me if he couldn't have me any other way."

"Don't wait until you're in bed, Tawny, to let him have it, like I put it. In the cold light of mornin', say like tomorrow mornin', you just lay it on the line. That you ain't goin' to behave like a wife if he so much as lays a rough finger on you. That if he ever does anything like that to you again you won't get into the same bed with him. Or even, you could threaten to leave him. To just walk out of the house and never come back! Stand up and let him know that you don't intend to be no slave, let him know that women have some rights in this world!"

Tawny thought of Evangeline. This was something Evangeline would have told her, in different words of course, but the essence of the advice was the same.

"It ain't your nature, Tawny, to be tough. But you gotta learn to be. You gotta toughen up!"

After a moment Tawny said, "I think you're right, Nellie. I think I'll try."

"Don't try! Do it!"

"First thing in the morning."

"And you know what might be an idea? To fetch yourself a blanket and go to bed right here on this lumpy couch. That'll be the first big hint about how you feel."

"But he might come after me, after I'm asleep."

Nellie got to her feet. She was smiling her awkward vee-shaped smile as she patted Tawny on the shoulder.

"Don't you worry about that, girl. I'll take care of that. Don't worry, I ain't agonna tell him what we talked about tonight, I won't let him know what I know. But I'll put it to him strong that you ain't well, that you gotta be by yourself this night. I'll tell him I gave you some sort of medicine and you mustn't be disturbed. I'll see to it he don't come near you with a ten-foot pole!"

"Thank you, Nellie."

"Now I'll go find a blanket for you and you just lie down there and start plannin' what you're gonna say and how you're gonna say it tomorrow mornin'."

Nellie found the blanket, tucked Tawny in as if she were a child, and put out the lights in the kitchen and living room. Fido lay down beside the couch. There was still a glow from the fireplace, enough light for one to get about.

"One more thing," Nellie called back from the door as she was leaving. "You make sure you get up first and make him a good breakfast. Don't start being tough right off the bat. But don't be too friendly, neither. Just be quiet and cool like. Understand?"

"Yes. I understand."

"Good night, then. Sleep tight and don't let the bedbugs bite."

Tawny laughed. "That's one problem I don't have."

Nellie shut the door behind her. Tawny lay there looking at the dying coals in the fire, planning her words for the morning.

She was still awake when she heard Bill at the front door. She closed her eyes and lay very still. She listened to his footsteps, heard them stop when he was halfway across the room and guessed that he was looking at her. Then he turned on into the bedroom. Fido had not moved. As Bill closed the door Tawny gave a sigh of relief and again thanked God for Nellie.

The next morning Bill was surprised to wake to the smell of coffee and bacon from the kitchen.

This had never happened before.

It had been a restless, tossing night. So strange to be alone in the bed. A dozen times he had reached out to touch Tawny—just touch her—and found his hand reaching into emptiness.

Nellie Fitzroy had indeed convinced him that Tawny was ill, that she must not be touched that night, but at the same time there was something in her craggy old face that made him wonder exactly what had happened between her and Tawny. She was not exactly unfriendly but neither was there the openhearted warmth that had always been there before. He washed and dressed and hurried out to the kitchen.

Tawny was by the stove, turning the bacon. With

her robe wrapped closely to the curves of her body, with her hair tumbling below her shoulders, she was so appealing. He would have liked to cross over and take her in his arms, but he hesitated.

She looked up. There were circles under her eyes. Her smile was vague, a ghost of a smile, so slight he wondered if he were imagining it. She said, "Good morning," and looked back at the bacon.

"Did you sleep well?" he asked.

"I slept."

"And how do you feel this morning?"

"Very well, thank you."

"I slept badly. Very badly."

"Oh?"

"You weren't there."

Still she watched the bacon. After a minute she said, "This is not quite ready but the coffee is. Would you like a cup while we're waiting for the bacon?"

"Yes, I would. I need a cup of coffee."

He started to sit down at the kitchen table but then she said, "It's on the stove. Help yourself."

Always before she had brought the pot to the table and filled his cup. He was about to ask her why she wasn't doing it this morning but something in her manner made him decide it would be smarter not to ask.

He watched her turning the bread that was toasting on the stove top next to the pan of bacon, and then fetching the butter and jam from the cooler, and lifting the bacon to drain. Her movements were swift and graceful; he had always enjoyed watching Tawny doing anything. This morning it was indeed like a performance inasmuch as she never looked directly at him.

Her hand on the cooler door, her back to him, she asked, "One or two eggs?"

"You know I always have two!"

Tawny caught her breath, restrained herself from making an angry retort. Nellie had said to be "cool like." She must keep on trying. She said, "Of course," in a modest voice, reached into the cooler and brought out two eggs for him, one for herself.

He was fussy about his eggs. She knew just how he liked them, once over lightly, cooked with lacy edges, which meant carefully splashing the grease up over the edges but not slopping it over the middle because he liked the yolk soft. Only rarely did she ever succeed in frying them exactly the right way. She hoped this would be one of her lucky mornings. If the eggs weren't right, he would let her know and she would again be obliged to keep a tight rein on her temper. Two of the eggs came out all right. The third, her's, was a mess, so she scrambled it.

They ate in near-silence, speaking only in regard to serving the food. They studied each other's faces, Tawny trying to guess her husband's mood. Finally, as they were finishing the meal, he asked, "Do you feel well enough to fix lunch for Lance again, or do I have to get Nellie over here?"

Lance. She had almost forgotten that he would be coming out again. "We've imposed on Nellie too long," Tawny said quickly. "I'll fix lunch. When do you think he'll be coming?"

"Any time now. When I took him in yesterday I showed him the general store and the livery stable so I imagine he outfitted himself yesterday afternoon. I'd best get to my morning chores before he gets here." He started to get up from the table.

"Bill . . ."

"Yes? What?" He was frowning.

"Don't go out just yet. I want to talk to you."

"Talk to me? About what?"

"Sit down, Bill. Please."

"I've got to feed the stock."

"They can wait. For once."

Slowly he sat down in his chair. "What the devil is it?"

He looked as cross as he could be, as if he would be outrageously unreasonable, but all the same she knew she must speak out. It was not a subject she could lead up to graciously; she must speak the truth and take whatever consequences there were.

"I slept alone last night not because I was ill, but because of a decision I had made."

His face paled. "A decision? What sort of decision?"

She folded her hands and put them on the table in front of her, let her hands cling to one another to give her the strength to speak.

"I've decided I can't go on living the way we have been for almost a year. I mean, I *won't* go on."

"What won't you do?" His voice was brusk.

"I won't go to bed with you if you go on slapping me, hurting me. Look!" As she had the night before for Nellie, she flung back her robe and revealed her breasts. The morning sunshine was sharp and cruel to the bruises on the tender skin. "You did that to me only yesterday!"

He reached a trembling hand across the table to touch them. "Oh, Tawny, my darling!" but she backed away, and got to her feet, wrapping the robe tightly around her.

"I'm your wife, but I am *not* your slave!" Tawny cried.

"It is only because I love you so much," Bill protested. "I can't help myself when we are in bed together. When I see you lying there naked something happens to me, something I am powerless to help . . ."

Despite his words, his tone and the expression on his face were that of Bill the wooer, the serious young man. It was hard, as Nellie had said, to believe that he could be physically cruel. But he had been, and he would be so again, if she did not stop him. "You're going to have to help it, Bill. You're going to have to stop being such a beast."

"What if I can't?"

Again she remembered Nellie's words of advice. "I shall leave you."

"No! Oh, Tawny, you wouldn't! You couldn't! Oh, Tawny, no!"

"I could. I would. I'd walk out of this house and never come back."

"But where would you go? What would you do?"

"Look, I may be your wife, but I am a woman, too. I am a human being. You are not my whole world. I won't grovel at your feet asking for favors. You are going to swear never to hurt me again. Only then will I be willing to share the same bed with you. And if once, just once, you start to behave as you have been, I'll leave you. I'll leave you—if it means getting out of bed and walking off naked into the night. Do you understand? Do you believe me now?"

Never had he seen her so angry. Never had she seemed more beautiful. Never had he wanted more to possess her.

"Oh, Tawny!" He got up and moved beside her, knelt down. "Oh, Tawny! I swear I will never hurt you again. Never!" He put his arms around her and buried his face in her lap.

At that moment there came the knock on the door.

6

By the time Bill opened the door for Lance, Tawny had fled to the bedroom. For a moment Bill almost didn't recognize Lance in his cotton pants and open-necked shirt, very much the same outfit that he himself was wearing.

"You're bright and early," was Bill's greeting.

"Too early?"

"No. Not at all." But Bill knew he was tense after that scene with Tawny and he knew that Lance was quite aware of it.

"I went to bed early," Lance told him. "Nothing much to do in this town. And so I woke up early. Well, at least I didn't get you out of bed."

"Oh, no. I've had breakfast already."

"And how is Tawny this morning?"

"All right. Look, would you mind waiting while I feed the stock?"

"Of course not. I've all the time in the world."

"There's coffee in the kitchen if you would like it."

"Thanks, I'll have a cup. I'm sure Tawny's is much better than what I had at the hotel this morning."

"Don't be too sure. Making coffee is not one of Tawny's prime achievements."

Lance walked into the kitchen. The dirty plates and silverware were still on the kitchen table. He took a cup from a shelf. It was cheap, heavy crockery. Again he was aware of how poor they were. He poured himself a cup of coffee, pushed back the dirty dishes to make room, and sat down at the table.

The coffee was good. He wondered at Bill's belittling remark, and other slurs he had made about his wife. He seemed to criticize her almost constantly. He had his back to the door to the kitchen and he did not see Tawny when she came in. But he had heard her footsteps and turned his head as they stopped.

Fido ran over and sniffed Lance's feet and Lance reached down to pet him. Tawny stood there as she had the day before in the front doorway, with the lilacs. Her eyes were startled, almost frightened as she looked at him.

He got to his feet. "Good morning, Tawny. Bill told me to help myself to coffee. It's awfully good."

"Thank you!" She was surprised and pleased. But she was embarrassed to have Lance here in her untidy kitchen. She said, "Sit down, finish your coffee. I'll just clear these away."

"No rush." He smiled at her. "Won't you join me?"

She hesitated, but the smile proved irresistible. She picked up her cup, went over to the stove and filled it, and came back to the table.

"How are you today?" he was asking. He had noticed the circles under her eyes.

"All right."

"That's what Bill said. But I don't believe either of you."

"Why not?"
"You look tired."
"Perhaps I am. A little."
"You work too hard, Tawny. You have too much work to do."
"It can't be helped," she said, resignedly, stirring sugar and cream into her coffee. "What's the old saying? 'Man may work from sun to sun but woman's work is never done.' "
"I like what Alexander Pope wrote better: 'Some men to business, some to pleasure take, but every woman is at heart a rake.' " His eyes were mischievous now.
Tawny looked down into her coffee cup, embarrassed. Was the way this man made her feel the key to her real character?
"This isn't where you belong, girl. This isn't the life you should be living. Or that you want to live. Is it?"
She didn't answer.
"If we can find that gold, everything will be changed. I can picture you and Bill in a fine house. I can see you, dressed to the teeth, playing the role of charming hostess—which I am sure you could play much better than you do the role of housewife."
Tawny tossed her head. "You don't think very much of me, do you? No more than you did the first time we met."
"What do you mean?"
"You know what I mean!" She got up and began clearing the table, putting the dishes into the sink. "Those lines you just quoted about men and women, that's what I mean. You look down on me. I'm not what you think I am. I am a respectable married woman!" He watched her attack the dishes as if they were her enemy, and in spite of himself he had to

laugh. He was still laughing when Bill walked into the kitchen.

"What's the joke, Lance?"

"Nothing much. Your wife said something funny. Are you ready?"

Bill gave one glance at Tawny's angry face. Then he said, "I'm ready if you are."

After they left Tawny mumbled "Something funny!" to herself. Something funny? She *was* a respectable married woman; she had been one now for almost a year. And she was a housewife. And she hated it. She hated both being respectable and doing housework.

Life fell into a kind of pattern. Lance appeared regularly every morning. He began bringing groceries to help repay them for the lunches he ate every day and for occasional dinners. Dining at the hotel was a lonely business and the food was terrible. Bill might criticize Tawny's cooking but Lance always praised it.

He was now exploring every acre of the ranch. Sometimes Bill went with him; sometimes he rode alone. He had learned from his talk with old California prospectors the various ways in which gold might occur in a lode. When it was discovered in California in 1849, the diggings had been in ravines with the ore lying concentrated on bedrock, exposed by eroding streams. Gold discovered on the Fraser River in Canada in the eighteen fifties had been in fine streaks in gravel and sand, through the terraces of hills and valleys running back from the river. So Lance began looking upward from the banks of the Green River.

The river bordered two sides of Bill's property and there was a lot of land to explore. He was able to ride horseback part of the way, but other parts were overgrown and had to be hacked through on foot. It was hard and frequently frustrating work. But he stuck to it. It was the first real challenge he had faced in all his carefree life and he warmed to it.

Occasionally he and Bill would go fishing, early in the morning, but soon Lance begged off. To him it was incredibly dull just to sit and wait.

Hunting and fishing were what he was officially doing here in Washington Territory. That was what he told the people he met in Littleton. Only the Fergusons and the Fitzroys knew about his search for gold.

Littleton had a name but that was about all it did have. It was not a town yet, only a crossroads. The postmaster doubled as manager of the general store. Many of the business people appeared to be related. The bartender, whose name he soon learned was Harry, was the brother of the man who owned the hotel; the owner's wife was the cook. Most of the town's residents lived out in the country on ranches. Often Lance was the only person in the saloon of an evening.

One rainy night the swinging street doors of the saloon were pushed open and a little gray creature slid in. That was Lance's first impression of the girl in a wet gray raincoat that was much too big for her, with a gray shawl over her head. She slithered over to the bar where Lance was leaning, but she did not look at him.

"Vivian, I told you not to hang around here," Harry said. "Your pa will have a fit."

"The old man's so drunk he doesn't know or care where I am. And I'm hungry. Can't you give me something? We don't have any food in the house and

Pa's been drunk all day. He spent all his money on whiskey."

"Okay, okay, this one time," Harry growled. "I'll see what's left in the kitchen."

Lance smiled at the girl and, very shyly, she smiled back. She pulled off the shawl and revealed a head of silky soft flyaway hair. Her face was thin and pale. It was a plain, unimaginative face.

"Would you care for a drink?" Lance asked her.

"No, thank you. I don't drink." After a minute she said, "You're new in town, aren't you? Or are you just visiting?"

"Just visiting."

She put out her hand. It was small, the fingers curved like a baby's. "My name is Vivian Norwood."

He shook her hand. "And mine is Lance Oliver. Pleased to meet you, Miss Norwood."

"Most of them call me Vivian."

Harry had come back with a plate full of scraps.

"Thank you, Harry."

She ate quickly, bits of meat and potato and onion, wiping the plate afterward with a piece of bread. Again she said, "Thank you, Harry. Good night." Then she turned and added, "Good night, Mr. Oliver."

"Good night, Vivian."

She vanished as quickly as she had appeared.

"Now you've met her," Harry grinned.

"What do you mean?"

"I mean she's the closest thing this town has to a whore."

"She doesn't look it."

"Nope, she doesn't. Kind of plain. And scrawny, for my taste. But the traveling men report she's not bad. Poor kid lives alone with a drunken father. A real bum. And I can believe she might be hungry, like she said, tonight. But my hunch is she really was looking for a man."

Lance thought: *I think she's got one for one of these nights.*

It happened one night when he had had dinner with Bill and Tawny, another one of those uncomfortable evenings with the two of them, an evening when he had been conscious of the tension between them—and of Tawny. He was aware of her body, aware of her hair and her eyes and her lips.

After dinner he had come back to town and left his horse at the livery stable and walked the few yards to the hotel. As he came up the hotel steps he saw the girl in one of the rockers on the narrow porch. She was curled up, scarcely visible.

She said, "Mr. Oliver?"

"Good evening, Vivian."

"I was waiting for you." She got out of the chair, moved closer to him, and looked up at him.

Lance smiled at her. "You're hungry again?"

Her face was very solemn. "No, I'm not hungry. Not tonight. I'm lonesome."

She was standing very close. As close as she could without their touching. Then she reached out and put one of those small curved hands against his trousers.

"Don't worry about the man at the desk," she whispered. "There's a back stairway. Just tell me your room number."

He laughed and whispered it to her.

First he went into the saloon for a nightcap.

When he reached his room she was leaning against the closed door.

Sleeping with Vivian was not the acme of satisfaction. As Harry had said, she was scrawny. Her breasts were no more than little buttons, her buttocks were bony. But she possessed the energy, the surprising strength that can sometimes belong to thin people. And she was the aggressor. It was immediately clear that she mated not just for money but for her own satisfaction.

She was out of her clothes within a moment after they had walked into his room and closed the door behind them, and starting to help Lance out of his.

"Hurry, Mr. Oliver, hurry! I want to see all of you!"

When his chest was bared she ran her little hands over it with contented sighs, nuzzling her nose against his hairs. She unbuttoned his trousers before he could reach them, pushed them aside, and knelt to kiss his penis.

"You are a beautiful, beautiful man! The most beautiful man I ever . . ."

He pulled her up to her feet and put his arms around her. He put his mouth over hers with a kiss that silenced her and when he finished he pushed her over to the bed.

They did not speak again. It was Vivian's night. He knew that when he saw her again by daylight he would be revolted by what they had done. But that night his body was ripe for fornication . . . with anyone.

Lance had fallen into the habit of delivering the Fergusons' mail on his daily trips out to the ranch. Not that there was much for them. Of course the only mail Lance received was the regular money from his father.

One morning there was a letter for Tawny with a New York postmark. Curiosity made him turn the envelope over and discover that it was from Evangeline McClintock. Good old Evangeline! He hadn't thought of her in months. He handed it to Tawny, watched her read the return address, and saw how her eyes lit up.

"From Wilma, I suppose?" Bill said.

"No, it's from Evangeline. I thought she'd never write!"

"Evangeline?" Bill puzzled. "Who . . ."

"Evangeline McClintock. The lady whose lecture back in San Francisco you refused to attend."

"*That* woman!"

"I went to the lecture. She was marvelous," Tawny said defiantly. "And I had breakfast with her the next morning."

"You didn't!" Bill gasped. "You never told me."

"Why should I have told you? You wouldn't have liked to hear about it. You didn't like the idea of her being a friend of mine."

"She's a friend of mine, too," Lance said, looking at Tawny. "That's why I attended the lecture."

Tawny did not return his glance. She was busy tearing open her letter. She began reading it as she walked away from the two men, out to a chair on the front porch.

My dear Tawny:

You would have heard from me long before this, my child, but I simply have not had time to write to anyone. I have been working with the suffragettes, with my friend Victoria Woodhull in particular. Victoria is quite sincere about wanting to run for President of the United States, but I am afraid in many ways the dear girl has been indiscreet. And having Horace Greeley in the running does make it difficult, and it's difficult enough for a woman.

I was happy to get the news of your marriage. As I told you that long-ago morning you are the sort of person who ought to be married. I can picture you in your little country home with, I am sure, a baby or so to brighten your days.

If someone like you should turn up on the doorstep of the Woman's Center today, alas the poor girl would not be rescued! The Woman's Center is no more. Politicians, mealymouthed ninnies, raised a hue and cry that forced me to close the establishment. Prostitutes condemned to be prostitutes for the rest of their lives. You were spared that fate, dear child, and I rejoice for you in your domestic bliss.

Do write me again with all your news and I promise not to be so dilatory about my reply.

My love, Evangeline.

Tawny folded the letter and slipped it back in its envelope. She sat there holding it in her hand, thinking: what sort of letter should I write Evangeline next time? Dare I pour out my heart to her, as I would if I saw her in person? Or must I keep up the pretense that all is well?

The men had come out of the house now and both stopped to look at her.

"Must have been an interesting letter," Lance said.

"I'd like to read it," Bill added. "I'd like to see just what kind of letter a woman like that one would write."

"You wouldn't be interested," Tawny said quickly, folding the letter and stuffing it into her apron pocket. Bill must never see that letter!

"How is Evangeline?" Lance asked.

"Fine," Tawny said. "And busy. With Victoria Woodhull."

"That one!" Bill snorted. "No, I guess I wouldn't want to read about that nonsense."

After the men had left, Bill off to the barn, Lance on his horse to do more exploring, Tawny sat for a long while, just rocking and thinking. She longed to pour it all out to Evangeline, the real story of her "domestic bliss." Tell her of Bill's physical and mental cruelty and her recent ultimatum. But she would have to request that Evangeline be discreet in her reply, lest the letter fall into Bill's hands.

She recalled his repeated expression, "Married people don't talk about such things." She could imagine him saying, "A wife does not talk about such things in a letter to an outsider."

She went back into the house and cleaned up the kitchen. The phrase "domestic bliss" became more and more ironic as she faced the morning duties. Suddenly she realized she wanted to be by herself, to reread the letter in solitude, to mentally plan exactly what words she would use when writing to Evangeline. She took off her apron and hung it on its peg on the kitchen wall, took the letter from the apron pocket and tucked it down her bodice. Then she went outside and crossed the yard to the barn.

Bill was just coming out. He looked at her in surprise.

"Where on earth are you going?"

"For a ride."

"Are you sure you're well enough?"

Tawny thought: *I'm well enough to cook and wash and clean and let you come at me in bed at night.* She said, "Of course I'm well enough!"

"I don't want you to get hurt again."

"That was a once-in-a-lifetime accident," Tawny said as she brushed past him into the barn.

He watched her lead Brownie out and mount. He looked up at her, his eyes pleading. "Tawny, be careful. Please be careful!"

She turned Brownie's head and galloped off, with Fido chasing behind.

Once on horseback some of the tenseness went out of her. In no time at all the wind had blown away her hairpins and her hair was flowing behind her like a defiant banner.

She passed the corner where the road led off to where the dog had frightened Brownie and she had been thrown. She turned Brownie toward the river, toward her favorite spot. Here she had sat on that long-ago January day when the snowstorm later overtook her. Now, in the summer sun, it seemed a different world. She sat on a rock, looking down at the water. Then she pulled out the letter and read it again. She would hide it from Bill until she had written an answer, and then she would destroy it.

When she heard hoofbeats she jumped to her feet and hurriedly stuffed the letter down inside her dress once more. It could be that Bill had followed her. It would be just like him to come after her.

It was Lance. He jumped off his horse in that quick way of his and walked toward her. "This is a surprise," was his greeting.

"I used to come out here often, before . . . my accident," Tawny said.

Fido was jumping up to be petted by Lance.

"It's a beautiful spot. And you're looking pretty beautiful yourself."

Tawny smoothed at her hair, nervously.

"Don't look so worried, Tawny. I have no intentions of laying hands on a respectable married woman. I should not have teased you the way I did that day."

"But you did!"

"I'm sorry."

"You made me remember . . . things I should not remember. Things Bill does not know about."

"I know. That's why I'm sorry."

He sounded as if he meant it. There was no teasing, no mockery now.

"I'd better get home," she said. "Get back to work."

"You hate it, don't you, Tawny?"

"Yes, I do!" she cried. "I hate it, hate it, hate it! Sometimes I feel like climbing old Brownie and riding far away, as far as I can go. Anywhere!"

"Poor Tawny. I think I understand." He put his arm around her shoulders. He could feel her trembling.

"And to get Evangeline's letter . . ."

"What about Evangeline's letter?"

"She wrote about what she called my domestic bliss. She thinks I'm so happy."

"She hasn't been here. She hasn't seen you as I have."

He longed to take her in his arms and comfort her; he had to remind himself sternly that this was his friend's wife. Even a kindly gesture of friendship, his arm around her shoulders, made his whole being come alive.

"I suppose I'm selfish and ungrateful," Tawny was saying. "He did marry me. He's given me a home. He provides for me."

"And loves you," Lance added.

"In his way."

It was strange to be standing there enjoying the

support of Lance's arm, strange to have him talking to her as a friend.

Lance was having something of the same feeling. He said, "If Bill saw us here, like this, he would be furious," and took his arm away.

For a moment they both looked at each other. There was no need for words, an emotion passed between them, an empathy that was as real as a kiss. They walked over to where the two horses were waiting. He watched her spring up into the saddle. She did not ride sidesaddle; her skirts were lifted, her lovely legs bared. With her hair down she looked like a primitive goddess of long, long ago, not at all like a respectable married woman, a rancher's wife who lived in an ugly farmhouse in the Far West.

He smiled up at her, admiringly. On impulse she blew him a kiss before she rode away.

The talk with Lance made Tawny feel better. She rode home and began preparing for lunch in an almost cheerful manner.

When Bill arrived he came straight into the kitchen. She was standing at the stove, stirring the soup. He came up behind her and put his arms around her, his hands covering her breasts.

"Tonight," he whispered. "Tonight, when we are alone."

She did not want to think about tonight. She had been happier out there in the sunshine beside the river, with Lance's arm across her shoulders!

"What's that?" Bill's hand had felt the crumpled letter she had tucked inside her dress.

"My letter from Evangeline."

"Why on earth is it there?" He took her by the shoulders and whirled her around.

"I took it with me when I went riding. To read it again."

"I don't like to think of it there. Next to your body." He started to put his hand inside her dress but she backed away.

She thought: I don't really need to keep the letter. I can remember all of it, all too well. She lifted one of the stove lids and then pulled out the letter and tossed it into the fire.

"There," she said. "It's gone!"

"Good. Gone and forgotten." He took hold of her waist and leaned over and kissed her, full on the mouth. Then he said, "I may not be able to wait until tonight."

She was quite sure he wouldn't. She was conscious of his eyes, all during lunch. When he had that look she knew he was ready, too ready, whether she was or not. It would be one of those times when he did not try to arouse her, when there would be no teasing period. He would take her, and take her quickly. She was aware, too, that Lance was watching both of them. She wondered if he were conscious of Bill's emotions of the moment.

"I'm going farther afield this afternoon," Lance said. "There's a section a bit south that I've put off exploring because the brush is so thick. Today I'll take an ax, if I may, and hack my way through."

Bill did not seem to be listening.

Tawny said, "He can borrow your ax, can't he, Bill?"

"What?"

"I need an ax this afternoon," Lance explained.

"Of course, of course."

"Want to come along, Bill? I'm going into new territory."

"Not today, Lance. I'm busy here, I'm afraid."

When Lance left that afternoon Tawny started to clear the table but Bill hurried across, took the dishes from her hands, put them back on the table. Then he took her in his arms and kissed her as he had that morning. Afterward he grabbed her hand and pulled her toward the bedroom. As he closed the door she gave him a warning look.

He told himself, *hold back! hold back!* His temples were throbbing with excitement as he begged her, "Please, Tawny, take off your clothes!"

Sunlight was pouring into the room, seeming to convey embarrassment; what they were about to do appeared wicked by daylight. She turned her head as she began to undress.

She was naked, lying on the bed, her eyes closed. She felt his touch, and opened her eyes long enough to see that he had only unbuttoned his trousers. There were no preliminaries, only his lips momentarily on her breasts, his tongue deep in her mouth, and then he parted her legs and his organ entered her, over and over and over again. Afterward they both fell asleep from sheer exhaustion.

They woke to a knocking on the door, to the sound of Lance calling out to them. Bill hastily pulled up his trousers, buttoned them, and stumbled out of the bedroom.

She was still not quite awake when Bill partly opened the bedroom door.

"Tawny, wake up! Tawny, come out and see!"

She sat up in bed, conscious of her nakedness.

"See what?" she asked.

Bill, too, seemed abruptly conscious of her nakedness. "Put on your clothes. And hurry. It's gold, Tawny. Pure gold! He's found it!"

PART IV

1873

1

They had the house built on the highest point of their land. From her front window Tawny could look down across the curve of the river, all the way to Littleton.

In a year's time Littleton had changed from a spot on the map to a town, spreading out north, south, east, and west, thanks to the discovery of gold.

Sitting there on the window seat that summer afternoon, with Fido at her feet, Tawny thought back on all the marvelous and not so marvelous changes in the past twelve months.

The vein of gold that Lance had discovered had stretched on beyond Bill's land, up into the hills. When the two men took samples of ore to the nearest bank in Twuylip, the news of the find spread like wildfire and people began pouring into the territory around Littleton. At first came the prospectors, but the second wave brought builders and shopkeepers, a doctor, a lawyer. Littleton popped up like a mushroom after wet weather; it became a place of excitement and constant celebration.

The vein of gold on Bill's land was the richest in the area; consequently, he became the richest man in town. He accepted the new role with delight. Lance became his silent partner. Bill turned the ranch affairs completely over to the Fitzroys, doubling their land and livestock. He still enjoyed hunting and fishing, but not as frequently as before. He was also less demanding in bed. Again, he had changed. Tawny sometimes felt that she was married to a chameleon.

She was now called upon to play the role of charming hostess, which Lance had said should be her rightful one. Their house was the biggest and grandest in the area. There were cupolas and curved bay windows, gingerbread carvings inside and out, enormous fireplaces in every room. Furniture, including a piano, was shipped from California and from as far east as Chicago.

"Why a piano?" Tawny had asked. "Neither of us plays a piano." Bill's answer had been, "Every proper parlor should have a piano in it."

Bill allowed Tawny to choose colors and patterns for all decoration and she reveled in that assignment. She was also in charge of hiring the servants. Among the people pouring in were those who came not to seek gold but to seek work, people who had lost their homes in droughts or floods, or in the War Between the States.

The first servant Tawny hired was Mrs. Higgins, who combined housekeeper, cook, and laundress. She was a large heavyset creature who loved cooking and who was such a mound of energy that she had to keep busy every moment she was awake. Bill agreed that she could live in what had been their former home. Mrs. Higgins lumbered up the hill early every morning so that when Bill and Tawny woke up their breakfast would be awaiting them. Mrs. Higgins sang religious songs as she worked: "Jesus Loves Me," "Jesus Wants Me for a Sunbeam," "Rock of Ages."

She sang a bit offkey but she sang lustily, and Bill and Tawny would laugh when they were awakened by "What a Friend We Have in Jesus."

One morning as they lay there laughing Tawny rolled against Bill in a way that sent him fondling her breasts.

"I just had an idea," she told him. "You know what I'd like to have? A maid. A personal maid to take care of my clothes and brush my hair and fix my bath." She was remembering the days on the road when she, as dressing woman, so waited on Amanda.

"Then have one." He kissed her quickly and got out of bed. "I'm meeting Lance at the new bank this morning. I've got to hurry."

Tawny folded her arms behind her head and lay back luxuriously. "How shall I find a maid? Nobody's been knocking on the door of late, asking for work."

"Put a sign up in the post office. That's what other folks do."

And it was there that Vivian Norwood saw it.

Among the many changes in Littleton there was the new Green River Hotel, built on the river, several stories high, with grandiose rooms, a long mahogany bar, a big dining room. The old Littleton Hotel had been discarded by its owners when they built the new hotel and degenerated to a shabby rooming house that was soon inhabited by a host of ladies of the evening.

Vivian found herself very nearly unemployed. The new ladies who had come to town were all more attractive than poor, skinny, little Vivian. That wonderful Mr. Oliver had a suite in the new hotel, but he never invited her to visit him. If he met her on the street he tipped his hat and smiled, and was polite, but that was all.

And so one shivery winter morning Vivian wrapped her shawl about her shoulders and walked all the way out of town and up the hill to the Ferguson house. The fat old woman who opened the door when she knocked looked at her suspiciously. "And what do you want, young woman?"

"To see your mistress," Vivian stammered.

"What about?"

"The job. I seen the sign in the post office."

Mrs. Higgins shook her head in doubt but she said, "You might as well come in out of the cold. I'll tell her you're here."

She left the girl in the front hall, opened the sliding doors to the parlor and closed them behind her. Tawny was curled up in a big wing chair in front of the fireplace, reading. One of the joys of being rich was being able to order all the books she wanted, and, furthermore, to have the time to read them. She was still in her robe, her hair tumbled about her shoulders. She bore little resemblance to the lady of the manor this morning.

"Mistress Ferguson?"

Tawny put her finger in her book to keep her place and looked up.

"Yes, Mrs. Higgins?"

"There's a girl here to see you. Says she came about the job."

"Oh, good!"

"I wouldn't know if this one's so good, Ma'am."

"Show her in, anyhow. It's for me to decide if she'll do."

"Yes, ma'am."

Tawny got up from the chair and put her book on

the table beside it, face down, as the girl was ushered into the parlor.

At first Vivian could only stare in amazement at the warm shininess of the room, such a contrast to the gray winter day outside. The firelight reflected on the brass andirons and the brass candlesticks on the mantel, the piano's mahogany gleamed. The wallpaper was blue and gold and the two colors were everywhere, blue velvet drapes, gold upholstered chairs.

Finally her eyes came to rest on the young woman. She was not at all the sort of person Vivian had expected to see. So pretty! So young!

"Mrs. Ferguson?" her question was a real one.

Tawny smiled. "Yes, I am Mrs. Ferguson. And you are?"

"My name's Vivian Norwood. I seen your sign in the post office about you wanting a maid."

The girl looked like a waif to Tawny, so pitifully thin, so pale, her hair hanging limply about her plain little face. She asked, "Have you worked as a maid?"

"No, ma'am," Vivian admitted. "But I kind of need a job."

"I see." Tawny admired her honesty. And she remembered when she had needed a job. Just the girl's appearance made Tawny pity her. "Sit down, Miss Norwood, and let me tell you what the job would be. And you can tell me if you think you could do it."

"Thank you." Vivian sat down on the only straight-backed chair in the room, holding her reticule in her lap, her small hands curled around the handle as if she were clinging to a strap in a carriage, or holding someone's hand.

"I can tell you all about it because I worked as a maid once."

Vivian's eyes widened. "You did?"

"Well, they didn't call me a maid. Because, you see, my mistress was an actress and I was called her dressing woman. I took care of her wardrobe, making sure her clothes were clean and pressed and mended if they needed mending. And I fetched things for her when she was getting dressed. And I ran her bath and laid out her underwear. And I brushed her hair. I even learned how to do her hair. It's things like that, things I do myself now. But I'm getting lazy."

"It don't sound like much work," Vivian said. "But I've got to tell you I've never done nothin' like that. There's never been women around me since I can remember. Only my old dad."

Again Tawny felt pity. And understanding. It might have been herself speaking, a few years back when all she had for family was Pa.

"You've only taken care of yourself, then."

"That's right, ma'am. I've had to do that."

"Do you think you could learn to take care of me?" Tawny smiled at her.

"I'd sure like to try, ma'am." Her returning smile was shy.

They chatted on for a while, getting acquainted. Vivian was seventeen, just two years younger than Tawny. Tawny learned that Vivian had not come to Littleton at the time of the gold rush but had been born there, and lived there all her life. That her father sometimes worked at the livery stable. Not very often because, Vivian explained, he liked drinking better than working.

Tawny asked her if she would like to live in. There was a room in the attic which could be furnished, but on this suggestion Vivian shook her head firmly. "No, ma'am, I like daywork better." When Tawny asked if it were her father who would object Vivian merely said, "No, it's not that. But daywork I would like better. I'll come early, whenever you say, I can stay late, if you want me to." So Tawny agreed that they would try it out on that basis.

For the first time Lance was beginning to enjoy life in Washington Territory. The Green River Hotel was new and bustling, the saloon always filled with adventurers; he was reminded of his voyage up the coast from San Francisco. Again he found himself in a motley crew with one thing in common, the love for a new place, a destruction of the past.

Now it was a pleasure to visit the Fergusons, to see Tawny beautifully dressed and often smiling. He was almost jealous of Bill for having such a wife, for having, it seemed, all that a young man could want of life.

One of the girls who now occupied the old hotel was a satisfactory companion on the rare evenings when he felt like indulging in that sort of thing. He was growing less and less interested in sex for sex's sake. The girl, whose name was Cora, had one attraction beyond her voluptuous body: a sense of humor. She made fun of intercourse, cracked little jokes about it, never took anything seriously.

Once he had asked her, "Cora, have you ever been in love?"

"Yup," was her answer. "But I got over it."

"Oh?"

"He beat me, love, with a buggy whip. Before and after he raped me. I was an innocent babe in the woods, an ignorant virgin. I thought he was the most wonderful man in the world. Until that night. Love? I outgrew it fast. Let's hit the hay, love, the wonderful soft hay—or is it feathers with which you line your lair?"

Cora was infinitely preferable to sad little Vivian. He met Vivian on the street the afternoon of the day she had been out to the Ferguson house. To his surprise she was grinning broadly as he approached her.

"Mr. Oliver!"

"Good afternoon, Vivian." As usual he tipped his hat. "You're looking remarkably bright-eyed today. Something has made you happy?"

"Something has, Mr. Oliver. I've got a job. A decent job."

"Congratulations. I'm happy for you, Vivian. "He really was. There was something likable about this pitiful little tart. "And what is your new job, if I may ask?"

"I'm going to be a lady's maid."

"Not really?"

"Really. At least I'm going to go to work; she's going to try me out and see if I do, and oh, I do want to do because she's such a wonderful person. And I'm not going to live in, like some maids do. I'll still be free at night to . . ." She broke off, a little embarrassed.

"To pursue your former occupation, I imagine," Lance said. "If the lady approves."

"She doesn't have to know what I do when I'm not at her house."

"I suppose not."

"She's so pretty and so sweet and she's not much older'n me. It will be fun to help her get dressed and brush her hair. She has such pretty hair."

"It sounds as if you've been hired by a paragon."

"A what? Like I said, she's a lady."

"Does she have a name?"

"Of course she has a name! Mrs. Ferguson. She lives in that big, big house out on the edge of town above the river. And it's such a nice house . . ."

Lance was scarcely listening as she rattled on. He was wondering what Bill would have to say when he found out who Tawny's personal maid was going to be.

That evening Mrs. Higgins was serving the Fergusons roast pork and sweet potatoes and apple sauce, and as usual Bill was praising her for her cooking. It made meals pleasanter than they had been in the old days, but Tawny could not help resenting the comparison. Conversation was never sprightly at mealtime because Bill preferred to concentrate on the food. Food had always been one of his passions, and now that he was not working on the ranch or exercising outdoors as much his stockiness was gradually turning to fat. He had a paunch, and was developing a double chin.

While the house was being built, while they were in the process of having furniture shipped in—all those months they had found plenty to talk about, even at mealtimes. But now there was little left to say. Bill did not care about reading and did not want her to talk about what she had read.

This night, after dinner, when they were in the parlor and he had lit a cigar, she told him, "I hired a maid today."

"Good, good." He seemed preoccupied and after a moment she knew why. He said, "You know, the trouble with Littleton is there are no social occasions."

"That's true. I guess the town is too new."

"Why don't we start a social season? Why don't we have a party, maybe a series of parties?"

"Who would we invite?"

"The new people. The doctor, the lawyer and their wives. Perhaps the man who opened the Emporium."

Tawny sat up a little straighter. It was beginning to sound like fun.

"And the Fitzroys. They'd love a party."

Bill frowned. "No, not the Fitzroys."

"Why not? They're our best friends."

"They wouldn't do. No, not for this kind of party. We might have them over for dinner sometime, just by themselves."

"Bill Ferguson, you're talking like a snob."

"Am I? There are times when one ought to be snobbish."

"Not for me!" Tawny cried.

Bill smiled. "My dear woman, you cannot help your background. But, as my wife, you should make some effort to rise above it."

"You have no right to say such a thing to me!"

"I have every right. I am your husband."

Tawny jumped to her feet, her fists doubled in anger. "You used to think you had the right to hurt me physically. Now you're doing it with words."

"Don't you remember 'sticks and stones may break my bones but words can never hurt me'?"

"All the same, words can."

"Tawny, let's not quarrel!" He put down his cigar and got to his feet and put his arms around her. "You married me for better or for worse, young lady, and tonight it seems to have been worse. But I'm serious. I want to be somebody in this town, and I want you to be somebody. Here we can be like reigning royalty, if we want to. We'll have something we could not have had in San Francisco."

She knew what he meant. There she would always be remembered as a onetime singing barmaid. Here she had no past. She was just the wife of a rich man. She thought: *I'll pretend to go along with him. But*

I'll go ahead and invite the Fitzroys anyhow. He wouldn't turn them away at the door.

"Let me get paper and pencil," she said by way of acceptance of his idea, "and we can make a guest list so I can send out invitations."

"Good girl."

She went over and sat down at the little escritoire in the corner. She wrote down the names as Bill called them out to her as he paced around and around the room. He was very pleased with himself for having thought of the party. After the list was complete and they had both sat down again in front of the fire he went on talking about it. "I'm sure Mrs. Higgins is capable of making delicious little sandwiches and cakes. I wonder if she knows how to make a really good punch. If not, I'll try to get a recipe from Harry at the hotel bar. Harry's an obliging chap."

"Maybe you'd like to invite him to the party."

"Tawny! There you go again! Harry is a bartender. People do not invite bartenders to their parties."

Again she thought *snob,* but this time she said nothing.

"How many people have we got on the list?" Bill asked.

"At least a dozen."

"I thought so. We may need extra help, serving and all that would be too much for Mrs. Higgins. Perhaps this girl you hired as a maid could also help with serving. Do you think so?"

Tawny laughed. "I really don't know. I don't even know how good she'll be as a maid. She's had no experience."

"No experience at all? Good lord, why did you hire her?"

"I felt sorry for her. And she needs work, poor little thing."

"Tawny, for a grown woman you are so irresponsible. People don't go around hiring servants out of pity, for pete's sake. Servants are hired because they are capable of doing the work you want done!"

"She's awfully willing. I thought it was worth giving her a try."

"Where did you find her?"

"I did what you suggested, put up a sign in the post office and she saw it. And walked all the way out here this morning, and you know how awful the weather was. If you'd seen her, you'd have felt sorry for her, too."

"Not sorry enough to hire her if I didn't think she was capable. How old a woman is she?"

"Seventeen."

"Good lord, an infant."

"Bill, you just called me a grown woman and I'm only two years older than Vivian Norwood!"

"Vivian *who?*"

"Vivian Norwood. It's rather a pretty name, isn't it? Bill, what is it? What's the matter? Do you know her?"

"Oh, my God!" He got up and went across the room to where the decanter of brandy was, poured himself a stiff shot, downed it, and then turned back to Tawny who was sitting there completely puzzled by his reaction to the girl's name.

"You ask if I know her, Tawny. Indeed I do not. But I know who she is as all the other men in town do. You know what you've done, my wife? You've hired for your personal maid the town whore!"

"I don't believe it!"

"Ask anybody." He laughed. "Ask Lance. He knows her."

At first Tawny could only stare at him in disbelief. Finally she said, "But, Bill, she doesn't look like that. She doesn't look at all like those women who came here after the gold rush, those painted women who live in the old Littleton Hotel. She's pale and thin and sort of mousy and very shy."

"She's not shy when it comes to men. I understand she slips into hotel rooms like a little mouse and pops into bed as easily and casually as if she were accepting a glass of water."

Tawny was remembering how adamant the girl had been about moving into the attic room. She kept saying she preferred daywork.

Again Tawny was identifying with Vivian, Vivian who had a drunken father. Perhaps her father made her do what she had done with the men of Littleton, as Pa had sent her that day to Lance Oliver's house. Poor Vivian!

"Well, what are you going to do about her?" Bill was asking.

"Do? What can I do now? She's coming out first thing in the morning."

"Fire her."

"Fire her before she's even started work? I wouldn't do that. I've got to give her a chance. I told her I would!"

"I won't have it!"

Tawny got to her feet and moved toward the door.

"Tawny, I warn you . . ."

She turned, her head held high. "Go ahead and warn me!" she said defiantly. "I'm warning *you*. I'm going to stand by my word." She thought of Evangeline and the Woman's Center. "If she has been what you say she has, I'm going to give her a chance to change. I think she deserves that chance."

Bill was positively glaring now.

"We'll be the laughingstock of Littleton."

"But we'll be doing the right thing."

"Tawny, you're a fool!"

"Good night, Bill." She opened the door and closed it behind her.

She was not quite asleep when Bill came to bed, but she pretended that she was. She was in no mood for continuing their argument or for his trying to make love to her to soften her up, to dominate physically, if he could not do so mentally. She lay on her far side of the bed and he on his. He had not bothered to kiss her good night. He never kissed her unless he was ready for all the rest. In a few moments he was snoring.

Tawny slipped out of bed and went over to the window in the cupola, curled up on the seat, leaned her forehead against the cool glass. Far below the moon was shining on the Green River. There was nothing green about it at night; the moonlight turned the world into black and silver.

Beautiful, yes, but what was she doing here in this far-flung, crazy, newly born town? Condemned to stay here for the rest of her life! She had traveled most of her years; she never had stayed in one place as long as this. Not even in San Francisco. San Francisco had been different; it was a city and somehow to live in a city was like traveling, in a way. In San Francisco, as in New York, a person could cross a street and be in a different world—an Italian world, a Chinese world, a German world. Littleton was Littleton, homogeneous. No change, except for the coming of the gold and the money. No changes as there'd been when she was on the road with Amanda's troupe, nor as there'd been when she was a little girl traveling with Pa.

She was restless. She was not sure what to do

about it except to rebel against Bill's domination, to defy him now and then, just to give herself a sense of independence, of being a person in her own right. She had a feeling that Lance would understand what she was doing.

Tawny and Bill were at breakfast the next morning when Mrs. Higgins announced the arrival of Vivian.

Bill, frowning, said, "Don't show her in just yet. Not until I've left." He hurriedly swallowed the last of the food on his plate and his coffee. "I'm going out to the ranch this morning, do a little shooting with Doug. Do those invitations, won't you?"

"I will. Maybe Vivian can help me."

Bill snorted as he dashed out of the room into the front hall. Mrs. Higgins had ushered Vivian into the parlor and told her, rather sharply, to wait.

Vivian, perched on the same chair where she had perched the day before, jumped to her feet as Tawny came into the parlor. "Good morning, ma'am."

"Good morning, Vivian. I suppose it's all right to call you Vivian now?"

"Of course, ma'am. That's how it should be."

There were shadows under Vivian's eyes, but she was holding herself rigidly erect, full of eager determination to behave properly. Tawny had an impulse to invite her into the dining room, serve her coffee, tell her what Bill had said about her, assure her that it wouldn't make any difference. But then she decided it was too soon for something like that. She would pretend ignorance for the present, pretend that Vivian was just a young girl who needed work.

She must also behave like a mistress. "Vivian, I think first of all we should do something about your clothes."

"My clothes?"

"Hang up your shawl in the hall and come back and let me have a look at you."

Vivian obeyed, and then stood there still clutching her reticule, looking embarrassed.

Tawny said, "You can leave your purse there on the seat of the hat rack. It'll be quite safe."

Again Vivian obeyed. When she came back her shoulders had slumped a little. She was wearing a faded but clean gingham dress. It clung to her small breasts and her bony back.

"I didn't try to dress up, ma'am. I thought maybe for working this would be best. Was I wrong?"

"No, not really. But I think, all the same, I'll send word to my dressmaker."

"But I . . ."

Tawny interrupted, guessing what the girl was thinking. "Don't worry, I'll pay for the clothes. I just like bright, new-looking things around my house. And that's the way I'd like you to look."

Vivian's eyes lit up. She liked the idea of new clothes. She said, "Thank you. Thank you very much."

"First, come upstairs and I'll show you around."

"Yes, ma'am."

They climbed the stairs side by side.

From that time on Bill stayed away from the house during most of the day. He did not even want to see the creature that Tawny had so willfully hired. Vivian's duties were really not too demanding and she left late in the afternoon each day.

One night on the way to bed Bill asked Tawny, "How is your bitch-maid doing?"

"Don't call her that!"

"I'll call her what I like. I call a spade a spade. Well, I asked you how is she doing?"

"Very well. She's learning fast."

"Has she stolen anything yet?"

"No. What made you ask that?"

"A prostitute has no morals. That's why I asked."

She looked at him in despair. She liked the girl, she respected Vivian—as Vivian respected her. So far she had done nothing wrong. She had even begun to care about her own appearance, brushing her hair one hundred strokes a night, as Tawny had instructed her to brush Tawny's each morning.

Tawny was slipping her nightgown over her head. He watched her arms' gesture with pleasure.

She said, "A prostitute is still a woman, Bill. A person. She need not be entirely sinful."

"To sell one's body is a sin."

As he took her in his arms she thought: *I sold mine to you. For a marriage license, for a wedding ring, for a home. I've never given myself to you freely. I don't think that I ever will.*

For the first time since the discovery of gold Lance saw that Bill was frowning. They were standing at the Green River Hotel bar late one afternoon, having drinks. "What is it, Bill? You look unhappy."

"It's Tawny."

"Tawny! In heaven's name what's wrong with Tawny? She's looking gorgeous these days. I think being in the money decidedly agrees with her."

"Perhaps it did at first. But now she's beginning to irritate me again."

"You can't complain about her housekeeping or cooking now can you?" Lance said slyly. "She isn't called upon to be more than a beautiful ornament. Which she is. I'm looking forward to your party."

"Lance, she has no taste. She actually wanted to invite the Fitzroys. She even asked if I wanted to ask Harry!"

Lance laughed. "I think, Bill, that your wife shows signs of being exceedingly democratic."

"Too democratic, for my taste."

"Bill, you didn't marry a duchess."

"I certainly did not. You've heard, no doubt, whom she hired as her personal maid?"

"Yes, I have. The lady told me so herself. I find it most amusing."

"I am not amused."

"You wouldn't be, Bill. Not much in life does amuse you. You're a very serious young man."

Bill swung around. "And what's wrong with that? Life's a serious business."

"Is it really now?" Lance's sharp blue eyes were twinkling.

"To me, it is. Look, Lance, I've come a long way from the college boy you used to know. Thanks to your discovery of gold I have become a man of property, a person in the community, a man of substance."

"Hear, hear!"

Bill ignored him and went on. "I have a home. I have a beautiful, if incorrigible, wife. I want children. At least a child. But I don't know if that's possible with Tawny. She is so . . . passive."

She was anything but, the time I was with her, Lance was thinking.

"You got her pregnant once, Bill."

"I know. But it wasn't easy."

"Not easy with a girl like Tawny?"

Bill looked at him for a long moment, pondering the words. Finally he said, "It's my belief that a woman should participate. In what some people put so vulgarly as 'making a baby.' She was that way once. One time. One night. But afterward, I don't think she wanted the baby. I think that's why she took that wild horseback ride and let herself be thrown."

"Bill, no!"

"She's a strange girl, Lance. I don't know if I'll ever really know or understand her. When I fell in love with her it was physical, purely physical, and at the time that was all that mattered to me, to have her as my own. I never guessed how impossible it would be to ever really know her."

Lance toyed with his drink, and then signaled Harry for another. "Women," he said thoughtfully, "are supposed to have mystery. Now, aren't they?"

"Maybe. But not your own wife. I'm never sure anymore when she's telling the truth. First she told me her parents had been theater people who were killed in a train wreck from which she escaped. Then, when she was pregnant, she told me she was afraid of childbirth because that was the way her mother had died, giving birth to her."

That was probably the truth, Lance thought, remembering the young girl who had walked into his study, at her father's orders.

"She said she made up the story about her parents because that was what she wanted to believe. Isn't that a preposterous way of explaining a lie?"

What she had wanted to believe, Lance reflected. Of course. Growing up with that father of hers had been no bed of roses. Of course she had made up a story about herself. Of course she wanted to escape from her memories of Jake McShane.

"That shows imagination, Bill. To make up her own past."

"It shows deception." He pulled out his watch. "Well, I guess it's late enough for that bitch to have left the house. I'll head for home."

Sitting there on the window seat in the summer of 1873 Tawny was remembering their first party. The party that had been the talk of Littleton for days.

The week before, Bill took her to dinner one evening at the dining room of the new Green River Hotel. As they walked in they heard piano music from the far side of the room. It was "Way Down Upon the Swanee River" played in a distinctive, flourishing way that she immediately recognized. Before Bill could seat her she dashed across the room, wending her way between the tables, to the piano.

It was Ned, good old Ned of The Golden Parrot, with his mane of white hair and his busy big hands. He was intent on his music, but when he finished the piece he looked up and saw her.

"Ned, what are you doing here in Littleton?"

"Playing the piano. Hello, Tawny, you're looking fine."

"I never thought you'd leave The Golden Parrot."

"Neither did I. But you see, the parrot died. Al sold out, and the new owners didn't want me. So here I am. A wanderer as I used to be when I was young." He took a sip from a mug of beer he had on top of the piano.

"Ned, it's so good to see you!"

"Good to see you."

Bill had followed her across the room and now was standing beside her.

"You remember Ned, don't you, Bill? And you, Ned, remember my husband."

"I certainly do." Ned was smiling but Bill was not.

Tawny said, "It's wonderful to have you here, Ned, to hear you play."

He flipped his finger lightly over the keys. "Care to sing a little ditty?"

Bill took her arm. "My wife does not perform in public."

Ned nodded.

Impulsively Tawny said, "Ned, I have a wonderful idea. We're having a party next week. I'd love to have you come and play for us. Wouldn't that be nice, Bill?"

Bill hesitated. Finally he said, "I suppose so. A little genteel music?"

"I'll stick to the classics, if that's what you want."

"Very well. Tawny, shall we go back to our table?"

"Friday, eight thirty," Tawny said to Ned. "Just ask anybody to point out where our house is."

Already Bill was leading her away.

The eagerly awaited party started off stiffly, but smoothly. Guests included the new doctor in town, John Edgars, and his prim little wife; Roger Dillingham, the solemn-faced lawyer and his wife, Ethel, a birdlike little woman with a bosom like that of a mother hen, close-set eyes as sharp as needles; Hans Knuppenberg, proprietor of the Emporium and his cheerful buxom wife. And of course Lance.

Tawny did invite the Fitzroys and they did come. The minute they walked through the door Tawny realized why Bill hadn't wanted to invite them. Even in their Sunday best they stuck out like sore thumbs. It was not just the way they looked; it was the very sound, not to mention quality, of their conversation.

"Tawny, honey, you sure be livin' in a palace!"

Nellie babbled, while Doug pounded Bill's shoulder as he boomed out with, "Livin' mighty high on the hog, ain't you, boy!"

Perhaps the other guests were not the true society that Bill wanted to entertain, but that evening, whatever their backgrounds, they were busy pretending to be complete ladies and gentlemen. When the Fitzroys were introduced they nodded and smiled, but made no effort to shake hands.

All but Lance.

Tawny would never forget how wonderfully gracious Lance was. He immediately asked about the ranch, about the animals and the crops; the Fitzroys, who previously had seemed a bit in awe of Lance, warmed to him immediately.

The incident of the arrival of the Fitzroys passed. And when, a few moments later, Vivian appeared with a tray of tiny sandwiches and passed among them, although it was a warm spring evening, there was a chill in the air. The women present did not recognize the girl. They scarcely noticed her; she was just a servant. They admired the sandwiches while the men looked at each other with raised eyebrows. All but Lance. He came over to Tawny's side, smiling, and stood beside her as Vivian and her tray reached them.

He accepted a sandwich. "Thank you, Vivian."

Her face glowed. "I didn't make them, Mr. Oliver. Mrs. Higgins did."

"Well, thank you for bringing me one."

"You're welcome." She moved on.

He looked down at Tawny. "I think you are doing a fine thing, hiring that girl. You make me think of our mutual friend, Evangeline."

Tawny, who had been watching the anger creeping over Bill's face, turned quickly to Lance. "Thank you, Lance. I appreciate your approval. I was thinking of Evangeline when I took Vivian in. Evangeline once rescued me."

"I know."

"Bill doesn't."

"I know that, too. There are a lot of things about you that Bill doesn't know, aren't there?"

She lowered her eyes. "Yes."

"Why?"

There were tears in her eyes when she looked up. "I wanted so badly to be married." Then, as she had said to Wilma long ago, "I wanted to be a wife, not a whore. But most of all, frankly, I wanted a man in bed with me at night." She did not add that it was he, Lance Oliver, who had aroused a passion for sex that she could not quench.

"I understand."

She was ravishing that night in an apricot silk that clung to her body. The low neckline created a temptation for any man who looked at her. Her dark red hair was piled high in what was an elaborate hairdo—Vivian's creation. Vivian had turned out to have a real talent for feminine embellishment. But the ponytail of dark curls at the back amounted to another temptation. Lance longed to pull down those locks, set them free, flowing behind her as they had that day he saw her on horseback, out on the ranch, the day she had blown him a good-bye kiss.

Bill is wrong, he thought. *She is not passive. Not in the least.*

"Thank you, Lance, for being so kind to the Fitzroys," Tawny was saying. "Poor folk. I knew Bill would be angry that I had invited them without letting him know. I knew he would be even angrier that I allowed Vivian to help with the serving. But those were two things I wanted to do—so much so that I can face his anger later this evening. But then, I've learned to live with his anger, along with a lot of other things."

"Tawny, I . . ."

"Never mind, Lance. Here he comes now."

She moved away from Lance and went over to the piano. Doug and Nellie were there watching Ned play, apparently fascinated by the sheer movement of his hands. Nellie looked up as Tawny came close to them. "This feller's been tellin' us how you used to be a singer. You never said nothin' about that."

"No, I didn't."

"Wish you'd sing somethin' now," Doug said.

As he finished the piece he was playing, Ned looked up at Tawny. "Well?"

"I don't think Bill would want me to." She shook her head. "You heard what he said the other day about his wife not performing in public."

"This ain't public!" Nellie cried. "This is your own house!"

Ned played, very softly, the opening bars of "Drink to Me Only with Thine Eyes." He said, "That's classical enough for your husband, isn't it?"

Tawny turned her back on the rest of the room and nodded to Ned. He started the piece again and this time she sang along with him.

There was applause when she finished.

Doug clapped loudest of all. Then he said to Ned, "Do you know the oldtimer about the dog?"

"Old Dog Tray?"

"That's it! Allus used to be my favorite."

Ned struck the chords. It was a duet this time, Doug's deep bass blending with Tawny's sweet, rich alto. Somehow from "Old Dog Tray" they slipped into "Old Black Joe" and then "When You and I Were Young, Maggie."

When they finished the last song, Doug suddenly swooped down his long arms and lifted Tawny to the top of the piano.

"Didden know you had it in you, gal. You're a humdinger!"

Bill was immediately across the room. He glared at Doug and at Tawny. He said, in a tense, terse voice, "I believe we have had enough music for this evening.

When the last guest had departed and the only sound was of Mrs. Higgins in the kitchen cleaning up, when Vivian had slipped out the back door and gone home, Bill and Tawny faced each other alone in the parlor. His face was white with fury. "I'll never forgive you for what you did tonight. Never! Never!"

"I knew you wouldn't."

"Then why, why did you do it? Why did you shame me in front of our guests? Why did you deceive me by inviting the Fitzroys, by allowing that slut to come into our parlor? By putting on that outrageous barmaid performance with Doug Fitzroy?"

"Because the Fitzroys are our friends. Because Vivian is a loyal servant. Because Doug and Nellie and Ned wanted me to sing."

"You only did it to embarrass me. That was your sole reason for your behavior all this evening. And you succeeded. You really succeeded. I should like to beat you, beat every inch of your body, make you cry out in shame, in apology."

His anger was not frightening her in the least. She felt no shame, no urge to apologize. "But you're not going to, are you, Bill?" she asked, with a little smile. "You know what I said I'd do if you ever hurt me again. And whatever you think of me as a person, as a human being, however much you hate what I do, you don't want to lose possession of my body, do you?" She was standing very close to him as she spoke.

"You bitch," he said under his breath. "Go to bed!"

2

One morning when Vivian arrived for work her manner was abruptly different. She was bright-eyed and excited and it showed in every movement of her tense little body.

"Before I start to work, ma'am, I'd like to talk to you."

She arrived when Tawny was still at the breakfast table. Bill had already left the house. Tawny was enjoying the first edition of the *Littleton Ledger* that Bill had brought home the night before. It was not much of a newspaper, a far cry from all those dailies in New York City that she had enjoyed at Evangeline's house. But for all that it was a newspaper, and to read it, lingering over coffee, was a luxury.

Tawny invited Vivian to sit down and have a cup of coffee with her. She rang the bell and Mrs. Higgins grudgingly produced another cup and saucer.

Tawny put aside the *Ledger* and smiled at Vivian across the table. "Well, what is it, Vivian? You have a problem? From the look on your face I wouldn't think that there was anything wrong."

"No, nothing's wrong, ma'am. Everything's fine. I just wanted to ask you . . . I just wanted to tell you that I've changed my mind. I think, if I could, I'd like to move into that attic room you talked about when I first come here."

"Well, well. What made you change your mind?"

"It would save the long walk out and back every day. And I wouldn't have to put up with my dad. Would it be all right if I did move in?"

Tawny thought for a moment. She decided the time had come for her to quit pretending ignorance.

"Of course it would be all right for you to move in. On one condition."

"What's that?"

Tawny looked her directly in the eye. "That you wouldn't entertain visitors."

Vivian understood. She cried out, "Oh, ma'am. Oh, Mrs. Ferguson, you found out about me and what I've done?"

"I knew all along, Vivian. Not when you first appeared on my doorstep, but that night. My husband told me about you."

"And still you hired me."

"And still I hired you. I never condoned what you did. That was your affair. I'd hoped that maybe you would change your habits—that perhaps I could help you change your habits."

"Mrs. Ferguson, that's just it! That's why I want that attic room!"

"You mean you are going to stop your night work?" Tawny gave a twisted smile.

"I already done that, ma'am. That's what I'm trying to tell you. I've got a steady beau."

"Good. Tell me about him."

Vivian leaned forward eagerly, more animated than Tawny ever had seen her.

"His name's Jim Jenson. He's just come to Littleton; his father has the new drugstore. He's just the same age as me and he's working in his father's store and he's real nice and shy, like nobody I ever knew before. He doesn't get fresh, he just holds my hand; he even asked if he could kiss me. And that was after the second time I'd seen him. We went for a walk down by the river. I met him, you see, when I was in the drugstore buying some medicine for my dad."

She paused for breath, and Tawny said, "I'm so happy for you, Vivian. He sounds very nice indeed."

"I only hope he don't find out about me. I hope nobody's mean enough to tell him the kind of girl I've been because I'm not going to be that kind of girl again. Never!"

"I hope so, too."

"And 'nother thing. I don't want him coming to my dad's little shack and seeing my dad. I don't like to be ashamed of my own kith and kin, but when he's drinking Dad can be pretty awful, and Jim is so nice I wouldn't want him to see. And he's invited me to a barn dance out in the country next week, and I'd much rather he came out here to this nice house to fetch me than to come to Dad's place. You see?"

Tawny nodded. Then she said, "And now, young lady, you better get to work and help me get dressed so I can go to town and fetch some furnishings for that room of yours. And while I'm doing that you can clean up the room. All right? It's never been used and it might have picked up some cobwebs and dust."

Vivian gulped the last of her coffee. "I'm ready, ma'am. Yes, I'm ready!"

By the time Tawny was dressed it had begun to rain, but that did not bother her. She would go to town anyhow. She was just starting to leave the house when Bill returned.

He frowned at her. "Where are you off to in the rain?"

"Shopping."

"Shopping! What on earth for? You've already got an armoire full of clothes."

"You might as well know. I'm furnishing the attic room. Vivian's moving in."

"Oh, God. In our house!"

"At least, Bill, she won't be out on the streets at night. And I made it a rule she could not entertain visitors."

He grunted. "I don't know how long that will last, with her reputation."

"Bill, she's a changed girl."

"So you think!"

"There's no use talking to you, is there?"

"There's no use talking to *you!* And there's nothing better to do on a day like this than head for the bottle."

He had been doing a lot of that lately—morning, afternoon, or evening. He opened the doors to the parlor and closed them behind him. Tawny shrugged and walked out the front door.

She was glad, glad to get out of the house, to be driving the buggy along the road to town. Glad, too, that there was such a place as the Emporium. The attic was bare, and she would need a bed, a chest of drawers and a chair. Maybe two chairs. She wondered if Vivian liked rockers. Linens, of course, she had, but she would also need curtains and a rug—a nice soft rug for Vivian's toes to wriggle to when she stepped out of bed in the morning.

She remembered mentally sketching the furnishings of the room for the baby that never was born. During that period she had been relatively content because she was busy planning. As she had been content when they were building and furnishing the house. As she was now, momentarily.

Everything in her life seemed to be for the moment only.

Bill had made vague suggestions about "making a baby" again but she had not responded. She was honest enough with herself to admit that she did not want to have his child. She did not want a child in his image. She simply did not love him that way.

Mr. Knuppenberg himself was there to greet her when she arrived at the Emporium. He was a plump little German who always seemed to enjoy himself. He particularly admired the beautiful Mrs. Ferguson and insisted on waiting on her himself, assuring her that the heavier pieces of furniture, et cetera, would be delivered promptly.

"You are redoing a whole room in your house, ja?"

"Not redoing. Furnishing for the first time. It's for my maid."

"Ja, your maid." He grinned, but she ignored it.

She was coming out of the Emporium, her arms loaded with some of the smaller packages, when she saw Lance.

He hurried toward her and reached for the packages. "Here, let me help."

"Thank you, Lance."

As usual, he was dressed impeccably; he might have been on a street in New York. Not since the first months out on the ranch when he was playing prospector had he ever reverted to rough country clothes.

He carried most of the parcels and she led him to the buggy and thanked him again. He helped her in and stood there looking up at her. She was wearing a rather plain dress, partly covered by her big rain-cape, the hood of the cape covering most of her hair. Still she could not help looking attractive.

"I guess I got everything I wanted," Tawny said. "So I better go on home." The prospect of home was not appealing. Bill would be sodden with liquor by now, perhaps passed out there on the sofa in the parlor. If he had not passed out he would be very poor company at the luncheon table.

"Tawny, I have a better idea. If you don't think Bill would mind."

"Right now he's in no state to mind about anything, is my guess. He was starting to hit the bottle when I left. What's your idea?"

"Did you know this town now has a restaurant? Somewhere to eat besides the hotel?"

"No, I didn't."

"It's not much of a place. I was there last night. It's run by a little half-Mexican fellow who says he used to have a restaurant in Los Angeles. Do you like Spanish food?"

"I've never had any."

"Would you like to try it? That's why I said I had an idea, if Bill wouldn't mind."

She smiled. "And I said he was in no state right now to mind anything. I'd love to try Spanish food. What's it like?"

"Hot, rich, seductive."

Tawny's eyes twinkled. "It would be fun to be seduced—by food."

"May I drive you there? It's at the other end of Main Street. Not too far from, but not too close to, the old hotel." He climbed into the buggy and she moved over and let him take the reins.

As they trotted along Main Street several heads turned, several heads bent together. And several people waved.

"We'll be the talk of Littleton," Lance chuckled.

"Bill says that we're the laughingstock, already."

"There's no harm in laughter," Lance said. "There should be a lot more of it. Everywhere. It doesn't matter what's being laughed at."

They rode along in comfortable silence for a while and then Lance asked, "Tell me, what were you up to buying out the Emporium? You must have made Hans Knuppenberg's morning."

"I did have to buy a lot of things. And what you see here isn't all of it. I've got furniture being delivered. I had to get everything to furnish the little attic room. You see, Vivian is moving in."

Lance's eyebrows shot up in surprise. "How on earth did that happen? How did you persuade her?"

"I didn't. She decided she wanted to. You'll never guess why. She's got a beau."

"She does?"

"An innocent lad, a newcomer in town, who knows nothing of her past. Of course she hopes he'll never find out. So she is reforming herself."

"Good for Vivian. I wish her luck."

Casa de Juan was a small, newly painted clapboard building. Lance hitched Brownie to the post, helped Tawny out of the buggy and they dashed through the rain, arm in arm, to the entrance. Inside there were booths with curtains that could be closed. As they passed the first one Juan himself was acting as waiter. He pushed back the curtain to deliver a serving and revealed the town's lawyer and his wife. They stared in surprise at Lance and Tawny before the curtain closed again.

"We startled the Dillinghams, didn't we?" Lance laughed.

"It's like putting up a billboard to be seen by Ethel

Dillingham. Or so I've heard." Tawny gave a little giggle as they sat down opposite each other.

She had thrown back the cape.

"Here, let me hang that up for you." He took the cape and stepped out of the booth to do so and also hung up his hat. He sat down again and looked across the table at her.

"I'm glad you're unconventional enough not to wear a hat. I much prefer you without one. Remember when I asked you to take one off?"

"I'd rather not remember that time," Tawny said gravely. But she had remembered it a thousand times, sometimes with shame, sometimes with a secret pleasure.

"So be it." He reached across the table and squeezed her hand.

At that moment Juan pushed back the curtain. "Señor Oliver! *Buenas dias*, welcome!"

Lance took his hand from Tawny's and she quickly put hers under the table.

"Good morning, Juan, and what do you recommend for lunch?"

"The specialty of the day. Chicken, Mexican style."

"Fine," Lance said. "Bring on the chicken."

"Right away, señor." Juan bowed formally and pulled the curtain shut.

Suddenly Tawny laughed, out of sheer exhilaration. "It's good to see you laugh," Lance said. "I haven't seen you do it much of late."

"That's true. I guess I haven't had much to laugh about."

Juan appeared with a bottle of wine and two glasses. "I've tasted better," Lance said. "But I didn't want to hurt his feelings by telling him so. To what shall we drink?"

Tawny lifted her glass and thought for a moment. Then she said, "To Vivian and her beau. May they find happiness together."

Their glasses clinked. They sipped the wine.

She was thinking: *I hope that boy really loves Vivian and that she really loves him, that she can have a happy future, that she can really forget the past.* She was no longer laughing, not even smiling. Her face was sad, particularly those strangely beautiful flecked gray eyes of hers.

Lance said, "You say Bill is drinking a lot these days."

"Too much. Far too much," Tawny nodded. "It's not good for him. But if I so much as suggest that perhaps he's had enough for an evening he'll pour himself another."

"Maybe I should speak to him," Lance wondered aloud.

"Perhaps. But please don't tell him that I told you about his drinking. He would be furious with me."

"I understand."

He could see fear in her face now. It was strange to think of her, or anyone, being afraid of Bill Ferguson.

The Mexican chicken arrived, steaming and pungent. Juan served the main course from a big bowl and then left it still half full in the center of the table.

After a time Lance said, "You're awfully quiet, Tawny."

"I'm sorry. I've gotten used to eating in silence."

"Why is that?"

"That is the way Bill likes it. When he sits down at the table he cares about nothing but the food in front of him. I think he's a little insane on the subject of food. Which is why he is getting fat."

"I've noticed that."

"He used to have something to say at mealtime," she said wryly, "even if it was only to complain about my cooking. But he can't complain about Mrs. Higgins's. It's too good."

"As I remember, yours was good."

"You were always complimentary, Lance."

"Perhaps. Partly. But to tell you the truth I was so blasted sorry for you when I first came up here. You had so much work, ugly dirty work you never should have been doing. Bill didn't appreciate what you had to put up with. It was one of the reasons why I was so anxious to find that vein of gold. It was not just the adventure, the fun of looking for it, it was thinking what money could do for both of you."

Mainly for you, Lance thought. *Bill was happy enough, playing at being a rancher, hunting and fishing. But you were miserable, girl, and it broke my heart to see you so.*

"So you found the gold." Tawny had put down her fork and was looking off into space. "You found the gold, and we were rich and we lived happily ever after. Only it's not so, of course. I'm still miserable, but in a different way. And Bill is unhappy and takes to drink. And it's my fault. I've disappointed him in so many ways."

"That's hard to believe," Lance said. "Don't blame yourself, Tawny. I think he drinks because of idleness. That can happen."

Tawny took a little swallow of wine, sat up straighter, and picked up her fork again.

Lance watched her, as she visibly controlled herself, and wondered what all there might be that she was not confiding in him.

"You were nice enough to ask me to lunch," Tawny was saying. "And here I sit complaining about my lot. It was rude of me. But I guess I am pretty consistently a rude person. As Bill says, I should try to rise above my background. But Bill doesn't even know my true background. I think I've come a long way from the daughter of a cheap medicine peddler."

"Put it behind you, Tawny. As Vivian is putting her past away."

"I've been trying to do that for a long, long time. Look, Lance, I am sorry for having poured out so much bitterness over such a nice lunch. But it's good to talk to a friend. You are my friend, aren't you?"

"Of course I am!" Again he put his hand over hers, again his touch sent shivers down her spine.

She said quickly, "I couldn't say all this to Nellie Fitzroy. She would never understand. No more than Wilma ever understood things I told her about myself. I think Evangeline did, most of the time. She was a true friend."

Lance was thinking: *I could be much more than a friend if she wasn't married to Bill.* Aloud, he said, "Did you ever answer that letter you got from Evangeline?"

"Yes. Finally. It was one of the most difficult letters I ever wrote."

"Why was that?"

"Because of what she had written me. All about my domestic bliss, children at my knee, things like that. I didn't dare write back and pour out the truths about my marriage, for fear she would make the sort of reply that would infuriate Bill, should he see the letter. So I wrote very carefully, hoping she could read between the lines. Perhaps I was too careful. She never answered."

"I'll ask Evangeline about it when I get back to New York."

Her heart sank. "You're going back to New York?"

"Soon, I think."

"But why?"

"Why should I stay on in Littleton? My prospecting adventure is over. Long ago. I'm restless again. Only this time I've made up my mind as to what to do about it. It's high time I quit sowing my wild oats. I'm going to go to work for my father, if he'll have me after all these years."

Going back to New York, she thought. *Back to that big house on Fifth Avenue. And back to his wife.*

"I'll . . . I mean *we'll* miss you, Lance."

"I'll miss *you.*"

You. He meant both of them, of course.

"Don't leave without saying good-bye."

He patted her hand. "Of course not."

Juan was with them again. "Will there be anything else, Señor Oliver?"

Lance did not take his hand away from Tawny's. "No, nothing else. The check, please."

When Juan had gone she said, "Thank you for lunch, Lance. Thank you for listening."

"Thank you for coming with me."

The rain had stopped when they came out of the restaurant and the drive home was pleasanter than the one coming into town. But again she thought that everything in her life was for the moment, or a few moments, only. The short time they spent at lunch had been delightful, in spite of her complaints about life in general. They talked little while Lance drove back to the hotel, where she dropped him off and took over the reins.

* * *

She stopped the buggy in front of the house and began carrying her purchases up to the front porch. She would send Vivian down to carry them to the attic. Fido was bouncing up and down in greeting. As she came up the steps with the last armful, the front door was flung open by Bill.

"Where the devil have you been?"

"I told you where I was going, Bill," she answered as calmly as she could.

"But it's past two o'clock. Past lunch time. The delivery wagon was here long ago, the men traipsing mud all through the house to get that damned stuff to the attic. Where were you?"

"I stayed in town for lunch. I didn't think you'd miss me. After all, you had your bottle."

"Lunch! At the hotel?"

"No. There's a new restaurant now in town. It's called Casa de Juan and it's run by a man who used to have a place in Los Angeles. It features Spanish food. I had Mexican chicken and it was delicious. I think you would like it." She walked past him into the house and took off her cape and hung it on the coat rack.

Bill had followed her.

She was smoothing her hair in front of the hall mirror.

"Do you mean to tell me, Tawny, that you went to that restaurant unescorted?"

"No." She still was looking into the mirror.

"Who took you there?"

"Bill, let go of me!" she warned.

He dropped her arm. "Tell me who it was!"

"It was Lance."

"Lance!"

"Yes. Our friend Lance. I met him as I was coming out of the Emporium and he invited me. He asked if I thought you would mind and I told him you wouldn't."

"But I do!"

The idea of her having lunch alone with any other man repelled him, but with Lance it was even worse. He had been aware of Lance's charm since he first knew him in college. He never had been concerned about him and Tawny because she had never appeared to be attracted to him.

"You mind my having lunch with your friend, with *our* friend Lance? Why?"

"It's unseemly for a married woman to be seen in a public place in the company of a man other than her husband!"

"In broad daylight?"

"At any time. Did anyone see you there together?"

"Well, there were people along the street. Lance drove me from the Emporium to the restaurant, which is on the other side of town." She remembered how she and Lance had laughed at the faces. "And then there was Juan."

"Juan?"

"The proprietor of the restaurant."

"Anyone else in the restaurant?"

"It's hard to say. The booths were curtained."

"That kind of place! You two were alone behind a curtain where you couldn't be seen."

"Juan was in and out all the time. Oh yes, as we came in he opened the curtain to a booth and we saw the people inside."

"Who was it?"

"The Dillinghams."

"Oh, God!"

Tawny finally turned away from the mirror. She had been staring into it to avoid Bill's anger. Now she determined to face up to it.

"Bill, why are you so upset about this? Everybody in Littleton knows how close a friend Lance is, as well as being your partner. What on earth is wrong with my having lunch with him?"

"Simply because you are my wife. I would like your behavior to be above suspicion. But you constantly undermine any respect people might have for you, or that I might have for you. You embarrass me, constantly. I think you do these things on purpose."

His capacity for exaggeration was boundless, and he obviously believed what he was saying. He was behaving in such a ridiculous fashion that she could not help smiling at him. "Perhaps I do do things on purpose, sometimes, when I'm sick and tired of your attitude toward me. And toward our marriage."

"My attitude is the normal one, the right one," he declared.

"In your opinion." She turned toward the stairs, to go up to tell Vivian about the packages on the front porch. She had one hand on the banister when he spoke.

"Tawny?"

"Yes?"

"One thing I want to make perfectly clear. You are not to repeat your performance of today. If you defy me in this matter, I shall go directly to Lance and place the burden of my decision on him."

She whirled around. For a long moment she stood there with her hand on the banister, looking down into Bill's flushed face.

The lord and master. She hated him.

Finally the words came, boiled up from within her, distilled through months of resentment.

She cried, "You'll never tell Lance Oliver what he can do or cannot do, you pompous ass!"

"Tawny!"

"That's what you are, Bill Ferguson. Mr. Know-It-All. Mr. I-Am-Always-Right. Mr. Propriety. You, the perfect gentleman, capable of physical and mental cruelty that you dare to put in the name of love. I'd like to shout to the world what kind of man you are, let the world know what you really are under that fat gentleman's skin."

His mouth had fallen open in surprise at her outburst. At last he licked his lips and said, surprisingly quietly, "Tawny, calm yourself. You're hysterical."

"I've every right to be!"

"Tawny, I beg of you, do not have lunch with Lance again."

"In case you care to know, the opportunity won't arise. Lance is leaving soon."

"Leaving?"

"He told me so today. He's going back to New York."

"Oh, no."

"Oh, yes. You'll lose a partner. I'll lose a friend. The only real friend I have."

She turned and hurried up the stairs.

Later that afternoon Vivian was busy arranging the attic room. Tawny, from her bedroom, could hear the footsteps overhead. The wine, the heavier than usual lunch, the scene with Bill, all had combined to weary her. She had partially undressed and lain down on the bed.

When she heard the knock on the door she thought it might be Vivian, but when she said, "Come in," it was Bill, with a sheepish look on his fat face. He came over and stood beside the bed, looking down at her. "Tawny, I came to make up."

"I see."

"You said some pretty dreadful things to me, girl."

"You've said many dreadful things to me, Bill."

"It's just, just that I love you so much I can't help being jealous of anyone at all being alone with you, anywhere!"

"Downstairs it was propriety. Now it's love." She turned her head.

"Tawny, look at me."

She did not try. She thought: *If he touches me, if he puts his hand anywhere on my body, I shall scream. I'll scream so loud that all the world will hear.*

Upstairs Vivian was singing to herself. The song floated out the open attic window and spiraled down to the open bedroom window below. "I lost my love in lilac time . . ."

It was midsummer, but both Tawny and Bill knew that the song rang true.

3

Their marriage existed now as a kind of armed truce.

Bill no longer harangued Tawny; in fact he scarcely spoke to her. And Tawny continued to be aloof. They took their meals together—silent, gloomy affairs. They slept in the same bed but he made no attempt to touch her. Both of them were mentally holding their breaths, waiting, wondering when a break would come in the impasse and they would either quarrel or make love, or both.

At the same time Bill stuck close to her. If she said that she was going shopping he immediately announced that he would accompany her. He was making sure that they would be seen together, always together, a loving couple. That was the way he behaved when he took her elbow as they crossed a busy street, the tender way he helped her in and out of the buggy. It was annoying to Tawny, but she preferred going out, even with Bill, to being left alone in the big house.

In a few days the truce was broken. But not in any way that either of them could have anticipated. They were riding home one afternoon when they came upon a crowd on the edge of town, where the road forked off to Twuylip and Wallula and the west. Bill slowed the horse to see what it was all about.

"Do you suppose there's been an accident?" Tawny asked.

Bill shook his head. "I doubt if an accident would draw this many people."

At last they were close enough to see what was happening. A man, standing at the back of a wagon, was making a speech.

Bill said, "I wonder what he's selling."

Tawny did not answer but she knew, the moment she saw the wagon, even before she saw the man.

"Let's listen for a little, anyhow," Bill was saying. "I think these quacks are funny."

They did not get out of the buggy. Tawny thought: *Even if Bill wants to, I won't go any closer.* So they sat there as Pa's familiar spiel roared out.

"And so, ladies and gentlemen," he was saying now, "I want to introduce to you a remarkable young lady. This child wonder is possessed of a power beyond belief. Yet if you want to see evidence of it, you must believe. By the magic of electricity she will, before your very eyes, arouse your spirit so that it will rise triumphant, mind over matter. Your headaches will evaporate in the breeze, your rheumatism will flow out of your veins, your broken bones will heal and mend like new again, your indigestion will melt as if you had taken a strong cathartic, but this will be painless and harmless. God has blessed this child with the gift of filling your mind with the power to overcome physical disabilities. All this for a small fee."

Bill turned to Tawny. "Did you ever hear such a pack of nonsense in all your life?"

"Let's go home, Bill. I've heard enough."

"So have I." He flapped the reins and clucked at the horse, and the buggy moved forward.

Just beyond the crowd there was a rise and a bend in the road so that they could look down on the crowd and the man and the wagon. The view now was of the side of the wagon. Although the sign was faded, the afternoon sunlight clearly illuminated the words MCSHANE'S MARVELOUS MEDICINE.

Bill read the sign aloud and laughed sarcastically. Then he repeated, "McShane—McShane! Tawny, could that possibly be a relative of yours?"

She did not try to answer. She said again, "Let's go home, Bill."

Bill looked into her face. "He *is* a relative."

There was no point in lying. "Yes," she said, "a close relative. My father, if you want to know."

They rode on in silence. Bill was stunned. Finally he said, "You lied to me, Tawny. You said your father was an actor."

"What else is he?" Tawny cried, her voice bitter. "That's all he is or ever was, a charlatan, putting on a show. I lived in that wagon for the first fifteen years of my life. I used to be his 'child wonder.' I was as blindly innocent as the poor kid he has in his wagon now. I was part of the show. That was where I first performed as a singer, as a curtain raiser to his medicine show. I sang, and I pretended to be a faith healer. I had to do those things to keep him from beating me. Now you know the truth, the whole naked truth about me!"

She began to cry as they rode along. Bill stared straight ahead down the road, not wanting to look at her, not knowing what to say. He felt as if he were riding beside a stranger. She had lied to him. God knows how many other lies she had told him. The story of her first marriage and the Indians killing her husband. Had it been another lie to explain why she did not come to him as a virgin?

As they drew close to their house they saw a buggy parked in front. Company. A rare caller.

Bill drew his rig up beside it and turned to Tawny. "Pull yourself together," he told her. "Stop that bawling. We're going into the house and we're going to pretend we did not even see that crowd, that wagon, that man. We're going to go on with your pretense together. You are going to behave like my wife."

Tawny dried her eyes and swallowed. "That I don't have to pretend. I am your wife."

"Yes."

"For better or worse, as you said the other day. Now you know the worst."

"I do, indeed." His voice was grim.

"Tell me something, Bill. If you had known long ago what you just learned about me today, would you have asked me to marry you?"

He hesitated for only a moment and then he blurted out the words: "I was so head over heels in love with you, I wanted you so badly, I probably would have asked you anyhow." He was cross with himself for having felt obliged to tell her the naked truth. His voice still gruff, he said, "Go on in the house and greet our guest while I put the buggy away."

Tawny got out of the buggy and climbed the steps slowly. She had not recognized the equipage and wondered who would be waiting in the palor. Fido was on the porch. She petted the dog and told him to stay outside.

Before he flicked the reins Bill watched her. Even her walk was beautiful—it had a rhythm to it, and a distinct grace. You would never have guessed that such a fine figure of a woman was the daughter of a quack medicine man, had once even shared his life.

Vivian opened the door for Tawny. "There's a lady come to call on you. I told her she could wait because I didn't think it'd be much longer 'fore you got here."

"That's right, Vivian. Did she tell you her name?"

"Nope, but she put her calling card there in the tray."

Tawny picked it up. "Mrs. Roger A. Dillingham."

Ethel Dillingham. The town gossip. *I'll have to be on guard.*

She took off her hat and hung it on the rack, removed her gloves and smoothed her hair, and then took a deep breath and walked into the parlor.

Ethel Dillingham was examining the velvet drapes by the window. She turned as Tawny came in and smiled, seemingly a bit apologetically.

"Good afternoon, Mrs. Ferguson."

"Good afternoon, Mrs. Dillingham. I'm sorry I wasn't here when you arrived."

"That's quite all right. Your little maid made me welcome." Somehow the way she said "your little maid" made it sound like an insult.

"Do sit down, Mrs. Dillingham. I'll ring for tea."

"Oh, that's not at all necessary, my dear Mrs. Ferguson. I only stopped by for a few moments. I was out driving along the river, and when I saw your lovely house I thought I might just drop in and see how you were. And, I must confess, look more closely at your charming home. It is hard to really appreciate a beautiful room like this during a party, don't you agree?"

"I do indeed."

Ethel Dillingham marched across the room looking very much like a hen. "I see you have a lot of books," she went on. "Quite a library. I had no idea that you were the least intellectual."

"I wouldn't exactly call myself an intellectual." Tawny smiled. "But I like to read. I always have."

"Indeed? Of course my husband, being a lawyer, reads a great deal of the time, great, heavy tomes. I am much happier with my embroidery. Of course it is nice to have a weekly newspaper now but I do wish the *Ledger* would have a society column."

"Society? In Littleton?" Tawny couldn't help an amused laugh.

"Why not, my dear? Why should we not read of the little soirees when they occur? Why should we not be informed of the goings on among our people?"

Tawny shrugged. "I suppose it would be interesting." *Particularly to you,* she thought.

Mrs. Dillingham had perched on the stiffest chair in the room. Tawny sank down on the sofa and wished Bill would come in.

"Speaking of people," Ethel went on, "I am given to understand that that nice Mr. Oliver is leaving us." Her sharp eyes were studying Tawny's face.

Tawny nodded. "Yes, he is."

The answer pleased the other woman.

"Do you know when?"

"No, I don't."

"I shall have to send him a note. I should like to have a little farewell party for him. He is such a lovely gentleman. Don't you agree?"

Tawny threw her a cold look. The woman was probing, digging, and at any moment Bill might walk into the room.

"Of course I agree that he's a lovely gentleman!" she snapped back. "He's an old friend of my husband and myself and we shall miss him when he leaves Littleton."

"I'm sure you will."

The silence seemed to last forever. It was still hanging there between them when Bill walked into the room. He bowed over Ethel Dillingham's hand as he greeted her. "What a pleasure to have you come to see us. I only wish Mr. Dillingham had accompanied you."

"He is a workingman, my dear Mr. Ferguson. Nose to the grindstone day after day. Not a free man, as you are."

Bill laughed, embarrassedly. "I've not always been free, as you put it. In my time I've earned my keep."

"Of course, of course!" She turned her face toward Tawny. "That little Mexican restaurant is an interesting place, isn't it, Mrs. Ferguson?"

"Yes, it is."

"Still, it does not really have the class that it should have. I mean someone should open a first-class restaurant here. I do miss the nice places we had back in Iowa. But in the meanwhile, we must make do with what we have. She turned her head again. "Have you dined there, Mr. Ferguson?"

"No, I have not. But Mrs. Ferguson has had the pleasure."

"I know," Mrs. Dillingham said with great cheeriness. Then she got to her feet. "I said I could only stay for a few moments. I really must be on my way."

"Please don't rush off," Bill told her, but his words only had the veneer of politeness.

Tawny had stood up, too. She forced herself to ask, "Are you sure you won't stay for tea?"

"I'm sure, my dear, I'm sure. I've had my little

chat with you, which was all I intended. So now, good afternoon to you both."

Bill walked with her out of the parlor and into the front hall, out the front door and down the steps to her horse and buggy. Once seated she picked up the reins and looked down at him.

"Your wife is a beautiful woman, Mr. Ferguson. You'd best keep your eyes on her." Then she clucked at her horse and was off.

Bill hurried back into the house and went straight to his brandy bottle. "You can't say I don't need a drink now," he said over his shoulder to Tawny. "I need one very badly."

Tawny was standing by the window, looking out. She said over her shoulder, "Perhaps I need one, too."

"Ladies don't drink in the afternoon."

She swung around. "This one does if she wants to!" She swept across the room and stood beside him, chin up. "Well, are you going to pour me one, or aren't you?"

He poured. He handed it to her, looking into her angry eyes. Tawny took a sip. Her bosom was rising and falling in accompaniment to her anger.

"That woman!" she cried. "That dreadful, vicious woman. I wanted to slap her across the face."

"That was what you wanted to do. But you didn't. That would have been the true Tawny expressing herself, wouldn't it?"

"Perhaps."

"She *was* rather unpleasant. But you asked for it. I told you that a married woman should not be seen in a public place with a man other than her husband."

"She had no right to come to my house and insult me with her suspicions!"

"There are people like Ethel Dillingham all over

the world, Tawny. You can't always strike out and scream for your rights, as your friend Evangeline McClintock would have you do. You must learn to be bigger than the unpleasantries of life. But I suppose that's a lot to ask of someone like you."

Slowly Tawny finished her drink, put the glass down on the table beside the bottle, and went back to the window.

"So you hate me that much, Bill?" she asked.

The sun was lowering in the sky and silhouetted her there, framed in the glass curtains and the drapes.

"No, Tawny, no! Of course I don't hate you! No matter what you've been, what you've done, who you are, no matter how you disappoint me, I can't hate you!" He came up behind her and put his arms around her, resting his hands gently on her breasts.

She was thinking: *He shouldn't have married me. When we first met, back in San Francisco, he should have seduced me, then and there. I was hungry for that. I had been alone for much too long. I should have told him all about myself, right then; he was mad enough about me in those days. We would have found out at the outset that we were not meant for each other, that we would not have to spend a lifetime of him trying to reform me, of my trying to defy him in every way possible.*

He was stroking her now, still very gently, but she felt no response, only a dead, desolate feeling of despair, near nausea.

Then they heard Vivian's small voice from the hall.

"Mrs. Ferguson? Mrs. Higgins says to tell you there's a man at the back door selling fresh eggs and do you want any?"

Bill let go of Tawny and turned around.

"Tell her to buy all the eggs she wants! But you get the hell out of here. This minute!"

Mrs. Dillingham encountered Lance on the street that afternoon. She was delighted. Now there was no need to write a note and wait for a reply. After polite good afternoons she plunged into the subject. "I understand you are leaving our fair city, Mr. Oliver."

"I am."

"What a pity! A lot of people are going to miss you."

"And I shall miss a lot of people."

"Before you leave I should very much like to give a small farewell party in your honor."

"Please don't, Mrs. Dillingham. I'd like to slip out of here as quietly as I slipped in."

"But I want so very much to do it! Please tell me how much longer you will be here."

"I cannot tell you that. I'm not sure. But no, no party."

Her eyes narrowed with displeasure. "But I . . ."

He interrupted. "No, Mrs. Dillingham. No party." He tipped his hat and moved on.

He had not been telling the whole truth when he said he would miss a lot of people. He certainly would not miss a crashing bore such as Ethel Dillingham, nor her stodgy, conceited husband. He felt as if his months in this part of the world had been like a long sea voyage. Land was in sight; soon the passengers would disperse and go their separate ways, with little chance of meeting again in the future.

But he would miss Tawny. Long, long ago he had looked upon her as no more than a tasty morsel of female flesh. Now he knew her as a woman, a beautiful, unhappy woman. Yet to be in her presence was always a pleasure. It was a pleasure just to remember different times and different places. Her singing in that little restaurant in San Francisco. Her riding horseback with her hair flying in the wind. At a party, bedecked with lace and ribbons.

Saying good-bye to Tawny would not be easy.

He was tired of walking back and forth on Littleton's few streets. He looked forward to New York again, where he could walk for miles, where he could leave one atmosphere and plunge into another.

There was still a bar in the old Littleton Hotel; it was where one went to meet the "ladies" who lived upstairs. But there would be no ladies there in the late afternoon. At that hour it was strictly a man's bar, with a slightly lower-class clientele. When he had walked the length of Main Street, Lance often stopped in for a quick drink before heading back to the Green River Hotel.

He remembered his loneliness when he first came to Washington Territory; nights alone in this bar with only traveling salesmen and good old Harry to talk with. It seemed much the same now as he stepped inside. Of course Harry was at the new hotel and the man behind the bar was a taciturn stranger. Lance was standing alone at the bar, at first. But before he had finished his drink the doors to the street swung open and another man came in. He did not turn to look at him; he was watching the entrance reflected in the mirror behind the bar. As the man came closer he began to look familiar, and the moment he spoke the rasping voice identified him, if the big ears and button nose had not.

"Double whiskey, please," was all he said.

Lance turned and watched him down the drink and when it was finished Lance said, "I do believe it is Mr. McShane."

Surprise was all over Jake's face as he studied Lance's. "And I know you. Just a minute, lemme think. Back East somewhere."

"Surely you remember?"

Jake pushed his hat back and scratched his head for a minute. Then he exclaimed in a voice loud enough to make the bartender look up, "Your name's Oliver. What the hell are you doing way out here in this hick town?"

"Visiting. And what are you doing here?"

"Got my wagon on the edge of town. Peddling my medicine, same as ever."

"Medicine and magnetic healing? Or did you give that up?"

Jake grinned. "Nope. Picked me up a new kid along the road. Does purty near as good as my Tawny did."

"You old crook," Lance mumbled.

"Watch out who you calling names, son. I'm no more a crook than most people in this world. A person'd be hard put to find an honest man, if you ask me. If a man tried to be honest he'd get took by another guy. I've lived long enough to know that. It's dog-eat-dog the world over."

"A *cynical* crook."

"Not sure what that means but it don't sound too bad. How 'bout me buyin' *you* a drink this time? Seem to remember that first time we met you was buyin'."

"I remember," Lance said dryly. He remembered actually being amused by the old codger. Here was McShane, smiling again in the same way, ready to let bygones be bygones, probably ready to offer the services of magnetic treatment with this new girl.

Before he could protest the offer of a drink Jake

had signaled to the bartender, and another full glass had been placed in front of Lance.

Jake lifted his new drink. He said, "Here's to Tawny, wherever she may be."

"To Tawny," Lance echoed. Then he added, "So you never found her?"

"Not hide nor hair. And I did my share'a lookin', too. That were three years ago."

Three years. It seemed a lifetime ago to Lance.

"Sometimes I get to worryin' 'bout Tawny." For once Jake was not grinning. And for once he sounded sincere. "Young girl like that, all alone in the world. She shouldn'a run off like that. She allus was headstrong. I mean to say she had lots'a crazy ideas. She was a smart kid though, allus with her nose in a book, or dreamin' about something. Sometimes I miss havin' her around. I raised her, y'know, all by myself. Her mother died abornin' Tawny. That made me kinda hate her at first. You know what I mean? 'Count of her mother dyin' that way. Her mother was an angel, a real angel, and a scrawny little brat like Tawny shouldn'a killed her."

As the old man rambled on Lance began to have a greater understanding of Tawny than he had had before.

"That scrawny little brat grew up to be a beautiful woman," Lance told him.

Jake looked at him. "She weren't no woman when you seen her in New York. She weren't no more than a kid, fifteen years old, although she kept givin' her age as almost sixteen, she was in such a hurry to grow up."

"She's nineteen now," Lance went on. "She's a woman."

"You mean you've seen her since that time in New York City?"

"I've seen her."
"Where? When? How is she?"
"Here in Littleton. A few days ago. Tawny is fine."
"I'll be damned. What's she doin' way out here?"
"She's living here. You don't have to worry about her, McShane. She's married."
"My little kid married? I'll be damned," Jake said again. "I think that calls for another drink."
"Not for me, thank you."
Jake was plainly getting excited now and Lance began to regret having told him about Tawny. She had run away from her father three years ago; certainly she would not want to see him now. He shouldn't have blurted out her whereabouts.
Jake reached for his drink and sipped it. His eyes were now darting about; one could almost see the wheels in his brain turning, turning.
"As I said, Mr. McShane, you don't have to worry about her anymore."
"I ain't worryin'. I'm thinkin'. Who'd she marry?"
"I'd rather not say. I've gone too far already, McShane."
"If you don't tell me, I'll find out all by myself. You might as well spill it."
Lance sighed. "She's married to a man named Ferguson. Bill Ferguson."
"That's a good Scotch name. Is he a Scotchman?"
"Of descent, perhaps."
"Is he a tightwad?"
"Are you a tightwad?"
"I ain't Scotch. I'm Irish! But is *he* a tightwad?"
No. He's a . . ." he hesitated. "He's a fine young man."
"Good. What does he do for a living?"
There was a laugh from the bartender, who had

gradually moved closer to them, listening to their every word.

Both of them looked at the man behind the bar.

"What's funny?" Jake asked.

"Bill Ferguson doesn't do nothin' for a livin'," the man explained. "He's the richest guy in town. The gold discovered on his land, why that's what made Littleton what it is today."

Jake grinned broadly. "Now, ain't that nice! I think I'll pay a call on Mrs. Ferguson. First thing tomorrow mornin'."

4

The next morning was gloomy from the beginning. A steady, dismal rain was falling. After breakfast Mrs. Higgins, who was suffering from a summer cold, asked to go home and to bed and Tawny agreed that she should. When Vivian had brushed Tawny's hair and laid out her clothes, she asked to be allowed to go to town to see her beau, and again Tawny gave permission.

Tawny and Bill were alone in the house, both in the parlor, Bill with yesterday's newspaper and Tawny trying to decide which book to read, when Fido's wild barking brought Tawny to the front window. McShane's Marvelous Medicine wagon was in the driveway and Jake himself was coming toward the house.

"Oh, no!" she cried. "Oh, no!"

"What is it?" Bill asked.

"He's coming here," she whispered.

"Who? What are you mumbling about?" Bill tossed the newspaper aside and got to his feet.

"My father."

The brass knocker was sounding now. Tawny

moved numbly out of the parlor and into the front hall. She opened the door and looked out at him.

"Well, Tawny, ain't you goin' to ask your poor old father in out of the rain?"

She opened the door wider and stepped aside. Jake came straight in, looked around, and hung his hat on one of the hat-rack hooks.

"Quite a place you got here. Quite a place."

She moved into the parlor, still not speaking, and Jake followed. Again he looked around and smacked his lips. Again he said, "Quite a place." Then he turned to Bill who had been standing there staring at him. "And you must be the fellow my little girl hooked."

Tawny managed to say, "Bill, this is my father, Jake McShane. Pa, this is my husband, Bill. Bill Ferguson."

Jake stepped forward with an outstretched hand. As he passed Tawny she could smell liquor on his breath and she noted that his movement was none too steady.

Bill shook the bony, damp old hand and looked with extreme displeasure at the man in front of him. It was incredible that this creature could be her father.

"Pleased to meet you, young man." McShane had spotted the brandy bottle in the corner. "This calls for a drink, wouldn't you say? Me finding my long-lost daughter after three years 'a lookin'?"

Bill poured him one, and one for himself. He did not offer Tawny a drink, but if he had she would have refused. She wanted her wits about her this morning.

Now Jake stopped inspecting the room and concentrated on Tawny. "You're looking fine, kid. You really are. The fellow was right when he said you'd grown up to be a beautiful woman. Your mother'd sure be happy if she could see you now, see how you turned out, how your life turned out. Like I always told you, she was a lady, a real lady. She loved me enough to run away with me, even though her family disowned her for it." He turned to Bill. "I want you to know I'm tellin' the truth about Tawny's ma. I can tell by the look in your eye that you ain't got too high an opinion of her pa."

Bill said, "I must say you come as a surprise, Mr. McShane."

"Long as you're my son-in-law you can call me Jake. If you want to."

Now he looked back at Tawny. "Yes, your ma was a lady. She went along with me but she never took to the gypsy life—like you did, right off, when you were a little nipper. You're a chip off the old block." He gave her a teasing slap on the cheek.

"Please, Pa, don't! Why did you come here?"

"Because I've missed you. Ever since you run out on me. Business ain't as good as when you were on the wagon. Besides, your poor old father just plain missed you."

"I find that hard to believe."

"S'truth, child. Honest truth."

"How did you find me? How did you know I was living here in Littleton?"

"Why, that fellow I was talking about. One who told me you'd grown up to be a beautiful woman."

"Who was that?" But she had begun to guess who it might be.

"Fellow named Oliver. You know, the one you gave the magnetic treatment to in New York City just before you run out on me. He didn't come out to the wagon, if you remember; I delivered you to his house there on Fifth Avenue."

Tawny said in a low voice, "I remember."

Bill turned abruptly back to the brandy bottle. He poured himself a drink and looked the other way as he drank it, trying to swallow his shock and his anger along with the brandy. After a moment he turned around and cleared his throat. "May I ask just what this treatment consists of?"

"Well, Tawny could tell you more about it than I could. She's the one who used to give the treatment. You got to have the proper touch to do it. It's a kind of magnetism, the way I understand it, like electricity. The right hand is the positive and the left hand is the negative; you run them up and down the patient's body and . . ."

Bill interrupted. "Never mind; I understand now." His eyes were on Tawny.

"Tawny here used to be real good at it."

"Stop it, Pa. *Stop it!*"

He shrugged. "I was just trying to explain." He held out his empty glass. "How about another, son-in-law?"

"Pa, I think you've had enough!" Tawny cried out. "I think it's time you should leave."

He put down his glass. "Damn poor welcome you give your poor old father."

"You're not old and you're not poor. Unfortunately you are my father. Now, will you please leave?"

"I got one more question. I'm not truly poor but I am a little hard up lately. Could you possibly loan me a few bucks?"

"I'll *give* you a few bucks. On one condition."

"Yes? What's that?" His eyes had narrowed.

"That you won't come back ever, ever again!"

"If you don't want me . . ." The sad look now. "If you don't want to see your own father, I won't come back."

"Come out in the hall, Pa. That's where my reticule is."

She hurried out of the parlor and he followed. As Jake reached for his hat, Tawny jerked open her purse and extracted a handful of bills. "Here!"

"Thank you, Tawny, thank you from the bottom of my heart."

She opened the front door.

"Good-bye, Pa."

He was leaning forward, about to kiss her, but she backed away. Again he shrugged, and walked out.

Tawny closed the door. She was trembling from head to foot. And now she would have to go back into the parlor and face Bill.

He was downing another drink as she came into the room. He threw the empty glass into the fireplace where it smashed.

"I'm sorry he came here, Bill."

"You have plenty of things to be sorry about, you bitch."

"Let me explain. . . ."

"What is there to explain? You've lied to me; you've cheated me from the very beginning. This magnetic treatment, what is it but an act of sex? Were you a child when he delivered you like a package to Lance?"

"I was fifteen, not quite sixteen. But I was innocent. I was a virgin."

"Not for long, if you gave that so-called treatment to Lance Oliver."

"That was a long time ago, Bill. Three years."

"That was how you lost your virginity, wasn't it? You made up that cock-and-bull story about having a husband killed by the Indians, to cover up the truth about yourself."

"That was not a cock-and-bull story. It was the

truth. I was married to Timothy Barrister. I was!"

"I don't care if you were or not. What I care about is how you've been cheating on me ever since we first met. God knows how many other men have possessed that body of yours. God knows how many times you were with Lance after he came to San Francisco, or after he came here. He didn't come here merely to look for gold; he also came because you were here. You were an easy target; he could have you any time he wanted. You . . ."

"Stop it, Bill! Stop it! I have never been with Lance since that one time in New York. I've never slept with any man except my first husband, and you. I have been faithful to you from the moment we were married."

"You're a liar and a cheat. You have the soul of a slut."

"Bill!"

He had crossed the room and was close to her now.

"Shut your mouth!" he commanded. "Shut your mouth and don't try to explain anything to me. Do you understand?"

He slapped her across the mouth. She cried out in pain and he slapped her again. Her lip started to bleed.

"This is what you've deserved for a long, long time, what you've been asking for!" He cuffed her ears as Pa used to do, so that they stung. Tears came into her eyes as he went on pummeling her, but he paid no attention. He was gripped by a fury such as he had never experienced before. Suddenly this woman before him was the enemy of all time; he must punish her for years of deceit.

Although it was of no use, she cried out for help, help from anyone, anywhere. She knew that Mrs.

Higgins and Vivian were gone. But still she cried out, "God, help me! Help me!"

"Shut up, you fool! God won't help you. No one will help you. At long last you're getting the punishment you deserve."

Outside Fido was barking wildly. Was Bill going to tear off her clothes? Was he going to rape her? Was all this violence a prelude, as violence had been before, to fornication? If that were the answer she would tear off her clothes herself; she would lie naked before him, anything, anything, to stop the pain of his blows.

She tried to move away from him but he grabbed her and flung her to the floor. Her hair tumbled loose and fell across her face. He knelt down and brushed her hair aside with a savage gesture. She looked up at him, pleading.

"Damn you! Damn your eyes!" He punched one and then the other as she screamed.

"Damn your breasts!" He struck them with his fists and again she screamed. He pulled her breasts free from her bodice, bent over and bit them, his teeth sinking into the soft flesh.

Next he was crying, "Damn you. You've sucked my life blood, my manhood; you've turned me into a beast. Because you're a beast. A beast! A beast!"

It took her a moment to catch her breath. Then, with supreme effort, she managed to raise one leg and kick him sharply in the groin. It was his turn to cry out as he pulled back from her. She rolled over and crawled for several feet while he was recovering from her kick.

There had been no use trying to talk to him, trying to reason with him, nor was there any use in offering herself physically to stop his cruelty. She was in the hands of a madman. There was nothing to do but to get away from him, as quickly as she could. She got to the wall of the room, and slowly pulled herself to a standing position. She leaned against the wall, still gasping for breath.

She was by the table where the bottle of brandy stood. As she watched Bill get to his feet and start to come toward her, she picked up the brandy bottle and threw it, with all her might, at his face. It struck him on his forehead. He was immediately drenched with brandy and, as he struggled to brush the liquor away and dry his eyes, she ran across the room and out the door, slamming it behind her.

She did not stop for a coat. She pulled her bodice in place, opened the front door and darted through that, slamming that door behind her, too, then fled down the steps, across the yard to the barn.

She did not try to saddle Brownie. She put on the bridle and reins and led the horse outside into the rain. Fido, who had been in the yard, greeted her excitedly and ran after her.

She did not know where to go, except away. Away, away! She was aching and weary and sick at heart. She would leave him now for sure. She would stay no longer in the same house. Never again would she submit to his violence or to his lovemaking. He had said, "Damn you." Now she damned herself too. She should never have married him; never have got herself into such a situation.

She was on the old road, headed along the river, past the Fitzroys' house, past the house where Mrs. Higgins now lived, their first home when they had come to this part of the world. She would go back to that spot by the river, what she had once thought of as "her spot." Bill, if he went looking for her, would not go there. He had never been there with her. It was her private world. Now it was her refuge.

The rain poured down upon her all the way. She was drenched, but in a way the water was refreshing. It swept the tears from her cheeks, it washed the blood from her cut lip, it cooled her anxiety.

There were trees by her spot by the river, heavily branched evergreens, between her and the rain. She found a dry spot for Brownie and one for herself, and lay down on the ground. Fido snuggled beside her, panting.

Lance had decided to leave Littleton the very next day. He made arrangements to take the stagecoach to Wallula the following morning. Then it was the boat down the coast to San Francisco and then overland by train. But today, this noontime, he must ride out to the Fergusons and tell them good-bye.

He was wondering, as he rode, if Jake McShane had gone out that morning to see them, and what the effect had been. He cursed himself a dozen times for having told the old man about Tawny. Bill would not be pleased to meet his father-in-law, Lance felt sure, and having met him he would not be the kindest of husbands, he also felt sure.

It was not too pleasant riding in the rain, but it seemed like one of those rains that would never stop. He must get out there; there were other arrangements to make back in town, such as selling his horse, settling his account at the hotel, packing.

He was almost to the turnoff that led to the Ferguson house when he saw ahead of him a figure on a horse, riding very rapidly in the other direction. As he came somewhat closer he realized that it was Tawny, riding bareback, her hair flowing behind her. He tried to call out to her but she was moving too rapidly and did not hear. He saw her disappear along the road that bordered the river.

He turned off at the Fergusons' gate, which was standing open, and went up to the house. He reined his horse to a stop near the front door, jumped off, and climbed the steps. He rang the brass knocker a number of times without an answer. Was Bill away, too? Was his trip out completely useless?

Finally he heard footsteps and the door opened. Something had happened to Bill. There was a bruise on his forehead, his face was stained. He reeked of brandy and his eyes had a wild, frantic look that Lance had never seen in them before. "What the devil are you doing here?" was Bill's greeting.

"I just came out to say good-bye."

"Then good-bye."

"Bill, what is it? What's the matter? Where is Tawny?"

"I have no idea where Tawny is. Perhaps you know. Perhaps you've known more often than I ever have."

"What do you mean?"

"You know damn well what I mean," Bill shouted. "I just found out today about you two. Her father enlightened me. That magnetic treatment business. That bitch has been deceiving me all along."

"Bill, wait a minute. Let me explain."

"Explain! I'm sick of explanations. Tawny was full of them. Where is she? I don't know."

"What happened?" Lance asked quietly.

"Her father came to call. Did you know that her father was a quack medicine man?"

"I knew."

"And you've known Tawny for a long, long time."

"Three years."

"Why didn't you tell me she was a slut and a whore?"

"She's no such thing, Bill."

"I say she is. And she's a liar, too. She's been lying to me ever since we first met. She taunted me with that body of hers; she cast a devil's spell over me until I had to have her. I thought she was mine after I married her, but all the while she was carrying on with you and God knows how many others."

"Bill, stop it. That's not true."

Bill did not seem to hear him. He was rubbing the bruse on his forehead and there was a dazed look in his eyes as he went on. "She threw the brandy bottle at me and then she ran away."

"Because you told her the things you have been telling me. No wonder she threw the bottle!"

"Not before I'd given her the beating of her life!"

"You *what*?"

"She had been asking for it, for a long time. Yes, I beat her. I gave her a beating she'll never forget."

For only a moment Lance stared at him with shock. There was a satisfaction on Bill's face that was even more cruel than his words had been.

Lance cried, "You drunken bum!" doubled up his fist and struck Bill with a blow on the jaw that sent him reeling back into the hall. Lance turned and started down the steps. Ahead of him, along the path, he saw Vivian coming toward the house. She smiled and waved up at him. He hurried down to her.

"Afternoon, Mr. Oliver! Oh, Mr. Oliver, I just got to tell somebody. Look . . ." She held out her skinny little hand. A small diamond glittered. "Me and Jim Jenson. We're engaged!"

"Congratulations!"

She looked into his face. "Mr. Oliver, what is it? What's the matter?"

"Vivian, I wouldn't go in the house if I were you. Not now."

"Why? What is it?"

"I think you might," he glanced back at the house, "might be in the hands of a madman. Your nice Mr. Ferguson has been behaving like an animal."

"What's he done to her?"

"Beaten her."

"Oh, no! Oh, I've got to go in to her!"

"She's not there, Vivian."

"Where is she?"

"I'm going to look for her."

"Oh, I hope you find her. She's been so good to me!"

"I know she has."

"Don't worry about me, Mr. Oliver. I'll slip in the back door and go up the back stairs to my room and stay there."

"Good girl." *She is a good girl,* he thought. *Because of Tawny.*

He ran to his horse and mounted. He would follow the river road. When he reached the fork in the road his horse would have preferred to head toward town, because of the rain, but Lance soon had him galloping in the direction he had seen Tawny going. The road was slippery wet, and he could not ride as fast as he would have liked. The usual roar of the river was augmented by the sound of rain splashing into the rushing water.

Never in a million years would he have imagined that quiet Bill Ferguson was a wife beater. From the way Bill had spoken, Lance guessed that this was not the first beating he had given her, just the worst. Lance had never struck a woman in his life. He could not imagine doing it. The very thought produced a shudder.

Another fork in the road. Which way would she have gone? Then he remembered the place, and the day he had met her, when he was out searching for gold.

The road narrowed as he came closer to the river; it was overgrown with brush. He wondered if he could find the place he remembered. Then suddenly, he rounded a curve and ahead of him was the road's end at the river's edge. He saw her horse and then he saw Tawny, lying on the ground, face down, sobbing. He could hear her above the noise of the river and the rain; it was a heartrending wail of anguish.

He jumped off his horse and ran across the space between them. Fido looked up at him and wagged his tail, but Tawny did not seem to be aware of his approach.

"Tawny! Tawny!" He knelt down beside her and put his hand on her shoulder. At first she cringed away from him; then she lifted her head and saw him.

Her face was badly bruised, her eyes were swollen, and there was a horrible cut on her lip. "Lance, I . . ." She closed her eyes. The tears still streamed down her face.

"Don't try to talk. Don't try to tell me anything. I've been to the house. He told me what he had done to you."

"It was so dreadful, Lance. I didn't think I could bear it. I was afraid I'd never get away from him."

"Try not to think about it, Tawny. Try to forget it." He sat down on the ground beside her and took her hand.

"I shall never forget it, as long as I live!"

"Has he beaten you before?"

"He has struck me, yes, but never like today. It was like he wanted to kill me, to destroy me, bit by bit. Before it was all part of his lovemaking."

"Striking you?"

"Being rough before . . . before . . . oh, that's what I want to forget. I don't want him to touch me, ever again. Oh, Lance, I want to die! I wish I were dead. I wish I had the courage to kill myself!"

He held her hand tighter. "No, Tawny, don't talk that way. Don't think such a thing." He was remembering poor little Sue Ellen with the usual surge of guilt and shame and regret.

"He said I deserved the beating today. Perhaps I should be punished."

"For what?"

"For never really loving him. I only married him because I wanted to be married. I wanted to be a wife, not a whore. I wanted another man, a man I could not have, and so I married Bill to satisfy that lust. And it was never satisfied, in all this time. Two years and only once, only once did I want him to take me. I was never the wife he wanted, so I have sinned as much as he."

After a moment Lance said, "Nothing you ever did, or did not do, can equal his cruelty to you today."

"Thank you, Lance. I'd better go down to the river and wash my face." She tried to smile.

"Wait. I'll take my handkerchief and bring the river to you."

When he came back with the west handkerchief she had pulled herself to a sitting position and was brushing back her hair.

They did not know when the rain had stopped. Miraculously, the sun was shining, glinting on that mass of dark red hair that tumbled across her shoulders reaching almost to those lovely upright breasts.

Lance sat down beside her and wiped her face very gently with the wet handkerchief, as if she were a child. He wished he could kiss away the bruises, the scratches. "Feel better?" he asked.

She nodded. "Do I look better?"

"Vanity, vanity, thy name is woman."

"You're teasing me."

"Yes. I want to make you smile again. I want to see you happy before I go away."

"You *are* going away, aren't you?"

"Yes. Tomorrow."

"Tomorrow!"

"That's why I came out to the house today, to tell you both good-bye."

"Oh, Lance, Lance! I shall miss you so!" She threw her arms around his neck and pressed her body close against his. He felt as he had the first time, back in his study in New York. He thought: *I want this woman. I have always wanted her. Just to touch her is to forget the world.*

"Tawny, I should like to wrap you up in a little package and take you with me when I go back to New York."

She caught her breath. She clung more closely to him. Then, with a sigh, she whispered, "But Lance, you're married. You have a wife."

"No."

She backed a little away and stared into his now very sad blue eyes.

"No?" she repeated.

"My wife is dead, Tawny. She took her own life because I deserted her. That's the cross I'll always have to bear."

"Poor Lance."

"Not poor Lance. Wicked Lance. For years I was no good. I was cruel and selfish, and lived for my own pleasure. I have sworn to bring an end to all that. I don't know how well I'll do at reforming myself, but I mean to give it a try."

She put her fingers to his hair and stroked it gently. "I wish you *would* wrap me up in a little package, and take me with you, wherever you go, whatever you do."

He put his hands around her slender waist and looked into those strange, exotic eyes. "Do you mean that, Tawny?"

"Of course I mean it! I have a confession to make."

"Another?"

"When I said I lusted after another man when I married Bill—you were the man."

His lips twisted into a strange little smile.

She went on. "After what happened in New York, Lance, I told myself over and over again that I hated you. I hated you as I hated my father, as I hated myself, for having let you take me that afternoon, for having been so willing. But when I saw you again in San Francisco I knew it wasn't hate, but desire. Desire, no matter how you looked at me or what you said. I knew on my wedding night, during the ceremony, when I looked across at you, that it was you and only you I had ever loved, or would ever love."

"Tawny, my darling . . ."

"Oh, Lance, kiss me! Please kiss me before I die of wanting!"

"Your lip . . ."

"Kiss me!"

He obeyed. She melted into his arms and they held each other close, listening to the beating of their hearts above the roar of the river.

PREVIEW

If you enjoyed *Tawny McShane*,
you will want to read

The Privateer's Woman

by June Wetherell

Following are the opening pages of Ms. Wetherell's recent bestselling second historical romance, THE PRIVATEER'S WOMAN,* *the exciting, hot-blooded novel of a young girl who refused to accept a life of servitude. Taking her fate into her own hands, she disguised* *herself as a boy and ran away to sea on a pirate ship, only to find her young, maturing body would betray her to the woman-hungry buccaneers.*

Desmond Duval's survival depended not on herself but on one man—Dragon—the mysterious, brooding captain of the privateers, the only man who could kindle the flames of desire in her; who taught her the meaning of passion even as he plunged her into an ecstasy of despair.

But who was Dragon? Where did he go those quiet nights when he turned his back on Desmond? . . .

* * *

"Boy—get down here!"

Desmond, blond hair blowing in the wind, looked down from high in the rigging. The men on deck had shrunk to pigmies, their bandannas, their broad brimmed hats, even their cutlasses were almost toy-size. This was the place to be, seated on the cross trees, in your own world of sky and wind. The ship was at anchor in calm waters; there was a sense of well-being in the gentle sway at the top. It was almost like being a bird, free and independent, breathing the clean salt-scented air instead of deck and cabin odors of rum, tobacco, sweat, and often blood.

From here the buccaneers formed a pattern of flamboyant color, nice little fellows dressed up like dandies, the sun glinting on their cutlasses and their pistols and their earrings. One was not close enough to smell them, to see their matted grimy hair, their scars, the missing hand or ear, the greasy blood-stained pantaloons.

The youngest, the smallest, the most agile, Desmond frequently was sent up the rigging to keep watch for other ships, or to hoist the skull and crossbones. But, when no ships were sighted, when no flag need be flown, the cabin boy was kept busy swabbing the decks, cleaning the pistols, or sharpening the cutlasses, gutting fish or birds in the galley, filling the rum bottles from the big cask in the cellar, cleaning muck from anywhere it appeared.

Desmond did the work, shared a small bit in the loot when a ship was captured, ate what the rest of them ate and for the most part was not mistreated. Sent on fools' errands sometimes, just so the rest of the crew could sit there guzzling rum and laughing their heads off. But the voice of the quartermaster, calling out just now, had had a different tone. Sharp, angry, threatening.

One hand was lifted to indicate the command had been heard, then Desmond turned and started the slow descent. A long-ago fall from the rigging, only a few feet above the deck, had caused enough pain to ingrain a habit of care. More care going down than in climbing up.

"Damn you, hurry!" the officer was calling again.

What mistake could I have made? Desmond wondered. What did I forget to do? Am I in for a beating?

It was late afternoon and the ship was at anchor. Most of the crew were on deck, leaning against the sides or squatting as they swizzled rum. They looked up as Desmond descended, an amused audience, as if they knew why Desmond had been called down so peremptorily.

"Yes, sir?" Desmond waited, trying not to show fright. I should not be afraid. To the best of my knowledge I've done nothing wrong.

Batham, the quartermaster, had only one eye, but it made up in malignity for the missing one now covered with a patch.

He did not speak immediately. He stood there in ominous silence, looking over Desmond as if that poor unfortunate were a slave he was considering purchasing. His contempt hung in the air between them.

"My boy . . ." The words had no touch of kindness usually held by such a phrase. "My boy, it is time you learned to fight."

Desmond had longed for this moment. It meant acceptance by the crew, it meant not being shoved aside when they captured a ship, but being allowed to join. And, most important, to receive a man's instead of a boy's share of the booty.

"I can wield a cutlass, sir." Eagerly. "I learned on the plantation. I cut sugar cane and small trees and they told me I was very good. May I show you?"

"I wasn't speaking of a cutlass. Any fool can slash about with a cutlass. Besides, you are too slight for that. First, the sword."

He pulled one from its scabbard, a weapon scarcely long enough to be called a sword. It was more like a stubby long dagger.

"As a young gentleman on that plantation, were you taught fencing?"

"I was not a young gentleman!" Desmond blurted. "My mother was . . . a servant. No, I was not taught to fence."

The sword. Sharp, sinister. Here, in front of those mocking pirates, would not be the place to learn. And not from that quartermaster who obviously, for reasons of his own, despised his cabin boy.

The officer tossed the sword, flipping the handle over, and miraculously Desmond caught it. Then the officer reached for his own weapon. Longer, sharper.

"On guard!" He was in position.

Desmond had played at sword fights with the "young gentlemen" on that plantation who *were* taught fencing, had watched some of the lessons, and had some idea of what was supposed to go on. Not easy, when you were trembling; only possible with the now engulfing bravado of fear. There were no buttons on the sword tips here.

"On guard!" A high-pitched echo of the officer's tone.

Desmond was agile. A tree climber, now a rope climber, arms and legs were under perfect control. Batham was bigger but clumsier. And Desmond began to realize that first, the man had been drinking rum, and second, that he was not fighting to kill. He was fighting as if he were playing a game. It was his method of wordless teaching. One should be grateful, one should regard it as a game and forget the expression on the quartermaster's face when he first said, *you must learn to fight.*

I will really be one of them now, Desmond thought. When they clamber over a prize vessel I shall be with them, sword in hand.

Whenever there was a successful parry of one of Batham's thrusts there was a roar from the pirates. Was it laughter, or was it an ironic cheer?

They circled around and around the deck in a rhythm that was almost like a dance, Desmond's slender bare feet whisking, over and over again, just out of the other's reach.

Then suddenly the dance Desmond was beginning to enjoy was shattered. A sudden lunge and Batham's heavier sword caught and swirled the lighter blade out of Desmond's hand and came straight for the heart.

Desmond leaped back but not quickly enough. The sword did not touch the flesh but it ripped open the shirt.

Her breasts—her small young breasts she had tried so hard to hide—were there in the heavy gold of the afternoon light, for all to see.

* * *

For two years Desmond Duval had been pretending to be a boy. Her yellow hair, bleached by the sun, had been hacked off shoulder length, as short as a man's. Her body, trim and slim, fit well into trousers and shirt, except for those breasts which lately had started to grow.

She would never forget the night she ran away from the plantation on Barbados, the long, long walk to the waterfront, sitting on the dock, hidden behind a barrel, waiting for the dawn.

She spent several nights on that tar and salt-scented dock. Each day she mingled with the seamen—old and young, some with rings in their noses, some with pigtails, some with long curly whiskers, all walking clumsily, as if their feet were unused to land.

Some of the ships were navy, others fullcrewed merchant ships. She tried them all, but nobody wanted a cabin boy.

Until one very dark night when a strange ship without a flag slipped into the harbor and anchored far out. A few men came ashore in a small boat. She watched them raiding a warehouse, and then they spotted her and asked her to help them. "Come on, lad, take a load there—we'll see you're repaid." And so she had helped them, load after load, and then, suddenly, while she was still aboard ship, a torch was spotted on the dock and the ship unfurled its sails and moved away.

The *Lady May*. A pirate ship!

Some of the food they had taken from the warehouse was spread out for a feast—salt pork, biscuits, brandy, pickled fruit—and ravenous, she had eaten with them and they had accepted her and adopted her as a member of the crew.

* * *

Until this moment when the shirt was ripped from her body Desmond had been sure she had fooled them. Now she realized that the quartermaster must have guessed her secret and chosen this way of revealing it to his mates. Clutching her shirt in front of her, she stood there defiant, looking at one face and then another. It was a man's world and when she was thought to be a male, everything had been all right. Now all had changed. The pirates' eyes had become the eyes of predatory beasts.

"I've done my job well, haven't I?" she asked.

Batham laughed. "You've done a boy's job, yes. But you haven't done *your* job. Not yet."

She knew all too well what he meant, what they all meant. She could not fight the lot of them, she could not hope that one of them would defend her.

Yet, even as her good sense told her she was helpless, she inadvertently took a step away from the officer.

His long arm shot out and grabbed hers, the one holding the shirt in front of her. He did not speak, he just held her firm.

"Try to get away from me. Just try, and you'll have the beating of your life."

A cheer rose from the pirates. "Rum! More rum!" one of them cried and others echoed. "Rum! Rum!" and there was the noise of empty bottles splashing overboard.

The quartermaster, gripping her arm so tightly that it hurt, told her, "Fetch rum. Fast!"

He let go of her, as he pushed her in the direction of the hold.

As she hurried past, two or three of the men reached out to grab at her breasts or pinch her buttocks.

"Wait!" A command from the officer. "Time enough for that!"

She got past them and started down the ladder into the darkness of the hold. She ran toward the huge keg of rum and then stopped. She reversed the shirt, back to front, and tied the ragged part behind her.

Then she began filling the bottles that lined the walls. *They want rum, I'll give them rum! I'll get them sodden, the way the master was each night back on Barbados. They'll never get me, none of them!*

Yet all the while her mind was racing with the possibilities of what might happen. Two of them would hold her while a third one . . . no, the quartermaster wouldn't let them, he wanted her for himself. But only first, she remembered. Some of the rum spilled from the spigot as she filled a bottle too full.

From the deck she could hear them calling, "Rum! Rum! Rum!" like birds cawing in the morning light.

She carried an armload of bottles up the ladder and set them on the deck. Batham was right there at the top of the ladder, waiting for her.

He grabbed her arm, but as she tugged to get away there was noise from the other side of the deck, the sound of scuffling.

Batham yelled out, "Stop that! Here's your rum!"

A few of the men moved forward but the two who had started to fight did not.

Batham dropped her arm and ran to intervene.

Desmond turned and as fast as she could, ran to the quarterdeck and along in the dark to the very end. She swung herself up on the rail.

The sun had set and the swift tropical dark covered the star-specked sky. Land looked a long way away, only a row of dark blobs of hills against the faintly lit sky.

There was nothing to do but swim for it. She prayed silently that somewhere over there was a beach, that it was not all rocks against the sea.

There was one feeble light along the shoreline, no bigger than a landlocked star, but it was *something* on . . . why, she did not even know the name of the island! All she knew was that she was somewhere north of Barbados in the West Indies.

She climbed the rail and jumped over the side, terribly aware of the sound when she struck the water, hoping it would not be audible to the men on deck.

Sharks? The boys back on Barbados had talked about sharks, way out where it was deep, especially in the dark. . . .

There was a strange light in the water that draped her arms with silver. Would they be able to see her, from the ship? So far she had heard no uproar, no one was calling after her. Perhaps it would take a while, with all that rum, before they started to look for her.

A flare in the sky behind her. Someone had lighted a torch. She slipped under water, down and down, held her breath for as long as possible. The shirt, torn earlier, washed free and floated away.

At last she surfaced. The flare was gone. Again she started swimming in the direction of that small light, long, slow, steady strokes; she must not get frantic and try too hard or she would soon be exhausted. Now and then she would stop for a bit, treading water, turning to look back at the ship. It was the only way she could tell how far she had gone—the land seemed as distant as ever, but the ship, thank God, was growing smaller.

The stars faded and the water, the sky, the whole world was consumed by black. The rain came first in such small drops that they might have been part of the foam. Then the drops grew in size and intensity, pelting down on the ocean with a roar of power; she could only try to go on steadily swimming. But the wind was whipping the water into crests that swept her with them—she could only pray it was in the direction of the shore.

She was getting tired; never had she swum so far, never in such an ocean. But still she kept on, doggedly, stubbornly, blindly. No longer was there any light visible anywhere.

Without warning a bigger wave, a mountain of water, swept over her and tossed her as if she were a piece of driftwood. She felt herself rise to the top of the wave and then tumble down and down until she was slammed against a boulder, and knew she had reached the shore.

At first she lay flat on her face trying to cling to the land. Land? It was nothing but shifting rocks, and each time the waves came they tried to pull her back into the sea, but each time the waters receded she managed to crawl another few feet forward.

The rain stopped, the stars began reappearing, and at last she reached a patch of sand, above the surf, above the water line. She burst into tears of gratitude and then, exhausted, she lost consciousness.

* * *